ANGLES OF DECEPTION

STUART MITCHELL

To Michael,
Best Wishes,
Stuart Mitchell
Dec 07

Stuart Mitchell © Copyright 2007

British Library Cataloguing In Publication Data
A Record of this Publication is available
from the British Library

ISBN 978-1-84685-894-9

First Published 2007 by
Exposure Publishing,
an imprint of
Diggory Press Ltd
Three Rivers, Minions, Liskeard, Cornwall, PL14 5LE, UK
and of Diggory Press, Inc.,
Goodyear, Arizona, 85338, USA
WWW.DIGGORYPRESS.COM

Stuart Mitchell was born in Edinburgh. After leaving school he served for fifteen years with the Metropolitan Police, before being medically retired as a Sergeant. He now lives in Lincolnshire with his wife and daughter and an assortment of pets. When not writing, he like to show dogs, socialise, read books, play pool and sleep, although not necessarily at the same time or in that order!

Special thanks must go to the following:

Carole Matthews for initial inspiration and a kick up the backside. Andrew and Dorothy for continued support, and finally my wonderful wife Wendy who is without doubt my biggest fan and main reason anything in my life ever gets done.

This book is dedicated to my Dad (I only hope you are allowed thrillers up there!) and to my beautiful daughter Paige.

Prologue

A wispy white, almost transparent snake of smoke filtered from the two black eyes of death at the end of the gun.

She had lived in her own private hell long enough. The years of torture, forced prostitution, drugs, beatings and public humiliation had finally taken their toll.

When the tentacles of morning sunlight squeezed between the bedroom curtains and danced along her bed, she'd woken with the sincere knowledge that today the abuse would finally come to an end.

The previous night's discovery that her husband was having another affair had finally rammed it home, that unless she made a stand, she would live in torment forever.

The clock on the wall ticked down the minutes that would change her destiny so slowly it felt as if time itself had decided to add to her agony.

Tension filled the room, so thick she felt she could see it hanging in the air, taste it on her dry tongue.

Frequently, cars drove past the house bringing with them false hope until finally she heard a sound that caused her heart to pump furiously, and her muscles to stiffen. Her husband had inserted his key into the front door.

Yet again she could tell he was drunk as he bounced and swore his way up the stairs, she slunk down under the bedclothes, trying to hide the surprise she had in store for him.

For a last surge of courage she briefly shut her eyes and recalled some of the heartless things he'd done to her over the years. Brian had fed her to his friends to be used as a sexual plaything, and stubbed out cigarettes on her bare thighs for fun. She shuddered at the memory.

Then he was before her, dressed in his Metropolitan police uniform, leering through yellow teeth. He would want sex now whether she wanted it or not.

She watched as he took out his penis and rubbed it to erection. It was his way to take her still dressed in his uniform. He'd once told her how this made him feel so powerful and added to his domination.

She remained still, like a small rabbit hiding from a hunting bird of prey, lay motionless like a statue until he was within a couple of feet, waiting for her moment of freedom to finally arrive.

He was almost on her now.

Wait.

Flinging back the covers, she was pleased to see his expression change from lust to abject terror as he saw the shotgun slowly rising to point at his waist.

What causes a human mind to break, or to lose track of reality?

Inside 17 Arcadia Drive, London NW9, Stella Blackmore had drifted over the edge and fallen into a vast catacomb of nothingness.

Her mind had been cleansed of pain only to be filled with a more powerful human emotion. As she pulled the trigger, heard him scream, noticed the pieces of uniform and flesh disintegrate before her eyes, all Stella felt as her husband Brain fell to the floor missing most of his lower body, was revenge.

1

Mickey Driscol was a hard man, and when one of his own men betrayed his trust, he was expected to dish out suitable retribution.

He smoothed his rough hands over his scalp, gently easing the few loose strands of hair back into the pony tail, which was tied tightly behind his head, held in place by a shockingly blue bobble.

Torture he thought was physically demanding work. Large beads of sweat had formed on his brow, and his navy blue silk shirt was now plastered to his back.

Before him, tied to a chair sat Derek Cutts, a pimply nineteen-year-old youth, who'd displayed the intelligence of someone much younger. He'd been given the relatively easy task of taking a package of ready cut heroin to one of the estates under Mickey's supervision.

Derek had delivered it to the wrong address, and to make matters worse, the people who lived there were members of a rare breed of human being residing in the area at the time. They were honest, law abiding citizens and had reported their surprise gift to the police.

Mickey had lost drugs with a street value of seventy-five thousand pounds, and this had seriously pissed him off.

Derek was now slumped forward unconscious. Dribble trickled from between his lips, and the legs of his chair were surrounded by a dark red pool of blood. Sticking out from this, two small white fragments of teeth resembling shark fins hinted at the brutality that had gone on before. Derek had been taken somewhere deep inside his subconscious by the time a few minutes of his beating had elapsed.

His guts impressed Mickey. He hadn't screamed like the pig his men said he would. They'd even had bets on how long it would be before he passed out. None had gone anywhere near the two minutes of agony Mickey had so far dished out.

Mickey looked down at Derek and smiled. He would be more careful next time. This lesson would never be forgotten.

He'd decided to finish his morning's work with something he'd seen done in a movie on satellite television the previous weekend.

Bending down he lifted the left knee up in the air so that it formed a right angle to the floor. Then with all his might he rammed a Phillips screwdriver straight through it.

Wherever Derek had been hiding, threw him back sharply and his scream made one or two of the watchers turn away to prevent them losing whatever breakfasts they'd eaten earlier.

2

The frail old lady was shakily holding onto the hot cup of tea the Woman Constable had made for her. Her thin fingers were covered in liver spots, and she looked as though she would drop her drink at any time.

At nearly eighty-three, Ethel Smithers had believed that she would meet her maker without having to go through anything this stressful again. Sobbing quietly, her small frame rocked back and forth as she fought back her tears. She was having great difficulty trying to understand how her God had allowed her husband to die during the Second World War, and now this.

She'd returned from one of her frequent trips down to see her brother in Brighton, and upon her return she'd had difficulty opening the front door to her semi-detached home in Muswell Hill.

Her neighbour, Jessica Donald, who worked for a large computer company whose name escaped her, often worked from home, and had forced her way through the door, only to find the house looking like a mini tornado had cut loose inside.

The police were doing their best to comfort her, but nothing they said or did could make her feel any less violated.

Upstairs Keith Greaves, the local Scenes of Crime Officer was dusting for fingerprints. He paid particular attention to the handles on the doors, the window ledges, and any other shiny surfaces, or possible points of entry, where it looked like tools had been used.

As he worked a glint of light reflected in his eye. Bending down to see what the offending object was, he picked up a gold chain. It was around fifteen inches in length and had a large oval shaped diamond hanging from the end. He'd attended a course on jewellery recognition the previous month, and knew from experience that this piece was very valuable. As he allowed the delicate chain to trickle between his fingers, and felt the weight of the stone, he estimated it to be worth somewhere between five and ten thousand pounds.

Holding it up he marveled at how the morning light danced and shimmied along its surface. He was still examining it carefully when he was interrupted by another male police officer entering the room.

"What you got there Keith"? The man asked.

"Something very nice mate," he replied smiling broadly. "Here what do you think?" He asked, as he lobbed the necklace over to the officer.

Catching it in one hand the younger of the two men said, "Might cheer her up a bit. She's in a right state down there."

Keith smiled at him. "You're so bloody slow Rod. It might cheer *us* up a bit you mean."

Rod grinned back. "Jesus mate, you're nastier than old Tony Asque."

"Only the devil's worse than him," Greaves laughed, before putting the gold chain in his pocket.

3

Detective Sergeant Billy Johnstone stood at the back of the *Maverick Club* watching the young and not so young gyrate the night away to the thumping dance music.

A knowing smile formed as he recognised various figures from the criminal underworld and the police force smooching cheek to cheek across the highly polished floor. Billy watched and waited.

The club had opened in the early eighties, and right from the start it had a reputation for drawing the local likely lads to it. Here they would meet up; strike deals and drink themselves into a stupor, as they planned their next illegal projects to make some money.

During the previous two decades it had escalated into one of the country's top clubs, and now within certain circles it was as well known for the names of the people who frequented it, as for the pulsating sounds being blasted out from the speakers.

Billy looked on as a girl of around twenty draped herself around Angus Sharp, like a piece of living jewellery. He knew that Angus was a Divisional Chief Superintendent from across the Thames, also that he was married and was well aware the girl glued to him like an over large stick insect was a prostitute called Sabrina. Sharp caught his eye and offered a half raised hand in a '*oh it's you*' kind of recognition salute. Billy nodded in acknowledgment, the smile on his face turning to a leer as Sabrina began to rub at the much older mans crotch.

These events were everyday occurrences within the club and in one way he felt secure that if his involvement ever became public knowledge he was in a strong position to bargain for his freedom, however on the other hand he couldn't help feeling that the more corrupt people there were the more chance everyone would eventually get caught. His logic stemmed from the fact that if so many were taking bites from similar pies, somewhere along the line mistakes would be made that could seriously screw the baker.

His thoughts were interrupted when a throaty voice from behind, informed him that *The Panel* were prepared to speak now.

Billy was led to the entrance and stared into the gloom inside the meeting room specially set aside for The Panel to conduct their business. It looked like a thick fog had formed inside, but he knew it was a combination of cigarette smoke and the dust particles catching the light from the two large spotlights at the front of the room. These were always on and shone brightly into the faces of the people who sat before the members, thus preventing them from ever seeing the identities of these mysterious and powerful men.

Billy unwittingly delayed his entry long enough for the bodyguard who'd ushered him in to become frustrated and he felt the hard shove in his lower back.

"Hey chill out," he said annoyed.

"Inside," the man built like a gorilla replied in a voice filled with menace.

Billy walked up to the hard wooden chair in front of the desk behind which these secret men sat. He stood like a schoolboy, hands behind his back waiting to be told to sit down. Without a word a hand sprung forward through the smoke like a cobra striking at its prey.

"Sit," a gruff voice ordered.

Billy noticed how thin and gnarled the fingers looked and wondered how many serious crimes the owner had been responsible for during his association with the club.

As he sat down the scraping sound from his chair legs on the floor reverberated around the room. "Sorry," he offered in an apologetic voice.

An eerie silence followed which unsettled him. He was thinking what he could say to break the tension that hung in the air like London smog, when another voice spoke out from the gloom.

"Billy you've been providing us with some quality girls lately. We're pleased with your input so far. We hope the high standard you've set will continue."

He tried to get a hook on the voice behind the compliment, but as usual it was being distorted somehow. Instead he merely said, "Thanks."

"The latest one...Mandy seems particularly well suited for our needs, and we see she's another copper. We take it she's a junkie?"

"Heavy habit, but she just loves the sex anyway. Like a rabbit on heat most of the time," Billy said, laughing at his own description.

No one else in the room followed his lead. "That's good Billy, but make sure she doesn't screw up otherwise..."

He knew the pause at the end of the sentence was a threat, and although he felt fear he didn't want to lose face and show any. "No sweat, she does what she's told," he answered as defiantly as he dared.

A long silence followed, Billy grew less comfortable with each passing second. Without another word being spoken a large brown envelope was pushed towards him. He waited for instructions. When he realised the interview was at an end he picked up the envelope, nodded his thanks and left the room.

Once outside he headed for the nearest toilet, found himself a cubicle and went inside, sat down and opened his gratuity.

"Jesus," was all he managed to say as he stared down at the half-inch thick pile of crisp new fifty-pound notes. Tucking it down the rear of his trousers for safety he came back out into the noise of the club.

Almost immediately he saw Sabrina and Angus Sharp fooling around on the dance floor in full view of anyone who cared to look. "It looks like someone else is going to be rewarded," he chuckled as he made his way out into the street.

4

Stella Blackmore wasn't unduly concerned by the noise her husband was making as he lay bleeding to death by the side of the bed.

Almost in a dream like state, she watched as the thick red liquid spread slowly from the massive wound that had once been his lower legs.

They'd spent a small fortune decorating the bedroom. It had been the room she'd wanted to look the best, somewhere for them to be alone, to make love, to start a family. Her heart sank when she remembered this. Brian had told her on their wedding night that he didn't want kids, not then, not ever. He'd purposely waited until they were married before telling her this cruelest piece of news. He had killed a part of his wife without even realising it.

The bedroom had a thick light blue pile carpet covering its wooden floorboards and Stella watched fascinated as the blood crawled slowly against the rub, like a steady flow of lava escaping from a volcano.

Without warning her husband let out one last pitiful moan and then was forever silent.

The only sounds left in the room were the beating of her heart, ticking alongside the small gold mantle clock shaped like the Eiffel Tower, which her sister had given them as a wedding present.

Stella hadn't moved since she had emptied both barrels of the shotgun into him, other than to let the gun fall slowly onto her lap. Now, she swung her legs over the edge of the bed and pushed her feet into a pair of fluffy pink slippers.

Slowly and with great care she tiptoed across the wet floor, trying to avoid putting her feet into the thick ooze that now spread to cover a large area of carpet. Not once did she allow her gaze to fall upon her dead husband.

Once out of the room she removed the slippers and taking careful aim threw them back towards the bed. One landed smack in the middle, the other fell short and with a loud plop landed in the sea of red. Stella stifled a laugh, although she didn't know why, as there wasn't anyone else in the house to hear her.

In high spirits she descended the stairs and entered the kitchen where she immediately filled the kettle with water and flicked the switch. Sitting down she waited for it to boil.

Leaning across the table she put a large helping of coffee into a bright yellow mug which had 'Happy 40th' printed in thick blue lettering down one side, the other having a display of fireworks bursting into life celebrating the happy event. Stella smiled broadly as she wished she had some real fireworks to commemorate her newly found freedom.

The kettle boiled and she got up and poured the steaming liquid into the mug. It was now time to implement the next stage of her plan.

She'd already worked out time was on her side as her husband had worked at a large police station and therefore would not be missed if he was away from work over a lengthy period.

Despite the lateness of the hour, Stella decided to prioritise this task. She picked up the telephone and punched out the numbers to his station.

The ringing went on long enough for Stella to wonder if she'd dialed correctly. She was about to replace the receiver when a young sounding female voice finally answered, "Westville Police Station, how can I help you?"

Stella didn't care for the overly happy tone in the girl's voice and wondered if she was one of the sluts her dead husband had been sleeping with.

"Hello, my name is Stella Blackmore." She paused and waited for a sign of recognition. Upon receiving none she continued, "Brian's wife. I'm sorry, but he won't be in for a while as we had some bad news earlier today..."

"Oh, I'm sorry to hear that, what happened?" the officer interrupted.

Stella somehow managed to prevent herself from laughing at the amazingly false concern in the woman's voice. She couldn't give a toss what the news was, and both she and Stella knew it. "It's his Dad. He passed away early this afternoon. Right out the blue. He was only here the other day for his dinner," she sniffed, pretending to be on the verge of tears. "Brian asked me to call as he's gone straight to his Mum's. He wants to take some holiday leave. Trouble is I don't know how much he needs. His Mum might need him there for a couple of weeks at least."

She listened as the woman scribbled down some notes. Eventually, just as she was about to ask if there was anything else she needed to know, the woman finally spoke. "Don't you worry yourself about it Mrs. Blackmore.   I'll let the Superintendent know in the morning."

Stella grinned as the conversation ended. She couldn't believe how easily the lies had come to her. She sat back and sipped at her coffee.

The house sat in its own acre and a half of secluded garden and was set well back from the road.   It was surrounded by a high security fence Brian had insisted he erected to protect them from the rougher elements of the neighbourhood. He'd always been paranoid. Arcadia Drive could be classed as one of the nicest residential areas in London.

When she'd told Brian that he was just a beat cop, she'd ended up in hospital with a broken rib from the severe beating he'd given her. *Fallen down the stairs, again* was the excuse she'd given when quizzed by the medical team. One of them had asked if they were particularly steep stairs as she had fallen down them a number of times during the past months. Stella had reddened and halfheartedly smiled. She'd wished someone had asked her out right and in Brian's presence if he'd been hitting her. She would have told them there and then.   No-one did and so she'd returned to more punches and more abuse.

If only someone had asked *that* question, Brian would still be alive (not that she cared much about that) but there would be no need for the others to die as well.

Stella looked out the kitchen window at her beloved array of exotic plants and flowers, and sighed heavily. Suddenly she felt very lonely. Her parents were dead and her older sister had kept herself to herself for several years now. Sadness began to churn inside her as she realised nobody cared. Nobody wanted her.

Finally, Stella smiled as she thought about how people would want her soon enough. Want her very badly indeed, as soon as her new game was fully underway.

5

Mark Carter slowly rubbed his forefinger and thumb gently back and forward across the top right hand side of the letter he was holding.   It was a deliberate action as if he was trying to coax some important information from it, but he knew enough already.

For the second successive year he had been turned down for promotion to Detective Chief Inspector. The letter as usual was devoid of reason, which he knew was a common police practice, but it still made his blood boil. Had he been turned down because he'd answered some questions wrongly or was it because he was too young, too fat, too thin or perhaps even too ugly?

He was forty-one, had a stocky appearance, although not overweight and had a mass of thick jet black hair, which no matter how hard he tried always found a way to look like a deserted birds nest. He refused to keep it short as this was his only dig at the establishment he worked for.

Carter's large hand roughly pulled open the drawer to his desk before he carefully removed a silver picture frame. He allowed his eyes to study the delicately carved dolphins that appeared to swim around the frame edges. Finally his gaze shifted to the photo of a beautiful woman with shoulder length blonde hair, bright sparkling eyes the colour of deep sapphire and a heavily tanned and toned figure that most models would cut their mothers throats for.

The lady was standing next to a man dressed in a light grey *Armani* suit. She had an arm loosely draped around his waist pulling him towards her. Their eyes reflected the early evening sun, in their gaze you could detect love and a hint of what the night ahead would bring. Carter traced a finger slowly over her clothing. She was wearing a short, mid-thigh, red silk dress that appeared to move in a slight breeze as you studied the picture. The couple appeared to be the picture of happiness.

Mark Carter let his emerald green eyes stare at the Polaroid, with such an intensity that he found after a while he lost focus causing him to blink in order to regain sight of the smiling woman.

The photo had been taken on their first holiday away together and Carter forced a smile as he remembered immediately after it had been taken, his girlfriend had dragged him down onto the beach, insisting that they went for a swim in the ocean.

When he had complained that they would ruin their clothes, she had grinned at him, before quickly removing her dress, and then running, squealing into the warm waters of the Mediterranean Sea. He'd joined her, and as he embraced her, all thoughts of swimming vanished.

Carter recalled the whole fortnight had been spent mostly in each others arms. He sighed heavily. It had been weeks since he had made love to her, in fact over the past months they had hardly spoken. Carter could not shake the feeling that perhaps she had found someone else to give her the physical needs she had always demanded from him.

He put the picture down in front of him and cupped his head in his hands as he glared down at her smiling face. She was his girlfriend and yet she demanded they kept the relationship a secret. When they'd met, she'd omitted to tell him she was at Hendon Police College, training to be a Police Constable. Somehow she'd known who he was and what rank he'd attained. Even at the early stage of her career she'd known relationships between young trainees and Detective Inspectors were frowned on within the service.

Carter had dated her for nearly three months before she'd told him the truth. By then he was totally captivated by the woman fifteen years his junior. He'd understood when she worried that she'd be constantly harassed owing to her involvement with him and he'd also had the sense to understand that the bureaucratic nonsense within the force would cause him problems as well. When they were established in what looked like a long term partnership, they decided to keep the relationship a secret from the Metropolitan Police Force. It had been Mandy's idea. Carter had felt obliged to go along with her wishes.

His head had started to pound. His love life was going downhill faster than an Olympic skier and his career had ground to a premature halt.

For the first time in his life, he hated it. Now in the photo she seemed to be grinning at him, as if she was the reason he had been turned down for promotion. Had someone connected them despite the charade they had put up? Carter lifted the picture frame, opened his drawer and threw it inside.

Dismissing the thought, he repeated his act of the previous year and screwed the letter into a tight ball, took aim and threw it at the battered metal bin that stood beside his doorway.

Just as last year the paper ball hit the rim, bounced in the air, looked like it would fall in, but at the last moment dropped to the carpet and sat there smugly in a final act of victory over him. Carter sighed heavily and pressed his intercom, "Sonia bring me a pot of coffee will you, please."

He didn't wait for a reply, merely let go of the switch, leaned back in his chair, shut his eyes and allowed his mind to drift back to his girlfriend's soft skin, her vivacious curves, her smiling blue eyes that on many occasions when the tension and pressures of life threatened to drown him, he'd found he could plunge himself into and completely lose himself.

6

Mike Grady sat at the battered looking table and watched his younger brother Jake chat up the pretty young barmaid. He smiled to himself as the scene unfolded before him like so many episodes from the past. Mike envied him the ease in which his brother attracted the ladies. He wasn't envious because Mike preferred learning how he could make himself rich. Money meant more to him than sex ever would and try as he might to convince Jake otherwise, the younger man still preferred the thrill of the chase.

Jake returned carrying two pints of beer and with a couple of bags of crisps hanging precariously from between his teeth. Even with his face contorted Mike could see the smile in his eyes that told him he'd arranged to see the barmaid later.

"Don't you get enough from the girlfriend?" he asked mockingly.

"You're just showing your jealousy now big brother. I can *even* fix *you* up with someone if you can't manage it yourself."

Ignoring the sarcasm, Mike grinned and took a long gulp of the cool beer. "That's nice," he said wiping the remnants of froth from his top lip. "So is she still doing a good job on the estate?"

Jake who had already drained more than half of his glass put it down with a thump, "You know she's good Mikey, no need to ask stupid questions."

"Not me asking though is it Jake?"

Before he answered Jake let what his brother had said sink in and felt the cold shivers of fear trickle down his back. "What are they trying to do Mike? Scare me or something."

"Hey calm down bro, there's no problem they just want to know she's still up to the task that's all."

"Yeah, well she is and if there was a problem don't you think I'd have told you?"

"Maybe. Let's be serious for a minute ok? You're in love with this one even though you want to dip anything with a pulse, therefore you might, and I *emphasise* might, just give her more rope than the Panel deems to be fit."

Jake studied his brother's eyes; the realisation hit him with a loud smack, "Bastard you're winding me up."

Mike took another slurp from his pint. "That's what older brothers are for Jake," he grinned, before he burst into uncontrollable laughter.

7

Chief Superintendent John MacDonald sat behind his desk studying the list of names presented to him on the A4 sheet of neatly typed paper which was encased in protective plastic sheeting. Sitting before him were four officers from the Complaint Investigations Bureau. He couldn't help noticing they all wore smug smiles on their faces. "So gentlemen, you seem to have named half my station here. Surely you don't suspect they're all involved in criminal activities?"

MacDonald had been introduced to the team of complaint officers when they'd first arrived at his station nearly two weeks earlier. As usual they'd stomped through their investigation sparing no ones feelings and already he'd lost any respect he may have had for them. Such was the animosity he now felt towards them he'd forgotten the name of the Inspector in charge who now stood up and walked behind him, where he gazed out of a large window. MacDonald was about to ask his question again when the Inspector spoke.

"I can understand your worries Chief Superintendent, but until I can say with certainty these names don't belong on my list. There they'll stay."

"Fair enough, but some of them are involved in some big cases at the moment. I don't want you interfering with any police work at my station."

The Inspector turned and smiled at him with perfect white teeth, "Don't worry we'll take the utmost care not to get in anyone's way." He returned to the front of the desk, nodded at his men and one by one like highly trained dogs they made their way out the office.

MacDonald muttered, "Wankers," under his breath as they disappeared from view.

Carefully almost as if he thought it would burn his fingers he picked up the alleged list of crooked officers names and allowed his eyes to take them in individually, trying to ascertain which if any he himself believed could be up to no good. There were a couple there that made him think hard, but on the whole he couldn't believe many of them were involved in anything serious enough to have teams of C.I.B. officers swarming around the station like demented bees.

Surprisingly he saw that all the officers were from the uniform section of his force and no detectives had been named. Normally it's from that sector within any police force that the bent officers can be found, as they have the biggest crimes to investigate and therefore are in the right or wrong place to be offered gratuities by the criminals to turn a blind eye. MacDonald scoffed and hit the button to his intercom "Marge, would you ask the following officers to come and see me at different times throughout the day. You pick the slots okay?" Having received acknowledgment from his secretary he proceeded to call out the officers names from the list. He was well aware this was the wrong thing to do, but he was determined his men and women should be forewarned of the investigations going on although he intended not to mention the fact they were the ones under scrutiny. He knew that doing it this way would enable him to see what if any actions they might take to cover up anything deemed illegal or improper. He had a reputation for being fair and he intended to live up to it.

WPC Mandy Burrows was disappointed Brian Blackmore would be away from work for the foreseeable future. He may be a lot older than she was, but she'd never met another man who could satisfy her like he could sexually, certainly not her current steady boyfriend or any of her lovers. Even without the pills she'd given him last time he'd made love to her like a man possessed and as the memories came flooding back, especially the recollections of the previous day she smiled in satisfaction.

PC John Reid walked past and caught sight of her. Mandy smiled seductively and blew him a playful kiss. A flush spread across his face, he would dearly love to tangle with WPC Burrows, but he was certain she would eat him alive. Feeling intimidated he gave her a half smile and carried on his way.

Mandy was annoyed more than upset by his rebuke. If

Blackmore wouldn't be in, John Reid at six foot three and fourteen and a half stone of solid muscle would have made an ideal substitute. The craving for sexual satisfaction was growing stronger with each passing moment. Climbing to her feet she made her way to the female changing room, went to her locker and with a look of sheer ecstasy took out her own police issue truncheon. In times of desperation it had never let her down.

8

Teresa Days' head felt as if someone had pushed large quantities of marshmallow into it via her ear canal. Her thought process felt muzzy and surrounding sounds were becoming slightly muffled.

The worse feeling however was the building pressure behind her eyes, which felt like it would push them from their sockets if the tension grew any greater.

Feeling distanced from her surroundings, she gingerly rose from her seat and with half closed eyelids to protect her from the intensely bright lights she slowly squinted at her table companions.

This was the first time she had been invited to come out with the senior partners of 'Hobson and Becket', a firm of accountants who had a reputation for doing the books for some of the largest criminal gangs in London, the emphasis on *doing*. This was a major and unforeseen change in her career as for the previous ten years she'd been a police officer and had only left the force owing to an incident in the back of a panda car with a married sergeant.

Teresa had a thing about unavailable men. They only had to show her a wedding ring glinting on their finger and she was smitten for as long as the men wanted to use her.

She watched as the vast area of drinks on the table grew smaller and smaller. She had consumed the best part of three bottles of house red and already her body had begun its admonishment.

Straightening up with the movement of a woman two or three decades older than her thirty-one years she rubbed her lower back and tried to stand tall. Her body ached and her upward motion relaxed her stomach causing her bladder to give the impression it was filled to bursting point. Gingerly she made her way to the ladies toilet, staggering into anyone who ventured within a few feet from her.

Once in the toilet she sat on the pan, bent over with her head in her hands enjoying the relief her emptying bladder gave. Without warning a sharp pain in her throat and tensing of her stomach told her she was about to vomit. Leaping up she turned around and stuck her head halfway down inside the bowl.

The liquid spurted from between her lips and for a brief horrific second, she forgot the wine and stared down at the sea of red forming before her eyes. When realisation finally dawned, Teresa managed a drunken giggle. She sat for a few moments allowing her stomach time to regain some calmness, pondering whether to go back and rejoin the others or quietly slip away.

The club had its usual cocktail of policemen, politicians, judges, violent criminals and famous celebrities. Who would miss her? After all she was merely the firm's receptionist. The latter option appealed more; still uneasy Teresa climbed slowly to her feet and walked out of the bathroom, aware of the other ladies disapproving looks as she stumbled by. She had after all made some strange sounds in her cubicle. Giggling she made her way back into the noise and lights that was 'The Maverick Club'.

9

Stella had spent what seemed like an age, sitting in front of the vanity mirror in the guest bedroom, applying her makeup. She had no intention of ever setting foot in the once happy marital room again. Had they ever been happy she thought and answered the question out loud, "Probably not." Her mind drifted back to some of the many beatings her husband had given her, some when he was fully aware of his actions and other times after he'd been swallowing or injecting his drugs. For days after Stella had sat in front of the mirror in her bedroom with silent tears trickling down her face as she looked at the bruises and teeth marks that covered her body, she also recalled all the lies she'd told to explain her injuries to others.

Stella shuddered as she came back to the present. Her hair had been given a slight curl and now hung loosely around her thin face creating an air of mystery. She wondered if she'd overdone the colour as it now shone with the brightness of a new copper penny. She'd removed her contact lenses which normally covered her rich earth coloured eyes, replacing them with a pair of sleek silver rimmed glasses which sat on the bridge of her nose. Ruby red lipstick had been applied sparingly and she'd added a touch off *Chanel No.5* to her neck and the top of her breasts.

The outfit she'd chosen complimented her slim figure and attractive face. A silk sparkly marine blue blouse hung loosely around the top of her hips. Her legs were encased in a tight pair of tan leather trousers and on her feet she wore black leather ankle boots.   Stella had always been a stunning woman and this fact had made the things Brian had done to her all the harder to swallow. Putting on a long cashmere coat she made her way towards her car and headed for 'The Maverick Club' where she was certain she would find what she was looking for, after all Brian had told her often enough when he'd left her alone to suffer another lonely night, that this was the place to be seen if you wanted anything...and he always added the word *anything* in a voice that had made her shudder. Somehow he'd managed to fill it with repulsion and filth. Even now fingers of icy cold tickled up and down her spine.

Pulling her coat tightly around her neck she pushed her foot down harder on the accelerator as if trying to speed herself away from the memory.

Teresa had stood leaning on one of the handrails overlooking the dance floor. She had always hated these types of places ever since her first visit in her teens. Nothing had changed; it still reminded her of a cattle market.

She felt better having cleared out her stomach and decided what she needed now was a breath of fresh air. Turning towards the exit she caught sight of a lady walking confidently towards her. Teresa thought she recognised the woman, but something was different. Was it the hair or the glasses? "Shit!" she said aloud, hating it when her mind had a momentary lapse, a blind spot, and couldn't throw forward a name.

Teresa was sure she should know this person. She was certain of it. The distance between them closed to a few feet and like a slap to the face the name leapt to the front of her head. "Bloody hell, its Stella bloody Blackmore," she screamed across the closing gap. She smiled at the fact she'd given the woman, now embracing her, a middle name.

"Teresa you look lovely, Christ it's been too long."

Teresa thought Stella looked overly pleased to see her and a quick shiver ran across her body. They'd been good friends once, but her addiction to married men had ended the relationship in a hail of tears and abuse. Teresa hadn't seen Stella for nearly three years.

"Aren't you going to give me a hug then?" Stella asked, her face breaking into the biggest smile Teresa had ever seen.

"Sure, it's just, you know, after what happened the last time we saw each other I kinda thought you'd always hate me."

Stella smelt the drink and saw how unsteady the other woman was. She was pleased as this would make her task a lot easier. "No, that was a long time ago. Time to make up," she gave a long pause before adding, "What do you say?"

Teresa choked and the tears ran down her face, she'd always felt guilty at what she'd done to her once good friend, "I'm sorry Stella," she muttered.

"Hey come on, don't be. Lets get you out into the fresh air and we can have a chat about old times."

Not waiting for a reply Stella put her arm around Teresa and led her out into the cold night air that filled the deserted alleyway at the rear of the club.

"It's bloody freezing out here Stella. Can we go somewhere for a drink or something?" Teresa asked through chattering teeth.

Stella looked into her old friends face and saw the happiness that meeting again after all these years had given her. She herself felt nothing but hatred. Maybe Teresa saw it too as she started to back away from her, but it was too late. Stella brought the sock filled with coins down on her head. Teresa collapsed in an unconscious heap onto the wet ground.

Stella bent down and examined the wound. Already a large lump had formed, while a slit like a grinning mouth had appeared on the top of it. A thin trail of blood oozed down across her forehead and began to puddle in the recess between Teresa's nose and her eye socket. She placed her arms under Teresa's shoulders and began to lift her up, but to her dismay Teresa's weight prevented her doing so. She sat down beside the limp body, head in her hands and started to cry. How could it all end before it had really begun?

"You okay love?" A mans voice above her asked.

Stella looked up and saw a young man of about twenty standing before her. Before she'd had time to say anything the man again asked her if she was okay.

"Not really," she answered. "It's my friend, she's so drunk she's fallen over and bumped her head. My car's just over there but I can't lift her."

The man's eyes sparkled in the moonlight and he smiled at her. "Come on between us I'm sure we can get her to the car."

Stella didn't say anything; instead she smiled and hoped she looked like a helpless woman just needing a little assistance.

Teresa was out cold, and even between them the lift was difficult. By the time they'd dropped her body into the car both were sweating and out of breath.

Stella stood on her tiptoes and, gave the man a quick kiss on the lips before driving away grinning like a Cheshire Cat.

Donald stood at the side of the road and gave a little wave after the red Mondeo. She was a beautiful woman and he'd noticed she wore a gold wedding ring.

As the car drove off into the night Donald envied her husband.

10

The Buckingham Arms public house had been the strong hold of Mickey Driscol's gang for as long as the local residents cared to remember. Not that many did. Mickey was a mountain of a man, weighing over 210lbs and at over six foot three his shadow blanketed most rooms he entered. The feature most recalled after meeting him for the first time was the zig zag scar that crossed from just under his right eye, over the bridge of his nose and down to the left edge of his thin, normally sneering lips. The cause of such an unsightly wound was never discussed, although rumour suggested he'd picked it up during a pub brawl with an off duty policeman years before he'd taken control of the North side of London.

The pub was quiet with only a handful of regulars dotted

about. In the furthest recess Mickey sat discussing a robbery with a small group of his men.

"So we all know what we're doing tomorrow?" he asked, slowly nodding his head and looking deeply into the eyes of each man as he allowed his question to sink in.

"Fairly straight forward boss," Tommy Black said, "Only problem I can think of is the area is normally covered by a lot of pigs."

Mickey let his head tilt back and leaned against the faded red velvet material that covered the lounge bar bench seats. "Don't you worry about that Tommy, its all sorted," he whispered to the ceiling.

A murmur of approval rippled around the table.

Alan Davidson, Mickey's driver, downed his third malt of the afternoon and shuddered as the whiskey burnt his insides. "We using the usual escape route?" he asked lackadaisically.

Mickey pulled his head forward and smiled at his friend, "Sure we are, however, I've also taken the liberty in asking the members of The Panel if they'll assist in the disposal of the gear once it's in our hands. They were very co-operative."

The mention of the most feared group of men in the capital both shocked the assembled group and excited them at the same time. Their gangland activities were large, but by involving the people who were the overlords to everything that happened in London the stakes had grown considerably higher.

"Why involve them?" Tommy Black asked in a fearful voice. "We run the North side and that's where the hit will be."

"Because Tommy I wanted to. Let's just say I have a plan that will get Bernie Reece off our backs and therefore allow us to run the South side as well."

The room broke into loud discussion as the men chipped in with their opinions. Finally Mickey intervened. "Enough of this shit. What's going down will happen because I say it will. Any of you fucks got a problem with that?"

Silence greeted him. "Good. I have contacts that're well in with the Panel and this gives us lots of possibilities, especially as the old bill will be distracted elsewhere when it goes down. Concentrate on doing your jobs right and its going to be a nice little earner...okay?"

Furious nodding of heads and mumbled apologies for the

earlier outburst filled the room. Mickey let his men talk and then shouted across to the barman for another round of drinks. Pretty soon he would be one of the strongest players in London and he couldn't wait for his moment of victory to arrive.

11

Teresa woke to a thumping headache for which she immediately blamed the drink she'd consumed the previous night. She tried to bring her hand up to rub at her aching temples, but couldn't. She screamed when she understood she was handcuffed to a chair which sat in the middle of someone's bedroom.

Vague images flickered before her eyes, disco lights, the ground coming to meet her as she fell, a hurried car journey, being helped from the car, a strange stairway; all of these images were intermingled with periods of darkness as though her memory had been erased at inappropriate intervals. She looked around, taking in the modern double bed with its black cast iron headboard, shaped into Gothic spikes. It was covered with a purple duvet cover and bright white lacey pillows, embroidered in the corners with small red roses. She saw the pine wardrobe, chest of drawers and the dressing table with an array of make up and grooming accessories.

Finally her wandering gaze settled on a wooden picture frame, the occupiers she recognised immediately. Brian and Stella Blackmore.

Her mind raced, heart pumping in fear, every sense telling her she was in danger.

Teresa screamed once more. Her bellow for help was cut short by the sight of the door opening and Stella Blackmore standing before her. Gone were the fancy clothes and the carefully applied make-up. They had been replaced by a dark track suit and a face that almost looked like it had been scrubbed too clean. As if the owner had wanted to remove the top layer of skin.

Teresa started to speak, "Stel..."

"Shut up!" Stella shouted as she walked towards her old friend.

Teresa desperately wanted to ask what Stella was doing, but she already knew her best course of action would be to do just as her captor suggested. She waited for Stella to say something.

"This is quite simple," Stella began. "You know how much of a bastard my ex-husband has been to me over the years."

"Ex!" Teresa butted in.

Stella ignored her. "I want you to tell me the names of everybody he slept with, bought drugs from and more importantly tell me how many times you slept with him."

"Stella don't be stupid. How the hell do I know any of that?"

Stella didn't respond verbally, she walked up to Teresa and slapped her with such force she rocked back and forward on her chair. "Listen bitch," she spat, "Don't give me the, I know nothing shit. He told me he'd shagged you, told me you were gagging for it. It gave him great satisfaction to tell me some of the names of his sluts as he rammed into me. Can you imagine what that feels like, having your own husband screaming the names of his lovers in your ear when he is having sex with you? Can you?"

Teresa looked into Stella's eyes and saw the truth. She hated her with every fiber in her body.

"Please Stella, I'm sorry. I can't help myself, you know that."

Another stinging slap stopped her talking, "You'll give me names or I'll kill you," Stella had bent over her to whisper the last three words. It had the effect she had hoped, Teresa started to scream.

"Carry on honey," she sneered. "Nobody will hear you here. I'll come back later and hopefully you'll have some news for me, eh?" and with that she retreated from the room.

Teresa watched her leave closing the door behind her. Before it had shut the tears had started to fall.

12

Mark Carter stood in his empty living room. His breath made patterns in the air as it swirled from his mouth, owing to the cold temperature he'd found inside the house.

He was confused by this. He hated it when he and his girlfriend were on opposite shifts, especially when he was on nights and she was on the 6am-2pm tour of duty. It meant they were like ships that passed in the night, never seeing even the other's shadow as one crept into bed and the other out of it.

Carter had expected her to put the heating on timer for when she awoke. The place was freezing and he felt sorry for her as he imagined how cold it must have been when she had risen earlier. He longed for her, wanted to feel her naked flesh next to his. Taking off his clothes as he went he crossed the hall to the bedroom, threw back the bed clothes and jumped in. The anticipated warmth he was sure she would have left him had been replaced by an icy cold that bit into his skin.

Mark Carter didn't need to be a police inspector to realise Mandy hadn't slept in the bed.

The pain in Teresa's throat was excruciating, having screamed continuously for the past four hours. She knew exactly how long she'd called for help owing to the large grandfather clock that sat opposite her. She'd noticed it had a painting of one of the Saints almost hidden behind the hands. Teresa was not remotely religious and could not name which Saint it was, but this one seemed to be looking down mocking her.

Her wrists were bleeding where she'd rubbed the flesh away, desperately trying to escape the handcuffs. It was a futile gesture, and she knew she was trapped like a fly in a large and sticky spider's web.

Stella had been clever because she'd tied her feet to the base of the chair and as it reclined slightly Teresa couldn't get any lift, therefore she was unable to move towards the door to see if she could get out that way or reach a window and yell for help.

Teresa's situation had sobered her up and though fear gripped at her heart causing her breathing to come in shallow bursts she began to rack her brains as to why Stella was doing this to her. After all it had been three years earlier that she had been having the affair with Brian. Surely, if revenge was the name of the game, Stella could have taken it much sooner.

Teresa knew Brian had treated her very badly, both physically and mentally, she also knew a lot of the names Stella wanted her to pass on, but what would she do to them if she did divulge the information?

More importantly what would she do to her? Teresa shivered as the cold night air nipped her skin through her clothes.

The clock ticked the night slowly away and it was now 4am. Stella had not returned and Teresa wondered where she was and what she was doing? The other thing that rattled around her head gnawing away at her mind was the emphasis Stella had put on the word 'ex' when she'd mentioned her husband. What had she meant? Maybe he had left her and this was the reason Stella had lost it. Maybe they'd decided to get a divorce.

Maybe she's killed him.

Teresa gasped as the thought entered her head, as surely as she knew her own name she was certain that's what Stella had done, and if she had killed once that meant there would be no hesitation to do it again.

Tears of panic cascaded down her cheeks as she tried to kick her legs free from their bindings and attempted to pull her wrists from the handcuffs. All she managed to do was twist them further into her bleeding flesh. She did not, could not, feel the pain such was the level of shock she was descending into. She would have to tell Stella something, give her all the names she could think of and although she didn't believe in God she would pray to him now. Teresa knew she would need all the help she could get.

Stella sat in the kitchen clutching another hot mug of coffee to her breast. She'd been listening to the screaming from the upstairs bedroom intermingled with cries of help for half the night. There was no need to worry about anyone hearing as the house sat well back from its nearest neighbour. Now silence was her companion.

She knew Teresa had a lot of Brian's ex-lovers names in her head, she also knew she could tell her who gave him the drugs. After all Teresa had been secretly swallowing tablets for years, and had tried on more than one occasion to tempt Stella.

Teresa had told her there were pills that would help her forget the beatings, help her to cope with his affairs. Stella grunted as she recalled this was before Teresa herself had ended up in bed with Brian.

Her calmness amazed her as she felt totally in control. She was sure she should be feeling anger towards her captive and worry at the situation she'd put herself in, but there were none of these emotions, gone was the bullied wife, banished the submissive woman who when asked to jump would ask 'how high?' Stella had a plan and she would carry it out. Perhaps then she would revive her senses which at the present time felt incapable of feeling anything. They were numb.

Sipping the hot drink, her mind ran over the next steps. Obtain the names from Teresa, find out where the people lived and pay them a visit. What happened next would depend on what was said and how well they begged for their lives. Stella took one last mouthful of coffee and then made her way back to where Teresa was shackled to the chair.

When she entered the room it was clear Teresa had worn herself out, as she sat slumped over, obviously asleep.

Stella walked over to her and lifted her head by the hair. Teresa stirred slightly, but not enough to please Stella. Dropping her head back down Stella then tipped the remaining coffee over the back of Teresa's neck.

The temperature had died slightly, but the liquid had remained hot enough to scald. Teresa screamed awake as her skin blistered. Tears of pain flowed down her face and terror pumped through her veins.

"Don't fall asleep on me now," Stella sneered.

Teresa found it difficult to reply, as her senses were fighting the burning sensation that raged from her neck to the base of her spine.

"Don't try and fuck with me Teresa or a minor burn will be the least of your problems."

Teresa exploded "Minor fucking burn!"

The fist hit her straight in the face and she heard the crack as her nose was pushed towards her brain.

"Tell me the names or this will only get worse."

Teresa coughed as blood from her nose ran down her throat; the pain was thrusting deep into her head. She could feel her body drifting away and knew she'd pass out soon. Looking up at Stella she saw once more the hatred in her eyes and knew she'd be dead soon whether she gave the names or not. The thought drifted away and with it went her consciousness.

Stella remained calm, she knew she'd not achieved what she'd wanted, but something deep inside her had taken over her actions. Normally she was not a violent person, but somehow new talents had risen to the top of her psyche. Had she lost the plot? Fallen down into an abyss of madness? Putting it down to the situation she found herself in she smiled and gazed down at the slumped body before her. Time was passing and she knew she needed the names. She went to the bathroom and filled a waste paper basket with cold water. Looking down she saw the water gushing out through the wicker basket and she cursed herself inwardly for being so stupid. Still if she hurried she would have enough to hopefully wake Teresa up. Frantically, she ran to where she sat still unconscious and threw it over her. Teresa sat bolt upright as if given an electric shock. Seeing Stella before her caused panic to rise and she once again began to scream.

Stella let her for a few moments and then she brought the basket down sharply on top of her head. It may not have been a metal bin, but the wicker made deep scratches in Teresa's flesh and thin lines of blood trickled down her skin. "Listen to me you stupid cow, I want names now. No more pissing about, understand?"

The pause caused Teresa to nod furiously and she started to shout out names, "Dave Bennett, Steven Reilly..."

"Wait." Stella said holding up her hand. "I need a pen or something to write these down." She left the room leaving Teresa crying with a mixture of pain, terror and frustration. When she returned she was carrying a large notebook and a bright pink pencil. "All I could find," she said in a humorous voice which was lost on the terrified Teresa. "Okay start again," she ordered.

Once more the names spilled from her mouth; one by one Stella carefully jotted them down asking whether they were sleeping partners or the people Brian had bought his drugs from.

After ten minutes and thirty two names Teresa had run out of information. "That's all I know Stella, honest to God."

Stella studied her face for a long time trying to detect any lies. Finally she said quietly, "Fair enough."

"What are you going to do with me now?" Teresa asked in a quivering voice.

There was another long silence during which Stella checked over the list of names before her. Most of them she knew or had known. Without looking up she answered the question, "Kill you of course."

Panic gripped at Teresa's heart and she struggled to catch her breath, finally she started to scream.

Still without looking at her face Stella casually walked behind her, pulled her head back and cut her throat with the large kitchen knife she'd placed there before her victim had even sat in her death chair.

Teresa made gurgling sounds as her life poured from the gaping wound, blood gushed down her blouse changing the colour in seconds and Stella held onto her head grinning to herself as her revenge on the cheating bitch was completed.

It only took moments for the body to go limp. Stella released her grip and watched the head roll forward, and then she went to make another cup of coffee.

13

Billy Johnstone glanced down at his gold Rolex and saw it was nearly six-thirty. The early morning sunshine caught the diamond encrusted hands and sparkled back at him. Billy smiled, remembering how he'd shown the watch to his colleagues telling them it was one of the best fakes on the market. He could hardly tell them the truth, that it was the genuine article, how would he explain such a watch on his pay? Nor could he mention it had been a gift from the members of The Panel.

Despite the early rays, the temperature in the car was still cold enough for him to watch his breath dance away from his mouth, turned into a frozen mist that swayed its way into oblivion.

This was the day that Mickey Driscol took charge of all criminal activities in London, supervised of course by The Panel. Billy knew they'd connections with every major crime organisation, both in the United Kingdom and worldwide, such as the Mafia. He was also aware of the arms deals to the IRA and how The Panel used these terrorists in jobs of their own.

The plan had been simple enough, using inside contacts a robbery had been set up at *Smyth & Jones*, one of the countries leading jewelers. Both Driscol and his opposite number from across the Thames, Bernie Reece had been supplied the information necessary to carry out the crime. Driscol however was the only one aware of the other gangster's involvement. It hadn't taken Billy long to work out what was going to happen at the scene. Mickey Driscol and his men would turn up armed to the teeth and murder Reece, steal the jewelry and set it up to look like Reece died in a bungled robbery. There was no other suitable candidates who could prevent Mickey taking over the dead mans patch.

The tension was mounting in his vehicle, any second it would all go off. The robbery had been arranged for just before quarter to seven and Billy's part in the operation had to take place just before then.

Checking again the time he saw only a few minutes had ticked slowly past, "Bollocks," he said to no-one in particular. The thin man bundled up against the elements sitting beside him looked across and grinned.

"Stay cool Billy it won't be long now," he offered, hoping to settle the nerves he could clearly see building up in Billy's face.

"Easy for you to say Tom, this is my baby and if it goes to rat shit, it'll be my fault."

"Nothing's going to go wrong. We'll be in and out in no time. The bastards won't know what's hit them."

Billy forced a grin to spread across his bluish lips. The cold was biting into his flesh and he badly wanted to switch the ignition on to warm up his stiffening limbs.

The silence was broken, when a voice crackled across the radio lying on his lap. "Alpha one. Alpha one. Go. Go. Go."

"That's us mate." The thin man gestured towards the house they were sitting outside.

Both he and Billy along with the two other men who had been nodding in the back seats burst out the car and sprinted across to number eighteen *Belvedere Road*. One of the men smashed down the front door with one almighty kick and they were inside.

Billy took the stairs to the top floor in leaps of three, shouting as he went, "Stephen, we know you're in here. Don't do anything stupid."

A spotty youth appeared before him at the top of the stairs. He was naked apart from a pair of boxer shorts. Billy noticed the small teddy bear heads that decorated them. "Nice," he said as he rammed his fist into the youths stomach. Stephen MacCulloch collapsed at his feet, gasping for breath. The others had arrived beside Billy. The thin man informed him the house was otherwise empty. Billy knelt down beside the prostrate youth and grabbing a handful of his hair pulled his head away from the wooden floorboards, "Stephen I'm afraid you're under arrest for burglaries at *Marks and Spencers, Boots the Chemist,* and *Tescos.* Anything to say?" Before his prisoner had time to answer he added, "Nothing...good." Turning to the thin man he said, "Take him down the nick. I'll stay here until we've searched the place fully."

"Okay Skip," the thin man replied as he dragged the youth away.

Detective Sergeant Billy Johnstone knew he'd done his job well. He'd arranged for three teams to systematically take out the members of the gang suspected of a range of burglaries across town. He'd been particularly careful to ensure most of the stations resources would be taken up by the early morning raids and that the operation was taking place across town from *Smyth and Jones.* This would ensure a poor response when the alarm at the said premises went off around 06.45.

The smile had returned to his face when he walked through to the kitchen and flicked the switch on the kettle. He fancied a hot drink to warm him up a bit, although the money he was going to earn from this scam would provide him with several trips to warmer climates. Billy was already planning his first holiday when a screeching female voice hollered across his personal radio that a major robbery was in progress at the jewelers. He'd sent his car back to the station with the prisoner so he was unable to attend. Sitting down he put his feet up on the kitchen table and waited for the kettle to boil.

14

Carter knew it was a risk as much as he knew she would not be pleased he'd phoned her at work, but he had to know where she had been the previous night.

His girlfriend came on the phone, "What the hell are you doing ringing me at work?"

He'd expected her to be annoyed, but the venom in her voice surprised him, "I was worried. You didn't sleep at home last night. Where were you?"

Mandy had rehearsed her reply in anticipation of the question, "I stayed at Sally's. Since when have I had to report to you?"

Again he was shocked by her tone. She was lying to him,

he could tell by the lack of emotion in her voice. She was giving him practiced replies. "I know you're lying to me. Where were you?" He hadn't meant to raise his voice, but was unable to prevent it. Looking around he checked no-one had walked past his office doorway before continuing in a quieter tone, "Well, I'm waiting."

The phone went dead at the other end and he listened to the constant drone for several seconds before slamming the receiver back down with such force he heard the plastic crack under the impact, "Bollocks!" he said loudly, not caring anymore.

Getting to his feet he made his way out into the corridor. There were a few officers milling around, but none took any notice of him. He knew his carefully hidden secret would be out in the open soon. The only way he could keep track of Mandy's whereabouts was if he came clean with his senior bosses and asked that she be transferred to his station on the grounds of his future happiness. Whether they'd agree to such a request after he had kept them in the dark was debatable, but Carter felt he had to try. How else could he prevent what he knew was already happening. Mandy was having an affair. What else could all the recent events mean?

***

Stella allowed her eyes to flick over the names, hungrily devouring the list that Teresa had supplied, believing that giving them would save her life.

Stella had mixed emotions as she studied the ex-lovers and drug suppliers who'd fueled her husband's vicious temper. The details were carefully scrawled onto the A4 pad she'd used. She was amazed to find herself staring at a list of over thirty names and allowed a brief smile to pass across her lips as she realised that Teresa, even fearful of her life had somehow managed to give the names in near alphabetical order. She noticed her handwriting was shaky to say the least and she remembered there were specialists who could tell a lot about a person's personality from reading their writing. She giggled wondering what they'd think of a housewife murderer.

Stella noticed that she'd put the pencil to the paper with her hand trembling so much that she had punctured the pad on numerous occasions, her writing looked like a drunken spider had dipped his eight legs in a pot of ink and gone for a walk across the paper. She studied the writing, which could hardly be recognised as her own, and decided it showed how much tension she was feeling in anticipation of the task ahead.

Happiness dominated her mind as names she knew stared back at her. They'd been faces Brian had introduced to her in the early days at social functions, when she'd believed life would always be a long line of parties and making new friends.

Anger trampled on her happy mood as she remembered where three of the names had been brought to her attention, Manville County Hospital Accident and Emergency.

Brian had beaten her to a pulp, breaking her wrist and causing internal bleeding where a broken rib had punctured her left lung, such was the force he'd put into one of the many kicks he'd rained down on her.

Stella stiffened as she remembered all that pain and suffering had been caused because he'd come home early from work and she hadn't finished cooking the dinner.

Yet again she'd told the doctors she'd fallen down the stairs. The police were there investigating a fatal road traffic accident in which a family of five had been crushed under an artic lorry. Brian had told her to stop crying from her minor injuries and think of the suffering the accident had caused other people.

"Minor injuries," Stella muttered. "Bastard!"

She recalled feeling sick to her stomach and being undecided as to whether it was the terrible death of the family in the crash or her bold as brass husband's attitude. He'd been so calm as he'd introduced his colleagues to her, totally devoid of worry that it had been him that put her there and he should now be accompanying these officers to the station on an assault charge.

The pain bubbled away, causing Stella to feel dizzy and breathless.

The list now lay on a small dark brown circular mahogany table. Stella sat beside it holding a glass of water tightly in her right hand. Her left hand was resting open on her lap and contained half a dozen headache tablets. The tension had slowly crept up from her lower back, gripping the muscles around her spine like powerful hands, before settling to gnaw at the base of her neck. Stiffness had joined the attack and Stella knew she must relax before deciding on her first victim from the list of names before her, casually like a small child picking a sweet from a bowl of candy.

A squad car had finally been sent to pick up Billy. As they pulled into the station yard it looked like all hell had broken loose. Dozens of police vehicles had been abandoned at random, some with their doors gaping wide open where the occupiers had decamped in a hurry.

"Jesus what's all this?" he asked the driver of the car.

"The robbery at *Smyth and Jones* turned into a fuck up from what we can make out so far."

"Go on," Billy prompted.

"Apparently Bernie Reece was shot dead by one of his own men, or so one of the security guards said."

Billy took a sharp intake of breath. There wasn't supposed to be anyone at the shop who could turn out to be a witness. "Security guard," he asked puzzled, "What was he doing there?"

The driver waited until he'd managed to find a space to park his vehicle before answering. "Unfortunately for him, he was just passing by from another job he does and saw the whole thing go down. Poor bastard got shot in the process. Told the first guys on the scene what he saw and then went into a coma. Pretty serious from what I've been told."

Billy felt slightly better. The guard could identify members of the Driscol gang and therefore make the job look very strange. Why would the two major players in the capital do the same premises at the same time? Coincidence or a set up? He knew where his money would go.

Climbing the stairs to the CID office he bumped into Mandy Burrows who as usual looked incredibly sexy in her uniform. He was sure she deliberately wore a size too small so it clung to her and revealed more of her shapely curves than it should. "Hi Mandy," he said taking in the fullness of her tight white shirt.

"Billy, have you heard about the robbery?"

"Sure sweetness, nothing for you to worry your pretty little head about."

"But if there's a gang war to see who takes over Reece's patch won't that affect the club?"

Billy looked around checking there were no prying ears listening to their conversation. "Everything's okay. The robbery was a set up so Mickey can take charge of Reece's territory. Nothing has changed; you'll still be needed to entertain selected clients."

Mandy smiled with satisfaction, her drug habit was growing stronger and she badly needed the extra cash to pay for her fix. Her boyfriend was growing suspicious and she could feel a parting of the ways there. That would leave her with nowhere to stay so she'd have to speak to someone at the club to remedy this. Perhaps Mickey Driscol himself would look after her; after all he seemed to enjoy taking her body when he felt like it.

Playfully she blew a kiss at Billy and skipped off down the stairs leaving him smiling after her as his eyes followed her tight skirt disappearing out of sight. The office was a hive of activity; detectives were talking on the telephone, listing the details of the stolen property from the jewelers, while others were still sorting out the evidence to put to the gang of arrested burglars from earlier. Billy walked over to his desk and saw Mike Grady reading over a witness statement, "Hi Mike, what've you got there?"

Detective Mike Grady looked up, Billy saw a worried expression on his face and noticed that his hands were shaking slightly. "This is the security guards statement. Says here he thinks he can recognise some of the men who did the robbery."

"So that doesn't mean he can say which gang they belong to. That's if he means recognise as in he knows who they are or just he'd be able to identify them from mug shots."

"Put like that I suppose it could be worse."

"Besides if there is a problem it'll be taken care of. Just focus on doing your job and don't worry. Big pay checks coming soon."

"Yeah, I'll need to use some of it to have my ulcer treated," Mike said sarcastically.

Billy squeezed him on the shoulder before walking off to see what the other detectives were doing. Once he knew the score he'd have to make a call to the club and see if things went according to plan or if complications had arisen apart from the wounded guard.

15

The tight lycra shorts stretched over her tanned and muscled thighs, filling every inch as if the material worn was a form of magic liquid.

Mandy studied herself in the mirror, she knew she looked good, and that was why Detective Wilson had taken her up on her suggestion the previous night to go for a drink after work.

Mandy had repaid his keenness with a thirty minute session in the back of his car that the married father of three would never forget and would surely make him come back begging for more.

Her boyfriend would swallow the excuse of staying with her friend when he saw her in her cycling gear, the sweat from riding home having made it even tighter, although Mandy doubted that was possible, and if he didn't that was his problem. She was tired of him anyway. Picking up her back pack she made her way out into the yard to where she'd previously padlocked her bike, aware of the many male eyes feasting themselves on her body as she crossed the forecourt to the bike shed.

Stella ran up to the young policeman just as he was about to turn the corner and come into the view of anyone looking out of one of the police station windows. He looked surprised at seeing her rushing towards him at such a speed, "Can I help you, Madam?" he asked in a helpful yet slightly surprised voice.

Stella waited for her breath to recover. "I'm sorry to bother you officer," taking in a large gulp of air she continued, "I've been sent here by my friend to meet Mandy Burrows. She's her mum."

"I thought her mum lived in Manchester?" the officer asked quizzically.

"Yes she does, but she'd arranged to come down today by train to meet Mandy. They were going to do a bit of shopping or something like that, anyway she rang me because I live here and unfortunately her train has been delayed. She hasn't got the number to the station so asked if I could come here and let Mandy know she will be late."

"Good idea," the policeman said with a smile, glad the woman before him did not want help with anything major as he was looking forward to going home at the end of his shift in less than half an hour.

"The problem I have officer is that I said I would relay the message, but it was only when I got here I realised I've never met Mandy. Silly I know but could you please tell me what she looks like?"

PC Griffon had a brief impulse to say 'sure she has tits that defy gravity, legs that go on forever and eyes that demand you do what she asks'. The moment passed and he merely said, "She'll be out in about twenty minutes on a red and gold mountain bike. You can't miss her she sprays on the outfit she wears home."

Stella didn't have time to thank the young man as he began to walk away from her as he finished his sentence. Glad it would be easy to identify Mandy she wondered why she'd decided to start with one of the names she didn't know. No immediate answer sprung to mind so she returned to sit out the remaining minutes before she came face-to-face with Mandy, in the comfort of her car.

When the woman on the bike shot out into the street, Stella thought how right the policeman had been regarding the spray on outfit Mandy would be wearing. From a distance it looked like one of the publicity stunts Stella had seen in one of her 'girlie magazines' as her dead husband called them, where a girl's flesh had been painted in the colours of a particular football team. Even the light wind made no impression on the material the cyclist was wearing such was the closeness with which it clung to her body.

Stella snapped from her thoughts when she became aware a gap of around a hundred meters had already been placed between her and the fast moving bike.

Starting her engine she glanced behind her to make sure the road was clear, before she pulled out, intending to catch Mandy Burrows up. No definite idea had been formulated in her head regarding killing the woman, however, she'd ruled out a hit and run. She was driving her husband's car and so couldn't afford any problems from witnesses who may see her running the cyclist over.

Her best bet Stella decided would be to stop Mandy, and spin her a story about how Brian wanted to meet her. That was the best idea, but as she sped along she wondered what she could say to make the WPC want to come home with her.

Mandy pedaled hard, enjoying the freedom her bike gave her and the sensation as the wind rushed through her hair, coupled with the invigorating feeling as it nibbled at her skin. Her lungs filled with the cooling air and her heart muscles pumped furiously in their efforts to sustain the speed her legs were spinning the bike pedals. The enjoyment however was being spoiled by the driver of the car behind, who'd come up too close and was now honking a horn at her.

Mandy's first impression was the driver wanted her to move closer to the kerb, so they could over take her, but the horn was being sounded in too friendly a manner for that to be the case. Mandy slowed down enough to be able to glance over her shoulder at the following car. She saw a lady waving at her, supporting a huge smile and indicating to her to pull over.

Mandy didn't recognise the driver, but couldn't imagine there was any danger in stopping to see what she wanted. Easing her pedal rate she pulled over to the side of the road and watched as the car passed her and came to a stop about ten feet in front of her.

Stella fought to control her nerves, which were causing a slight trembling in her hands. This needed to sound perfect if she had any chance of persuading Mandy Burrows to come home with her. Taking a deep breath she made her way towards the place where Mandy stood leaning her bike to one side, allowing her to place her left foot firmly on the road.

Stella began hoping the other woman would fail to notice the hesitation in her voice. "Sorry to stop you like this, but my husband Brian asked me to catch you after work. I was daydreaming and only just noticed you had come out and were cycling up the road. You must be very fit to ride that quickly." Stella watched with fascination the change in the woman's facial expression as she spoke. It had gone from curiosity at being stopped to one of amazement as the wife of the man she had slept with wanted to pass on a message from him to her. Stella couldn't suppress the smile that exploded across her face.

"Brian?" Mandy asked in a voice filled with surprise.

"Yeah, he wants you to come back with me to see him. Says you have something he wants."

Mandy nearly choked. "What do I have that he would want?" She asked in a voice she hoped would be taken as one filled with surprise. She didn't like the way Brian's wife was now staring at her.

"Come on Mandy, I know all about you and Brian. I know about the drugs, the sex, everything." She waited for her words to have maximum impact before continuing. "Let's not play games here. Brian wants some more pills."

Although Mandy had not been a police woman for long she'd heard of elaborate stings where the Complaints Investigation Bureau set officers up to catch them carrying out illegal activities. Surely this couldn't be one of those. After all it was only uppers and downers she dealt in. Not prepared to take any chances however she asked, "Where's Brian now? I can give him a ring on my mobile to see what he's talking about because I haven't got a clue what's going on her."

Stella was getting annoyed. "Oh come. Have you got some gear for him or not? I'm sure you're not the only bit of skirt he plays with who can supply what he wants."

Mandy had been hurt to the quick. She was not naive enough to believe Brian had only slept with her, in fact knew this to be the case, but to have his wife be so insulting to her and to make it sound as though she was nothing to Brian got under her skin. Forgetting her previous worries she said, "I've nothing on me. I'll come round in an hour. I thought he was up at his mum's though, will he be there?"

Stella felt proud of herself for having won the mental battle. Mandy's self importance had cost her dearly. "Course he'll be there. He came back for some clean clothes and he needed some of your magic pills. Don't worry about me being there as well, we've a very open marriage; he does what he wants and so do I. I'll bet he told you I was some sort of ogre eh?" She grinned at Mandy.

Taking a chance to even the score a little Mandy replied. "No, he's never mentioned you."

Smug bitch, Stella thought. Still she wouldn't be that way for much longer. "Okay, I'll tell him to expect you later. Like your outfit by the way."

Mandy was about to reply, but the other woman had turned her back and begun walking to her car. Funny, she thought, Brian hadn't said much about his wife, but she was amazed he hadn't mentioned how hard she was and had kept secret the fact they both had affairs. Shrugging her shoulders Mandy climbed back onto her bike and began to pedal home, this time it wasn't the wind that gave her warm sensations, it was the thoughts of what she and Brian would get up to in less than an hour. Smiling broadly she pedaled faster.

The telephone call had gone well, Billy hadn't been allowed to speak to any of the members of The Panel, but he'd been informed the guard would be taken care of if he ever came out of the coma he was now in. The hospital doctors had told one of the nurses on The Panels payroll that it looked very doubtful, owing to his internal injuries.

Everything else had gone well. Driscol had fired the bullet that had killed his rival and four other members of the Reece gang had been blown away. The rest apparently, when they found out what was going down were glad to switch their allegiances to Driscol, especially when they heard the job had been sanctioned from inside the bowels of the Maverick club. Billy was informed the jewelry haul was around two million in diamonds, so all in all it had been a very successful day's work, and he was to call into the club when he decided it was safe to do so and collect his share of the proceeds.

At times like this he loved the role he'd taken on. He'd enjoyed being a straight policeman, but knew he'd never be rich doing just that. Then a fellow officer told him about the rewards of turning a blind eye, at first he'd been intrigued, then hooked and now he'd plunged himself in at the deep end. He was happy and it wasn't going to end now. The Panel was strong, and if he was ever uncovered they'd look after him. Safe in this knowledge he went to pass the good news on to Mike Grady.

16

The house had grown colder since she'd left earlier, and Stella's breath created clouds of icy vapor before her. Fascinated she blew out as hard as she could and watched the white mist dance before her.

Her heart still thumped furiously with a mixture of excitement and anger at how the meeting with Mandy Burrows had gone. She'd sensed the other woman's suspicions from the start and thought she'd done well to suppress them, however her fury was directed at how well Mandy had taken the news she was aware her husband cheated on her and how coolly she'd accepted her invitation to come and see Brian at her house. It had all been so matter of fact, as if these things happened every day. Stella thought that at her dead husband's police station perhaps they did.

She looked up at the clock and guessed Mandy would be on time, which gave her precious little breathing space to prepare. The plan was simple, tell Mandy that Brian was in the bedroom waiting for her, let her walk in and see the dead body on the floor and when she screamed and turned around to get away *bang*, it would all be over.

What Stella had to do before she arrived was to place a plastic sheet under the rug at the bedroom door so any blood would not stain the carpet and would allow her to move the body easier later. One of the ideas she'd had was to position the bodies on the bed in such a manner as to suggest they had been having sex when she caught them, and then in a rage shot them. It would be a crime of passion, but then she'd realised there would be more bodies at different places and it wouldn't matter about the two found at her home. Besides, Stella knew how she was going to commit all the murders and get away with it.

The hot water pummeled Mandy's neck and shoulders, she sighed as the tensions of her day were beaten away. She was surprised at the mixed feelings that flowed through her veins. She felt guilty at the way she was treating Mark, even though she was thinking about ending their affair, and total disbelief at the relationship Brian had with his wife. Mandy was also shocked at how calmly his wife had invited her to visit him later for sex, after all what else would he want her for?

It was the guilty feeling that troubled her most. Mark still meant something to her, in fact if pushed she had to admit she still loved him, but he was not enough for her, no man was or ever could be. She'd thought he was different and shuddered as she remembered how she'd convinced him to allow her to move in so soon after they'd met. She'd always acted on impulse, but now regretted doing it.

Mandy felt trapped with a man she loved, but couldn't remain faithful to or stay with him for the rest of her life.

She'd nowhere else to go if she finished with Mark. Perhaps she should stay and continue the life style she'd grown accustomed too. Use him and abuse him.

Mandy smiled as she started to think about Brian Blackmore and the last time they'd had sex. The store room had been filled to the brim with different boxes of files, assorted papers, stacks of pens and magic markers, but somehow they'd found a space large enough to squeeze in their rampant bodies, which also provided minimum cover should anyone else enter the room.

Mandy grinned and relished a repeat performance later. Who knows his wife wasn't bad looking, maybe they could persuade her into joining in with the fun.

Mandy started laughing. All her thoughts of guilt over Mark forgotten.

Stella watched as Mandy slowly poured herself from her blue BMW convertible. The young police woman was dressed like a two bit whore and as she walked up the drive way, the wind caught under her flimsy dress and blew the material up around her waist, her struggles to cover up did not prevent Stella seeing the frilly suspender belt holding up the dark seductive stockings. "How can she be so brazen?" Stella muttered, her anger rising. She'd known Mandy would take her up on the offer to meet Brian, but she was stunned at how she'd dressed for the occasion. Mandy had come making a statement. Stella read it as, *I'm younger, better looking and far sexier than you are or could ever be.*

Stella *had* taken time with her own clothing, needing Mandy to believe she might join them in bed, but her idea of sexual clothing remained several levels below the woman ringing the doorbell.

Stella opened the door and saw that Mandy was grinning like a Cheshire cat who'd found a never ending supply of cream. "Hello Mandy, come in please," she offered as she stepped aside and let Mandy walk past. "Did you have difficulty finding the house?" she asked, trying to make polite conversation to control her building rage. She didn't want to kill Mandy anywhere other than outside her bedroom.

"No, I've been here lots of times," Mandy replied casually, her smile this time showing her beautifully white teeth.

"Really, I wasn't aware of that," Stella mumbled, swallowing hard as the younger woman revealed the fuller details of Brian's infidelity.

"Yeah, you know how Brian is when he gets the urge, don't you?" She gave Stella a slight dig in the ribs to encourage a reply.

"Yes I do and I know he has an urge right now. He's upstairs waiting for *us*," Stella whispered the last word to emphasize to Mandy she was going to be part of the game. She wasn't prepared for Mandy's next movement however, as she leaned closer and gently stroked Stella's right breast, "I thought you were game Stella, by the way you acted earlier. You're quite a bonus. Brian never mentioned how filthy his wife was."

Stella felt sick, "I bet he didn't, he likes to keep me a surprise."

"Great idea, I can hardly wait. What about you?"

Moving as if she'd been bitten, Stella pulled away. "Come on save it for upstairs," she managed to say before pushing Mandy in the direction of the bedroom.

"Hey, you're in a hurry," Mandy said misreading Stella's body language.

In a rush they arrived at the bedroom door. Mandy turned around to see Stella slowly dropping the zip on her dress, causing it to fall to the floor. She was naked underneath apart from a small pair of pink pants. "Wow, you're gorgeous," Mandy gasped and moved to touch her.

"Inside," Stella said seductively, pointing to the closed bedroom door.

Mandy was now so turned on by what she believed was about to happen, she failed to hear the rustling of the plastic sheet under her footstep, failed to see the shotgun propped up against the dark mahogany chest, which stood beside the bedroom entrance, and most importantly of all, was so oblivious in her hurry to open the door, didn't see Stella move to pick it up and level it at her back.

Mandy turned the handle and pushed open the door.

At first her eyes didn't grasp the sight before her. Her lover Brian was lying beside the bed, except it was only about two thirds of him. He was lying on a carpet of red and his eyes were blank staring orbs. The sight that started the scream to rise from deep inside her throat was his gaping open mouth, as if he was shouting at her to help him.

Mandy turned to run, but stopped when she felt the cold steel of the barrel from the shotgun dig into her flesh. Lifting her gaze she saw Stella before her. This time Stella was the one grinning.

"Screw my husband, you slut? Now you're the one who's screwed."

"Please, Stella, let me go," Mandy mumbled through her tears, as her plight became so terrifyingly obvious to her.

"Might have done if you hadn't turned up here bold as brass, expecting to sleep with him again with me here."

Mandy opened her mouth to speak again, but Stella cut her short when she pulled the trigger.

A macabre painting of death erupted onto the walls, bedroom door and carpet. Mandy stood upright for a brief moment, a hole as big as a basket ball blown through her midriff, and then she crumpled at the feet of the grinning Stella Blackmore.

Stella looked down at the dead body of one of her husband's lovers. She had to admit to herself Mandy had been both very pretty, with a toned and trim body most men would have wanted, and had an attitude that would challenge them to try their luck. Now naked herself she went into the guest bedroom and stood before the large vanity mirror. For her age she still looked good enough, and she'd avoided cellulite around the areas women have been battling to keep smooth for many years, the hips, thighs and buttocks.

Turning to look at her bottom she clenched her cheeks together and was delighted to see tight skin and a smoothness that surprised her. Her breasts felt firm to her touch and her hair felt silky as she ran her fingers through it. Mandy had the edge owing to her sexuality, Stella felt most of hers had been beaten out of her over the years. It was now time to re-establish herself. She could learn from Mandy and use her body to entice her victims into situations she would be able to manipulate to her advantage. Perhaps use it as a weapon to seduce them to their deaths?

Stella carefully placed the gun back against the wall and went downstairs to the kitchen, where she flicked the switch on the kettle before retrieving her list of names from where she'd thrown it earlier. Scanning down it quickly, she located Mandy's name and with great care she drew a line of black marker pen across it, as if doing so would erase any recollections of her from memory. Stella put the list down and sat on one of the pine kitchen stools waiting for the kettle to boil. She felt hungry and needed to eat. Somewhere she recalled she'd watched a film or read a book that stated when you do some thing which is so intense, so totally out of character your body demands nourishment soon after the event. Stella, at that precise moment, knew it to be true.

Mark Carter had finished his shift over two hours ago and now felt totally drained. He'd put in some extra hours to try and help ease the pain he was feeling over Mandy's deception. He'd returned home expecting to find her waiting for him, anticipating the row he knew she'd demand as punishment for his phone call earlier in the day. He now sat motionless in an old black leather reclining chair which he'd purchased for £15 at a car boot sale nearly ten years ago. He'd loved the feel of the soft leather as it seemed to wrap itself around him the first time he'd sat in it. The chair was one of the few things he'd kept that reminded him of what life was about before he'd met Mandy. Long days searching for second hand furniture to fill his bachelor flat, hand in hand with whoever he was seeing at the time. He'd always found walking through rows and rows of bits and pieces from other peoples lives exciting, and tried to picture who'd owned the articles. Sometimes the person he was with joined in with his game, but most tended to think he was a tad sad and let him get on with it himself.

Sunday morning was his favourite time, especially if he'd been out drinking the previous night; it allowed time for his head to clear. Mandy at first loved to play along, but the novelty soon wore off on her and she would complain almost constantly at how bored she'd become with the whole scene. Carter could not remember the last time they'd gone to a boot sale together. He had difficulty recalling the last time they'd gone *anywhere* together.

On finding the house deserted he'd looked for a note on the dining room table, which was where Mandy left messages if she was going out. He'd found none.

Searching the house from top to bottom he'd located nothing that told him where she'd gone. He did know, however, that she'd been in the shower and had taken her time before deciding what to wear. Damp towels lay strewn across the bathroom floor and several discarded outfits were hanging from the bed and dressing table as if she had thrown them around in an effort to create a statement of modern art.

One by one and with great care he had folded each dress, blouse and jacket and placed them back where they belonged, the wet towels he popped into the washing basket. The air was heavy with Anais Anais, Mandy's perfume she saved for special occasions.

Mark picked the bottle up and threw it across the room where it exploded against the far wall, causing shreds of glass and perfume to ricochet around the bedroom. He screamed in anger knowing only too well that Mandy had gone to meet her lover.

Carter walked to the hallway where he picked up the telephone and punched out the numbers to Susan Murray one of their few joint friends who knew their situation. Tapping the side of the phone to his ear he waited for her to pick up. The ringing stopped and a friendly voice filled his head "Hello, Susan here."

"Hi Sue. It's Mark."

"Well hello stranger, great to hear from you. How's Mandy?"

Mark paused long enough to think what to say "That's why I rang Sue. Look there's no easy way to say this. I think she's having an affair...!

Susan cut across him. "Mark what are you saying? She loves you."

Mark let out a sad laugh before replying. "Maybe, but she's out there now with someone else."

The anger in his voice both scared and surprised Susan. "What makes you think that's where she is?"

"She's spent ages getting ready to meet him; the bedroom smells like a whore's parlour."

"Oh come on, maybe she's just gone shopping with one of her friends."

Mark sighed. "Susan, you and I both know she wouldn't do that. It's not her scene. Anyway, normally she'd tell me what she was doing, but not this time. This time she's just vanished."

"Christ Mark, I don't know what to say. I promise you she's said nothing to me. Mandy always tells me how happy she is with you."

Mark hoped Susan was telling the truth. "Yeah I know. Listen thanks for being there."

"If you need anything just call, and if Mandy rings I'll get back to you."

Mark said his farewells and dejectedly hung up the phone. Deep down he'd known Susan wouldn't know anything, but he'd wanted to hear a friendly voice. His girlfriend was having an affair and she wasn't going to tell a soul, that was the nature of the beast, totally secretive.

He went to the drinks cabinet and poured a large measure of whisky into an Edinburgh crystal glass before returning to his chair. There was nothing he could do but sit it out. He hated confrontation, but this time he couldn't think of any other course of action, except wait for Mandy's return.

Taking a large sip from his drink he settled back for what he assumed would be a long and lonely evening.

17

Stella had eaten a simple meal of baked beans on toast. She'd found her appetite larger than usual and needed the whole tin, followed by another two heavily buttered slices of toast to satisfy her hunger. Her third cup of coffee sat half drunk before her and she absentmindedly allowed her fingers to play with the handle of the cup.

She felt invigorated by how easily her plan had fallen into place, although she'd now definitely decided not to carry out her earlier idea, regarding finding the lovers together and shooting them in a fit of rage. She realised this wouldn't work as she'd studied the list of names Teresa had given her. So many deaths could not be put down to mere rage. Stella knew she'd be hunted down as a deranged killer, who could expect no mercy if she was ever caught, but she already knew how she'd avoid capture.

The next name on the list was Tony Asque who Stella knew from previous gatherings Brian had organised at their house.. He had, on numerous occasions, when filled with drink, tried to make a pass at her, and on one occasion when she had allowed him the honour of a slow dance, he'd quickly grabbed at her buttocks, and she recalled how he'd pulled at her flesh, in his efforts to get closer. Stella had allowed him to carry on for fear if she made a fuss, Brian would have accused her of leading him on, and he would've demanded retribution later. Stella winced, at the thought of how he'd have beaten her badly and then told Tony that's what happened to an unfaithful wife.

Getting Tony alone would not prove difficult. All she had to do was put herself on offer. He'd made the list through Teresa telling Stella he'd supplied some of the drugs Brian had used and that he found her dead husband some of the prostitutes he especially liked, the ones who suffered pain and humiliation for money.

Teresa had told her how he'd beaten them nearly to death, and how Tony was the one who took them to hospital and paid them off before squaring up with Brian later. Teresa, when asked why none of the girls ever complained to the police about what Brian had done to them, told Stella that Tony made sure the girls were heavily dependent on his drugs, and if they'd said anything he would've stopped their supply. Teresa had said the girls would die before doing without their daily fix.

Stella stood up from the table and pushed the unfinished cup of coffee away from her. Making her way to where Mandy lay, she bent over the dead police officer. She knew she could make herself sexy enough for Tony, but wanted him to be like a salivating dog, which would make getting him to where she wanted that much easier.

Mandy had fallen revealing her lacey underwear and stockings. Stella once had such sexy attire, but Brian had burnt them all because she'd told him how much she enjoyed wearing them, had told him how sexy she'd felt knowing men would like to see her in them. Brian had slapped her across the face and had told her she was his and his alone, he'd pushed her to the ground, lifted her skirt and ripped off her stockings, suspenders and pants. He'd then pulled open her blouse, tore off her bra and stormed up to their room. Stella had run after him only to see him take all her underwear out of the drawer, push past her on his way to the garage, where he poured petrol over the clothing and burned them to a pile of black ash. From that day Stella was only allowed to wear what he wanted when he wanted. If she ever wore stockings he tore them off at the end of the evening and threw them in the bin. He told her he wouldn't have his wife wearing '*sluts*' clothes when he wasn't around.

Stella smiled, realising he would never be around again. Slowly she bent forward and started to undo Mandy's suspenders, taking time not to snag one of the stockings as she removed them. Luckily only a few drops of blood had splattered onto the silk material and she knew they'd wash off easily.

Stella would wear Mandy's stockings when she killed Tony Asque. This made her laugh so much she thought her sides would burst.

Billy Johnstone watched in fascination as the capital of England grew smaller before his eyes. Although born in Kingsbury and having spent all his life in London, he'd never been one to visit tourist attractions, and was only now standing inside one of the orbs belonging to the London Eye because he'd been unable to turn down the personal invitation he'd received to sample its wonderment. The journey round according to the guide who'd assisted him on, would take around thirty minutes. He glanced down at his watch and saw already they'd been spinning at a snails pace for nearly three-quarters of an hour. Realisation dawned that in fact they were now stationary.

"How the hell do you manage it?" he asked smiling at the only other person with him on the ride.

Mickey Driscol laughed heartily." Money not only makes the world go round, it can stop it as well."

It was Billy's turn to chuckle. "Okay, this is very nice and you've filled me in with how well the robbery went, but why all this secrecy and why the hell up here?" he asked as he made a sweeping gesture over the city hundreds of feet below.

"I like you Billy. You're one of the few people in life I feel I can trust completely. I just want your opinion on something."

Billy nodded without taking his eyes of the miniature buildings below. "Shoot," he offered.

"The Panel, how strong do you think they are?"

The question took him totally by surprise. He continued to try and recognise the famous buildings below him for several seconds before replying, "Why do you ask that?"

"Need to know how big a problem I'd have if I was to try and take them out."

Billy spun round like a guardsman on the parade square, "Tell me you're winding me up Mickey?"

Mickey could see the fear in Billy's face, "No I'm not," he said quietly.

Billy slowly slid down the side of the orb and sat with a bump on the shiny floor surface. "You couldn't win a war with them if that's the question you want answered."

Mickey grinned, "Might be fun trying though. Are you with me Billy?"

Billy couldn't believe he was hearing this, just when his life was getting better with each passing day, a giant spanner had been thrown into the works. "Do I have a choice?" he asked in defeat.

"You could always grass me up," Mickey said sarcastically.

Billy sat dejected and rubbed at his face.

A sharp bump caused movement again and they began the slow journey back to earth. Neither man spoke. Driscol was thinking he had a new strong man on his team, Billy was trying to figure out which side he'd be best to serve. He was certain of one thing. He'd be dead if he tried to double cross Driscol. He was also well aware that if he kept Driscol's intentions from the Panel, and they ever found out, he would also forfeit his life. By the time they reached the bottom and Billy stepped out, he was a very unhappy man.

18

Scenes of Crime Officer, Tony Asque, looked at his reflection in the dirt covered toilet mirror. Someone in a fit of rage had taken a disliking to what they saw in the reflective surface and had punched a large dent which was surrounded by dozens of fine cracks positioned exactly where Tony Asques nose would normally be. "Shit," he said aloud as he stared at something resembling a glass spider's web in the area where his face should be.

At forty-seven he was wearing well, with his silvery grey hair still long enough for him to tie it in a sleek pony tail, his bright blue eyes and almost wrinkle free face allowing him to pass for someone at least a decade younger.

He badly wanted to check on his nose as he was certain that the last remaining cartilage in the middle, separating his nostrils, had finally given up the battle against his never ending cocaine habit. Tony gingerly felt the gaping hole with his left index finger. "Shit, shit, shit," he repeated over and over, knowing his career was about to end in humiliation and disgrace. The police force hated bent coppers, and now after twenty years of deceit his past had finally caught up with him.

In a temper Tony added his fist imprint to the one already in existence. He was reasonably well off owing to the various scams he'd been involved in, theft, burglary and drug dealing had all supplemented his pay. Westville Police Station had been a den of iniquity for as long as he could remember. He allowed himself a brief smile as he remembered the Commissioners new Policy statement to stamp out all the crooked cops. Asque knew he could half the dodgy deals just by closing down and locking up 90% of the Westville force.

Looking down at his fist he saw he was bleeding from three knuckles. He brought the injured hand up to his face and licked the blood away before tearing a paper towel from the wall and wrapping it around his hand.

Asque knew he would need to talk to Brian Blackmore as soon as possible. He was the main man to talk to regarding whatever action would be going down next. If his nose was knackered, he'd need to do outside jobs to keep the lifestyle he enjoyed going at its current pace. Perhaps he could still turn up at burglaries as the SOCO, do the dusting and at the same time steal some nice trinkets.

Asque laughed, deciding his situation wasn't as bad as he first feared. So what if he lost his job. There were other opportunities for a man with his unique skills.

Checking that the bleeding had stopped he returned to his place at the bar. Tony saw that John the Nags Head pub landlord was staring at his hand. "Sorry mate got involved with the mirror."

John, a portly gent of fifty-six wasn't going to upset Tony over a broken toilet mirror. Tony had been drinking in his pub for nearly ten years and John knew he was not a man you would knowingly upset. Tony, John knew, had friends in very influential places, not all of them good. All it took was a word here or there and the health inspectors, VAT men or Drugs Squad would be hammering at his pubs front door, or worse, some of his thug friends would turn up to rearrange the place. "Hey, I can fix a mirror. Besides it was smashed anyway."

Tony grinned. He liked John, as he kept himself to himself, served the beer and *never* asked anything he shouldn't. Many a time Tony had dealt in stolen gear from the pub and John had turned a blind eye. He respected him as well, so much so that when requested not to bring drugs into the pub Tony had agreed, although he knew both Billy Smythe and Anna Thompson did just that every Friday and Saturday night. "Hey John, my glass is empty. Bung a pint in and top up yours while you're at?"

"Sure, cheers."

Tony thought for a minute and then said to John. "Does my nose look crap?"

John looked up from pouring the beer and grinned from ear to ear. "Think I've just found somewhere to park my new Galaxy," he joked.

"Fuck you." Tony moaned.

"Hey, come on, the birds won't see it if you keep your head down."

Despite feeling low, Tony burst out laughing. "Maybe I can get plastic surgery," he said hopefully.

"Why bother? You were an ugly bastard anyway."

"Sometimes I don't know why I drink here," Tony said feigning disgust.

"Cos I let you do what the hell you want and I serve the best beer," John called as he walked to the far end of the bar to collect some empty glasses.

"Fair enough," Tony agreed. "Listen I think I'll swallow this and head off. I'll need to think of what I need to do regarding my future career."

"Christ Tony, I hadn't thought of that."

"I had. That's the reason I slapped your mirror."

John gave him a worried look before going to serve another customer. Tony needed to speak to Brian Blackmore so he pulled out his mobile and tapped out the numbers..

Stella's heart nearly stopped when she answered her phone to hear the man she was planning to kill next on the other end of it.

"Stella. It's Tony. I need to speak to Brian on the hurry up." She detected his urgency and wondered what he wanted. Her delay in answering caused Tony to speak again.

"Stella, are you there honey? I need Brian."

"Sorry Tony, he's not here right now."

The silence was deafening. Finally it was broken. "Where the hell is he?"

Stella remembered what she'd told his station. "His Dad died and he's gone to comfort his Mum."

"Why didn't he phone to tell me? Why haven't you gone with him?

Stella could hear the doubt in Tony's voice. She knew this was a crucial part of their conversation.

"It was very sudden Tony. He just rushed off. You know what he's like, didn't want me fussing over him I suppose." She could almost here Tony's brain ticking over before he replied.

"When's he back. I need to speak to him urgently?"

Stella knew it was time to play her Ace card. "Not for at least a week. I wish I'd gone now, it's ever so lonely here without company." She knew she had him, heard his large intake of breath, heard the sigh as he prepared to speak, imagined him licking his lips.

"Do you want me to come over for a bit, I've got nothing on?"

"Don't make it sound as if I'm a last resort Tony." Stella prayed she hadn't pushed him too far. Tony had a temper like her dead husband.

"That's not what I meant you silly cow. I meant just to talk, pass the time, you know?"

Stella knew all right, he already sounded well on the way to being drunk. If she risked bringing him to her home he might force himself on her. He was a big man and she didn't want to take any chances. "Tell you what; meet me in the Hong Kong Garden tomorrow night. I fancy going out, besides it'll make a nice change."

Tony couldn't believe what he'd just heard. On numerous occasions he'd tried to get inside Stella Blackmore's pants without success. Brian had told him that he'd drug her up for him so he could do what he wanted, but somehow the idea didn't do anything for him. He'd always wanted her awake and kicking. "Sure sweet thing, I'll be there," he said quietly trying to contain the excitement in his voice.

When the conversation ended, Stella sat back leaning against the hallway wall. One more day would be sufficient to get her mind around what she intended to do with Tony.

Already her mind was buzzing. First she would shower, and then she would spray her body with sweet smelling perfume before finally dressing in the most revealing outfit she had. The most important part of the agenda was to make Tony want to take her in the back of his car. That is where Stella intended to slit his throat.

19

Carter jumped awake, the pins and needles immediately bit into his upper thighs, the result of sitting in the same position for too long. With one hand he rubbed furiously to chase them away, while at the same time he tried to focus on his other wrist to read the luminous digits on his watch.

He'd been asleep for nearly three and a half hours. "Mandy!" he shouted into the darkness. "Mandy, you home yet?" The silence was like a knife through his heart. Although it was barely early evening, the fact his girlfriend still hadn't returned or called to say where she was started to ring alarm bells in his head. Yes, he was now certain she was having an affair, but he believed he knew Mandy well enough to know she wouldn't just up and leave him. She was a highly emotional creature who'd want to try and explain what had gone wrong with their relationship. Besides, she would really enjoy telling him it was his own fault. Mandy never admitted that anything of her doing was wrong.

He'd not yet decided to do anything that might give away the fact that he was her partner, but decided to use his rank to see if he could get any information as to where she'd gone.

Hastily he punched out the numbers to Westville Police Station and did not have to wait long before a cheery female voice answered.

"Westville Police Station. How can I help you?"

"Ah, good evening, it's Inspector Carter from Merrywell. I need to contact a WPC Mandy Burrows regarding a court case she's involved in." Carter hoped the officer at the other end would not ask for details of the fictitious case.

"I'm sorry Sir; she went home at 2pm today."

"When will she be back on duty please?" He asked, hoping his voice sounded ok, and did not really have the edge he felt it had.

"Back on at 6am Sir, would you like me to give her a message to call you?"

Carter quickly decided it would seem odd if he declined the offer. "Yes, that would be great. Thank you."

"No problem, Sir. Good night."

"Yes...right. Good night officer." He replaced the phone and looked down at his shaking hands. Mandy had been given a nickname by him during their early courting days. She'd appeared to sleep almost all the time. Every time he called her, no matter what time of day or night she would always say she was in bed, he now wondered possibly who with! Carter, because of her sleeping habits had named her 'dormouse' and used to tease her relentlessly every time she told him she needed to sleep.

Carter knew if Mandy was on an early shift she would need to go to bed around 9pm. That meant that if she was coming home tonight he only had two hours to wait. Looking at the whiskey bottle, he resisted temptation and headed for the bathroom. Perhaps a shower would wash away the worries swirling around inside his head. As the water charged through the temperatures from very cold to hot, he doubted it very much.

20

Mark Carter nervously rubbed his sweating palms together as he sat outside the Chief Superintendent's office. He shifted position often and realised why prisoners being interviewed fidgeted so much during questioning. The brown plastic seat he sat on felt like concrete and although he'd only been waiting twenty minutes he could feel the numbness creeping over his buttocks and up into his lower back.

He'd waited at home until 9am for the call from Mandy he was sure would arrive. When she failed to ring, he again phoned her station in a pretend official capacity. On being told she hadn't turned up for work and had failed to report in sick or otherwise, Carter had felt the hairs on the back of his head spring to attention and the beating of his heart speeding up considerably. Deciding he needed to go to her station to try and find out what the hell was going on, he swapped his white cotton dressing gown for jeans and a dark blue polo shirt. Before he left he stood before the full sized mirror in his bedroom, drinking the umpteenth cup of coffee that morning and stared at his reflection. Worry was etched over what he saw. Something bad had happened to Mandy and all his years of experience couldn't make him think otherwise.

Carter had walked into Westville police station, introduced himself as Detective Inspector Carter from Merrywell and demanded to see the Divisional Chief Superintendent immediately. He was told the Chief Super would be in around ten and that he could wait outside his office until then. A young WPC brought him a coffee and then left him to sit alone with his thoughts.

The moistness from his hands seemed to be spreading upwardly and he wiped cold sweat from his brow. What was he going to tell the Divisional Chief about his relationship, and the fact he felt Mandy was in some sort of trouble. He rehearsed a few introductions to what he would say and was formulating a game plan when a loud, strong Scottish voice which he recognised at once boomed at him from along the corridor.

"Mark, what's all this I need to see the boss urgently crap? Why didn't you call me on my mobile? You've got the number."

Carter looked up to see Chief Superintendent John MacDonald striding towards him like a giant from a children's story. At well over six feet and two hundred pounds he cut a ferocious sight as he stomped along. Carter had known him all his service and somehow every posting he'd received always followed the big Scotsman. He liked him immensely and felt he could trust him more than any other senior officer he'd ever met. Most, he felt were after what they could get and how high up the promotion ladder they could go. Carter knew John MacDonald only wanted to rid the streets of the villains who lived on them.

"Morning Sir," Carter said in a quiet voice.

"What's up Mark? You look done in."

Carter looked deeply into this great policeman's face, hoping to see answers before he'd even asked the questions. Blankness greeted him. "Mandy Burrows, a WPC at the nick has gone missing..."

"Yeah, I know. The desk sergeant downstairs tells me who's absent everyday when I get here."

"She's my girlfriend." The last word was almost unheard as he bent his head forward and said it to the floor.

John MacDonald stared at the man before him for a considerable time. "She's *your* girlfriend! That will come as a big disappointment to many of the male officers here. Why have you kept it a secret?"

"You know how it goes with young WPC's and senior officers. We met while she was at Hendon and decided to keep it quiet so as not to interfere with my career and to stop her having the piss ripped out of her for having me as her old man. Stupid I know, but that's not the problem..."

"Before you go any further Mark, I have to say I'm disappointed. As your area Chief Superintendent, I would have thought you'd have seen fit to tell me about the relationship. After all it could have caused problems for everyone both in a professional and private capacity."

Carters head felt as if it was going to explode, "I wanted to be near her, and was worried one of us would be posted elsewhere. You know what the politics of senior officers dating young women are. We never expected to get found out in this way, I had already decided to come clean next month once Mandy finished her probationary period."

"Might not have finished it on time Mark, I'm afraid."

The response was totally unexpected and briefly Carter forgot why he was in the Chief's office. "What do you mean?"

"Mandy has been under investigation from Complaints for some time. Mind you, not just her, we have some serious criminal offences going on at this police station and we're about to name names. Mandy was one of those names."

Carter slumped into an old leather armchair positioned at the far side of his bosses' office, "What's she done?"

"Mark, if it was anyone but you I wouldn't say until the investigation was complete..."

"Gov!" Carter pleaded.

"Let me finish Mark, please. Mandy was suspected in a drugs ring operating within this station and outside. She was a bit player, but none the less part of the game. I think she was involved enough to have been placed under arrest at the end of the day. Her career was finished. Now you tell me she's your girlfriend. Can you see the world of trouble you've just landed at my feet?"

The headache was now so strong it felt it would burst out his skull at any moment. Carter massaged the sides of his head slowly in deliberate circles. "Was my name ever mentioned in any of this? Is that why I failed promotion again?"

"Don't be a prat, you failed because you're not a yes man. No more, no less."

Carter let out a long pained sigh. "What am I saying? Who cares? Mandy failed to come into work today and she didn't come home last night. I think she was having an affair, but for her not to come home and then not be here, on top of what you've just told me, suggests something terrible has happened."

MacDonald could see how upset Carter was becoming, "Okay, let's get onto it then shall we?"

Carter looked up; MacDonald could see the tears forming at the sides of his eyes.

"You mean I can get involved here?"

"For now, I won't mention what you've told me regarding Mandy being your other half until we find her. Then I'll decide what to do. In the meantime I'll telephone your nick and get you posted over here on some task force or something."

Carter stood up and offered his hand; MacDonald looked at it without response for long enough for Carter to consider dropping it. Finally the older man gripped his fingers, "Mark she may be a bad one, but for your sake I hope we find her soon."

"Thank you so much for giving me a chance to find her."

"Mark knowing you as I do, you'd have gone off and done your own thing anyway. At least this way I can keep some sort of eye on you."

Carter saw the smile begin to form on MacDonald's face and allowed himself to grin back. Mandy was out there and when he found her she'd have a lot of questions to answer.

Providing she was still alive

That thought entered his head so easily Carter shuddered violently as he walked out the office door.

21

The journey to the Chinese restaurant was a strange one for Stella. Her emotions were in turmoil, the previous twenty-four hours had seemed like an eternity as she'd tried to come to terms with what she was about to do.

The earlier murders had been easier because she was the

same sex as her victims, and if difficulties had arisen, she'd reckoned her levels of strength would have matched those of Teresa and Mandy Burrows. Stella knew Tony would be a totally different proposition if she failed to carry out her attack successfully on her first attempt.

She noticed her knuckles had gone white with the pressure she was exerting on the steering wheel. Taking a deep breath she tried to relax, but was only too aware of her trembling body. She needed to try and calm down otherwise Tony might suspect something was wrong.

The tall oak trees that lined much of the route passed in a blur. The tall wooden soldiers gave protection to the large detached houses on either side of the road. Prevented prying eyes from taking in much of the impressive details of the buildings or gardens, stopped potential burglars obtaining easy access to the properties. On many occasions as Stella had driven to the local supermarket she'd wondered who lived in such huge dwellings and dreamed of one day maybe being able to own a home like these.

Removing her right hand from its grip on the leather steering wheel she rubbed her thigh, feeling the softness of her dress and the little bump where she'd attached Mandy's stockings to her suspender belt. The dress was a deep blue colour, with small yellow flowers running up both sides to meet as they ran over her shoulders. It was her favourite and she'd bought it to look good when accompanying Brian to one of his many police do's. He unfortunately told her she reminded him of a tree trunk with all the flowers growing over her, and had forbidden her from wearing it. The dress had remained neatly folded at the base of her wardrobe for the past two years. Luckily Stella had taken care to wrap it in soft tissue and now it looked as good as the day she bought it.

She felt good wearing it and had to admit she also felt very sexy wearing Mandy's underwear. The few blood spots had come off easily and although Mandy had been slightly smaller, her stockings fitted Stella's legs well. She hoped Tony would see the suspender straps through the tightness of the dress. Tony had to want her badly enough to be distracted and off his guard when she attacked him.

Her heart hammered against her rib cage as she pulled into the small car park beside the Hong Kong Garden. She'd always believed the name was totally unoriginal, but had never the less enjoyed eating there on the few evenings Brian had spent any money on her during their initial romance.

Stella slipped back into the past; briefly trying to remember what it was about him that had caused her to fall so madly in love. She quickly gave up, guessing her mind was concentrating hard to keep her from running away, as the intense fear built up inside her, so that she couldn't think about anything else.

Stepping out of the car her feet made loud crunching sounds on the gravel. She bent down to straighten her dress and nearly collapsed when a voice from behind her cut into the silence of the evening.

"Stella, you look good enough to eat."

Turning around she saw Tony Asque leaning against his car bonnet. How she'd failed to notice him when she drove in to the car park was beyond her. She couldn't help noticing the leer that stretched across his face. "Hi Tony," she replied smiling, before adding, "Just thought I'd get tarted up a bit to cheer myself up that's all."

"Well girl, you've certainly cheered me up and that's no lie."

"Are you going to stare at me all night or are we going inside?" Stella asked, amazed at how calm she sounded, surprised owing to the fact her insides were doing cartwheels every time she opened her mouth.

Tony continued to gaze at her and Stella could feel his eyes trying to undress her where she stood. Finally, he moved closer and gently placed his arm around her waist. Stella mentally fought with every sinew as she struggled not to shrug him off.

"Come on sexy," he sneered. "Let's get some grub."

Stella forced herself to look at him and smile, "Sure, let's enjoy ourselves eh?"

Almost before she'd spoken the last word Tony's hand slid down from her waist and squeezed her buttocks, "Lets," was all he said before steering her towards the door.

Stella noticed the hole under his nose and felt the repulsion rise in her throat. His attitude towards her as he continued to grope at her even as they were shown to their seats inside the restaurant killed any doubts she had left. Cutting this bastard's throat would be a pleasure.

The waiter had tried to sit them opposite each other, but Tony had rudely pushed him aside and sat in the seat beside

Stella, pulling it across the floor so that he sat as close as the space allowed. Immediately Stella felt a warm hand on her thigh.

She turned to face him, "So Tony how've you been?"

The question surprised him for a moment and briefly he stopped rubbing her leg. "What do you mean?" he asked resuming his hand action.

"Nothing, I haven't seen you for a while, just asked. You don't have to tell me if you don't want to." Stella caught the angry look flash across his features. He didn't like his life pried into and briefly she thought he'd blow up and her chance to remove another name from her list would be gone.

"As you can see from my face, things haven't been going too well of late. Still with you here to cheer me up I'm sure things are about to change sweetie."

His expression was changing all the time and Stella wondered if he was high on drugs. She grimaced as she felt his hand slide up her leg, heard him gasp as it reached bare flesh and then felt the strength of his fingers as he tried to open her legs wider.

"Not in here Tony please," she said in a hopeful voice.

"I just want to touch you. Come on nobody can see us."

Stella felt like a prostitute, but not wanting to lose her chance she slowly parted her thighs a little. Immediately his hand moved up and rested on the thin material of her pants. Stella felt nauseous as Tony ran his fingers over her most private place. "Please, Tony stop," she whimpered.

Tony placed both his hands onto the table before him, interlocking his fingers. "I've lost my appetite, for food anyway." He grinned at her. "Let's leave now and just play."

Stella felt her blood run cold. This was what she wanted, but her nerves were already shredding. "I want to Tony, but please don't tell Brian ok?"

Stella pushed her chair back and stood up. "Let me powder my nose before we go." Before waiting for a reply she walked slowly away, trying to sway her hips slightly knowing his eyes were boring into her back.

Tony couldn't believe his luck; she wanted him as much as he wanted her. What had changed her mind towards him? He knew Brian treated her badly; maybe she just wanted to have someone treat her nicely for a change? He smiled broadly as he saw her re-entering the main part of the restaurant. He devoured the way her body swayed as she moved gracefully across the crowded Chinese restaurant, admired her long legs, and noticed she was gathering lustful looks even from the men eating with their wives, girlfriends or lovers. For the first time in a very long time he felt good about his life.

Stella noticed the cool look on his face, took in his relaxed mannerisms, and knew he was going to make this easy for her. Seizing the mood she leaned forward placed a hand on his shoulders, and in the sexiest voice she could muster whispered in his ear, "Let's go then."

Tony pushed the table away from him so quickly several glasses fell to the floor. A waiter hurriedly approached and asked if everything was alright? Stella tried to hide her embarrassment as Tony grabbed her elbow, pushed the man out of the way and then shoved her towards the door.

Outside it had started to rain. It was a fine mist that appeared to be harmless, but they both knew if you stayed out in it long that within seconds you're soaked.

"My car," Tony shouted and pushed her in the direction of his shining black Porsche Carrera. Stella wondered how he could afford such a luxurious car on a police civilian's wages.

The central locking clicked and she climbed into the passenger seat and closed the door. Turning to speak to Tony she saw that his eyes were firmly focused on her legs. Looking down, she noticed that in getting into the vehicle her dress had ridden up her thighs and the dark bands of her stockings were on show as was a large expanse of bare thigh on her right leg. "Do you like my stockings then?" she asked in a sarcastic voice.

Tony laughed loudly which unnerved Stella, before he reached over and rubbed her leg, pushing the thin material higher and higher until the white lace of her pants came into view.

"Tony not here it's too close to the restaurant."

"Okay I'll take you back to my place then if you're going all shy on me."

"No don't do that!" Stella almost screamed.

Tony gave her a puzzled look.

Stella reached across and squeezed his leg. "What I mean is I can't wait till then, I'm on fire now. Brian hasn't made love to me for weeks. Tony just drive over there to the dark end of the car park where we won't be disturbed and make love to me...*please*."

"You sure about this. You seem tense?"

Stella panicked. Had she scared him off? "Nothing's wrong. If you don't fancy me anymore forget it. I just thought you had always wanted to...*screw me*." Stella spat the last words at him hoping it would get the desired response.

"Hey I didn't say I didn't want to. I'm just curious as to the change from quiet housewife to raving nymphomaniac."

Stella laughed so hard tears trickled down her cheeks.

"What's so funny?" he asked.

Stella wanted to scream at him that she was far worse than that. She was a murderer and he was the next victim. Instead she just said, "Drive the car over there Tony before I change my mind."

Tony, with anybody else, would have lashed out at the way she'd just spoken to him, but he badly wanted her, "I'm going to make you scream, when I do this."

"I'll make *you* scream louder." was the strange reply she gave him.

The car journey from the front of the car park to the more secluded spot at the rear took no more than thirty seconds. Stella could feel the tension building up inside her with each passing tick of the Porsches interior clock. Tony Asque still had a hand on her thigh and his warmth burnt into her flesh. At least while he was driving the hand remained reasonably still on her leg.

The darkness fell over the vehicle as though someone had thrown a black blanket over them. The car engine stopped and Tony leaned forward and flicked the cars reading light on.

"No, turn that off, Tony. I don't want some peeping tom getting a free show."

"*Free show* Stella? You're going to give me a good time right here in this car park?"

Stella rubbed at his trousers. "Take them off Tony," she urged. "Show me what you've got."

"Ladies first, Stella," he said and turned full on to her.

Stella could barely see his face even under the light which Tony hadn't switched off as requested. What she did see made her wonder about her sanity and ask herself if she really believed she could go through with this.

Tony reached across and began to ease her dress down over her shoulders, lightly kissing them as they were revealed. Stella sat back wondering when her opportunity would present itself, realising she hadn't thought through the complications of her task. Mounting fear rose from the pit of her stomach as he touched her breasts and she heard the low grunting sounds coming from Asque as he began to enjoy his opportunity. Stella felt his hands roughly try to lift her bottom off the seat so he could remove her pants. She also noticed his breathing becoming frantic as his intensity grew.

Stella knew she wouldn't be able to make it too difficult for him otherwise he would possibly sense something was wrong. His fingers reached under the elastic of her underwear and he started to pull her pants down.

"Tony!" she almost screamed.

"What?" He yelled with mounting frustration and anger in his voice.

Stella needed to take control of the situation before it got out of hand. Forcefully she pushed him away and reached across with both hands. She slowly slid down the zip on his black cord trousers and fumbled her way inside his boxer shorts. He was as hard as an iron rod. "Mmm is that all for me?" she asked in a voice she hoped sounded playful.

"We can get someone else here for you as well if you want to be really bad." Tony leered.

"No, I want it all."

"Show me Stella. Show me how much you want it." He said as he pulled her down so that her face hung over his lap.

Stella could smell the odour of sexual excitement oozing from him, could feel the pressure he was exerting on her neck and knew she'd played this part of the game very badly. There were no alternatives. To stop now would show Asque she didn't really want to be with him.

She closed her eyes and lowered her head, hearing him sigh with pleasure. She felt angry Asque was receiving pleasure from her before he died. She didn't feel any repulsion, and believed her coldness could work for her in the future. Stella smiled inwardly at her thoughts. She tried to sit up, but Tony had other ideas.

"Where the hell do you think you're going? Get back down there baby and finish what you started."

Stella managed to squeak out *"but"* before he started to manhandle her back over his groin.

"No buts. Don't come up until you've finished this time."

Stella felt the force increase on the back of her neck.

Frantically she wondered what she should do. The answer, when it came pleased her immensely. The passenger door was unlocked and she had her handbag beside her on the floor. The large kitchen knife was waiting inside, Stella bit down with all her might.

Things went ballistic, Tony screamed and tried to beat at the back of her head with his fists, but as she bit down she'd pushed the door open and his blows skimmed off her head. The flesh had been bitten into very deeply and Tony could see the blood pumping from the wound. He could see Stella standing at the side of the car grinning at him.

"Bitch!" He screamed into the night as he stumbled out of the drivers' door. "I'm going to kill you, you insane bitch."

Asque staggered round the side of the car to where he'd seen Stella standing. When he got there she was gone. Only darkness greeted him. "You can't hide, you're dead meat."

Stella came at him from his right and he saw a shape coming towards him out the corner of his eye and turned to look. Was it the same woman that had been with him in the car moments earlier? Her face was contorted in rage; her hair was swept madly around her face. Too late he saw the blade raised above his head. Stella rammed it between his eyes. She felt the blade bend as it cut its way into his head, felt it stop moving when the hilt of the knife reached Tony Asque's skull. Stella released her grip on the handle and watched as Tony momentarily stood before her with the knife sticking out of his head. She laughed loudly as he looked like a *Dalek* from *Dr Who*.

Tony Asque's eyes were bulging from his head with shock. A thin trickle of blood ran down from his forehead, along his nose and into his gasping open mouth. With great determination he lifted a shaking hand and tried to grab at Stella's face. She calmly stepped out of range as he let out a long last pitiful gasp and fell to the ground.

Stella stood over the dead body for a minute regaining her composure. Not because she'd just killed another human being, but because she'd enjoyed it more than she'd imagined. Finally, she carefully removed the weapon and returned it to her handbag. Looking around the empty car park she was certain her actions had gone unnoticed. Happiness overflowed from her as she climbed into her own car and made her way home.

22

The body of Scenes of Crime Officer Asque had been found at 3am by the manager of the Hong Kong Garden as he locked up and checked everything was in order before he went home for the night.

Both PC Wilson and PC Grant recognised the deceased at once and had called their station immediately. Carter was woken from a disturbed sleep by John MacDonald who'd told him to go and take charge at the scene; this would give him more of a reason to be working at Westville, rather than at his own.

Carter arrived less than ten minutes after his call to find a handful of detectives already hard at work securing the scene and looking for the murder weapon.

Blue and white *Keep Out* police tape had been crudely tied around a lamp post, a dustbin and a tall tree to form a triangle around the body preventing the usual onlookers who always came out the woodwork on such occasions, from seeing any part of the grizzly scene. Dozens of flashing lights illuminated the car park making it look like a secret policeman's disco.

Carter's footsteps crunched loudly as he approached the body. MacDonald had told him what he would find, but nevertheless when he first saw the dead body of Tony Asque it still caused shivers to run up and down his neck. He was lying on his back as if he had just lay down and gone to sleep. The two things that gave the true situation away were the large cut that stretched from the top of his nose to midway up his forehead, and the bloody area around his crotch where his penis should have been. Carter also noticed the missing piece of cartilage from Asque's nose, although he knew that it had nothing to do with the crime that had been committed. He wondered as he stood in the flashing lights if the deceased had been one of the officers under investigation.

His thoughts were interrupted by a young detective who called over to him as he walked towards the Inspector. "Hello Gov. What brings you over to our patch?"

Carter knew Detective Constable Reid from a training day he'd carried out earlier in the year, "Morning Jason, I'm the O.I.C."

The young detective pulled a surprised face before replying, "Great to have you on board Sir."

Carter grinned, "What have you got for me so far, hot shot?"

"Not a lot to be honest. He's been dead for a couple of hours, sharp pointed knife, possibly a large kitchen knife. His penis has been hacked off and taken away with the murder weapon, and as it stands we haven't been able to find either. Early enquiries have turned up a Chinese waiter who went to serve him in the restaurant, but he and his date left before he offered them a menu. Only problem is he can't really give us much of a description owing to the fact they left so quickly. He said she was pretty, around her mid thirties, light brown to dark hair and a looker. Other than that he can't remember much. Saw so many people last night because the place was packed."

Carter pulled a face as he thought over what he'd been told. "Okay speak to him again in the morning and see if he can remember anything else. We need the names of everyone who ate there last night and find out if anyone at the station knew who he was dating. Is a team trying to locate the weapon?"

"Yes. Billy Johnstone's looking with five others. At the moment they're over in the woods at the front of the car park. I don't think we'll find it here though Gov. Whoever did this has taken it with them."

"You're probably right Jason. If they find anything let me know straight away."

Carter decided there was nothing he could do that wasn't already being taken care of so told DC Reid he would see all the team back at the office at 7am.

He walked away and within seconds he'd lost the illumination of the blue lights that had been cutting into the blackness of the night and found himself engulfed in total darkness. "Shit!" he muttered as he stumbled towards his car. Fumbling for the lock he heard the scratching of paint as his key missed it by inches. "That's just great." He moaned. The key finally slipped into position and he opened the door and climbed in. Less than twenty-four hours ago he'd sat in his boss's office, telling him he felt his girlfriend was in some sort of danger. Now, with the finding of a murdered police SOCO his level of certainty that Mandy was in danger had hit red.

He decided to put out a news bulletin as soon as he got back to his house. First he would call John MacDonald and run the idea past him. He'd need senior officers' approval to release details to the press and television companies so soon after a crime had been committed. Two people connected to the police force dead or missing would be a huge media event. What he wanted to say was that a body had been found and a WPC was missing. Perhaps if it was someone with a grudge against the police, the oversight in not revealing the dead man wasn't a police officer would prompt some sort of reaction. Even if it meant he found out Mandy was dead, at least he'd know and that as far as Carter was concerned was a hundred times easier than the void he currently felt himself wrapped up in.

After a ten minute drive he pulled up outside his home in Wilson Street. As he walked up the drive he thought how lonely it would be if Mandy never returned to it. He knew instinctively that he'd have to sell it. He couldn't live there without her as there would be too many memories. The key turned in the lock and he felt the tears run down the side of his face. He loved Mandy with all his heart and the pain inside him was tearing at his very being.

All his years of police work investigating numerous murders and kidnappings told him something big was happening right now, and whether he really wanted to be involved or not, he was going to be the man to sort it out.

The hot water came up to her neck and provided her aching muscles with some relief.

Stella was surprised at how her body felt the morning after she'd murdered Tony Asque. She felt as though she'd spent a long day in the garden, mowing the lawn, planting new seeds and doing the job she'd hated doing all her life, weeding. Sitting up she took a long drink from her mug of coffee and listened to the song that played on the background radio. It was the theme to *Mission Impossible 2* by *Limp Biskit* and Stella chortled at her mission the previous evening. "Nothing impossible to me," she said with an air of confidence.

The song finished and the early morning news came on.

Stella's ears pricked up as she listened for anything that might connect her to Tony Asque's murder. She was amazed to hear both her crimes being discussed. She'd expected

Tony's body to be discovered, but was surprised to hear anything about Mandy Burrows. It was only her disappearance that the radio news reader mentioned, but even that hadn't been expected at such an early stage. Were the police suggesting she was dead and wanted someone to come forward and tell them?

Stella pushed herself deeper into the water, subconsciously trying to hide from the policeman who was now talking on the radio. Her curiosity made her sit back up and she listened carefully as the man in charge of the case answered some questions about the missing police officer. Stella was careful to make a mental note of the detective's name...Inspector Mark Carter.

23

The following morning Carter was introduced to the detectives Chief Superintendent MacDonald had laid at his disposal. He met each one individually in his office before he gave an office meeting on the previous night's murder.

The team consisted of five male detectives and three women. This could be construed as a relatively small unit of police officers to deal with such a crime; however Carter knew resources at the station were limited, so was aware he'd been given all the manpower that had been available to MacDonald.

Leaning on a desk, he began his briefing, "Thanks for allowing me to have a brief chat with each of you before we started this morning. Hopefully you will all have seen the photos and detailed reports of the crime scene." He looked around the room as he spoke and saw the nodding heads acknowledging his statement. Continuing he said, "Tony Asque was known to all of us through his work as a Scenes of Crime Officer, some of you were friends of the deceased. Some of you will also be aware that certain police officers at this station are being investigated with regards potential involvement in criminal offences. I have the Chief Superintendent's permission to tell you Asque was one of these officers."

Gasps arose from around the room and Carter heard someone mumble "Never!" under their breath. He continued, "Whatever the implications of that investigation, Tony Asque should have his murder investigated to the best of our ability. Does anyone disagree?" He knew the room contained strong minded officers who lived by certain rules of conduct both inside and outside the station, but he'd wanted to show he was willing to listen to any views they might want to put forward. No-one disagreed with his question and he let the murmuring die down before continuing, "Okay, we know he was seen with a lady at the restaurant, we know over thirty people saw them together and witnessed the fact that they left within ten minutes of arriving. What we need to find out was what they saw and heard. Did anybody hear them argue, etc. etc. I also want as many detailed descriptions of this mysterious woman as possible."

"Gov, have any prints or other evidence turned up?" asked WDC Forsyth.

"There were dozens of fingerprints both on the outside and interior of the car. None of them are identifiable prints. There were a few brown hairs on the seat of the car, but as yet we don't know if they're from the killer."

"Anything else to go on?" a male voice asked commandingly.

This time it had been DS Johnstone the oldest member of the team who'd spoken. Carter had worked with him on a previous murder and had found him an excellent foil for his ideas.

"No Billy, that's it so far I'm afraid."

"What's your take on his penis being cut off?"

"Trophy maybe, but I'm not going down that path yet. All I do know for certain is the killer is one sick bastard we need to catch quickly."

Billy Johnstone nodded in agreement. "Okay troops," he said, "Let's get this show on the road."

Minutes later the office was deserted and Carter sat down at one of the desks and placed his head in his hands. Nothing excited him more than the chase of a villain. This time however, he felt numb and wondered desperately if he could carry out the job before him while his thoughts were on his missing girlfriend. He was a thoroughly professional police officer and despite the strain he felt under he'd give it his best shot. Nothing else would do and if his fears for her proved to be correct, he needed to be on the ball to catch the bastard who'd killed Asque and possibly... quite possibly killed Mandy as well.

Stella spent the day after killing Tony Asque trying to bring order to the mess she'd caused in her main bedroom.

She forced herself to go back in, because when she'd returned the previous night, the smell had been so thick and heavy, she felt she could've cut it with a knife.

She felt no remorse when she saw the corpse of her husband in the early stages of decay. Teresa caused her to flinch a little, as at one stage in her life she'd been her best friend. Mandy Burrows caused her heckles to rise. She'd been a slut who'd deserved all that had come her way.

The first task had been to move the corpses from the room. At eight and a half stone Stella was not built to move heavy objects without a great struggle. The awkwardness of the bodies made the task much harder. Firstly she'd placed the remains of Brian onto an Egyptian rug and pulled it out of the room to the top of the stairs where she'd then pushed him off the rug and watched his corpse bounce haphazardly down the flight of steps. Two further journeys later both Teresa and Mandy lay on top of Brian in a heap of rotting, twisted limbs.

Moving the bodies had caused the smell to increase and Stella felt the vile stench stick to the rear of her nose and throat making her gag.

She'd removed all her clothing before the gruesome task began, so she could try and minimise the risk of evidence being found on her clothing at a later stage, she had no such thoughts regarding the house. It would take a major cleaning company several days to remove the blood and other human debris that now littered most of the upstairs.

Stella wasn't unduly concerned with this as she fully expected to be named as a suspect when her husband failed to return to work. Her only aim at present was to try and nullify the horrendous smell that currently filled her nostrils.

Climbing over the decaying corpses she went into the kitchen and flicked the switch to the kettle. Waiting for it to boil she took a full bottle of *Bells No.8* whiskey from the cupboard and poured a very generous measure into her mug. The whistling sound from the kettle cut into the silence and she topped up the remaining space in the mug with boiling water. Taking a small sip which scalded her bottom lip, Stella cursed her stupidity. She went and poured some of the liquid down the sink and topped it up with water from the cold tap, taking another drink she smiled this time, as her drink slipped down her throat.

Almost immediately the sour smell of blood and dead flesh was rinsed away. Stella started to laugh a low chuckle as she caught a glimpse of the bodies lying at the foot of the hallway stairs. Brian lay under both Teresa and Mandy and Stella couldn't help thinking he'd have loved to have been in that very position whilst alive.

The laughter stopped when she realised it may have happened without her knowledge as so many other things clearly had.

She lifted the mug to her mouth and in three gulps, downed the remaining liquid. The whiskey burnt its way down slowly, causing her to cough severely. "Shit!" she moaned as she wiped the dregs from her lips. Placing the empty mug in to the sink a smile returned to her face as she made her way back out into the hallway.

Straining with every movement and with sweat pouring from every part of her body, one by one she placed the corpses back onto the rug and pulled them out the side door which led to the garage. Each journey caused her back muscles to ache and her legs to turn to jelly, as first the strength in her muscles slowly slipped away and then the pain set in. It wasn't long before her breathing became laboured, and her fingers grew numb such was the tight grip she needed to pull the corpses out of the house. She had to stop at regular intervals to catch her breath and furiously rub her lower back before it seized and brought a dramatic ending to her day.

She began to wonder, as she had Teresa half way to the garage, if the task was beyond her. Her body had begun to seriously object to the pressure it was under. Her heart pumped with so much urgency she started to worry it might explode leaving her to die on top of one of her victims.

Slowly she dropped the weight and listened as her body screamed with relief. She returned to the kitchen, grabbed a clean mug and retraced her steps of making herself another Irish coffee minus the cream. There was no hurry to finish anyway; the smell seemed to be growing weaker as she grew used to it.

Stella decided to enjoy her task and would have a break between corpses.

Once more her laughter filled the room up as she thought how her drinks could be her way of toasting the people away to hell.

The second and third whiskey slipped down easier than the first and as she poured out a larger fourth drink she didn't bother with the water. Tilting her head back she took the whiskey down in one mouthful, feeling the heat increase as it ran down her throat and felt the explosion when it hit her stomach. This was promptly followed by a huge spluttering fit, interlaced with loud hacking coughs.

Stella allowed the fit to pass, looked at the bottle before deciding to leave number five until she'd finished with Teresa. As she made her way back into the hall she could feel the drink induced haze starting to cloud her mind and looked forward to the time, when everything she did would be done as if she was floating outside her body.

At nine thirty that evening, the detectives involved in the murder enquiry of Tony Asque returned to the incident room to discuss the day's investigations.

Carter began, "Right, so far we've managed to locate and interview twenty three people that were enjoying the delights of the Hong Kong Garden last night. The bad news is for all the fact that most of them saw the lady who was Tony's guest, none of them could give us a description that's good enough to take us any further to identifying her."

"Gov, what seemed to be the reason behind their lack of memory?" a young heavily spotted detective by the name of Redman asked.

Carter sighed heavily before replying. "Basically, the men didn't see anything above her waist such was the outfit she was wearing, and the women were too busy bitching at what a tart she looked like in her...and I quote," and he made quotation signs in the air with his fingers, "clinging so tightly you could see what she had for dinner dress."

Laughter filled the room.

"This isn't the start I was hoping for, but let's go over what we do have on this woman."

DS Johnstone opened up a black leather note book and started to read aloud. "All we have after putting all the information together is that the suspect is around 5 foot 3-5 inches tall, average to slight build, brown hair, likes to dress very sexily and doesn't seem to care if most of her underwear can be seen through her clothes."

"My type of woman then," DC Dwyer said in a sarcastic voice.

"Anything with a pulse is your sort of woman." Someone whispered behind him. The room briefly filled with laughter.

"Is she a prostitute?" WPC Forsyth inquired, bringing things back to order.

Carter nodded his head suggesting maybe his train of thought was going the same way. "Looks that way, but nothing suggests that for certain. Let's not get lost on a wild goose chase here. Take a look at it from all angles...okay."

"Sir." came at him in unison and he smiled at how easily the team had taken him on board as the O.I.C. He wasn't the man in charge normally at this station and he'd expected some mistrust or suspicion especially now that the whole station was aware that the Complaints Investigation Bureau was in town.

"Right, we'll get together at 9am in the morning. Get a good nights sleep, I've a feeling tomorrow could be a long old day."

Carter said his goodbyes and made his way out into the cold evening air. He had mixed feelings about where the case was going. Something wasn't quite right and he couldn't place his finger on what. There had been no real descriptions of the mystery woman, she hadn't done anything unusual to make her stand out, which suggested she was uninvolved or so cool it would need *her* to make a mistake to give them any chance of catching her. He also wondered if Mandy could have been kidnapped by a woman. Mandy was very strong for her size and build and could detect if someone was spinning a line. If the woman in the restaurant was the killer, what had she done to get to Mandy without an apparent fight?

He reached his car, but before unlocking it heard DS Johnstone shout out the office window. "Gov, Hawkins has found the knife."

Carter felt his heart leap, at last a break. He turned round and retraced his steps back to the main incident room. "Go on," he said.

"It was about three hundred yards from the corpse, deep in the bushes. The uniform missed it first time round, but I had our lads go over the scene again."

"Well done. Where's the knife now?"

"On your desk Gov."

Carter walked to the desk with a spring in his step in anticipation at seeing the knife which had killed Tony Asque.

Also he felt they'd needed a break to put them on the right direction both regarding the murder and the main event as far as he was concerned, Mandy.

The knife sat in an exhibit bag in the middle of his desk. Picking it up he twisted it round in his hands studying it closely. The knife could have been jammed in his heart for all it mattered when he realised this weapon wasn't the one that had killed the SOCO.

"Bollocks!" he shouted at nobody in particular. He felt the eyes boring into his back, turning around to face Johnstone and DC Gregory, the only two officers left in the office he said, "This isn't it."

"How can you know that?" Johnstone asked surprised

"Look at the width of the blade. Think about the wound in Asques head. This is no where near wide enough."

Both Johnstone and Gregory looked at the blade which was still in Carter's hands. It was the younger man who said, "Shit."

"Have it printed anyway, but I'll bet you a tenner this isn't it."

"All bets are off," Johnstone moaned.

"At least we're turning something up," Carter mused to no one in particular.

All three left the light blue coloured office together, each lost in thought. The knife had been discarded in a drawer to come out for fingerprints at a later stage. All three knew it was a waste of time as far as this case was concerned.

24

Even at two thirty in the morning, the Maverick Club still heaved to the beat of pulsating music and young flesh swayed around the dance floor. Tucked away in a corner booth, Billy Johnstone, and Mike and Jake Grady sat at a table, drinking the array of drinks that had been put into place before their arrival.

Billy watched Jake twisting the small gold hoop that pierced his top right eyebrow. "Jesus that turns my stomach," he said and if to emphasise the point he let out a loud belch.

"Trendy nowadays though, isn't it Jake?" Mike asked his younger brother.

Jake was too far down the road to care and just smiled from behind a pair of bloodshot drunken eyes.

"He shouldn't mix the drugs with booze Mike. It'll be the death of him."

"Try telling him that. All he wants to do is get high and laid. Nothing else matters to him anymore."

Billy sighed, "He needs to take care Mike. If he screws up, your position as a copper won't save him. I hope you understand that."

Mike took a long drink from his pint of beer, rolling his eyes as he did so. "What can I do Billy? It's his life."

"Sort him out son otherwise he won't have a life, will he?"

Jake at this point made his exit by sliding off his seat and falling face down onto the floor, knocking several drinks from the table as he did so.

"Fuck sake Mike, pick him up or we'll all be in the shit."

Mike bent over and with a great effort pulled him back onto the seat where he lay unconscious beside him. "I'll take him home," he said in embarrassment.

"Listen before you go; is he all right to deliver the drugs for his missus to flog on that shit hole of an estate?"

"Sure no problem, I'll make sure it's done properly."

"Don't get caught with the drugs Mike."

Mike looked at Billy and sighed, "I'm not stupid Billy," he said in a huffy voice.

"I know, but you need to be very careful at the moment what with Carter here and that C.I.B. crowd looking for any excuse to bust someone. On that front I've had an idea."

"Go on," Mike prompted.

"Well you know we have a killer to track down..."

"Mmm," interrupted Mike.

"I thought we could turn that to our advantage."

"How the hell do you propose to do that?"

Billy's face beamed with happiness at the thought of his own brilliance. "We muck up the investigation if we can, that way it'll take ages to catch anyone and in the meantime the C.I.B. won't be able to take us off the case to interview us."

Mike slumped back in his chair, his bottom lip curled up over the top one in concentration. "How're we going to do that then?" he finally demanded.

The smile was still on Billy's face. "Done it all ready haven't I?"

"How?" Mike gasped.

"All the witness statements at the restaurant weren't all crap. One gave us a brilliant description of the woman Asque was with."

"I didn't see that one," Mike said puzzled.

"That's because she gave it to me and I forgot, accidentally on purpose to mention it."

"Bloody hell!" was all Mike could add.

"Lady by the name of Susan Snead, meant to meet up with a fella, but he stood her up. She decided to have a meal anyway and so when Tony and his bit walked in, they had her undivided attention for the whole time they were there. Susan even heard some of the conversation. Quite rude it was to. She saw him feeling her up, thought the woman seemed very tense or scared and gave me a brilliant description of what she looked like. Funny thing is I think I know her."

"What Susan?"

"No you idiot, the woman with Asque. Can't place her yet but I will."

"What are you going to do with the statement?"

"Nothing, I doubt she'll come in and ask if it helped us catch the killer. Do you?"

Mike shook his head. "No, but it's dangerous."

"Danger is my middle name, Mike, besides the best is yet to come."

Before continuing, he pulled out a sealed plastic evidence bag from inside his jacket pocket and threw it on Mike's lap.

Under the dim lights of the club, Mike couldn't see properly what was in the bag, but recognised it as a piece of very bloody meat. "What the fuck's this?" he asked in a disgusted voice.

Billy grinned at him. "Asques cock."

The words reverberated around Mike's head like the steel balls in a game of pinball. Nausea swamped over his body, the room started to spin and for a worrying moment, he thought he'd join his brother in the world of unconsciousness.

Billy seeing how pale he'd gone returned the offending article to his jacket pocket. "You okay?" he asked smugly before adding, "Look like you've seen a ghost. Or part of one anyway."

Mike tried desperately to find the humour in the remark, but was in turmoil. "You cut Tony's prick off?" he muttered in total disbelief.

"It was covered in lipstick and bite marks. That was when I had the brainwave to screw with the investigation. No cock...no evidence."

"How the hell did you manage to do it with all the others there?"

Billy's smile appeared to be growing wider. "I was on my way home when the call came out. I always keep my radio on until I get there. I was the first officer at the scene. Sent the chinky guy back to the restaurant to brew a cup of tea for the officers arriving...well it was freezing. Did what needed to be done before anyone got there. Close though, I'd just got the thing off when the crazy gang turned up."

Mike's colour was slowly returning, "It's you that's crazy. I suppose you've taken all the DNA samples away then?" he said matter-of-factly.

"This could keep C.I.B. off our tails Mike. We need to be stronger here...okay?"

Mike nodded his head.

Billy continued, "Now go and take the drunken bum home before he's sick on the upholstery."

Mike stood up and manhandled Jake to his feet. "See you at nine then," he said as he half carried his charge across the dance floor. Billy waved a hand casually in their direction before happily helping himself to another drink.

25

Sunlight broke through the heavy green velvet curtains, bright shafts of light danced on the sleeping face of Stella Blackmore. Slowly the temperature of the suns rays stirred her from a drink induced sleep.

Stella rubbed her eyes, turning away from the morning sunshine as she did so. Her head felt as though she'd banged it against something heavy, such was the throbbing sensation that had engulfed it. Moaning, she tried to sit up, but straight away the room started to spin. She moaned loudly as everything went out of focus. Lying back down on the sofa where she had fallen asleep the previous night, a result of the drink and hard physical effort she'd put in throughout most of the day and into the early evening hours.

Stella closed her eyes and tried to think of the names on the by now grubby piece of paper she'd fondled to a great extent, deciding in which order she'd carry out her plan. Fighting back nausea she forced herself to remember the next name on the list.

She managed to grin when she recalled it was a teenage girl who lived just around the corner, on one of the council estates. Teresa had added her to the names because she knew Brian had not only slept with her, but she'd supplied him with drugs. Teresa was also certain the girl had supplied stolen goods to him on many occasions. What had annoyed Stella more than anything was the fact Teresa had told her this girl had given Brian the ruby ring he'd given Stella for her last birthday. It'd been stolen the previous week from an old lady who'd been beaten up and robbed in the street. Teresa told her Brian had known this, but told her he wasn't prepared to waste good money on Stella. Stella had been over the moon when she received the gift. When the truth had been revealed, she felt sick.

The painful memory caused the pain floating around in her head to magnify. Burying her head into the soft linen of a sofa cushion, she tried to push the demons of drink away and conjure up blissful sleep, where she hoped dreams of her next killing would help see her through the next few hours and bring her back to the land of the living.

Annie Walsh was in a happy mood. Her boyfriend Jake had just left and as usual, he had brought her something nice as a surprise gift. This time it was a small, gold jewellery box that, when opened, played the theme music to Swan Lake, while a small, delicate ballerina danced around in never ending circles, 'Well, never ending until the music stops," Jake had joked.

Annie toyed with her gift while she looked at the more important reason of his visit, a large quantity of heroin she had to cut and sell, making a huge mark up profit in the process.

Annie quickly worked out she'd make over four hundred pounds from the deal, which was a very small percentage of what the drugs would bring in for Mickey Driscol the main supplier of the drugs on the estate.

Annie had just turned nineteen, and had been a drug addict and prostitute for most of her young life having been sexually abused by both her parents from an early age. When she finally told the police and her parents were taken to court, her relationship with them had ended.

Foster home and step parents saw her through life until she reached sixteen, when she'd ran away from home and met

Jake, who'd been her boyfriend and pimp ever since, Annie having started on the game at twelve to see herself through care. Somehow she'd needed a way to get cash to buy cigarettes and fuel her early heroin habit.

She put the jewelry box down and opened one of the bags of crisp white powder. Licking her finger, she stuck it into the small hole she'd made. Carefully she pulled out her finger and slowly wrapped her tongue around it, removing the drug in one continuous lick.

Sitting down she waited for the buzz to come and fill her head with sweet thoughts, replacing her usual feelings of depression and sadness. She loved Jake, but knew he used her; she had no friends and no family. The council kept threatening to throw her out of the flat if they received any more complaints from her neighbours about late night callers banging on the doors and shouting abuse when she'd refused them a fix. Luckily they didn't know the reason for all the trouble; otherwise she'd already be homeless.

The effects of her quick fix had taken hold; Annie smiled as she recognised good gear. She would enjoy the next few hours, without a worldly care. Then she'd carry out her job, mix the heroin with baking soda to make the stash last longer. Once done she'd go out into the night and locate her usual punters before they turned up on her doorsteps, banging, hollering and screaming abuse at the residents who wanted her out. Annie wouldn't give them the satisfaction. She intended to live here until she decided it was time to leave.

Stella woke and was amazed to see she'd slept for nearly a further twelve hours, where the bright early morning sun had been, now the moon had taken its place.

Her headache had gone and all she felt was hunger as it nibbled her insides.

With a new supply of vigor she jumped up and headed to the kitchen, where she pulled open the fridge door and looked inside. She groaned at the lack of food. She'd not shopped for several days and her fridge was practically empty. She withdrew a lump of mature Scottish cheddar and a half a loaf, which she noticed had sections of green mould at the edges. Her hunger out maneuvered her worries about food poisoning, and she buttered the bread and carefully cut thin slices of the cheese, placing them on the bread in such a way as to cover the mould. Settling down at the kitchen table she started to eat her sparse offering. The food tasted great despite the mouldy bread, and she smiled as each mouthful was gratefully swallowed, without being fully chewed.

Half an hour later and fully refreshed, Stella dressed in casual jeans and a bright yellow woolen jumper and headed out, her intention being to visit the *Green Man* public house and find the girl she knew was called Annie Walsh.

The Green Man sat comfortably in the middle of the Stonewall estate. It was a huge eatery with three bars running off the main restaurant, each serving a particular function.

Stella had a quick look into the sports bar, which had two snooker tables and half a dozen pool tables crushed together in such a way, the players had to wait until the person on the table next to them played their shot, before they could get down and line up their own stroke. Stella noticed that the green baize on all the tables had seen better days, each had small cuts and dents in the cloth and the cigarette ash was so thick on the tables that each shot left a trail in the grime.

Stella glanced at the players; all were youths of about eighteen to twenty-five and had a look in their eyes that suggested serious money games were being played. Drugs would not be wanted in this bar tonight.

She went to the lounge and was surprised to find it empty apart from an elderly couple in their seventies, who were carefully guarding two halves of stout and who looked up nervously when she entered the room. Stella held up a hand to say hello, both residents dropped their faces into their drinks. She sighed, nobody trusted anyone anymore which she found sad.

The public bar was the complete opposite, as it was packed with people of all ages. Stella went to the bar and ordered a whiskey and coke. Taking the drink she found herself a seat to the rear of the bar, which gave her a perfect view of the goings on before her.

Her gaze fell upon a couple sitting to her left who were heavily engrossed in conversation. They looked about seventeen or eighteen and by the look of them hadn't washed in weeks. The girl had on a pair of very faded light blue jeans, that if the sun hit much more would almost certainly turn white, she had a red vest on, which did little to contain her breasts, and her forearms were decorated by hundreds of tiny flower tattoos. Stella watched with fascination as the girls breasts bounced up and down in time to her conversation. Her hair was tied back in a loose pony tail, which revealed a long sleek neck and very bony shoulders. The part of her anatomy Stella was particularly interested in, apart from the bouncing breasts, was the girls forearm. Even at a distance of six or so feet she could see the track marks running up her arm.

The boy looked different. He too could have benefited from a hot bath, but he had a healthy look about him where as the girl looked half dead. Stella saw he wore black leather trousers and a pair of ankle boots that matched. His torso was hidden under a blue denim shirt, which did little to hide his bulging biceps. The shirt sleeves were down depriving her of any signs, but she only had to look at his eyes to know he was an addict. It looked as though he wore a heavy dollop of black mascara under each eye, and his face appeared too gaunt for the size of his head. Stella knew she'd found a perfect way of identifying Annie Walsh.

She returned to the bar, taking in some of the other customers as she went. Several looked as if they were in need of a fix. The bartender, a dizzy blonde looking creature of barely eighteen smiled at her as she reached the counter. "Hi," she said,

"Can I get you a drink?"

"Another whiskey and coke please."

The barmaid gave a fake smile and went to get the drink, leaving her to lean against the bar and continue her observations.

Teresa had given her descriptions of people on the list she hadn't known, Annie Walsh being one of them.

Her eyes scanned the bar, hopeful of seeing a girl who'd match the rough mental picture she'd painted of her.

An hour and three whiskeys later, Annie Walsh walked into the bar. Stella was certain it was her the minute she saw her. Without going near the counter to order a drink, Annie approached the young couple Stella had targeted as potential buyers. She craned her neck in an effort to hear what was being said. Above the music and chatter that filled the smokey atmosphere, she listened intently as the conversation reached its end.

Annie Walsh hated doing deals in public, but as usual she'd been ordered to sell the gear as quickly as possible. It was strong stuff and one hit would be enough for some newcomers to the game to be hooked for life.

She'd known Janice and Steve would be in the pub as they were most nights, sitting out the cold with a drink before them, only taking a sip occasionally so as to make it last for several hours. Once outside it would be back to their freezing squat if they'd been lucky enough to secure a place in one. Otherwise it was a night under the stars, fun in summer, but potentially fatal in winter. Annie knew they took the drugs to deaden their senses to the hand the world had dealt them.

"Hi Jan, hi Steve," she began in a quiet happy voice. She genuinely liked the couple.

"Hi Annie," replied Janice in a shaky voice, her mounting need to score already affecting her speech. "Got any?" she asked in such a pleading voice it cut at Annie's soul.

"Sure sweetness," she responded. "Nothing but the best for you two." finishing off the sentence with a smile. Carefully she took out two small cellophane packages and under the cover of the table passed them to Steve. The act was repeated in reverse and Stella assumed, although she didn't see, that payment was made.

Annie her first sale of the night completed, kissed Jan and Steve on the cheek, said a quick goodbye and moved with the sleekness of an alley cat to a table further away from Stella, who got up and walked to an adjoining table in the hope of seeing another deal done. She hated drug users, but not as much as she detested the people who supplied them their misery.

This time no conversation took place, the deal was done quickly, without any fuss.

Stella felt her bladder tighten and left Annie to deal while she went to relieve herself.

The toilet looked like something from inside a derelict building. Flakes of pink paint hung like giant leaves waiting to drop from a colourful exotic plant, a fine covering of water lay on the floor, caused by overflowing toilet bowls, the result of cigarette packets and used tampons being rammed down them over time. Stella guessed the management hadn't been in here for days. The smell was as bad as anything she could remember and she chuckled when she recalled the reason she felt it had been necessary to remove the corpses of Brian, Teresa and Mandy. The smell of death lost in a straight battle against piss, butt ends and used sanitary towels all mixed together in a hellish soup.

Her thoughts were broken when a voice from behind startled her.

"You a copper?" It was a direct question and as she turned to answer, she found herself face to face with Annie Walsh.

"Jesus girl, you nearly frightened me to death."

"Well are you?" This time the voice was threatening although Stella didn't feel bothered by the tone.

"Do I look like a copper?" she asked.

Annie studied her before answering. "Don't know, could be."

"Listen love even if I was, which I'm not, you'd still supply me with some shit. Wouldn't you? I mean you did my husband."

Annie looked doubtful and seemed to be searching Stella's eyes for the truth.

Stella interrupted her thoughts. "My husband, Brian, bought stolen goods from you. He bought drugs as well and for all I know he slept with you too."

Annie cut in, "I don't know what you're talking about."

"Oh come on, don't give me shit. I'm not a cop, do you really think if I was, I'd be in this filth hole talking to you. Bearing in mind I've seen you dealing in the pub. Come off it girl, you know you'd have been nicked already."

Annie looked at the floor. Stella watched as she pushed a blue and white Nike trainer deeper into the layer of water. "Okay, so you ain't a copper. What do you want?"

"How do you know I want anything?" Stella asked quizzically.

"You were following me around the pub. You must want something."

The trap was set. Stella knew Annie would play along. "Listen, my husband said you were good. Know what I mean?" She watched a smug smile cross Annie's lips. "I want some myself and I want some gear to make it sweeter.

"I don't do women, only good friends."

Stella could feel the anger building inside.   She'd practiced all her conversations in her mirror back home, taking the words from television programmes and films she'd watched on lonely nights, left alone while Brian had no doubt been out screwing someone else. The words didn't come easy to her and she was beginning to feel the strain. "Look honey," she said, "I'm clean, not too bad looking and I'll pay you well. Surely you can have a hit and then just do like I ask?"

Annie hesitated.   "Okay, but it'll cost you big.   I don't enjoy doing it to people I don't know."

Stella threw back her head in victory, hiding her winning smile. "Sure I understand, but hey, the money will be worth it. Who knows I might teach you a few tricks."

"Doubt it." Came the sarcastic reply.

26

The morning office meeting wasn't going well. The interviews had produced no leads and the murder weapon still hadn't been located. Worse; all the prints found in Tony Asque's car had been contaminated at the scene by moisture from the drop in evening temperature, which had crept in through the open car door. The fingerprint men had only lifted partial prints, which at this stage were no good to anyone. Nobody mentioned the missing penis, such was the horror and disgust they all felt.

Carter had spoken to John MacDonald earlier, and had been told the Commander was getting anxious. Carter had told him there were no leads, on the murder or the missing WPC.

Interrupting the loud conversations going on before him he said, "Right, this isn't going as well as I would've liked. All we need is a break and I'm sure the information will fall into our laps. What I want done quickly, is for all the records of female murderers to be retrieved out of storage and cross checked against any who have just been released from prison. Also look at any lists we have containing details on suspects who remove body parts." He heard the mumbled groans of disgust, could feel the hatred towards the killer. "There can't be too many of those, so it shouldn't take long. I also want further house to house checks done along the whole route WPC Burrows took the day she went missing. From what I've been told she used to cycle home quite slowly, so someone must have seen her."

"Especially if it was a man following her before she disappeared, Gov," DC Kent hollered across the room.

"What's that supposed to mean detective?" Carter asked trying hard to control his fury.

"Well Sir, I don't suspect you met her, but by Christ she was a prick teaser of the highest order. If a man had been behind her she'd have cycled with her arse stuck so far up in the air, he wouldn't have been able to miss it, nor forget it either."

More laughter filled the office and few detrimental remarks regarding Mandy Burrows were thrown in for good measure.

Somehow Carter managed to remain calm until DC Kent shouted. "Mark Allen over there can tell you more Gov, he was shafting her. Weren't you boy?"

"Enough Kent, do you find this funny? A WPC from your station is missing, chances are she's dead. Are you a moron?"

DC Kent hung his head in embarrassment, "Sorry Sir, I didn't mean any disrespect. I was only trying to lighten up the situation."

"Well don't and if you do so again you will be off this investigation. Do you understand me?"

"Gov," Kent said in barely a whisper.

Carter looked around the office to see everyone staring at him, but he didn't care. If Kent had been there alone he would've smashed his face in. "You've all got work to do. I suggest you get on with it." He didn't wait for a response, merely turned around and went into his office where he slammed the door behind him.

Taking a plastic cup from his drawer he poured a large brandy from a silver hip flask he kept in his briefcase, a habit he'd developed early in his career. The liquid made him gasp as it was swallowed quickly. He filled up again and repeated the process, this time sipping the drink. Throwing the beaker into the waste paper bin, he put his arms on the desk and rested his head on them.

It wasn't long before his anger was replaced by sleep and he nodded into the land of dreams, although for Carter, there were only nightmares.

The cold night air, caused clouds of vapour to escape from

their lips, as they walked the five minute journey from the
pub to Annie's flat.

Stella listened to the multitude of different sounds being
carried on the evening breeze. Her mounting tension caused
her heart to thump against her breast bone, making such an
imaginary loud noise, she was sure Annie would hear it
through the thin material of her sunshine yellow jumper. A
faint jingle jangle from gold bracelets slipping up and down
Annie's forearm as she purposely swung her arms like a
marching soldier to quicken her step in an attempt to stop the
chilly wind biting into her skin punched out a rhythmic beat
taking Stella towards her next kill.

She wondered why it seemed to be only personal sounds
that entered her head so clearly. Everything not connected to
them seemed somehow muffled, distant, and unimportant, as
if they weren't part of the larger picture.

No conversation took place until they stood on the porch
entrance to the council block of flats where Annie's life
evolved.

Stella watched Annie, the drug dealer prostitute slip her
master key into the lock.

"Glad to be inside getting warm," she muttered through
chattering teeth. "This is going to cost you lady," Annie told
her in a voice as icy as the night air.

Stella smiled. "Don't worry, I'll take care of you, but only
if you take good care of me," she said, enjoying her
performance.

Annie gave her a look that suggested pity, sadness, but
above all, disgust. Stella knew she'd play along, because she
needed the money to supply her drug habit.

The door to the flats stood open before them. Annie
waved her through and side by side they began the climb to
the third floor where she lived.

Almost immediately the smell hit Stella, dog and cat
urine, mixed with heavy cigarette smoke filled the air.
Alcohol fumes and a sweet aroma of cooking battled to fill her
nostrils. She thought the hallway smelt worse than the pub
and for a brief moment she thought about letting Annie live
as she caught a glimpse into the young girl's life. The image
faded fast as she remembered why she was here and she
quickly blamed the other woman for her own circumstances,
after all nobody forced her to sell drugs and her body. With
that thought she continued the climb, arriving outside the

purple, paint chipped front door to Annie's home, both angry and a little out of breath.

"Quick inside before the neighbours see you," Annie whispered.

"Oh come on," Stella said in a mocking voice. "They all know what you do."

"Just get inside," Annie rasped.

Stella brushed past her and found she was standing in the main room. A quick glance around told her it served as living room and bedroom, the large unmade bed taking up over half of the floor space. A door led to a small kitchen unit and she could see through a partially open door.

"Sit down," Annie ordered, pointing to the bed. "I'm going to get myself ready." and with that she headed towards the bathroom.

Stella watched her go with a surreal sensation building up inside her. She was alone with her next victim barely twenty feet away. In her haste to get out and find her she'd forgotten to bring along her knife. Stella couldn't help the laughter that escaped her lips.

Standing up, she knew she'd made a huge mistake and that things could go seriously wrong from this point forward. Looking around she tried to focus through tears of frustration on anything that remotely looked like a murder weapon. Apart from the bed, the only other items of furniture in the room were a small wooden table that had strips of its veneer hanging off, and two large pink armchairs that now had so many stains on them it looked like abstract patterns had been drawn into the fabric. She shuddered as she tried to imagine what had caused the marks. A small twelve inch television completed the room's decor. She was about to go and look in the kitchen, when she heard the toilet door open and Annie reemerged.

The transformation took Stella by surprise. Gone were the faded casual clothes, replaced by a black bodice which was transparent enough to allow Stella a view of dark hair surrounding Annie's most intimate place and her hard dark nipples pushing out from behind the lace. The young woman's face now resembled one of the many Stella had seen gazing back at her from glossy magazines. Stella stared open mouthed at the creature before her. She'd never felt sexually aroused by another woman before and when Mandy had touched her earlier she'd felt physically sick. Every nerve she had, demanded she now go and touch her.

Annie couldn't fail to smile at the open mouthed customer before her, "Like it then?" she beamed.

"You look beautiful," Stella replied and meant it. Her mind raced, what was happening to her?

Annie came forward, her hips swaying seductively. Stella could feel goose bumps springing up all over her body. She felt like a teenager again, waiting for that first long, passionate kiss.

Annie pulled her close and their lips touched, sending waves of electricity through Stella's body, taking her breath away, causing her mind to spiral out of control. She felt the blood drain from her limbs as a probing tongue forced its way into her mouth, gently caressing her teeth and lips. Caressing hands kneaded her bottom, and she could feel Annie's hips grinding against her own.

A hand took a tight grip on her forearm and she allowed herself to be taken over to the bed, offered no resistance as her jumper was slowly pulled over her head, revealing her naked breasts to Annie's gaze.

Stella lay down on the bed and let Annie remove the rest of her clothes. Butterfly kisses were evenly spread over her, each one providing magic.

Stella gasped and grabbed at Annie's hair as her passion rose. She'd never fully enjoyed sex with Brian as it was only a means of his own satisfaction, he didn't care if Stella enjoyed herself. When the waves of her orgasm burst through her, she prayed the feeling would never end.

Annie sat up and Stella could see the smug look on her face. She didn't care if the younger woman was mocking her. Stella was lost in her first really enjoyable sexual experience since her early days as a teenager. Her fun had ended the day she got married to Brian.

"You can pay me and go," Annie sneered at her.

It was as if someone had slapped her hard across the face, dragged her off the bed and screamed at her to tell them what the hell she thought she was doing. She was there to kill this scheming, lying, drug taking little whore, and what was she doing? She was having sex with her.

Stella, shocked at what Annie had said and horrified at what her own demons had told her, sat bolt upright on the bed and punched the unsuspecting Annie with all her might.

The blow was hard enough to push her nose back into her face and Stella felt it shatter under her knuckles. Blood splattered at first and then poured. Annie taken by total surprise, looked at her in shock, before the pain registered and she drifted into unconsciousness.

Stella sat slumped on the edge of the bed, resting her head in her hands. She'd checked for Annie's pulse and was disappointed when she'd found one. She knew it would've been lucky if her blow had killed her, but it would have finished things quickly.

Still naked, she padded her way across the linoleum and into the kitchen. It was a small place and Stella could imagine her victim trying to cook a meal in such restricted circumstances. Annie had taken her time when she'd decorated in here. Pastel yellow paint made the room warm, three hanging baskets of dried flowers hung from the ceiling giving it a peaceful feel. Dozens of small spice bottles were carefully positioned along all sides of the work surfaces and she noticed two blue and orange stuffed elephants peeking out at her from behind a coffee jar. The more she looked, the more cuddly animals she found returning her gaze. She began to open drawer after drawer, trying to find what she would use to finish Annie. The third drawer provided what she was looking for.

The handle was dark brown, made of hard plastic, but it was the blade on the meat cleaver that had taken her eye. It was eight inches long, and as she twisted it in her hand the reflections from the kitchen light danced along the shiny surface. Stella ran her thumb along the blades edge and felt her skin slice under its power. Taking the cleaver back into the bedroom she noticed Annie squirming on the bed as she regained consciousness.

Annie opened her eyes and saw Stella closing the small gap between them, "What the fuck did you do that for? You've bust my nose."

Stella sat on the bed beside Annie and gently turned her face towards her. She noticed for the first time how large, brown and beautiful the young woman's eyes were, but she could also see sadness and deep set pain held in her stare. Keeping her voice hushed, Stella said, "First orgasm I've had in years, thank you, but the truth is I came here to kill you."

Annie's eyes screwed almost shut and her mouth opened

as if to speak. She'd only been half listening to Stella between sobs and stabs of pain. Only the last few words set of the alarm bells in her head. Pushing Stella away, she tried to get off the bed. As she moved to stand she saw the flash of metal above her head as Stella swung the cleaver towards her. Annie threw herself off the bed and hit the floor with a loud thump.

"No escape honey," Stella laughed, standing over her.

"Please, I've got money, lots of money. You can have it all, it's in a jar in the kitchen...please don't kill me."

Stella bent over Annie. Tear tracks had formed where they'd washed away the blood from her face, the make-up she'd carefully applied was now spread everywhere, looking like an abstract painting tattooed onto her skin. Sobs cut across deep breaths and again she felt pity for the girl. She couldn't allow her to live though, not now. Stella bent forward, keeping the cleaver out of sight as she did so. "Tell you what, I'll take the money and we'll call it quits. What do you say?"

Annie didn't answer; she crumpled before her in relief, the tears flowing faster than ever.

Stella helped her to her feet, tucking an arm under her so she remained close by her side. She edged her over to the bed. "Sit down here. I'll get some tissue paper for your nose eh?"

Annie gazed at the woman before her, wondering how her mood swings could be so violently different, thinking maybe she was insane, relieved in the knowledge she'd saved her life by offering the cash and knowing she'd gain her revenge by having the shit kicked out of her by her employers and then grassing the bitch to the police.

Stella hadn't left her side and as she studied the battered face of Annie she could almost read her thoughts, "Do I detect revenge in your pretty little head?" she asked in a knowing voice.

"Revenge for what?" Annie replied in a meek manner.

"Don't be a smart ass, people don't like smart asses."

Annie was about to reply when she felt the blow to her side, felt the hot pain as the cleaver entered her body, and looked up to see the smiling woman before her.

"Time up," Stella whispered.

Annie tilted her head to where the blow had struck her. She wanted to scream when she saw the width of blade embedded in her side, but the blood rushing into her lungs prevented her doing so. Mesmerised she watched the blade being pulled out, saw the blood run down her side and felt the second blow hit her between her shoulder blades.

Annie looked around for the last time, her vision blurring as her life force prepared to leave her body. Her gaze fell on the open kitchen door and she tried to focus inside.

Annie Walsh saw her beloved cuddly toy animal collection piled high on a stool, and although in considerable pain, was horrified to see they'd all had their heads removed. These lay in a separate bundle at the foot of the stool. "Bastard!" she somehow dragged from deep within.

Stella sat down beside her. The girl would be dead soon. She pulled her head to her and let it rest on her shoulder, knowing there would be no resistance this time. She waited for it to end before lifting Annie back onto the bed before she lay down beside her.

When sleep came it took her back to before she'd murdered the girl, back to the time when waves of pleasure washed over her body, back where her game no longer mattered, where she'd been lost in a world she never knew existed.

27

A solitary table lamp fought gallantly to bring light into the lounge, where Mark Carter was lying on a pale blue Italian leather two seater.

He stared into the darkness, his right arm dangled over the edge of the couch; in his left hand he tightly gripped a three-quarter full Edinburgh Crystal glass that contained a twelve year old malt whiskey. The coffee table beside him was littered with empty bottles of beer, a half finished Indian take away and the remains of a bottle of Vodka he'd started his evening's entertainment with.

Hours had passed in total silence as he poured one drink after another, first into his glass and then just quickly down his throat. He'd been putting off the thought that Mandy was dead, covering it up with all the positive police talk he could muster, but tonight when he'd sat at his office desk, analysing the evidence so far, he'd asked himself the most searching question he could think of.

If someone else was missing, would you still believe she was alive?

The answer had slapped him in the face with such force he felt the shock waves wash over his entire body.

Mandy was dead.

It didn't make any sense to him, but his feelings when he woke to the truth were of devastation, but there was also relief. He assumed, admitting to himself what he'd known from the start, opened him up fully to the pain he knew would follow, but also allowed him to get on with finding the person who'd shattered his life, with no hidden secrets anymore.

Carter sat up; taking a large mouthful of whiskey he swallowed hard and immediately felt the warmth as the malt found his stomach. He knew he should be drunk, but his emotions were keeping him sober. It wasn't what he wanted. He needed to find oblivion so he could forget that his heart ached with such a deep intensity that his brain hurt with the knowledge the murderer was still at large, and they hadn't a clue as to who he or she could be.

Questions rattled around his head, each one feeling like someone was inserting a hot needle into his brain.

Why was someone killing cops?

Why was Mandy targeted?

Why hadn't anyone seen her being kidnapped?

Did she know the killer?

Was it anything to do with the corruption inside Westville Police Station?

These and more continued to spin around inside his head like an angry tornado, causing bolts of pain as they twisted him into knots.

Carter's body ached with grief, and still there was no sign of the alcohol coming to his rescue.

It was then that he started to cry.

When Stella awoke it was 3.27am. She'd been asleep for nearly five hours. Her immediate thought on waking was where was she? Pins and needles played with her arms and she realized she'd fallen asleep with her fingers linked behind her head.

As she tried to regain control of her tingling limbs, her eyes focused slowly on the situation around her, finally her gaze fell on Annie Walsh who looked as if she too was in a deep sleep. Stella laughed, knowing that the girl would be sleeping forever.

The small clock on the wall told her she needed to move quickly if she wanted to leave under the cover of darkness. Rising to her feet she dressed and tidied herself up. Moving to the kitchen she poured some water onto a dish cloth and returned to the lifeless body.

Carefully she washed Annie's body. She didn't know exactly what evidence the police could retrieve from a corpse, but she wanted to put the odds in her favour of them finding nothing.

When she'd finished, Stella washed down all the surfaces in the flat that she could recall touching. Once done, she found an old carrier bag and dropped the wet cloth inside. She felt confident her fingerprints had been removed from the scene.

Next she squeezed in the cleaver, followed by all the clothes Annie had been wearing both earlier in the evening and her black lace body stocking that's had seduced Stella earlier.

The task took longer than she'd anticipated and when Stella looked back at the clock she found she'd been cleaning for nearly an hour.

With mounting urgency she stood beside the bed and looked down for the last time at Annie Walsh. Slowly she bent forward and gently, almost lovingly kissed the dead girls lips. Somewhere deep inside she was forced to admit regret at killing Annie. Maybe if she'd thought it through, Annie would've been one of the last on the list. These were the people who may yet escape death. Stella knew that if she made a mistake her list may not be completely erased.

Jake Grady's head felt like someone was following him as he climbed the stairs to his girlfriends flat, and that with each step the pursuer would bring a hammer down on his cranium. He'd spent a small fortune getting into the state he was in and badly needed to get some cash at the same time as obtaining his next fix. It was nearly first light, and he knew Annie would be angry at the lateness of the hour. With relief he finally stood before the door and fumbled first getting the key from his pocket and secondly in finding the keyhole to open the door. Finally, he staggered inside, trying to be as quiet as possible, but knowing he was too drunk to manage it. When he fell over in the darkness, he howled with pain.

Stella was almost at the other side of the door when Jake pushed it open. She hadn't heard him reach the doorway, but had heard the scraping sounds as he'd tried to insert the key in the lock.

Panic had rushed through her veins, her throat had tightened and her mouth went dry as a desert as she felt wave after wave of nausea mounting.

Dropping the bag containing the evidence she'd made her way back to the bedroom area and had jumped in beside Annie, pulling up the sheets to provide cover. Immediately she'd realised she'd left her weapon in the bag. Defenseless, she waited for whoever had come into the flat to find her.

Jake slowly picked himself up, and rubbed his lower back, which sustained most of the impact from his fall. He was surprised Annie hadn't come to see what had caused the noise, but assumed she was asleep and that his ungainly entrance hadn't disturbed her.

He made his way over to the bed and fumbled in the darkness as he tried to find the top of Annie's head. "Jesus," he mumbled when his fingers caressed the hair of two people. He pulled his hand back as if he'd touched something hot and moved away from the bed. Jake was aware that Annie took on an old client sometimes, but she knew he no longer approved, now that they were more than friends. Even drunk he knew from the smell radiating from the bed, the other person was a woman.

Normally he would have found this exciting, but his head ached so much all he wanted to do was score and then retreat somewhere quiet to sleep it off. The warmth of the kitchen floor would suffice until Annie's friend left.

Trying to be as quiet as possible he found the stashed drugs and taking out a syringe he started to process his fix. He was oblivious to the pile of decapitated furry animals, lying on a stool before him, their heads neatly stacked.

Stella felt the hot breath from the mouth of her new flat mate tickle her neck, as whoever it was lent over her. She could smell alcohol and cigarette fumes in the air, and when the person uttered the one solitary word that pierced the quietness of the night, she knew it was a man.

She lay still, silently praying he wouldn't decide to climb into the bed beside her and the blood coated body of Annie Walsh. Her chest felt as if something very heavy had attached itself to it, and was now trying to push her heart out through the centre of her back. Each second brought increased pain as her muscles fought to control the mounting terror.

The man seemed to take an age to back off, finally she heard him cross the floor and enter the kitchen. From the sounds he made Stella guessed he was staggering so knew he was either drunk or high. This she hoped would give her the advantage to escape.

She waited a few minutes and then slowly, taking care not to make a noise, she lifted herself from the bed.

From her position she could see into the kitchen. The man was squatting on the floor, cross legged and appeared to be engrossed on a task. She saw a match light up and then a silver spoon placed over it. He was fixing himself a shot of heroin, and while he was busy, Stella figured she could slip out the front door, picking up her bag containing the evidence and flee.

Jake was having difficulty focusing, and although he badly needed a fix he knew he was fast approaching the point where he would just fall into unconsciousness.

In his haste, he placed his fingers to close to the tip of the burning match and he yelled, "Ouch!" as it burnt his skin, before he dropped the spoon with a clatter that in the darkness sounded like Big Ben.

Jake turned round expecting to see movement from the bed, but instead caught a glimpse of Annie's friend sneaking towards the front door. "Hey wait a minute," he shouted. Unsteadily he got to his feet and as fast as his wobbly legs would allow, he made his way to the front door.

Stella had picked up the plastic carrier bag and was about to open the door when she heard the man shout after her. Her composure seemed to have returned, and she calmly slipped her hand inside the bag and removed the cleaver that had butchered Annie earlier.

She kept facing the door until she felt the man's presence, and then she spun around, raising the cleaver at the same time.

Jake was too drunk to understand what was happening and in the semi darkness of the flat had no way of comprehending what was about to happen. He saw the woman turn, saw she'd raised her arm above her head, but had no idea why.

Stella brought the weapon down with such force on the unsuspecting Jake, that it almost carved his head in two. Horrified, she watched as his face halved before her like a ripe apple, before spewing the insides of his skull over the floor. Amazingly he remained standing for long enough to frighten Stella. She moved forward and gave him an almighty shove. The body toppled over and crumpled at her feet.

She knew her time was up and that she couldn't clean up this mess. She felt confident as they'd had little direct contact she still hadn't left any traceable evidence.

Minutes later, Stella was happy to get out into the fresh air and was delighted to find it was still reasonably dark. Her heart still thumped furiously inside her rib cage, and she felt sick, but she knew she'd make it home before daylight, and more importantly, she could remove another name from her list.

28

Chief Superintendent John MacDonald sat in the station canteen and looked down almost lovingly at the plateful of bacon and eggs, sizzling before him. He'd watched a programme on television the previous evening, concerning the increasingly worrying statistics regarding obesity in the UK. MacDonald didn't believe in all that nonsense and enjoyed his food, but as he placed a large piece of bacon in his mouth, its fat dribbling down his chin, he wondered if perhaps the time was right to have his own cholesterol levels checked.

Inspector Ascot and Sergeant Green from the Complaints Investigation Bureau sauntered over to where he was sitting.

MacDonald saw their approach out of the corner of his eye. He allowed his eyes to flick a look at the clock on the wall and noticed it was only just after six fifteen in the morning. He'd come in early to catch up on the murder enquiry, why the C.I.B. were in so early was beyond him.

"Morning Sir," Ascot said in a booming voice.

"Bit early for your lot, isn't it?" MacDonald sneered as he popped some fried egg between his lips.

Green smiled at him briefly, "Early bird catches the worm Sir," he said in a very sarcastic voice.

Before MacDonald could respond to the obvious dig at his officers, Inspector Ascot spoke. "Sir, we've been given some information from an outside party that perhaps you'd care to look at?" He placed a brown file before the Chief Superintendent before continuing. "Some of the names in there are prominent detectives at this station. I know there's a big investigation going on, but I really need to speak to these officers as soon as possible."

MacDonald opened the file and at once saw the names of most of his senior detectives staring back at him. "Jesus Christ," he gasped. "This is nearly the whole Criminal Investigation Department. Surely, you're not telling me they're now all crooked as well as the entire uniform branch?"

"No Sir, I'm not. But from what I've been told, quite a few of them may be involved in serious crimes. Obviously we need to sort it out quickly."

"Can I ask who gave you the names?"

"You can ask Sir, but don't expect to get an answer," Ascot grinned in response.

"Fair enough then, let me finish my breakfast and I'll get right on it."

The C.I.B. officers left and MacDonald pushed his half eaten breakfast away from him, "Damn!" he said aloud and stood up, pushing the table across the floor as he did so. Angrily he stormed off to his office, with the brown file tucked roughly under his arm.

Stella sat in her kitchen, with both hands tightly holding onto a mug she'd filled three-quarter full with whiskey. Droplets of pale liquid splashed onto her knees as she desperately fought to control her shaking limbs.

She'd made it back just before the sun had cast its morning glow across the city.

Neighbours were already up and about, and she saw Mrs. Donnelly through her fine net curtains setting the breakfast table for her five children and drunken slob of a husband.

Stella had always wondered how such a family managed to get a house in Arcadia Drive. Now it seemed funny, seeing as they now lived near a serial killer!

A few other lights were on, but she felt safe that no-one had spotted her early return.

Stella knew if she'd been seen a lot of questions in the street would need to be answered. Everyone understood she wasn't allowed out without her husband. Brian had seen to that.

She placed the drained mug onto the kitchen table and rubbed the palm of her hands along her thighs. Her feet were playing a rapid tune on the linoleum; such were the tremors running through her body.

Stella assumed she was shaking with relief, that she'd done managed to do what she'd set out to do, and then made it home safely.

Rising to her feet she went to where she'd left the bottle of whiskey, before bringing it back and filling the mug once more, this time to the top. As she raised it to her mouth, she caught sight of the answering machine sitting on the footstool in the hall. "Oh no!" she said aloud, realising she hadn't checked it for nearly a week. Pushing her drink from her she rushed into the hall to check it. Her heart sank when she saw blinking red light telling her she had messages.

Her hand shook horribly as she pressed the play button, and waited to be told she had three messages. She held her breath as the machine started in a robotic voice.

First message: Stella, its Sergeant Wilson from the nick here. Can you please give me a ring ASAP as I need to know when Brian is likely to be back, as I want to sort out his duties? Ta very much. Bye.

Stella felt her blood go cold.

Second message: Hi Brian, it's Billy here. We had a meet tonight, remember? Give me a ring otherwise you know what's likely to happen.

She sat down hard on the blood soaked carpet, and swallowed hard.

Third message: Hi, it's me again. I need to speak to you

or Brian today. The Chief Superintendent is concerned Brian is okay. Give me a ring otherwise I'll pop over sometime tomorrow for a chat. Cheers.

Stella pressed the off button and sat in silence. A clock ticked loudly from the kitchen. It seemed to Stella to be counting down her future. If the duty Sergeant turned up and she let him in, he was going to see the mess in the hall, created when she'd pulled the bodies out into the garage. If she didn't phone him and sound convincing her game would be up before it had really started.

Panic clutched at her throat when she remembered she hadn't listened to the machine for days. When had he rung? Had he called around already? Had he seen anything suspicious?

The policeman was bad enough, but what did the second message mean? Was Brian involved in something bigger than she'd thought? Who was Billy?

Stella wearily pulled herself to her feet. Her body hurt all over, making her feel decades older than she was. She retrieved her drink and climbed the stairs to the bathroom, where she turned on the hot tap to fill the bath. Pouring in some *Radox,* she undressed slowly, putting her discarded clothes into the linen basket. As she replaced the lid, she wondered if perhaps she should dispose of them. Stella was starting to believe she'd need to leave her house and never return.

The water filled the bath and she climbed in. The heat soothed her immediately and her muscles relaxed. Leaning her head back she supported her neck on the cold enamel, her thoughts already turning over what she had to do next.

Stella lay in the bath for over an hour, topping it up with hot water when she felt the chill start to nibble at her limbs.

Over and over, she retraced what had happened so far, going through all the details of each victim's death, trying to find a mistake with which the police could attach the crimes to her. Obviously if they came to the house and managed to get into the garage to search it, the bodies of her husband, Teresa and Mandy would greet them. There was nothing she could do to prevent that as she wasn't strong enough to physically remove the corpses. Briefly she had the idea of cutting them into manageable chunks, but her stomach had turned at the very thought of it.

The murders of Tony and Annie had gone as well as she could have expected, given the slight problems she'd given herself with each one, and the unexpected guest who'd turned up.

The concern that kept coming back, no matter how hard she tried to pull a veil over it, was the phone calls left on her answering machine.

Stella wished they'd had an updated version, one that gave the date the caller had rung. Unfortunately, the one they owned was almost a relic.

There was nothing for it, she'd have to leave and make her base elsewhere. She knew how she would escape the police, once she'd finished what she'd started, but in the meantime she had to remain out of their clutches.

What she needed was time, time to carry out the remaining murders, without the police looking for her. Stella needed to throw them of her trail; she needed to make it appear that she too could be a victim of the madman going around killing people with no discrimination.

Stella let out some of the cold water for the last time, before turning on the hot tap with her toe and settling back into the bath, waiting for inspiration on how she'd deceive the Police long enough to make her escape permanent.

She lay struggling for the solution for some time, thoughts floating between the murders and whether the feelings of intense stress building up inside her were signs she was about to fall from the cliffs of sanity, before drowning in the waves and deep depths of the madness she feared was creeping up on her, like a hungry cat ready to pounce on a large and juicy prey.

29

Billy Johnstone trod carefully as he walked slowly along the muddy path which circled the outskirts of Gibson Park. He'd felt cooped up in the canteen and decided twenty minutes in the brisk afternoon air, eating his ham and tomato sandwiches would give him a chance to think things through.

When Mickey Driscol told him he was going to take the Panel on, Billy now understood that he'd gone into mild shock on hearing the audacious plan. The Panel were a very strong opposition to try and defeat, and if Mickey was to win, it would be through deception and guile, rather than sheer brute strength. In a physical confrontation there were too many irons that the secret society could bring to the fire against him.

Billy smiled at an elderly lady walking towards him with a dirty white, West Highland Terrier trotting along beside her. He wondered when the dog had last been bathed?

He was earning very good money from his dealings at the Maverick Club, running the drug racket on the Stonewall Estate, but was well aware he'd never be offered anything else, especially while still employed by the Metropolitan Police. If he left the force and began to work from within the club, he knew it wouldn't take long for the police to come looking for him. After all, the club was frequented by both criminals and members of the force. If he was seen in there, looking like he was making money, somebody somewhere with a grudge would drop a few hints here and there and before long he'd find himself under investigation. This was the reason he'd had the brain wave to tamper with the evidence from the murder enquiries currently being undertaken. He needed to be able to work the fiddles while still a police officer.

If he went along with Mickey, however and helped him take the Panel on, perhaps there would be more opportunities to advance down the road to his ultimate utopia. More money than he could spend in his lifetime.

He was smiling like a man possessed when he passed the lady and her dirty dog again. Gibson Park wasn't very large. The dog gave him the usual once over before snorting at him and shaking his head. Billy had a brief suspicion the dog knew he was crooked.

Billy dropped his lunch wrapping into the waste basket at the exit to the park and headed back to the station. He felt tense. No decision had made him feel any easier. Not to tell the Panel about Driscol's plans would be very dangerous, but so was double crossing one of the most violent men in London.

As he reached the entrance to Westville Police Station he'd decided to play the waiting game. See what Mickey intended to do and then make a calculated decision as to what action to take.

Walking along the corridor he was drawing strange glances from the officers he passed.

Billy realised he was smiling to himself, like a man who knew he'd win in the end.

Her hands cupped the steaming mug of coffee almost as if she was holding a valuable heirloom carefully between her fingers.

Stella looked out through the grime stained windows of *The Tastie Café* and watched the streams of people wander past. It was as if she was privy to the worlds largest television screen, broadcasting one of the many daily soap operas.

She saw the bus stop with the large group of school kids pushing and jostling each other as they fought to get on the number twelve. She caught sight of an old man walking his even older looking poodle, as the dog stopped directly outside the window to urinate against the lamp post. For a fraction of a second Stella wondered why dogs are so attracted to these concrete trees. She saw a young mother, wearing faded jeans and a bright pink sleeveless blouse, dragging two screaming under five's behind her, smiling at her as the kids tried to pull their mother in the opposite direction, and she watched a large black man with several chunky gold necklaces almost fill the café window as he stopped to light a cigarette.

The images crossed in front of Stella, she took them in, but gave no thought to who these people were, nor did she care.

When she'd woken in the early afternoon, lying on a sweat drenched couch, shaking uncontrollably, salty tears streaming down her cheeks, she realised her situation had started to take its toll, more than she'd thought. Immediately she'd dragged her tired body from the sofa, had showered, eaten some breakfast and walked out into the biting morning air.

Her footsteps had eventually led her to the bus stop in Lighthouse Avenue, the road that lay parallel to her own. She'd climbed on board the first bus that had pulled up, paid the fare, and around thirty minutes later she'd alighted in Kentish Town. Why she'd chosen to get off when she did eluded her, but she'd begun to slowly walk up Highgate Road until she'd stumbled across the tiny café, sandwiched between a solicitors and a betting shop.

On entering she'd discovered just how small it was, with four tables crammed into the tiny room. The proprietor offered her a food stained menu and she'd requested a bacon roll with a mug of strong coffee. The food and drink had helped her snap out the dream like state she felt herself to be in. Now as she sat with her third coffee, she pondered over her scrambled emotions.

When she'd married Brian nearly ten years earlier, she'd been an outgoing young woman with a large circle of friends and a bubbly personality. Brian had swept her off her feet with his strong character and handsome looks. Friends and family warned her he was a womanizer who'd one day break her heart. Stella had refused to accept this until after one beating too many, she'd finally understood her situation.

She was no quitter however, and strongly believed that marriage was for life no matter what kind of matrimonial bed you found yourself lying in.

When she'd began to think that perhaps her life didn't have to carry on going the way it'd progressed so far, she found to her horror that when she thought about leaving Brian, she'd look around her beautiful home, see the many antiques, the expensive paintings hanging from the walls, sink into the burgundy leather sofa and drink her fill of fine Italian and French wine, while at the same time weighing up whether the beatings and sexual torment he put her through were really bad enough for her to sacrifice the lifestyle she enjoyed so much. The more she dwelt on it, even the sex with some of his friends had its moments.

Stella shuddered as she remembered how on many occasions he'd brought four, five or more back with him to use her as they thought fit. Those were the times he made her drug up first, so she couldn't remember afterwards, but also to make her susceptible to the men's wishes.

She took a long drink and pulled a face as the cold liquid ran down her throat. Turning round she held the light blue, chipped mug up and waved it in the direction of the owner of the café.

Her drink refreshed, her thoughts drifted back to the moment she'd killed her husband. At the time she believed she'd gone mad, killed him suffering from a stress related illness, brought on from years of suffering. But now she wasn't sure. She'd enjoyed a lot of what had gone on, and certainly was happy with what Brian had provided for her within the home. She'd had to make personal sacrifices like losing all her premarital friends and not making any new ones unless her husband had said it was okay to do so, but in a way that too had seemed fair enough. She enjoyed her own company and found friendship on the Internet, when playing with the top of the range computer he'd bought for her last birthday.

What was eating her most was deep down when you pulled away the rubbish, she'd known all along he was a bent copper, she'd almost grown to love everything about her life, with the exception of the beatings and drug induced rapes.

Perhaps the mists of madness had momentarily descended on her when she'd pulled the trigger on him, but what about the other people? What about the ones she still had every intention of killing?

Had she been mad when she'd blown her husband of nearly ten years almost in half? Or had she descended into the pits of hell as a result of that first killing?

The only thing she was sure about now was that to kill another human being in cold blood, madness was certainly a pawn you brought to your side of the table.

The bodies of Detectives Ascot and Green were found just after 6am, by a jogger, who'd braved the wet, thin mist that had blanketed the area during the evening.

Both officers had been dead for only a few hours when their bodies were found. They were naked and their throats had been cut cleanly from ear to ear. Death, however, had been caused by a bullet through the head at close range, some considerable time before they were mutilated further.

Chief Superintendent MacDonald stood over the corpses with his hands plunged deeply into his cashmere overcoat. Great bellows of air left his lips as he sighed heavily at the scene before him. "Christ, Mark. We need to catch the bastard who's doing this and bloody quickly."

Mark Carter's head felt as if it had been surgically removed and replaced facing the wrong way, such was the degree of pain his hangover was causing him. Fighting back nausea, he merely nodded in agreement. One of the dead policeman's open eyes stared up at him, as if asking, 'Why?' Carter shook as the cold air bit into him and he whispered to the dead man, "Sorry," before shrugging his shoulders and turning to face MacDonald saying, "We need more men now. This is way out of control."

"Tell me what you need and I'll make sure you get it Mark. I've already spoken to the Deputy Commissioner and he's happy to let you remain in charge. He'd heard about some of your good work apparently."

Carter huffed, "Didn't help get me promoted though."

"And you know why, so forget that and catch the nutter who's doing this," MacDonald replied as he waved a hand over the bloody scene before them.

"We can't keep this a secret from the press anymore."

"No, we can't. I'll have my press secretary sort out a release when we get back. Come on let's leave the crew here to sort out what they need to do. You and I need to have a chat about other things now."

Carter followed his boss back to the squad car and climbed into the rear with him. MacDonald nodded his head and the driver pulled the car out of the children's park play area where the bodies had been draped over the roundabout, and headed back to the station.

"We have to assume Mandy is dead," MacDonald said quietly without looking at Carter.

"I know," he replied in an equally hushed tone.

"I've been thinking about this and it's up to you. We don't have to tell anyone the whole story if you don't want to."

Carter leaned back into the seat before saying, "Thanks. It might be better to leave it alone. The people who matter know."

"We'll have to do the full works regarding a police funeral. It's going to be very hard for you to deal with."

"Not any harder than for the other relatives and friends of the other dead officers."

"Very true," MacDonald added reflectively.

The vehicle moved slowly through the morning rush hour traffic, edging its way nearer the station.

"Can't we go any bloody faster?" MacDonald bellowed at his driver, who shook his head in defeat at the jam in front of them.

The rest of the journey passed without conversation between the two men. MacDonald worried about the press, the man sitting with his eyes closed beside him, the reaction the force would have to the latest murders, but most of all what would happen to his career if they failed to catch the person responsible.

Carter's only worry as they moved along with intermittent stops was would he make it back without throwing up and whether his head would ever feel normal again.

Detectives were hunched over desks, studying photographs of the dead officers. Some were flicking through mountains of witness statements, trying to uncover something they may have missed during a previous reading.

Dozens of civilian computer operators were searching data bases for links between murdered cops, current suspects recorded anywhere who'd a grudge against policemen, had threatened violence towards them, sent hate mail or were just warped enough to be in the frame for the current crimes.

Carter watched them scurrying about like rats in a medical lab, trying to find there way out the maze so they could eat their reward.

He was going to catch the killer, if it was the last thing he ever did as a detective. What buzzed around inside his head like a demented wasp was the fact they'd no evidence whatsoever linking anyone to the deceased.

He stood watching, leaning against the wall, feeling the tension in the room, interspersed with hatred towards the person killing the policemen.

Carter also felt wound up, although hatred wasn't one of his feelings. He had numbness towards whoever was committing the murders. Perhaps, when he finally came face-to-face with the person responsible it would be different. He shrugged at his thoughts, maybe it was his way of coping with the fact he knew Mandy was dead. He was still lost in his own reminisces when Constable Brian Peachy burst through the double swing doors that led into the main incident room.

Peachy was breathing heavily from excitement. "Another two bodies have been found. This time it's a hooker and her pimp from one of the flats on the Stonewall Estate. One of her customers found them about an hour ago."

One of the other officers who was hunched over a scaled down map of the play ground area where officers Ascot and Green had been found, shouted, "So what? That's got nothing to do with the dead police officers we're dealing with in here. Get one of the CID from the main office to deal with it."

The young constable waited until his breathing slowed down sufficiently enough for him to enjoy his reply, "That's just it. The girl's body has been wiped clean. There's not a trace of any evidence on it, apart from the wounds caused by whatever killed her. The pimp looks like he disturbed our killer in the act of doing it, or getting away. The duty officer thinks they've been killed by the same person who murdered Tony Asque."

The room went silent together, as if someone had removed the needle from a playing gramophone record.

"Jesus Christ!" WDC Forsyth muttered to no-one in particular.

Carter could feel all eyes on him, moving from the wall he'd been leaning on to the centre of the room, he sat down on one of the lime green plastic seats, that somehow always manage to appear in major incident rooms or at school fairs. "Okay, Billy, you and Mike to the scene. Take great care to go over everything with a tooth pick. Somewhere there must be a clue to who's doing this. The rest of you, tool up with enough paper and pens to do house-to-house through the whole estate." He let the groans die down before continuing, "Somebody out there saw or heard something. We need a break here people and we need it now, before another cop or member of the public gets wiped out."

Nods of heads and spoken acknowledgments greeted his speech. He knew the job would be carried out professionally, despite the murmurs of discontent.

30

Billy Johnstone looked across at Mike Grady as he drove to the scene of the latest murders. Both men knew who they were going to find as victims. "I'm sorry Mike," Johnstone offered.

Mike remained quiet for a while before letting out a loud sigh, "I know Billy, thanks. Who the hell do you think did it?"

It was Billy's turn to remain silent while he thought about the question.

"Well?" Mike asked agitatedly.

"Not sure Mike to tell the truth. I would have said the same person who did Asque, but now with the C.I.B. boys getting clobbered as well, I'm not sure of anything just yet."

"Bloody hell Billy, my brothers been butchered. I need to find out who killed him." Tears started to well up in the younger mans eyes.

"Don't worry son, we'll find whoever did it. Christ, Carter will die trying and if he comes up empty I'll speak to Mickey and then the panel. Okay?"

Wiping his face with the back of his jacket sleeve, Mike managed to nod.

"Do you want to wait in the car while I take a look?" Billy asked him.

"No I need to see what the bastard's done to him."

"Fair enough mate, but remember the uniform will be there and you can't let on who's in there."

"Fuck sake Billy, I'm not an idiot am I?"

"No mate you're not, but it'll be hard in there, especially if...you know?"

"Yeah, he's lying in bits all over the floor."

Billy could feel the anger mounting and prayed that Mike would be able to control himself. If he was linked to a dead junkie and his prostitute lover, he'd most certainly be investigated by the Complaints Investigation Bureau and that could lead them to him. If he started to lose it, then he'd have to think of a way to get Mike out the flat.

Ten minutes later the police car came to a halt outside the block of flats where Annie and Jake had been murdered.

Billy switched off the ignition and turned to Mike who was staring blankly out the front window. "You sure you want to do this?" Billy asked in a concerned voice.

"Think so," was all the younger detective could mumble back in response.

Both men climbed out the car and began the walk up the drive to the entrance to the flats. Mike took each step on the stairs as though he was climbing the guillotine to his own execution. Billy reached the top and turned back to see Mike had only reached half way. He knew he would crack inside the flat when he saw his dead brother. Taking that possibility out of the equation, Billy shouted down at him, "Mike go and knock on the neighbours doors will you? See if they heard anything."

Mike looked up, a mixture of surprise and relief spreading across his face. He made no comment when he saw that Billy had shouted out the instruction in front of two uniformed officers who stood guarding the entrance to the murder scene. He merely turned into the hallway of the lower level and started to knock on the doors.

Billy sighed heavily, he felt as though he'd added to Mike's pain, but the risk to him was too great. Nodding to the two men on the doorway he entered the flat.

A hive of activity greeted him. Scenes of Crime officers were gathering evidence from every available inch of space around the bodies, finger prints were being lifted, pieces of fabric were being cut away for analysis later, and the drugs found in the kitchen were being sealed and numbered as exhibits along with anything else found which was believed to link the killer to the scene. Detectives from the station who hadn't been drafted into the team hunting Asques killer were present at this one, along with, Billy noticed a couple from C.I.B.

He walked over to the bed and looked down on Annie Walsh. She'd been a pretty girl and he couldn't help feeling some pity, as he thought about the life the young girl must have led, before she was butchered to death, for no apparent reason. The body of Jake Grady was the worst of the two. His head resembled a chopped melon. Where he'd fallen from the blow that had split his skull in two, brain and blood surrounded his upper body. His legs were spread-eagled at an unusual angle and the smell of death hung heavily in the air. Billy was glad he'd made Mike go elsewhere.

There was nothing he could do at the scene, so he left it to the men already dealing with it and went to find Mike. He found him sitting on the top step of the second floor landing.

"You didn't want to go in there Mike," Billy ventured.

Mike slowly shook his head from side to side, "You're probably right. Did he...look really bad?"

Billy merely nodded his response to the question before adding, "Come on let's go grab a pint."

The two men left the building in silence, Mike still churning over who might have killed his brother, Billy Johnstone feeling decidedly uneasy about the whole situation.

31

Stella rubbed her body dry, furiously. She'd always taken a hot bath if she'd a problem that needed sorting. This dilemma was huge. Her head raged with the effort she'd been putting into trying to come up with a way she could throw the police off her scent.

Nothing had sprung to mind and now she felt angry and frustrated at her lack of imagination.

Stella slipped on a toweling dressing gown, and walked into the guest bedroom where she sat down in front of the vanity mirror.   Her reflection gazed back, she looked exhausted. Large black circles, around her eyes dominated her face and her hair looked even darker than its usual auburn brown. She rubbed her face, disappointed at how puffy it both looked and felt. She sighed, admitting that the events of the previous week had caught up with her. She hadn't been eating or sleeping normally and her main pastime recently, apart from murder, seemed to be drinking coffee and gulping down large mugs of whiskey.

Stella stood up and promised to take better care. A smile returned to her tired face and she went down stairs to the kitchen. Opening up the cupboard above the cooker, she found herself a tin of tomato soup and poured it into a pan.

While she waited for dinner to heat up, she played with the lid of the tin, slipping her finger through the ring and spinning the lid, as she tried to solve the problem she was in. Absentmindedly she brought her hands together, forgetting she'd the sharp lid attached to one of them. Immediately she felt the pain as the serrated edge sliced into her finger. Looking down she watched, fascinated as bright red droplets of blood fell from the cut, before bouncing on the kitchen floor.

Stella jumped to her feet and moved to the sink, where she quickly turned on the cold tap and stuck her injured finger under the gushing water. She watched the small flap of skin on her finger hang as the water cleansed her wound.

The bleeding stopped. Stella took a plaster from a drawer and wrapped it around her finger. Like a bolt of lightening flashing across a stormy sky, inspiration hit her full in the face. The cold water had numbed her wound to such an extent she'd forgotten the earlier pain. She'd repeat the process, but in reverse order. First she would numb her whole hand under the tap.   Then she would cut herself sufficiently to provide enough of blood to enable her to smear it around the house. The police would find the bodies, but they'd also find her blood. They might think she'd injured

herself killing her victims, *but* they might just as easily
assume she was a victim of the killer. This would give Stella
all the time she needed to plot her escape.

Stella laughed so hard her sides ached. Tears streamed
down the side of her cheeks, her body jerked as she inhaled
great gulps of air, trying to calm herself down.

She was still laughing hard when she switched on the
television to catch the early morning news. Puffing up two
beautifully, hand stitched hunting scene pillows, on which
she'd spend many a lonely night forcing her embroidery
needle through the thick fabric, she settled into the leather
couch and waited for the programme to start. She knew the
news might contain some details of her crimes, owing to what
Brian had previously told her when he'd worked his CID
attachment. The news reader might, however, bend the facts
to suit what the police the public to hear or they might even
keep the whole thing secret until they had something concrete
to tell.

With her dead husband's words ringing in her ear she
listened to the introductory music and watched scenes of
London illuminate the screen.

*'The Metropolitan Police Force is this morning
investigating the murder of three male colleagues, while
fears are growing for the safety of a young WPC who is
currently missing.'*

The newscaster droned on, but Stella didn't hear anything
else being said. She churned over again and again his opening
words, trying to make sense of it all. He had definitely said
three male officers, which she knew couldn't be right. Apart
from Brian, the only other man had been Tony, Mandy was
the missing WPC, but none of her other victims had anything
to do with the police. Not from an employee role anyway.

Teresa had worked for them in the past and Annie had
been arrested by them on a number of occasions, but Stella
couldn't come up with three dead male officers.

Were the police trying to catch *her* out? Did they have a
hidden agenda which might trick her into making a mistake?

Quickly, Stella flicked through the channels and waited
for the news to be broadcast again. The lady reader this time
went into more detail and named the three men. Stella had
never heard of officers Ascot and Green. She sunk into the
couch as details of Manor Park children's playground floated

out from the screen. Each word filled her with a new sense of panic, amazement and total disbelief. What was going on? She hadn't murdered the two men, so if she hadn't, who had?

She clicked the set off and sat in silence. Stella needed to think.

Her mind raced, battling with questions that dropped into her head as fast as grains of salt falling through a timer. The questions came, but the answers remained hidden. She had the urge to call the police and tell them she'd had nothing to do with the two men found dead at the playground. What stopped her were the facts she didn't want them to know the killer for the other murders was a woman, and she intended to carry out her original plan regarding her list, and also follow through with her latest *brilliant* idea, of using her own blood to throw the police off track.

Stella decided to make her next move. Packing a large hold-all with clothes and toiletries she put it by the back door. Returning to the kitchen she took out a sharp knife and laid it beside the sink. Turning the tap on again she immersed her hand under the water, feeling its power beat against her skin.

It didn't take long before the numbness reached a sufficient level, which allowed her to drag the blade across the fleshy bit at the bottom of her thumb.

A cut of about half an inch caused the blood to flow freely.

Stella watched each drop land in the small jam jar she'd washed specifically for collection.

Time ticked slowly as the jar filled. She fought the inclination to cut herself deeper to hurry the task along. A wound that might cause infection later was not a good idea, so she waited in silent frustration.

Stella knew that blood spills always look worse than they are, from personal experience of having many nose bleeds, caused by Brian's punches. When she had roughly a couple of inches in the bottom of the jar, she bandaged her thumb carefully. Taking the jar, she went into the hall, where she poured some blood on to her hand, before she smeared it along the banister and flicked some of it with her fingers onto the wall at the bottom of the stair. She took great care to ensure some of it ran over some blood stains the others had left, when she'd dragged them downstairs.

Finally, using some of her catch, she spread it on the kitchen table and down the leg of one of the chairs.

Satisfied, Stella retrieved her bag, dropped the jam jar

into it, and without a second glance behind her at the house she'd lived in all those years, she walked out into the morning sunshine.

Silence sat heavily in John MacDonald's office. He looked across his desk at Mark Carter, who was reading through the list of witness statements gathered at the Chinese restaurant after Tony Asque's murder. "You trying to memorise them son?" He asked in a fatherly voice.

Carter looked up and smiled, "Sorry, it's just with so many statements I can't fathom out why no-one got a look at the women with Asque before he died. Good enough to give us a description to go on anyway."

"What do you mean?"

"Well we've over two dozen people in a reasonably small restaurant eating a meal. From what I can gather, Asque and this women have an argument or at least some heated words with one of the waiters as they leave. This is barely five, ten minutes after they've arrived. Don't you think someone would have been nosy enough to watch these events take place?"

MacDonald slumped into his chair. He could see where Carter was coming from. "Seems strange. My missus would have seen it and that's a fact."

"Sir, can I ask you something sensitive?"

"Go on."

"My team...are any of them being investigated by C.I.B?"

"Why do you ask that?"

"Something's bothering me with these murders. Do you think someone at the station could be involved?"

MacDonald nearly choked. "Killing fellow policemen, you mean?"

"Probably not the actual crime, but involved to a degree?"

"No I most certainly do not. Some of them maybe on the take, but I can't believe they're murderers."

"What about tampering with evidence to keep us all busy while they carry on with whatever it is they're doing?"

MacDonald sighed. "I can't rule that one out, but I know, none of the CID officers I placed at your disposal, were on the list of officers under suspicion."

"Doesn't mean they're clean though does it? Maybe that's

why Ascot and Green were bumped off. They were about to name other officers."

"Good God Mark, it's not some sort of conspiracy theory going on here. It's just a bit of dope or something equally small being pocketed."

"You sure?"

"Yes I am."

"Fair enough, we'll leave it at that, but I want you to tell me if anything happens that suggests otherwise. I want to catch the bastard doing this before anyone else gets killed."

"Me too son. Me too."

Carter stood up and placed the file containing the witness statements in front of the Chief Superintendent, "Have a read through these, and I think you'll understand where my suspicion comes from." With that he turned and left the room, leaving MacDonald sitting in stunned silence.

Stella drove to the train station and abandoned her car in the long stay parking zone. She didn't bother to pay for a ticket as she wanted the police to believe the killer had stolen it.

Her last act was to wipe the dregs of blood from the jam jar over the passenger seat.

She crossed the forecourt and bought a rail ticket from the machine on the wall. She'd always thought these modern ways to buy your ticket were very impersonal and took away the opportunity to chat to the ticket seller. Now she loved the fact she could buy a ticket and no-one would know where she was going.

Keeping her head down to miminise the risk of anybody remembering her, she boarded the train which would be the first step of her journey.

The train left the station on time; she took off her coat, folded it up into a pillow and leaned it against the window before resting her head on it. Stella was heading to the New Forest, having telephoned ahead and rented a caravan on the site at Deep Dean near Brockenhurst. For her stay she'd be called Debbie Russell, a name she'd picked out of a magazine she'd flicked through whilst sitting in the *Tastie Café* in Highgate earlier in the week. She'd stayed there once before, three years earlier with Brian, and she remembered that it was very secluded, with a minimum of security. No-one would question her name and she could pay cash for the rental. The owner of the site had told her it was very quiet at this time of year and she could just pay for a week or longer stay in advance as she went. There was no limit on how long she could remain. It was an ideal place to lose her identity.

The train's movement caused her eyelids to feel heavy and she gave in to the temptation to close them. Her last thought before drifting into a deep and dreamless sleep was to wonder what the other person killing police officers would think if he knew his competition was a woman.

32

Sergeant Paul Wilson was overweight. He'd been slowly piling on the pounds ever since he'd hurt his back and been given a desk job, which he hated.

Not knowing precisely where in Arcadia Drive the Blackmore's house was situated, he's parked his car at one end and decided on walking up the hill, checking the house numbers as he went. Now as the sweat poured from his brow and his heart thumped against his chest, he promised himself he would lose some of the extra weight if it was the last thing he ever did. Finally, he stood outside number seventeen, looking up the long driveway.

The first impression that hit him was that the garden looked untidy, which surprised him, knowing how meticulous Brian Blackmore was. The lawn had been neglected, and now if you stood on it, you would lose your feet, such was the depth of the grass.

The curtains had been pulled tightly shut, offering no glimpses of the interior inside, and there were no lights on, giving it a deserted, spooky feel, and the gravel crunching under his feet seemed to be making a louder noise than it should have, as if warning the people inside, that intruders were approaching.

Wilson felt uneasy as the gap between himself and the front door closed.

He struggled to keep his mounting anxiety in check, fought with the urge to turn and run, and couldn't understand why he felt so strange.

He cursed himself for not coming during daylight, but as often happened; his shift had disappeared under a mountain of paperwork and officers pestering him for time off.

To make matters worse, the Chief Superintendent had demanded the month's duty roster for the uniform branch a week earlier than usual. He'd been behind schedule all day because of this.

Meaning to come and see Stella Blackmore after lunch, he'd to wait until everything else was finished and had, therefore, decided to pay the visit once he'd finished for the day.

His fingers bunched into a fist and he rapped on the door, jumping when the knock reverberated around the house.

He'd never had any premonitions in his life, being a bit of a sceptic regarding such things. Now, however, as he stood on the front step of seventeen Arcadia Drive, he knew something was terribly wrong.

His knocking went un-answered.

Wilson moved along the front of the building and tried in vain to see through the slightest gap that had been left in the curtains. Sometimes people in their haste to block out the world, leave just the thinnest crack through which an intruder could spy on their lives. This was not the case here. Finding nothing he went around to the rear of the property. The result was the same.

Pulling on the handles to the garage door, he found it locked. He was about to give in and go and speak to the neighbours, when he caught a whiff of a smell he knew well. It was the sickly aroma of death.

The light was growing darker, with each passing second and he didn't feel very brave. Taking out his mobile phone he punched in the numbers to Westville police station.

A civilian station officer came on the line, "Westville Police. How can I help?"

The words were barely out his mouth when Wilson screamed at him, "Listen, it's Sergeant Wilson from duties here. I'm at seventeen Arcadia Drive. I don't know exactly what's happened here, but I want back up. There's a horrible smell coming from the garage at the rear of the house. I think it's a dead body."

"Sure thing Sarg. Someone will be with you in minutes."

Wilson wanted to shout 'Make it seconds' but instead said, "Okay."

The phone went dead and he was alone.

"Shit!" he said aloud. "What if it's a dead dog or something?" Realising he may have called for help without establishing the facts, knowing he'd never live it down if it turned out to be the carcass of a dead animal, he sat on the rear porch and waited the arrival of the cavalry.

He could hear them coming before they'd reached the street where he waited, his heart beating faster with every breath. The police sirens cut into the night, bouncing off each house and causing Wilson's pulse to quicken some more.

He hadn't expected the response to be so overwhelming, and when the four vehicles screeched to a halt at the foot of the drive, he began to pray with all his might, that whatever it was he'd smelt was something so terribly horrible, that it deserved the show of strength that had answered his request for back up.

When Detective Inspector Mark Carter climbed out of the second police car, Wilson thought he would die.

"Sorry to bring you out here Sir. I know how busy you and the team are at present."

Carter looked at the ageing officer before him, and realised he felt he was about to waste the detective's time, the worry of the situation masking the officer's usual cheery face. "It's okay Paul. I needed to tag along just in case. You know how these things go.?"

Wilson offered a weak smile, "Yeah, just don't know what's here yet."

"No problem. Show me where you think the body is."

Both men walked around to the rear of the house, where the side entrance to the garage lay. Carter could smell the odour as soon as he drew level with the door. Its pungent arid smell filled his nostrils and bit at the rear of his throat. Turning to one of the uniform officers beside him he said, "Kick the door in."

A loud sound of splintering wood flooded their ears. The door fell inward and immediately the smell increased to such an extent, most of them had to turn away from the shattered entrance.

Only Carter and the now confident Wilson edged forward.

The bodies were in a pile in the centre of the garage, they hadn't been covered, just left to rot where they lay.

Wilson screamed, bent over and lost control of his stomach.

Carter stood motionless, his eyes glued to the face of Mandy. Her eyes were shut and he was grateful for that small mercy.

Mandy had been placed on the top of the pile, symbolic he thought of the place she'd held in his heart. Even dead she seemed to have an aura, with her blonde hair lying seductively around her face. He saw she was wearing one of her favourite dresses she kept for special occasions, ones where she wanted to show off, both her confidence and her figure. He wondered why she'd be wearing it now? The position in which she lay prevented him from seeing the large hole in her stomach. He fought the urge to run to her body and hold her tight.

Pain drove its way deep into his heart as he recalled what he'd thought, what now seemed an eternity ago, back in his office. That she was having an affair. Had she died on route to meet her lover? Was the man responsible for her death?

Looking at the other two bodies he realised he knew them. Officer Blackmore from the station and the lady's name was Teresa. He couldn't recall her surname, but remembered she too was once a police officer.

A voice from behind him interrupted his thoughts.

"What do we do now?" a young constable asked, his voice quivering with shock.

Carter turned to look at him and saw the look of horror held in his face. "Call out the rest of my team please. In the meantime don't let anybody in here. Understand?"

The young man nodded and made to contact the station.

Carter turned to Wilson who now stood leaning against the wall to the house, his face ashen white. "Are you alright?" he asked.

"No. Not really. Not what you expect when you come to visit someone is it?"

"You've done well. If you hadn't turned up God knows how long their bodies would have remained undiscovered."

"Doesn't make me feel any better," Wilson muttered.

Carter sighed, "We need a police surgeon down here, also about twenty uniforms to do house-to-house. Think you can manage it?"

Wilson looked up at the Detective Inspector, "Still a policeman, you know."

Detecting the bitterness in the reply, Carter said, "And a good one at that. I'll leave it to you then."

He left the duty sergeant to call for the back up requested and walked down to his car. Once inside he let the tears he'd been fighting so hard to control, flow freely. He'd known she was dead, but now there would be no little doubts he could cast, which is what he'd been relying on to see him through this terrible ordeal.

Carter was still sobbing silently when the other detectives turned up ten minutes later.

The journey had passed without any problems. Stella had kept herself to herself and apart from a visit to the dining car to pick up a roast chicken sandwich and a small bottle of mineral water, she hadn't ventured from her seat on either of the two trains that had been necessary for her to reach Southampton.

From there she'd made her way to the small village of Lyndhurst by taxi, the driver having appeared to be high on some illegal substance. Stella had ignored his ramblings and had focused on the beautiful scenery as they drove through the forest of oak, ash and willow trees. Such was the natural beauty of it all, she'd almost forgotten why she'd come to such a peaceful place. The driver dropped her at the entrance to 'The Deep Dean Caravan Park', where she'd made her way to reception.

The employee in charge was captivated by a football match he was watching on a small television set he'd installed inside the portacabin, which served as both reception, and information desk to the many holiday makers that used the site.

Stella stood for several minutes before she coughed politely to gain the youth's attention.

Without looking away from the screen, he leaned backwards to reach a selection of paperwork, including fire regulations, entertainment for both inside and outside the camp, a key to the caravan and a map of the surrounding woods. "Keep any barbeque's away from other peoples pitches and remember we lock the front gate at midnight. If you're going to be out after that, you need to tell someone so they can arrange to let you back in. That only applies if you have a car obviously, as you can get in on foot twenty-four hours a day."

Stella listened amazed as he rattled off his instructions without once looking at her. She felt her anger grow, but was also glad he seemed so disenchanted with his job, as she knew her coming and goings from the site would go totally unnoticed. She didn't bother to thank him after picking up the pamphlets from where he'd thrown them down.

Walking carefully to avoid tripping into any of the pot holes that littered the well-worn tracks, which led campers into the site, she made her way to her caravan.

The key turned stiffly in the lock. Giving the door a hard shove she finally gained entrance to her new home.

Pulling on the light, the caravan was filled with a warm orange glow. Everything was as she remembered from her solitary visit with Brian. Caravans hadn't suddenly changed beyond recognition like so many other things in life.

The place was dusty, giving it an un-kept atmosphere, but she felt safe once she'd closed the door behind her. There was clean linen, cutlery, some toiletries and more important than any of that, the bed felt divine. She still felt incredibly tired and knew she must rest to recharge her batteries.

Setting herself down at the table she took out a small bottle of whiskey from her bag and removed the top, before pouring a generous amount into a blue and white china cup. Savoring the biting drink as it passed her lips, she sighed contentedly, safe in the belief she'd escaped the police for good. Rising, she went and plugged in the TV set, before returning to her seat.

Taking large sips from the cup she watched a program about the fate of British Farmers and felt sadness at how such a way of life, soaked in British history seemed to be going to the dogs. How she wondered, could people purchase foreign meat when there was plenty in the UK?

The news followed and she hoped to hear more about the two dead officers found two days earlier. What she didn't expect it to contain, was 17 Arcadia Drive as the main feature.

More than an hour after she'd switched off the box and tried to digest what she'd heard, Stella still sat in total disbelief.

The finding of the bodies so soon had come as a great shock. The police hadn't mentioned her at all, not as a victim or as a potential suspect. That's what bothered her the most. Were they looking for her or not?

The announcer had given a brief history of the three

deceased. She'd choked when he'd described Brian as a loyal and loving husband, who'd served the force well. Teresa and Mandy were described as young women with their whole lives before them. The deaths had been linked to Tony Asque and a prostitute murdered alongside her pimp on a council estate, near the latest murder scene. Stella thought it strange they didn't name the exact location, seeing as; Stonewall was the only council estate in the area.

Nothing was mentioned this time about the two police officers found in the park. Again she thought that strange. Something was going on, and she hadn't a clue what it could be.

Refilling her cup Stella took three large mouthfuls in rapid succession. The next name on the list was Meredith Rogers. She was a solicitor, who Brian had been sleeping with on Tuesday nights, when he was supposed to be out with his mates.

Teresa had told Stella that Meredith was married, but she and Brian had been having liaisons for two years, ever since she'd prosecuted a serial burglar he'd arrested. She'd also suggested Brian used her to cover some of the underhand dealings he was involved with.

They met on Tuesdays because he was supposed to be at darts and she'd signed up for a fictitious night school class, doing calligraphy.

Stella had thought through carefully how she was going to get to Meredith. Now it was time to implement her ideas.

33

The briefing took place just before nine in the evening. The detectives had been on duty since early morning and looked fit to drop, red tired eyes peered out from sunken black sockets.

Carter looked across at MacDonald and could read the expression on his face, which seemed to ask him, "How could they be working so hard if they were doing something to jeopardize the case?" He gave a shrug of his shoulders and MacDonald frowned in response.

Carter waited for the few stragglers to take their seats before he opened up the meeting. "Okay, we now have three more dead bodies making the total eight. All with the exception of Annie Walsh and her pimp whose name we haven't been able to ascertain yet, were police officers or worked for the force in some capacity or in Teresa Day's case *had* worked for us. That would lead me to believe we're looking for someone with a very large grudge against anyone connected to the law. Anyone disagree with that theory?"

"How would the two found on the Stonewall Estate tie into that theory Gov?" asked one of the detectives.

It was Chief Superintendent MacDonald who walked to the front of the room to answer the question. "Inspector Carter believes officers at this station could be linked to the deaths." A loud selection of muttered comments and disgruntled noises came back to him in response. "Before you all shout no way, let me explain why we've had so many C.I.B officers at the station for the past month or so. They've been investigating serious allegations of corruption within this station. I've a list of those suspected in my office and let me tell you ladies and gents, it doesn't make pretty reading. Now, as I told Inspector Carter earlier today, I don't personally believe these killings have anything to do with any of my officers *but*, and I stress *but*, I can't rule it out, especially as two C.I.B officers have now also died. What that tells us I'm not sure, but I intend to find out. In the meantime I want you to work until you drop, until we get to the bottom of this sorry episode. Do I make myself clear?"

The officers said, "Yes," in unison.

"Right, I'll leave Inspector Carter to carry on."

Carter could feel all eyes boring into him, demanding to know why he thought there were dishonest officers amongst them. He decided to gingerly cover that question and stick to the facts of the case so far. "We need to find out if there is a connection between the dead officers and the two butchered in the flats. If yes, then we'll know there is someone inside the force involved. If not, then we need to find out why these two were killed and if they were the victims of the same killer. God help us if we have two murderers on the go.

Billy Johnstone spoke up, "Gov, I feel we have a right to know if you suspect anyone in this room of being involved in anything illegal."

"I can only say I've seen the list that was provided to the Chief Superintendent. None of the officers involved in this case were named on that list. That still doesn't explain why two of the investigating team were shot though does it?" He felt great satisfaction in the answer he'd given. It would create unease amongst the team. Now the honest ones would be looking out for anything suspicious, while the rotten apples, if there were any involved might possibly make mistakes trying to cover their backs. "Okay, if no-one has any more questions I suggest we put this to bed and have a bright and early start. You all know what needs doing."

Carter waited until the room had emptied before flopping down on one of the seats, wondering if he'd just stirred up a hornets nest and concerned he might have just put his own life in danger.

The music seemed incredibly loud inside the club. Billy found himself screaming at the barmaid as he ordered a pint of beer. He'd phoned Mickey Driscol as soon as he'd left the station yard and arranged they meet at the Maverick Club. Billy was early and swallowed his pint rapidly before yelling across the bar for a refill. By the time Mickey tapped him on the shoulder he'd downed four pints and had a glazed expression.

"What time did you get here? You're pissed already," Mickey asked grinning.

"You won't be smiling when I tell you what happened earlier today."

Mickey merely nodded at the pretty blue eyed barmaid knowing she'd give him his usual double Vodka and coke. He tilted his head in Billy's direction and she filled another pint glass for him. "Come on Billy, let's take these and go into a back room for a chat. You can tell me what's got you so wound up in private."

Billy had known Driscol for years and liked him immensely, however sometimes his over confident attitude got right up his nose. In a way he was looking forward to knocking him out his stride a little.

Mickey helped the slightly drunk and staggering police officer into a small room towards the rear of the club, pulled a chair out from under a desk and sat him on it. "Okay Billy, what dragged me out into the cold at this God forsaken hour?"

Billy gazed into Mickey's eyes, saw he wasn't taking this very seriously and let rip, "Brian Blackmore is dead, so is

Mandy, and two Complaint Officers have just joined them. My bloody Inspector suspects someone at the nick is involved in the murders. I don't, but I'm shitting myself that my involvement with you and the Panel will all come out in the wash. Do you know what happens to ex coppers in the nick? *Do you?*"

The fact he shouted the last two words told Mickey just how worried Billy was. Normally he'd have slapped him for his lack of respect, but the news he'd just been given was serious enough to have caused his outburst. He thought briefly before casually suggesting, "Why don't we arrange to bump the Inspector off then?"

Billy sighed and shook his head. "Because Mickey, that would bring the cavalry in quicker than would've saved General Custer at Big Horn. Besides he's told my Chief Superintendent his suspicions, so God knows who else he's told."

"Why do you think the police aren't involved?"

"Because I *know* who the killer is."

Mickey sat on the edge of the table and looked down at Billy, "Sometimes you amaze me, Billy," he said. "Tell me then, who's the killer?"

Billy had a sudden urge to say he was keeping it a secret, but knew this wasn't the time to be funny. "Stella Blackmore," he whispered, immediately wondering why he'd whispered as they were alone in the room.

Mickey Driscol stared at him for a few seconds before bursting into uncontrollable laughter. Billy found it infectious and soon he too was having hysterics although he was at a loss as to what they were laughing about. Without warning Mickey stopped. "Stella Blackmore, the lady he used to get high so we could have her, the lady who wouldn't say boo to a goose, the lady he battered like a second hand punch bag. Jesus Billy, I think you need to go back to training school and learn how to be a copper all over again."

Still smiling, Billy said, "I know it sounds ridiculous, but think about it. She's gone, vanished. We have a witness statement from someone who saw her with Tony Asque the night he died, where was Brian then? She telephoned the duty skipper to tell him Brian needed time off work as his dad had died. I spoke to his dad yesterday and he seemed very much alive to me."

"Interesting Billy, but what about the other deaths? You telling me she stiffed them all?"

Billy let out a loud sigh, "I don't know about the others, but seeing as Mandy was found with Brian I think she found them sleeping together and blew them away with a shotgun. If she killed Tony, maybe it was revenge for something. Maybe he had her when she was high. Can't just have been us. The worrying thing is the two Complaint officers. I doubt that was her and if not who the hell was it?"

"The Panel should be told Billy. On the other hand, maybe I can use this unexpected information to my advantage later if I don't tell them."

"Eh!" Billy sounded shocked.

"Might be worth holding on to that gem a while? What're you going to do now?"

"I'm going to help Stella Blackmore as much as I can. While she's out there creating havoc the heats off me. I also need to find out who did the other jobs. It wasn't *you* by any chance?"

"Why the hell would I bump off two cops?"

"Well didn't you tell me you were going to take the Panel on? Maybe it was a show of strength."

"You're way off the mate. I'm not that stupid. Now get your ass out of here and find who's responsible."

The drink had taken more effect now and Billy needed help to get up. Mickey shook his head, before he called two of his men in from outside. Between them they helped Billy out into the street where they left him to stagger his way home.

Carter had been sitting at his desk, alone in the office for most of the night. The clock opposite him read 4.15am.

Sleep had been hard to find, after the discovery at Arcadia Drive.

Thankfully MacDonald had rescued him from his misery, taking him to La Tosca, one of the best Italian Restaurants in central London. There they'd discussed events so far. Both men were in a situation neither had been in before. Carter had told his boss he'd been surprised when he'd mentioned his suspicions regarding the potential involvement of officers from the station. MacDonald had pointed out that as he didn't think there was any chance of it, he'd seen no reason not to mention it. Besides if Carter was correct, the crooked officers might make mistakes now they were under the microscope. Carter was forced to agree it was an idea that might flush someone out.

Now, as he sat in the stillness of his office he ran the case through his head. The death toll stood at four police officers, a civilian Scenes of Crime Officer, an ex-police woman and a drug-craved prostitute with her boyfriend/pimp. The last murders had raised the question, could there be two killers? What did Annie Walsh and the so far un-identified male deceased have in common with Mandy, or any of the other victims? Was there anything to link them? If there were two killers, what was their motivation for committing the crimes?

He'd dined royally, finding it strange how hungry he'd felt. He'd devoured a huge plate of garlic mussels, followed by a pile of Spaghetti Bolognese, all washed down by two bottles of house red.

Although exhausted he couldn't help churning the murders over and over, spinning the evidence round and round like a great big washing machine inside his head, hoping to stop the cycle with the answers on who killed which victim.

Nothing made sense. The only connection so far between the victims, was the fact that at some stage they were either police officers or had in some way been connected to the force, either as employee or criminal.

MacDonald had confirmed one of his suspicions. Ascot and Green were investigating three of the victims. Brian Blackmore was on top of their list, Mandy was a bit player, and Tony Asque was suspected of dealing in drugs.

Carter also had to contend with the fact that Blackmore's wife was also missing. He felt there were several avenues of investigation they could take here. Stella Blackmore was either dead, with the killer as a hostage or she was the murderer. He'd never met Blackmore's wife, but from all accounts given by people at the station who'd met her, she was a very quiet woman, totally dominated by her husband.

Carter therefore felt for the time being until evidence suggested otherwise, she was either dead or in the hands of one of the killers. "God help her," he said aloud.

It had been MacDonald's idea not to let the media know another victim was missing at this stage. The less room for hysteria the better had been his reasoning. Carter saw no reason to disagree..

One or two killers, that was the crux of the case as far as

he was concerned. That, and whether or not somewhere deep in the mire, hiding like a poisonous snake waiting to strike, lay a crooked police officer who'd stop at nothing to achieve their place in history.

The tiredness that had eluded him for so long crept up without warning. He put his arms onto the desk, and rested his head on it. Thoughts of Mandy tried to prevent sleep, but minutes later he drifted into a worry filled world.

34

Meredith Rogers parked her midnight blue, three series BMW in her allocated space, beneath Rogers, Rogers and Bullman, her place of work since she'd qualified to be a solicitor twelve years earlier.

Her father had been one of the most successful solicitors in the country and he'd insisted that both her elder brother and she joined the practice as soon as they were able.

Meredith had loved her father; right up until the day he died from a sudden heart attack, whilst trying to pitch a nine iron onto the thirteenth green on the Dukes golf course at Woburn. The significance of the number had appeared lost on everyone except her.

Five years had passed since then and during that time she'd seen her marriage collapse into a sham of pretence, her older brother getting a partnership, when really it should've been her, as she was by far the better lawyer, and to cap it all, just a day earlier she'd heard on the news that the only good thing in her life had been snuffed out by some deranged killer.

Fighting back the tears that'd flowed almost constantly since she'd heard the newscaster break the news, as if personally to her, she got into the lift, which would take her four flights to her office.

Meredith was tall at five foot ten inches. She had a full figure which she battled with constantly to keep down to a size fourteen and short cropped mousy brown hair. Her eyes were a darker brown and were underlined by a series of fine laughter lines, although she'd had little reason to laugh these past five years. People said she was pretty, although she herself thought her position of power made them cast the niceties that often came her way.

The lift hit the floor she wanted and wearily she came out into the plush hallway that led into the main entrance to Rogers, Rogers and Bullman.

"Hi Meredith," her secretary Fiona greeted her with a smile.

"Hi Fi. Any messages for me yet?"

"Yes there is. Bit of a weird one really. A woman rang just as the office opened. Seemed a bit tense, but wants to arrange an appointment to see you. I didn't know what to do because she wouldn't tell me why she wanted the appointment, nor would she tell me her name, just said it had something to do with one of the dead policemen found at Arcadia Drive. When I queried what she meant, she just said you'd know. Said I'd get back to her once I'd spoken to you. Hope I did the right thing?"

Meredith digested the information before she replied, "Sure no problems. Fit her in at her earliest convenience. Do me a favour though. Make sure I'm not the only one left in the offices when she turns up."

Fiona waited for an explanation, but could see none would be forthcoming, "I'll call her back then," she said in a slightly huffy voice.

"Please," Meredith replied before heading to her office.

Once inside she sat down before her legs gave way. She'd visited Brian at his home on numerous occasions and had recognised the address Fiona had given her. She knew who the woman was going to be as sure as she'd known anything before in her life. Stella Blackmore was going to pay her a visit.

What she wanted to know was why. According to Brian his wife knew about his affairs. He'd even told Meredith that he'd told Stella the details of their sex lives to turn her on, she liked to listen in intricate detail to what he did to his lover. Meredith had thought that kinky, but somehow she too had enjoyed the fact someone shared their love-making.

Years before at college she'd experimented with her sexuality and had enjoyed more than one bed time romp with a member of the same sex.

Maybe Mrs. Blackmore wanted to see for herself the woman behind her husband's stories. Maybe she wanted a piece of the action. Meredith smiled as she remembered seeing a photograph of Brian's wife on one of her visits. She was a very beautiful woman.

Meredith decided there was nothing to worry about; in fact the visit could be a very enjoyable experience.

Flicking the intercom she asked Fiona not to worry regarding her request not to be alone, in fact she would prefer it if she was.

Meredith laughed away her secretary's concerns and told her not to be so silly.

When Fiona buzzed her back less than five minutes later to tell her a Mrs. Whitemore would be coming to see her at 5.30 that evening, Meredith had nearly screamed with laughter. Mrs. Whitemore, indeed, she thought.

Her next move was to look through the clothes she kept at the office. She attended many special social events throughout the year and as many were evening affairs after a busy day at the office, she needed a supply of fresh clothing for her to change into. Mrs. Whitemore or Blackmore would be greeted by the woman she'd heard all about in her husband's fantasies.

Stella had known Meredith would see her from the information she'd gleaned from Teresa before she'd killed her. According to her now dead ex-friend, Meredith was a professional lady of the highest caliber, who both looked and acted the part very well. Teresa had informed her she liked a good time and until recently could be found at one of London's top clubs most weekends, and in fact often visited the Maverick Club. Her marriage had faltered since she'd returned home early from a conference and caught her husband in bed with the maid. From that moment on she'd gone all out to seek revenge. Brian happened to be in the right place for her, but at the wrong time for Stella.

They'd conducted an affair for a long time and Teresa had told her that both of them had enjoyed nights at swapping parties and that it was known Meredith enjoyed the company of women almost as much as she liked to be under a man.

It was *that* piece of information that'd given Stella her idea on how she was going to kill Meredith, especially as she'd found herself having so much fun with Annie. This was the reason she'd chosen her as the next victim.

Mark Carter sat in the small interview room, just inside the main entrance to Westville police station. Beside him sat DS Johnstone, who was gently tapping his fingers on the dull plastic desk before him. Opposite sat Mickey Driscol, one of the hardest men Carter had ever come across.

Mickey Driscol had murdered his own younger brother ten years earlier because he'd failed to properly arrange the contract killing of a rival gangster, who'd been stealing funds from the Driscol gang's drug empire.

Mickey had calmly told him he expected better from his brother, and that he'd have to set an example to his men, one which made it totally clear to everyone that he would not tolerate failure, from anyone. He'd then shot his brother through the head.

The story was one from which local legends grew. Nothing had ever been proved and Mickey never went to trial for the offence. Since then most of the major deals that had gone down locally had been masterminded by Mickey Driscol.

Carter had arrested him on numerous occasions, but had never managed to get any evidence strong enough to put the man away. During the years he'd grown to almost respect him, although one day he swore that Driscol would serve time behind bars, the result of one of his investigations.

Mickey Driscol smoked a Benson and Hedges cigarette, slowly blowing the smoke over his head. Carter studied the man before him, noticed his size at around sixteen stone, his greying hair pulled tightly into a pony tail, and at fifty-seven years of age thought he looked much younger. His grey eyes peered at you constantly, as if trying to catch you out on a lie. One for which you could lose your life. Carter knew the story behind the scar on his face and smiled back at the constant sneer on Driscol's lips. He sat slouched in his chair, leaning back, portraying an air of total confidence.

Carter wished he felt half as cool as the man before him looked, "Mickey nice of you to drop in. I don't suppose it's a social visit, now is it?"

Driscol grinned, showing a row of sparkling white teeth, "Mr. Carter, can't a man drop in to say hello to his friends?"

"Friends," Carter said sarcastically, "Have you got any of those?"

"I have many friends officer. You know that. Some of them would die for me."

"Like your brother?" Johnstone asked sharply.

Carter saw the look change on Driscol's face, from one of sarcasm to anger. Before the conversation grew heated he said, "Okay, Mickey. What brings you here today?"

Mickey held up his hands in mock surrender, "I thought you might like to know who's killing your colleagues.

The words cut through the air like a hot knife through wax, before reaching the astonished detectives.

"And why would you want to do that?" Johnstone asked doubtfully.

"Let's just say it would cause some folks who I *don't* consider to be on my list of friends, a world of inconvenience."

Carter sat back, "Okay then Mickey. Tell us what you know."

"Nothing for nothing Mr. Carter. Whilst I appreciate that it would seriously piss off these guys, it would be far better for me if I could also gain something from our little chat."

"Go on," Carter prompted.

"Davie Grant is down stairs sitting in one of your cells, no doubt picking his nose and chewing on the snot. He's here because he did a job over on Smithy Street. Nothing big you understand, but needed to be done. He walks from here with me, otherwise no deal."

"I don't recall asking you here to talk deals Mickey. You came here of your own accord."

"True, but I know how badly you'd like to catch the people responsible for killing the two cops. Me, I couldn't really give a shit."

Johnstone tensed in his seat, Carter believed he could feel the rage building in his fellow detective and had no doubts if the last remark had been said outside the confines of the station, Johnstone would have assaulted the man sitting opposite, smugly smoking on his cigarette. Unknown to Carter, Johnstone's tension was caused by what his friend, Driscol was trying to do, what he knew he was about to say.

"Billy, what's Grant in for?" he asked trying to calm the other man down a little.

Johnstone relaxed slightly. "Burglary, criminal damage and assault. Punched a security guard so hard they had to operate to rewire his jaw back into place."

Carter blew out hard, "Mickey your man is screwed. There's no way I can help him leave the station."

Both Carter and Johnstone were surprised at the reaction Carters speech received.

"Don't get if you don't ask my mother used to say. Okay let's talk murder then shall we?"

"After you Mickey," Carter said, gesturing with his hand for the other man to begin.

"The two cops, Ascot and Green, wasn't it?"

"Yeah," Johnstone said, backing up his reply with a sharp nod of his head.

"Well the pair of them were running a protection scam down by the river..."

"No way!" Johnstone interrupted.

"Way!" Driscol replied in a raised voice. "It's been going on for a number of years. Not just them mind, others as well. Some of them still at this nick I'm afraid."

Mickey Driscol waited for the last remark to fully sink in before continuing, "Anyway the set up was they protected the girls for a share of their earnings. Some of what they made had to be handed over to a group of men who I believe you call the Panel."

Billy gasped openly.

Mickey Driscol continued, "The stupid bastards paid up for a while, then decided they'd keep all the money. Thought they were above the law of the street. The Panel had them shot."

Carter had heard of the secret society that ruled over London, allowing men like Driscol to run certain areas, like a general in battle. He'd never seen them, arrested them, or had anyone try to grass them up before. Informers would be executed for even thinking about doing it. The members of the Panel were, like Driscol, hard cases, who'd stop at nothing to keep their empire running. Shooting two policemen wouldn't be above them.

"Okay, so if it was these men, what about the other officers involved?"

"They still pay their dues so no problem."

"Who are they?" Johnstone wanted to know.

"Sorry, you'll need to find that out for yourselves."

"We'll need proof, Mickey. We can't go in without evidence."

"Listen, it's well known within the proper circles that most of the crimes the Panel undertake get videoed, especially all the hits they order. It gives them a chance to watch the

people die, so I've been told. I'm sure you've someone who
can get the tape for you."

"The sick bastards," Carter muttered.

"They do every kind of tape you can think of boys, or
didn't you know that?"

Ignoring the question, Carter asked, "What about the
other murders? "The ones found at Arcadia Drive and Tony
Asque. Did they have anything to do with those?"

"I doubt it. That Blackmore cop had fingers in a lot of
pies so could be he upset a lot of people. But you already
know that. He was being investigated anyway. By Ascot and
Green if my information serves me correctly"

"How do you know that?" Carter asked astonished at
Driscol's knowledge.

"Make it my business to know these things *Mark*."

Driscols smugness and leering face was beginning to get
on Carter's nerves and he felt if Johnstone didn't thump him
he would if he remained in their presence for much longer.
"Okay Mickey, we'll take it from here. By the way what do
you gain if we break up this operation?"

"Come on, surely you don't expect me to tell you that?
Let's just say with them out of the way I can concentrate on
tasks at hand."

Carter rose from the table, ignoring the outstretched
hand, Driscol stuck out in front of him, "Come on, Billy, we've
work to do."

As the door to the interview room closed behind them,
both heard Driscol mutter, "Wankers!" under his breath.

Carter smiled at Johnstone as they made their way back
to the incident room, where he would tell his squad about the
breakthrough that had unexpectedly landed on their laps.

Billy Johnstone suspected Driscol had played his ace
card. Billy had acted out his own part well in the interview
room and doubted Carter would suspect any links between
him and Driscol. He would need to speak to the gangster soon
though to ascertain how he was going to prevent the panel
from knowing he'd tried to stitch them up.

Meredith waited patiently for the arrival of Stella Blackmore.
She gave a low chuckle at the false name Stella had given
when she'd called earlier in the day.

Why she'd done so, didn't really matter to Meredith, all she wanted was to meet the wife of her dead lover. She wanted to know if what Brian had told her about her was correct. Did she really want all the details of their sex sessions? Was she really up for a bit of fun?

Meredith had dressed in what she thought was a smart, but sensual outfit. She'd chosen a cream coloured silk blouse, which when she stood beside a bright light, turned almost totally see through. She wore a knee length, tan leather skirt with a pair of dark brown snake skin boots. Her hair, usually neat, had been ruffled into what she hoped would give her a sexy look.

Meredith had applied bright red lipstick to her full mouth, and had darkened her mascara, which in turn made her brown eyes stand out more. She felt ready for her visitor. Meredith knew she looked great.

At just before five-thirty, the intercom on her desk beeped. She pressed the button to answer and heard Fiona tell her that Mrs. Whitemore had arrived for her appointment. Meredith stifled the laugh, she'd felt rising in her throat all day, every time she heard the false name.

The door opened and Fiona was followed into the office by a woman, who like Meredith had dressed for the occasion.

Meredith liked what she saw. Stella was dressed in a light blue suit, consisting of three quarter jacket and short skirt. Her feet were neatly encased in a pair of black leather heels, adding several inches to her height.

"Mrs Whitemore," Meredith said as she beckoned Fiona to leave them alone, "How good of you to come and see me so soon after the death of your husband."

Fiona wondered what her boss was talking about, owing to the fact Meredith hadn't mentioned she knew the lady when she'd finally given her name to book into the appointments diary. She was even more surprised by the way Meredith almost pushed her out of the office before shutting her door behind her. Annoyed, she went and sat at her desk.

Meredith gestured Stella to sit, while she herself walked around and perched on the front of her heavy oak desk, directly in front of Stella. "Let's stop the pretence shall we? I know you're Brian's wife."

Stella looked up and caught her eye, "Okay, fine by me."

"Why the false name, anyway?"

"Haven't you been watching the news lately? The police haven't mentioned me. That suggests I'm presumed dead, or

I'm a suspect. Either way I thought I'd play along. Also depending on what you tell me, will depend on whether we can do business together or not."

"Business," Meredith asked puzzled.

Stella knew she'd laid her trap well. "If I'm a suspect, I'll need a lawyer. Seeing as you knew Brian so well, I thought you'd help me. If I'm not a suspect, but presumed dead, I thought together we could try and find out who killed him. I could be your ghost so to speak."

Meredith laughed a hearty laugh. "My you have been thinking hard, haven't you? Brian told me you were a kinky bitch and liked to hear what we got up to, but he didn't say you were a clever little cow too."

"Takes all sorts to make life interesting," Stella said, deliberately crossing her legs slowly, letting her skirt ride higher up her thighs.

Meredith inhaled sharply as her gaze fell on the expanse of flesh Stella had revealed, "Certainly does, doesn't it?" was all she could mumble in reply.

"Are you in or not?" Stella enquired, keeping control of the situation.

"I don't see why not. I don't think you're in the frame for his murder. The police would have put out your description by now. I mean it's not just Brian who's been murdered is it? No of course not," she answered herself, before continuing. "Therefore they think you're dead, or at the very least you've been kidnapped. Whatever they think, it would be a good idea for you to play my *ghost*."

Stella knew this was her opportunity to get Meredith out of the building. "Let's get out of here. This place seems too busy to me."

Meredith hesitated before saying, "No-one will come in here without my permission. We can talk openly here."

"Who said anything about talking? I want to see what interested my husband for so long, and I know you like women, so don't go all shy or defensive on me."

Meredith felt like she'd been hit by a sledge hammer. Her dead lover's wife was coming on to her faster than an express train and it didn't seem to matter she hadn't as yet even buried her husband.

In a way that scared her, but it also turned her on more than at any time of her life. She knew she'd like the danger in a relationship with Brian's wife. "What else have you got in mind?" she asked in a quivering voice.

"Oh come on Meredith, you know what I like. Come on, let's go."

Meredith leaned forward and kissed Stella fully on the mouth, "I'll get my coat."

Fiona briefly saw them as they entered the lift, laughing and giggling like a couple of school girls. She wasn't aware it would be the last time she saw Meredith alive.

The journey down the four floors took less than a minute to complete. As soon as the doors closed behind them, Meredith moved closer to Stella, taking her head in her hands she kissed her on each cheek before slowly tracing her tongue around her lips.

When she finally pushed her tongue into Stella's mouth, pressing her lips hard onto hers, Stella gasped in both horror and surprise. She felt repulsed at what was happening to her, the same sensation she'd received when Mandy Burrows had come on to her. It was nothing like the feelings she remembered when alone with Annie Walsh.

Stella wasn't in control here, in this confined space, where she'd no escape and she hated it.

Meredith, taking the intake of breath as encouragement pulled Stella closer still, her hands kneading at her buttocks, rubbing the material of Stella's short skirt higher and higher with each movement from her hands.

Stella felt flesh on flesh and tried to pull away, but Meredith had her in a vice like grip. She mumbled for her to back off, as Meredith kissed her hard and she felt her tongue darting in and out of her mouth.

Panic gave her the strength she needed to pull herself away, the material of her clothing returning to where it had been, making her feel safe again, in more control.

Meredith had a shocked look on her face, and Stella knew she needed to do something quickly or lose the situation she'd wanted to build up. "It's okay; I just want to wait until we are somewhere a bit less....dirty. The lift will open at any moment and we don't want to get caught doing things we shouldn't, not here, now do we?"

Before Meredith could answer, the metal doors opened, revealing two men in navy pin-striped suits, carrying black leather briefcases and supporting the reddest ties Stella had ever seen.

"Hi Meredith," one of them said, "You look flushed, are you okay?"

Stella could have jumped out and kissed him, unwittingly he'd handed control totally back to her.

"Yeah Steve, I'm fine, had to run for the lift upstairs that's all."

Steve appeased at her response nodded and the parties swapped places.

"Now what would you have said to him, if the door had opened just two or three seconds earlier, when you had my skirt up around my waist?" Stella asked, hands on hips, seductively licking her top lip as she waited for the reply.

"I'd have asked if he wanted to join in, must admit he's a hunk." Meredith laughed and Stella found herself joining in. "Come on, let's get to my car. We can carry this on in private."

Stella nodded in agreement and followed Meredith to her BMW.

The electric doors clicked and she climbed into the passenger seat.

"God Stella you've got great legs," Meredith said hungrily.

"I know," Stella replied before leaning over to kiss her. "Nobody can see us in here."

Meredith smiled; at the same time she pushed her seat backwards to give her more room. "I knew the tinted glass would come in useful one day," she said humourlessly.

Stella smiled; she hadn't taken in the dark colour of the windows. They would most definitely be an added bonus.

Meredith moved closer, running her warm hand along Stella's thigh.

Meredith's touch once again pushed Stella over the edge, where panic, along with uncertainty began to nibble their way through her thoughts. Her stomach was turning over and over, nausea built up; she could feel her body involuntary trembling. She didn't understand why Mandy and now Meredith repulsed her so much, whilst Annie had turned her on to feelings she hadn't known existed. Her feelings were scrambled beyond recognition.

She'd wanted to go home with Meredith, had wanted time to carry out the killing at her own pace, but now as she felt the hot breath of her victim nibble at her ear, felt the fingers edge under the thin material of her skirt, sensed the increase of pressure as Meredith tried to prise her legs apart, Stella knew for her own sanity she needed to end it now.

She turned full on to Meredith, trapping her hand tightly between her thighs.

"What're you doing?" asked Meredith in a quizzical voice. "You're hurting my hand."

Stella forced her mouth onto the other women's lips, hoping she would relax under her kiss.

Meredith tried to move away, her hand was still trapped between Stella legs and from the way she sat; there was no way to pull it free. Pain shot up her forearm as her wrist bent to a greater degree as Stella moved closer. She let out a shriek of agony as Stella tightened her grip.

Stella broke away, saw the tears welling up in the other woman's eyes, relaxed her thigh muscles and felt the hand being quickly removed.

"What the hell do you think you're doing? You've nearly broken my wrist."

Stella knew what was going to happen next. Meredith lifted both hands to wipe away her tears. This was the opportunity she had hoped for. Seeing Meredith's full ribcage open up as a target before her, she thrust the kitchen knife deep into her chest. The blade disappeared through flesh and cloth.

Meredith let out a gasp of shock, rather than a scream.

Stella quickly removed the blade before plunging it once more deeply into Meredith's body. There was little sound this time apart form a long slow sigh, as Meredith's life drained away. Stella watched with fascination, as all the pain, emotion, and finally realisation she was about to die, registered in Meredith's eyes. The dead solicitors last action was to slump forward onto her brown leather steering wheel.

Stella coolly replaced the knife back in her handbag, got out of the car, making sure the central locking clicked on as she shut the door. Calmly, now and in complete control she walked back to her hire car. The illuminated clock on the dashboard told her it was nearly 6pm. Her whole visit to Rogers, Rogers and Bullman had taken a mere thirty minutes. She was amazed at how little time had passed.

Owing to the location of Meredith's car and the darkened windows she hoped the body would remain undiscovered till morning. Driving out of the city she parked in the first available parking zone she came to. Switching the engine off, she sat back into the seat. She quietly remonstrated with herself over what had happened before calming down to realise, that less than two weeks previous she'd been this timid little mouse of a woman, dominated by her thug of a husband, and with no life to look forward to whatsoever.

Something had changed her and she was grateful for whatever it was. It had brought out the powerful, intelligent, cunning, sensual, happy woman she could and should have been. She'd decided that perhaps the idea of using her sexuality as a weapon had run its course. The mixed emotion she'd felt when alone with Mandy, Annie and now Meredith had made her believe she should now just concentrate on killing her victims quickly.

Looking sideways she saw the rubbish bucket beside the car. Checking to see there were no other vehicles in the lay by, she removed the short cropped blonde wig she had squeezed her own hair under, popped out the stark blue contact lenses she'd installed and whipped off the thin gold rimmed spectacles she wore, which had clear glass lenses installed, such was the direction fashion had been taken recently. It was trendy to be seen wearing glasses now. Finally she took of her high heels, which added at least four inches to her already above average height. Putting all her accessories into a *Marks & Spencers* carrier bag, she placed them all into the bucket, before adding some more rubbish she'd brought along specifically for the purpose of covering her tracks. Satisfied the bag would not be detected she resumed her journey back to the New Forest.

Fiona Webster had been Meredith Roger's personal secretary for three years, during which time she'd grown to like her boss a great deal, despite her tantrums and quick temper.

She couldn't remember a time when Meredith's behaviour had been so out of character and pondered what the relationship with the strange Mrs. Whitemore actually was.

The heaped pile of files, searches and financial documentation that had greeted her arrival at work that morning, had covered her in-tray completely, such was the volume of paperwork that needed attention.

Fiona had a date arranged for seven o'clock at Berger's Wine Bar, with her boyfriend, John. By 10.45am she had called him to ask if he'd mind making it around 8.30pm as there was no way on God's earth she was going to get through the work before her by close of day.

Now, as she put her lap top into its case and tidied up her desk she was pushing it to make the bar on time for their later arrangement.

"Shit," she moaned, safe in the knowledge she was the only person left on the floor dedicated to Rogers, Rogers and Bullman.

One last look around the reception area told her she could now leave. She grabbed her coat from the stand at the entrance to the lift and pushed the button to take her to the basement car park.

As she made a dash for her car she noticed Meredith's BMW still in its usual place. Fiona started to walk to the car and was within twenty feet from it when her mobile phone started to play '*Roll Over Beethoven*'. Stopping she took it out of her handbag.

"Hello," she answered.

"Hi, it's me. Any chance you'll turn up sometime tonight?"

Fiona recognised John's voice and the sarcasm that filled it, looking at her watch she saw it was already 8.45pm, "Sorry sweetie, I'm on my way. Be with you in less than ten. Okay?"

There was a long pause until John replied, "Oh I suppose so," in a playful voice.

"Order me a rum and Coke, will you?" Fiona said, as she turned away from Meredith's BMW.

"Sure, see you soon," said John.

"Soon," Fiona gasped. She'd already started to run towards her car, thoughts of her boss's behaviour now replaced with how she was going to pacify her boyfriend for her being late. It would take her at least ten minutes to get to the wine bar. She knew he'd be furious, but she also knew what she was going to whisper in his ear, suggesting what she planned do to him later, knowing this would kill his annoyance stone dead.

With that thought raging in her head she started the car up and left the car park, without a second glance behind her.

35

Chief Superintendent John MacDonald was sitting behind his desk, studying the file Carter had given him the last time they'd been together, when the Inspector gave a sharp knock on the door and walked in without waiting for a reply.

"Your secretary told me you were alone. I need to speak to you urgently."

MacDonald looked up and could see Carter was eager to talk. "More grief for me son?" he asked with the slightest smile on his face.

"What would you say if I told you I'd received information from a reasonably reliable source that both Ascot and Green were on the take?"

MacDonald casually threw the paperwork he'd been reading onto his desk, leant back in the chair, placed his hands behind his head, "Go on," he said in an intrigued voice.

Carter pulled up a chair and sat down, "Mickey Driscol came in earlier and wanted to tell me who'd killed them, Ascot and Green that is. He reckons it was a hit, sanctioned by members of The Panel. He waited for that piece of information to sink in before continuing, "I asked him why he was telling me this, and from his response I get the feeling he wants to run London on his own. From what I've heard the Panel just give hand-outs to people like him and rule the capital with an iron fist. It's this that leads me to believe he's telling the truth."

"Mark, Ascot and Green were two of C.I.B's top men. Surely you don't believe they were crooked?"

"Why not? Maybe they were involved in some massive scam involving the officers here. I mean, can you explain why they've been here for over four weeks and haven't found any evidence against any officer to link them to a crime?"

MacDonald leaned forward in his chair, "Okay Mark, I'll let you pursue this line of investigation, but for Christ sake be careful. I don't know much about this so called Panel that's genuine, but from the rumours I've heard over the years, they're a really dangerous bunch. Also don't stand on C.I.B toes if you want to still have a career at the end of this case."

Carter grinned, "Thanks for the warning boss. I'll be as careful as I need to be."

"Before you go any news on the other murders?"

"Nothing, as soon as I know anything I'll be right here."

"I know you will son, that's why you're on the job."

Carter returned the chair he'd been sitting and left the office. If he could tie everything together his career would go wherever he wanted it to. This was a once in a life time opportunity and the fact he could nail the bastard who'd murdered Mandy in the process made it all the sweeter.

Billy Johnstone had rang Mickey Driscol's pub *The Buckingham Arms* to arrange a meet several times over the past two hours. Each time he'd been told Driscol was unavailable, but would get back to him soon. When Billy's mobile finally rang, he nearly jumped out of his skin as he'd been nodding in his car outside the police station. He'd told one of the detective's that if anyone came looking for him, he'd gone to get a breath of fresh air.

"Billy!" Driscol's voice came over the phone.

Billy pictured him sneering at him from the other end of the mobile. "What in God's name was that all about earlier?" he demanded, fully aware Driscol might just tell him to piss off and hang up.

"Billy...Billy, I'd have thought it was obvious. I told you I was going to screw the Panel and I will. The old bill will try and find evidence to arrest them on suspicion of murdering the two cops, I'll make sure I throw a few spanners in the works and in the meantime all the shit created will help you my friend keep clear of the stink."

"What about the video of the killings? Does one really exist?"

"Don't be so bloody stupid Billy. For all I know Santa Claus killed the coppers."

Billy gave a slightly demented laugh then said, "If they find out you're a dead man."

"Well let's make sure they don't then."

Billy heard the click at the other end and knew he'd been cut off. He felt as if he was going to explode such was the fear and tension building up inside him. He needed Stella to commit another murder, so the heat would be directed back to where he felt it safest. If Mickey and The Panel clashed he had a horrible feeling everyone involved would burn in hell.

Fiona felt happy as she parked her old Black Capri 2.0 litre Ghia in its allotted space.

Her evening with John had been a great success and the sex they'd shared later at his flat had somehow felt better than it ever had in the past. She'd put that down to the fact she'd felt so tense beforehand, what with Meredith's strange behaviour and her work causing her to be late for their date.

As she walked toward the lift she saw Meredith's car already there. Looking at her watch she saw it had just gone 7.50am. Her boss was at work more than half an hour earlier than she'd normally put in an appearance.

Fiona made her way to the fourth floor, where all the offices were set aside for the sole use of Rogers, Rogers and Bullman.

Flinging her overcoat onto the back of her chair she went and knocked on her boss's door. Receiving no reply she pushed the door ajar and looked in.

The office was empty and looked as if no-one had been in since Meredith had left it the previous evening with the strange Mrs. Whitemore.

Returning to her desk, she shrugged her shoulders. Meredith must have gone with the woman in the other lady's car.

Sitting down she started to open the outstanding mail that had arrived in the morning's post. As she sorted the items into their respective piles, she wondered if she should ask her boss who the mysterious woman really was.

At 10.30am Geoff Bullman came into the reception area and headed for Meredith's office door.

"She's not in yet, Geoff," Fiona said, intercepting him.

Geoff looked at her with a puzzled look on his brow, "What do you mean? She's not in yet. We've an urgent meeting with Bill Nixon regarding his takeover bid to sort out."

"Sorry Geoff, I see it's in the diary for today, but what can I tell you? She hasn't turned up yet."

"Have you rang her at home?"

"No, I didn't think it was my place to do that."

"Probably not, ring her now while I'm here, will you please?"

"Sure," Fiona replied as she punched out the number to Meredith's luxury flat on the Thames. She let the phone ring for a couple of minutes, hung up, then tried her on her business and personal mobile phone numbers. Meredith didn't pick up.

Fiona looked up at Geoff, "No reply to all her numbers. The answering machine at her home isn't on, which is weird. Listen I hope I don't sound strange, but something happened yesterday that seemed odd to me."

"Go on," Geoff prompted.

"Well this lady telephoned to make an appointment. Something to do with her dead husband, but she wouldn't leave a name. Just a contact number she said was a hotel phone. I told Meredith and she went white, told me to book her in, but not when she'd be alone with whoever this woman was. When I booked her in at 5.30pm, she told me her name was Mrs Whitemore. Meredith's whole attitude changed to such an extent she said she now *wanted* to be alone with her. The woman turned up on time, I showed her in and less than five minutes later they left, all friendly and laughter. It didn't make sense to me Geoff."

"That does seem strange Fiona. Listen, if she hasn't turned up by midday, give me a buzz." Geoff walked back to his office leaving Fiona to mull over what'd happened. Try as she might she couldn't come up with an answer to what would have changed Meredith's attitude so quickly.

At midday she called Geoff as instructed. He came straight through. "Listen, I've spoken to her brother in France. He said if she hadn't appeared by twelve we were to report her missing to the police."

"Police!" shouted Fiona hysterically.

"He's very worried. Like us, he's been trying to reach her all day with no luck."

Fiona ended the call and immediately dialed the local police station. She was told someone would be there shortly. Less than ten later, DS Johnstone and DC Grady were discussing the disappearance over a cup of tea in Geoff's office.

"Fiona," asked Grady, "Apart from what you've told us already, is there anything else you think might be useful, anything at all, no matter how silly it may seem?"

"No not really. The fact she went in someone else's car is a bit funny. Meredith loves her BMW. I wouldn't have said she'd have been too happy leaving it downstairs all night."

Johnstone stood up, "I'll go and check the car. Maybe she's left us a hint as to where she went."

Grady turned to Fiona, "Okay, tell me if I get anything wrong, tall white woman, about five feet eleven inches tall, wearing a light blue two piece suit. She had gold rimmed glasses on and you think she had very blue eyes. She had short cropped blonde hair..."

"Natural I'd say, there were no roots showing."

"Ok, could be important. The lady had a black bag and you reckoned she was about a size 10-12. Have I missed anything?"

"No, that's it I think. She was only here for minutes and as I said, Meredith practically pushed me out the door as soon as I showed her in. Can I ask you something detective?"

"Of course you can."

"Well, when I told you Mrs. Whitemore's name, I couldn't help but notice the glance you and your colleague gave one another. Does it mean anything to you?"

Grady was about to give an explanation when Johnstone reappeared at the door, "Mike, can I have a word?"

As Grady approached the detective sergeant he saw from the look on his face something was up.

"She's in the car. Stabbed through the chest and I suspect she's been there all night. Mark's on his way with the doctor."

"Christ, this is getting scary, all these dead bodies."

Fiona had come over to ask what was happening. She looked firstly at Johnstone and then at Grady, "She's dead isn't she?" She asked in a knowing voice.

"I'm sorry Fiona, yes she is," Mike Grady said as he put his arm around the grieving secretary and led her back into the office, where they were met by the stricken face of one of the firm's senior partners.

"Have you found her yet?" he asked.

"She's dead, Geoff," Fiona mumbled between sobs.

"Sir, I know this is a hard time for everybody, but I have to ask the question. Did Meredith have any enemies that you knew of?"

Geoff looked up as if he'd just been asked the most stupid question of his life, "Enemies, no everybody loved her. She was such a wonderful lady." He then broke down, crying unashamedly into his hands.

Grady left Fiona and Geoff comforting each other and quietly closed the door behind him, before joining Johnstone in the wait for Carter.

The detectives stood on the right-hand side of the BMW, watching the forensic team looking for early clues. The body of Meredith Rogers had already been removed and the vehicle would follow shortly for a fuller examination.

Carter, Johnstone, Grady and Forsyth stood in a huddle and stared at the grisly scene.

Carter whispered to his colleagues, "Have we any similarities between the description of this woman and the one who attended the restaurant with Asque?"

"No Gov, this is a blonde and the other was a brown-haired lady."

"Could be a wig," Forsyth offered.

"Listen, for Mrs. Whitemore substitute Stella Blackmore. Go with Janet on the wig theory, add the fact we've no idea where Blackmore is, indeed we've no idea if she's alive or dead, and this gives me a very strong hunch she's our killer."

The other three detectives remained silent for a long time. He tried to read the expressions in their faces to see if he could detect signs they thought what he'd suggested was wrong. He couldn't tell.

Billy Johnstone needed to create doubt in everyone's mind and was first to speak, "Okay, we've a lot of circumstantial evidence here, but nothing that could be proved in a court of law. Besides, everyone that we've spoken to regarding Mrs. Blackmore have all said she was a very quiet woman who was well and truly under her husbands thumb."

"Wouldn't be the first person who'd deceived people with there character." Carter prompted.

"Yeah I know, but this is a serial killer, someone who as far as we know has murdered nine people, leaving us squat to go on. Do you really think she could be the one?"

"Listen, what about Dennis Neilson? He served in the army and the police force. If you'd asked his family and friends, do you think they would've said he was capable of murdering at least fifteen victims, before he chopped them up and buried them in his garden?"

Grady responded this time, "True, but he had police and military training. You're talking about a middle-class housewife, whose biggest task of the day was washing the dishes or a bit of ironing."

"Sexist pig," Janet Forsyth muttered.

"You know what I'm getting at Janet. Don't give me a hard time."

"Joking Mike, ease up."

"Sorry."

Carter could feel the tension mounting, after all, the body of Meredith, when removed from the car had been a horrific sight, "All I'm saying is perhaps we should look at the possibility, perhaps put out a press release asking if anyone has seen her. Keep it that she's merely missing. After all she could've run off with another guy and not even know her husband is dead."

Johnstone nodded his head at the Inspector, "I'll get on to that straight away. Mike and Janet can go round the office block here and see if anyone else saw our lady."

"Good idea Billy. While you do that I'll go and speak to Mr. MacDonald and discuss our, *my* latest theory!"

"It's okay Gov, I like the idea as well," Grady said.

"Thanks Mike, I appreciate that."

Carter watched the detectives go. He remained at the murder scene perhaps twenty-five minutes longer, waiting to see if any forensic evidence turned up.

He walked away disappointed.

36

Stella was woken by the cold eating at her left leg, which had found its way out from under the protection of the bed covers. Quickly she pulled it back into the warmth, shivering as she brushed it against her otherwise warm body.

"Shit, it's freezing today," she muttered between chattering teeth.

Stella pulled the covers up to her neck and sat up so she could look out the small bedroom window that provided minimum light to the room.

A mist had fallen during the night, making it difficult to see more than three or four feet. Stella slipped back down the bed. Although cold, she felt in a good frame of mind. Her newly found confidence and the way she'd so far handled the names on her list had impressed her greatly. As she lay in bed marveling at where her hidden skills had come from, a brief worry started to niggle at her. Would people say she'd gone mad? She rolled over onto her right side and picked up a half full can of beer. Taking a long sip, she wondered if perhaps she was.

Maybe when things get so bad and you finally crack, you *are* letting the insanity seep from your bones. The thought caused a hearty laugh to rise from her belly. She didn't really believe she'd lost it completely; she'd just bottled up all the abuse that'd been thrown her way over the years and had now decided to take it to the garbage and dump it.

No she wasn't mad, she was just getting even.

MacDonald listened closely to what Carter had to say, nodding his head in all the correct places.

Carter told him that although there was no concrete evidence to support his theory, he couldn't shake the idea from his head.

"Mark, I can see why you feel this is the way forward, I mean Whitemore, Blackmore it's a huge coincidence. We haven't found Blackmore yet, which leaves her just as much a potential suspect as a victim," MacDonald hesitated as he searched for the correct words before continuing, "But, don't you think people will think we're clutching at straws if we name her as a suspect based merely on the similarities of the names and the fact she's missing?"

Carter shook his head. "I don't want her named as a suspect. Let her believe she's just a missing person we need to speak to. Like I said to the team earlier, maybe she's run off with another man; maybe she doesn't even know Brian is dead. Who knows, but we need to find her, dead or alive to eliminate her from the enquiries."

"Okay, Mark. Give out a press release along those lines.

Carter locked himself in his office and sat down at his desk. His gut feeling was Stella Blackmore was a large part if not the only part of this case. True, the only evidence they had was circumstantial, but it was all they had, and he intended to go with his hunch.

Mary and Glen Gage lay in a pool of sweat. Their lovemaking had been intense and now their bodies glowed with satisfaction.

Early morning light filtered in through the lace net curtains and danced on Mary's naked hip.

Glen Gage was a fifty-one year old accountant who lived

for his career and wife, and who until recently had committed no deed that might affect the quiet life they'd built together during their twelve years of marriage.

Three weeks previous they'd been invited to a party by one of his friends at work. What they didn't know before they'd arrived, was the party was full of people eager to swap partners for the night, and it didn't matter what sex they went with, as long as it wasn't their respective other halves.

At first Glen and Mary had been shocked, but as the drink flowed and the pressure to join in mounted, they'd discussed the possibility of experimenting just this once, after all as Glen had said through drunken and lust filled eyes as he watched scantily clad women dance around, "You only live once."

He'd enjoyed his time with a pretty brunette called Alex, while Mary had ended up in tears having been treated very roughly by a man who claimed later that he was a policeman. Glen had refused to leave and so she'd taken a taxi home on her own with the so called policeman screaming obscenities at her as she was driven away.

During the past weeks, Glen had tried very hard to make it up to his wife for that one moment of madness that he would regret until the day he died.

His wife was ten years younger than him and as she lay contently dozing beside him he could feel the tears of regret building up in his eyes.

Mary stirred and looked at him through sleep filled eyes, saw his tears and pulled him closer to her, "Hey come on, it wasn't your fault. I could have said no."

"I shouldn't have been tempted in the first place," he retorted.

"Come on lie back down and I'll go get us some orange juice, okay?"

"I love you," he whispered.

"And I love you too honey."

Mary rolled over and kissed the top of his head before climbing out of bed, her naked body shivered in the morning light.

"Put your dressing gown on before you catch pneumonia," Glen said softly after her.

Mary returned with two glasses of orange and a packet of biscuits.

"That'll do my figure good," he joked.

"You'll always be a hunk to me," Mary answered as she gently ran her fingertips across his naked chest.

"Will I ever stop feeling guilty?" he asked her.

"Probably about the same time I stop. Come on we both regret it and if we just put it down to the drink and our own stupidity then we'll be able to forget it and move on."

Glen Gage smiled lovingly at his wife. He could feel the emotion building inside; he could feel his heart knotting with the love he felt towards her. Somehow he managed to speak calmly as he took the glass of orange juice from her. "You're right as usual. Now put the biscuits down and come here. I still have fifteen minutes before I need to get ready for work."

"That's all a man of your age will need," Mary said cheekily before she was pulled down onto the bed and smothered in kisses.

37

The news broadcast took Stella by surprise. She'd assumed the police would've traced her blood type from the amount she'd poured around her house, and from the car she'd abandoned at the station.

The broadcast had stated the police suspected her to be a missing person; they hadn't mentioned the house, the car or suggested she was suspected of foul play.

Stella wondered if perhaps they hadn't *found* the false evidence she'd tried so hard to leave them, but quickly dismissed the idea as stupid.

The police and now the population who'd seen the programme would be looking for her with renewed vigor. There was nothing she could do now, but sit it out and wait for the search to die down slightly.

She was confident no-one knew she was at the caravan site. She'd paid the rental for the forthcoming month and could stay locked inside for the duration if needs be.

The attendant hadn't paid her any attention when she'd booked herself in and as yet she doubted he'd even looked in her direction on any of the occasions she'd passed his reception window. Maybe he's gay she thought to herself and chuckled. As far as anyone on the site knew, Stella Blackmore was anywhere, but amongst the happy campers.

She decided it was time to change her appearance again as the more deception she could lay before the world the longer she believed she'd remain free. She'd bought various hair dyes from a chemist in London, choosing a large department store to lessen the chance of the sales assistant remembering her. Heading into the bathroom she decided to be a redhead for this transformation, and so spent time hacking at her hair, giving it a spiky modern look, before dying it with the chosen colour.

Finally, satisfied at the look she'd achieved she smiled at her reflection. The next stage of her game would need to wait a few days, until then she'd have the chance to think carefully about what she would do if the police drew too close to her.

A distant rumbling sound from deep inside her stomach reminded her she hadn't eaten for hours; her body had begun complaining bitterly at being so neglected.

Stella opened the fridge and bent down to look inside. Her disappointment at the near empty shelves caused her to sigh heavily, "Damn," she said, "I forgot to get any shopping."

Reaching to the back of the fridge she pulled out a packet of ham slices, noticing there were only four squares remaining. Hungrily she devoured each waver thin slice individually, savouring every morsel. Stella sat uncomfortably, her insides had started to cramp such was her hunger. Perhaps she could risk a trip to a local shop later in the day, once it had grown darker outside, in the meantime there was nothing she could do, but retire to bed and try to sleep the pains away.

Detectives worked night and day in their efforts to track Stella Blackmore down without success. She appeared to have vanished off the face of the earth.

The blood (believed to be Stella's) at the house and inside the vehicle belonging to her found abandoned at the railway station, only served to discredit Carter's idea regarding her as a suspect. No sightings of her in the past three days did anything but support his cause.

"Doesn't look good, does it Gov?"

Carter turned to see Johnstone leaning over his desk, studying the lab reports on the blood found at the scene.

"We know the samples are Brian Blackmore, Teresa Day

and WPC Mandy Burrows.   The other must be Stella Blackmore's because of where it was smeared, there's no way the killer could have left such stains in the act of killing his victims."

"Could they have been planted?"

"Gov, don't you think you're trying too hard?"

"No, the killer's Stella Blackmore, I just need to prove it, connect her to the crimes."

Billy Johnstone looked at his boss with a worried expression on his face. Carter was determined Stella was the killer and Billy knew he needed to make him think otherwise.

"Why don't you go home and rest for a bit, I can handle it here for a while."

Carter smiled at his sergeant, "Thanks Billy, I know you're only trying to help but I'm okay, really."

"Fine by me, just worried you're getting too stressed out over all this."

Mark Carter for the first time since he'd found Mandy stacked like hay in the garage, badly wanted to tell someone the truth, but knew he couldn't. His deception would have to be held within for the rest of his time with the police. To tell anyone now would destroy the trust he'd built up with his fellow detectives over the years.

Besides he didn't want pity, he wanted to catch the bastard responsible.

Three days locked in a space no larger than a prison cell, was time enough to reflect, or to feel the tensions rise to a highly flammable level.

For Stella it was the latter.

She'd dared to find a small grocer shop in an out of the way village, somewhere deep in the heart of the forest, where the people who lived there, had forgotten what life was about, outside in the real world.

She'd only purchased food to last for the duration of her imposed solitary confinement. Today was the fourth day since she'd been plastered over every news bulletin as a missing person, wanted in connection with the deaths at Arcadia Drive. The reports hadn't said it so bluntly, but she'd read between the lines.

This morning as she brushed her teeth and saw the pale lifeless reflection staring back at her in the dirty bathroom mirror, she'd known that her body craved freedom and that she badly needed to feel the cold air on her face to provide life to her flagging spirits.

If she stayed cooped up any longer she was in danger of just curling up into a ball and dying where she lay.

Her neck muscles ached with the stress of waiting. Headaches had become her everyday companion. What she hadn't picked up during her previous trip to the stores chemist were any pain killers, and this was a very stupid mistake on her behalf, after all she'd practically lived on the little white pills when she'd lived with Brian. It had been her only way to numb the agony caused from the constant beatings.

Stella once washed and feeling slightly better sat at the table with a cup of hot tea in one hand, the list of death in the other. She sat in silence, concentrating on the remaining names, trying to make one of them jump out from the page screaming, *'Pick me. Pick me'*.

Running a slender finger down the page she studied the small notes she'd scribbled beside each name. Brief details Teresa had provided on each potential victim.

Near the bottom sat the names of Glen and Mary Gage, the only married couple on the list. Teresa had said Brian had been involved with Mary, but only on one occasion. She had apparently hit him when he'd attempted to force her to have oral sex with him. Before he could gain his revenge she'd fled in a taxi.

Teresa had told her, he'd said Mary was very quiet and reminded him of Stella.

Stella tapped on the names with her nail so hard she put her finger through the thinning paper. "Oh bollocks," she moaned

Her head felt ready to burst with the anger and frustration she was feeling at her whole situation. Stella screamed as loudly as she could into one of the cream coloured couch pillows, her cries of anguish suffocating in the velvet material. The release gave her a wave of confidence she hadn't enjoyed in the past three days. Picking up her coat she decided to go and pay Mr. and Mrs. Gage a visit, now while she felt so invigorated.

It had rained heavily during her stay at the caravan site and as she drove along the thin dirt tracks that lay between the individual living areas, large puddles of mud filled water splashed up from beneath her wheels, painting filthy muck filled abstract paintings on the sides of the white vans.

Stella wondered why nearly all caravans were white. Surely she thought, darker colours would be more practical.

She reached the entrance and kept her head down as she drove past the reception hut. As usual the person inside paid her no attention. Smiling she turned left and headed along the country road to travel the three miles which would lead her to the motorway and her meeting with the Gages.

Flicking on the radio she listened to the music as she drove. None of the tunes were familiar to her. Stella liked the Beatles and had enjoyed Abba when they were a huge success. Recently she hadn't had the time to listen to anything and had therefore lost touch with the music industry.

The tunes came and went, almost as quickly as the countryside passed by her windscreen. Everyone sounded the same and it wasn't long before she preferred to drive in silence.

Less than three hours later she reached the outskirts of Watford, a town she'd visited only once before. That had been to do some Christmas shopping with her sister in 1994.

As she drove around the one way system, she hardly recognised any of the buildings she passed such had been the development since her last visit to the town.

It always saddened her when great hulks of concrete swallow up whole areas of country side, or small communities. Everything it seemed was for the benefit of large co-operations making more money and to hell with the small businesses that died in the process.

The map she had was over ten years old and as she drove through the busy town centre, she worried she wouldn't be able to find the street she wanted.

Her fears were groundless, as she passed a large warehouse that sold second hand furniture; she spotted *Oak Avenue* on her left. Slowing down to make the turn, she eased the hired Ford Focus down the street, studying the house numbers as she went.

Number 89 lay pushed slightly back from the road, unlike most of the other houses in the street. She'd almost driven past, receiving a loud blast from the vehicle behind as she'd stamped on her brakes to prevent her passing the address.

Stella caught the one fingered salute the male driver gave

as he drove past. She smiled pleasantly back, which seemed to make him madder, as the finger doubled in number.

Stella parked up and eased herself from the car. It had taken nearly three hours to reach the address in Watford, and now as she glanced at her watch, the dial told her it was 11.43am.

Stella hoped Mary would be at home, she was assuming Glen would be at his place of work.

38

It had been a bad morning for Mary Gage, only ten minutes after Glen left for work she'd stumbled down the stairs and smashed her face against the banisters at the foot of them.

She sat on the small step that led into their bathroom, holding the tea towel, filled with crushed ice, tightly against her swollen lips. Dried blood stained her yellow T-shirt, her running mascara had left tell tale signs on her cheeks where the tears had trickled down, joining the blood spots in an unholy alliance of suffering.

Mary sniffed away new tears that threatened to fall. She wondered if she should call Glen or perhaps her doctor, as her face had really started to hurt now.

The doorbell rang in the recesses of her mind; however it was only when the person standing on her front porch failed to remove their finger from the bell, that the sound penetrated far enough for Mary to hear it.

Climbing slowly to her feet, she headed to the door.

Before opening it she took stock of the damage to her face in the hallway mirror. She looked like a female version of the elephant man; such was the level of swelling around her mouth and under her eyes where she'd cried herself dry.

Mary thought about not opening the door and if the person standing on the other side hadn't been so persistent with their finger, she may have walked away.

Truth was the sound was getting on her nerves.

Opening the door she expected a sales person. After all who else rings at that time in the morning?

The smartly dressed woman standing before her took her by surprise.

"Hello, its Mary isn't it?"

Mary took a step back. She didn't recognise the person in front of her and was shocked to learn she had the advantage of knowing *her* name.

"What happened to your face?"

The second question hit the mark, "Nothing for you to concern yourself about. Who are you anyway?"

"May I come in before I explain; it's rather chilly out here."

Mary studied the outfit the woman was wearing. It consisted of a black leather jacket, over a white shirt or blouse, a pair of faded blue jeans and ankle high black leather boots.

She did look cold. "Not until you tell me who you are."

"That's fair enough. My name is Stella Blackmore."

At first the name meant nothing to Mary, then something from deep within her subconscious started to burn.

"Are you related to a policeman called *Brian*?" she asked in a concerned voice.

"I'm his wife."

The words felt like a hammer blow to Mary's head and her stomach dropped at the same time as she tried to slam the door shut. "Go away; he was trying to force me into doing something I didn't want to do. I've done nothing wrong."

Stella put her full body weight behind the closing door and pushed it back, at the same time forcing her way into the house.

Mary stumbled and fell backwards onto the floor, hitting her head on a small telephone table as she fell. She screamed out in pain.

Stella slowly and deliberately closed the door and went and stood over Mary.

"What's the matter? Why did you try and shut me out?

Mary rubbed the back of her head and felt the lump already forming, "I don't know, maybe you're here to cause trouble."

"Trouble, not really. I came to tell you he's dead."

The words stabbed at Mary, almost as if Stella had run her through with a sword.

"What happened to him, I mean how did he die?" Mary asked shocked by the news, and suddenly feeling guilty for trying to slam the door in the woman's face.

Stella squatted down so that her face was only inches from Mary. "I killed him."

Mary gasped and felt her chest tighten. "You what?" she managed to gasp between breaths.

Stella smiled happily. "I said he's dead. I killed him."

Mary panicked and tried to get to her feet, at the same time as kicking her legs frantically in Stella's direction.

"What the hell do you think you're doing?" Stella shouted. "You're here to kill me as well, aren't you?"

Stella so badly wanted to say *yes,* but something in the sad eyes of the woman scrambling around on the floor like a wounded animal made her hold her tongue for the time being. "I came here to talk, that's all. Why would I want to kill you? What have you done to hurt me?"

Mary let out a deranged laugh, "I slept with your husband. Isn't that enough?"

"Maybe," Stella whispered as she stood up straight.

"Oh God please don't kill me...

Stella slapped her hard and opened up her busted lip and again. "You're not going to die if you shut up and tell me what I want to know," Stella said calmly, but with a hint of menace. "Tell me why you find it necessary to sleep with other people's husbands?"

Mary dropped her head onto her hands and pulled her feet up so her chin rested on her knees. "I don't *need* to do it. It was the first time I'd ever done anything like that and I won't ever do it again. It was all a mistake."

"How can opening your legs for somebody else's husband be a mistake?" Stella asked angrily.

Mary started to sob, "We didn't know the party was going to be like that, we were drunk. I couldn't stop it happening. What would you have done?"

Now it was Stella's turn to laugh like a banshee, "Done, me. I would've blown him apart with his own shotgun. *Hey*, that's what I did."

"What are you talking about? I only did it because I was drunk. He did it all, I just lay there trembling."

Stella abruptly stopped laughing. The room went deathly quiet, before she spoke again. "Let's talk a while, until your man gets back. Then the fun and games can start eh?"

"I'm sorry," Mary whispered.

"Say it again."

"I'm sorry."

"Sorry for what? Sleeping with my husband or because you're going to die?"

Mary looked deeply into her eyes, "Sorry I slept with your husband."

Stella sat down beside her and for the first time really saw the damage that had been caused to her face, "Did he do that?" she asked and stretched out a hand to gently touch Mary's face.

"No of course not, I fell down the stairs."

"Yeah and I'm the Queen of England?"

"I did fall down them. Why don't you believe me?"

"Because I used that same excuse so many times, I wore it out."

Mary was looking at her with a blank expression and Stella found it disconcerting. The tears had started to fall again and Stella remembered her own experience with drugs, brought on by her bastard of a husband.

She put an arm around the grieving woman. "Do you still love him?" she asked.

Mary sniffed, "Of course I love him."

Stella cradled the injured Mary in her arms and rocked her back and forward. Both sat in silence until exhausted Mary, surprisingly fell asleep. Once she'd drifted off, Stella rested Mary's head on her jacket and left her to sleep away some of her bad memories.

Her own head started to spin. Mary seemed to be a carbon copy of the person she'd been, and not too long ago, someone who was beaten black and blue, used as a punch bag by her husband for his own pleasure. They would have a lot more in common soon enough. Both would be widows.

When Mary awoke less than twenty minutes later her neck felt stiff and detached from her body, such was the angle that she'd fallen asleep in.

It took her a few seconds to remember what had happened and where she'd been when the stress induced sleep had descended on her.

Quickly she glanced around, there was no sign of her captor, but she could hear the faint sound of people talking in the front room.

Aching all over, she slowly pulled herself to her feet and went to see who it was.

Pushing the door open she found Stella spread eagled on the floor watching the afternoon soaps on the television.

"I thought Glen had come home early," Mary muttered quietly.

"No such luck baby," Stella said without taking her eyes from the program she was avidly watching. "Back about six, is he?" she added in a nonchalant manner.

Mary felt as though she was in a dream as she stared down at the woman lying on her carpet. Maybe she should try and escape? Make a run for it, get help? Then she realised if she did and Glen turned up he'd be in terrible danger. After all, the woman was clearly mad. She decided to play it really cool and try and warn Glen the minute he showed up. "Fancy a cup of tea?" she asked in what she hoped sounded a friendly voice.

"Sure why not," Stella replied, wondering how she was going to be able to pull the trigger when Mary's turn came. She could feel the pity she felt towards her building as she gazed at her injured face.

When Mary returned the late afternoon news was on. Mary wasn't paying much attention as she concentrated on pouring the tea. It was only when Stella said, "Hey look, I'm on telly again," did she take notice.

The newsreader was asking for witnesses who'd seen anyone resembling Stella Blackmore to come forward as she was still missing and the police wanted to question her regarding serious offences.

"My God, you're telling the truth. You have killed your husband."

Stella laughed and rolled onto her stomach before pulling out the shotgun she'd retrieved from the car, while Mary had slept, "Yep," was all she said.

Mary started to scream and made a dash for the kitchen. Stella shouted after her, "Stop or I'll shoot you now."

Mary stopped and turned around slowly. Her legs were shaking and her face had gone ghostly white.

Stella grinned at her; she hadn't even bothered to point the gun at Mary.

"Bitch," Mary whispered and started to cry.

Stella stood up and was about to speak, when she heard the key turn in the front door.

The door opened and a man's voice called out, "Hey honey, it's me."

Mary woke from her silence and she screamed at the top of her voice, "Get out Glen, there's a woman..."

Stella hit her over the left hand side of her skull before Mary could add anything else. Mary was out cold before she hit the carpet. Glen either from disbelief or bravery, burst into the lounge where Stella stood looking down at the prostrate Mary. He had no idea who the woman standing over his wife was, but yelling, he charged across the room, closing the distance between them in rapid fashion.

He had nearly reached Stella when she brought up the shot gun and pulled the trigger.

The noise in the enclosed semi-detached house sounded like an exploding bomb.

Glen screamed as the shot burst him open just above the belt of his trousers. He looked down to see his large intestine hanging over the top of his trousers like some macabre piece of clothing. A waterfall of blood cascaded from where his stomach had been. Glen looked at Stella and then fell dead to the floor, where he lay beside his wife.

Stella's heart thumped against her breast bone, the sound reverberated around the room, her throat was so dry it felt as if it had been cut open, perspiration ran down her forehead and in rivers down the middle of her back.

The shotgun hung heavily in her left hand. She still had her finger on the trigger, white smoke floated out the barrel as she stood over her victims.

Finally she felt calm enough to reload the weapon. Mary had stayed unconscious throughout the shooting which would make her next task easier.

Carefully she placed the barrel of the shot gun on to Mary's temple and exerted pressure to the trigger. She felt it reach its biting point, ready to release its deadly payroll, her finger twitched nervously on the thin strip of metal.

Hell is waiting for you Stella if you pull the trigger and you know it.

Her finger squeezed a fraction more; the bullet would fly on the final journey soon.

Bang!

The explosion rocketed round the room, Stella almost fell backwards under the impact she hadn't anticipated. She'd been deep in thought as to whether she should pull the trigger or not, when the gun had gone off.

Her gaze fell to the floor and she picked up the burn marks in the carpet to the side of Mary's head.

Mary's destiny had been in another's hands.

Stella bent down and whispered in her ear, "I don't know if you can hear me or not, but I'll let you live if you promise not to tell the cops it was me who did your old man. I can always come back."

Bending lower she kissed Mary on the left cheek, she then headed for the door, listening to the distant sound of police sirens approaching as she made her escape.

39

Early investigations to try and find out who the members of the Panel were had drawn a blank. Carter called an office meeting to share all the input obtained so far. He sat and listened as one-by-one his team told him they'd failed to discover anything useful and that the capture of these men would not be easy. Finally it was Billy Johnstone's turn. Carter had asked him to call on The Maverick Club because he knew it was frequented by both police officers and sections of the underworld. He had hoped Johnstone would be able to dig out a lead.

"So Billy, how did you do at the Club?"

Billy took out his small black leather bound filofax and flicked it open before scanning down the page. "Sorry Gov," he said. "As I told you earlier, I often go to this club myself as does most of the team here. Yes, sometimes you see interesting faces, but there's nothing to suggest a large criminal organisation has anything to do with the place."

"Did you get a chance to speak to everyone you wanted to?"

"Yeah, everyone I thought might know something all came up blank. I've left my card with quite a few of them so if anything does turn up they'll call me."

Hiding his disappointment, Carter said, "Okay people, we need to keep looking. Use your informants to dig deeper, there will be a reward for information that leads us to any arrests. I've already spoken to the Area Commander regarding this, so it'll be well worth them helping."

"Gov, if these men are as bad as we think they are, I don't suspect anyone will tell us anything."

Carter looked at WPC Forsyth who'd spoken the words he felt all his officers were itching to say, "That may be true

Janet. But we have to do something." Carter shrugged his shoulders at her as if to say *'what else can I do?'* Nobody else spoke and he let the silence drift over them for a moment. "Okay people let's get on with the task in hand." He left them to it, went to his office, closed the door behind him and slumped into his chair. The case was beginning to get out of control and sooner or later he suspected officers from larger squads would be brought in to sort it all out. Carter felt he could easily lose charge of the case if he didn't start getting results quickly.

Mike Grady had never been summoned to meet with the members of the Panel before, and as he sat outside waiting to be called in, he could feel his stomach churning with nerves, caused by his fear and anticipation. He'd asked Billy what to expect so knew he'd be blinded by bright lights which prevented anyone from seeing the faces of these powerful men. Billy had also told him their voices were distorted so he wouldn't recognise these either. He sat twiddling his thumbs for what seemed an eternity, before finally the door to the room opened and he was beckoned in.

Immediately he blinded himself by looking directly into the light at the front of the room, muttering to himself he fumbled his way to the chair in front of the desk and sat down. He had a panic attack when he remembered Billy telling him to wait to be asked to sit. Show respect he'd been told. Pushing the chair backwards he made an attempt to get back to his feet.

"Remain seated Mike. We understand these occasions can be...nerve racking," a quite, but firm voice joked.

Mike thought he heard muffled laughter, but couldn't be sure. "I came as soon as I was asked," he volunteered, trying to sound calm and helpful.

"We know Mike and we thank you for your prompt timing."

Again he heard the muffled giggles from before him, "Why am I here?" he asked, the fear in his belly growing stronger with each passing moment.

"We're sorry to hear about your brother. Tragic waste of life and it's caused us a lot of problems as well as a great deal of pain to you."

Mike sniffed hard.

"Mike we need someone on the Stonewall Estate to do the work Jake and Miss Walsh so ably carried out. Do you think you can arrange this for us?"

Mike couldn't believe what he was hearing. The Panel wanted him to run drugs on the estate. This was Billy's territory and he wondered why he was being overlooked this time. "What about Billy?" he asked.

"Let's just say he'll be doing other things. Besides we feel as reward for your sacrifice you deserve to be given more responsibilities."

"Thank you, thank you," Mike mumbled under his breath as he tried to think how Billy would take the news he'd lost the income generated from running the drug supply to the sad junkies on the Stonewall Estate.

"Before you go Mike, tell us what's been happening at the police station."

Puzzled, Mike looked directly across at the hidden men, "What do you mean?"

"Tell us about the murders."

Shrugging, Mike replied, "Not a great deal. We haven't got the foggiest who's killed the two Complaints Officers, but we're pretty certain we know who killed the others."

"Billy has informed us of his plan to interfere with the evidence so we can all get on with our lives easier."

Mike laughed, "That's one way of putting it."

"Anything else you want to say to us Mike?"

Mike could feel they were probing him for information, but he had no idea why, nor what they hoped he'd tell them. Struggling to say anything useful he said, "Mickey came in the other day to see Billy. He spoke a long time with Carter as well. Don't know what it was about. Part of Billy's plan to screw the case I shouldn't wonder."

There was a long silent pause during which time Mike sat and listened to his heart thumping against his rib cage. Finally, "Thank you Mike you've been very helpful. Take this small token of our appreciation. Close the door on your way out."

Mike got up, taking the package before him. He walked out backwards practically bowing at the faceless men as he went. Once outside he ripped open his gift and whistled when he saw the crisp pile of twenty pound notes staring up at him. He thought although it wouldn't bring his brother back, it *would* allow him to drink and sniff sufficient quantities to question whether he'd ever had a brother in the first place.

When he returned to the station he sought out Billy, who he found drinking a cup of coffee in the canteen.

"How did it go?" Billy asked without looking up.

Mike sat down before replying, "I was shitting myself Billy, I can tell you that."

Billy this time did look up, "And?"

"They asked me to organise a new dealer on the Stonewall Estate."

Billy put his cup down, "They what?" he demanded to know.

"I asked them why it wasn't you anymore and they said you were going to be doing other things."

"Like what?"

"They didn't say, Christ Billy I didn't ask for the job. How much were you making anyway?"

"Piss off Mike," was all he said as he hurriedly stood up and jogged from the canteen.

"Only asked," Mike shouted after him.

Billy went into the toilet and entered a cubicle where he sat down, leaned forward and put his throbbing head in his hands. What did all this mean? He could feel his pulse racing. Did the Panel suspect him of something? Billy wondered if he should go and tell them Driscol was stirring it or should he just continue to play dumb. After a long time he decided it was best to say nothing and see how he was treated the next time he went to the club. Perhaps he was going to be rewarded with a cushier number. After all he was making over three grand a month from his dealings on the estate. It was income he'd grown used to and he didn't want it to stop now.

He could feel his breathing slowly returning to a regular pattern. Rubbing his palm across his forehead, he wiped away the cold sweat that had formed on his worried brow. Leaning forward once more, he sighed heavily. Mike's news had taken him totally off guard.

It would be several minutes before he regained his composure completely and left the sanctity of the male toilets.

40

Heavy drizzle had started to fall, making the morning even more depressing, if that was at all possible.

Mark Carter stood with his hands stuffed deep into his long black raincoat, droplets of water running off the end of his nose.

It was worse than he imagined.

The force had requested that the relatives allow a funeral, where all the murder victims could be buried together in a specially purchased plot at Ashridge Cemetery bought specifically for the purpose.

It was the police way and although he could see why it should be done in the manner asked for, he'd badly wanted to bury Mandy privately.

The deception they'd hid behind, for all this time had finally bitten back.

Mark stood alongside MacDonald and DS Johnstone, there were nearly two hundred other officers and civilians, standing on one side of the open graves, whilst the family members of the dead, stood equally sobbing on the other.

Carter looked up and saw Mandy's sister Rebecca watching him. He could read what she was feeling in the pale complexion of her face. Like him, she was heartbroken, her world ripped apart at the seams.

He tried to raise a smile, to help her, but he thought he grimaced instead.

Mandy's parents had been killed in a car accident six years earlier and the only other close relatives who'd turned up were her Uncle George and Auntie Katie, both of whom Mark liked immensely.

He was glad many of their friends had stayed away as he'd asked, during the many phone calls to explain what had happened.

His own family was absent as he hadn't told them yet, for fear of breaking down in front of them. His courage didn't stretch that far, and he was relying on the fact they paid no attention to worldly events so most probably were unaware of the current drama unfolding in London.

He glanced round at the saddened faces, each a picture of the individual's grief. He knew he would need to be strong for his colleagues, for Rebecca, but it was difficult standing inside a funeral party, watching your girlfriend being buried, with only a select few being privy to such information.

He listened to the words in a dreamlike state, shutting his mind off to their meaning as the minister said each one carefully over each coffin, before they were lowered into the dark, musky damp earth.

Only once did he falter. It was when he heard the words, *Ashes to ashes, dust to dust*, it made it so final. Mandy was gone forever.

MacDonald sensed his weakness and subtly took hold of him below his right elbow, offering the support he badly needed.

The rain fell heavier towards the conclusion, people dropped red roses on top of the coffins, and then the mourners started to drift away.

Carter stood beside the grave long after everyone else had gone. How he'd got through without breaking down amazed him. Each beat of his heart caused the level of pain and loss to increase.

He was soaking wet and shivering with cold.

Rebecca had gone, taking Mandy's Aunt and Uncle with her, she'd not spoken to him. He felt deserted at the time he most needed to talk, to let out his true feelings. Carter didn't want to feel so alone.

Silent tears began to roll down his face, he took in large gulps of air to calm himself, but it was no good.

Crumpling in a heap, at the side of Mandy's grave he broke down into the man he should have been portraying at the funeral. He was now, properly, the grieving partner.

By the time he'd removed his soaked clothing, filled the bath with hot water, climbed in and allowed the temperature to defeat the army of goose pimples that had covered his body, he was beginning to feel as if his grief had started to subside to a manageable level. He lay with the water up around his chin, his breath causing small ripples to float away from his nostrils, as if chased by a fiery dragon.

Sweat formed on his brow and the skin on his hands started to wrinkle as the minutes ticked slowly past, as he sat in silence enveloped by the dark.

Over and over, he turned and tossed the facts of the case around in his head.

Stella Blackmore had allegedly been transferred from a shy, mild mannered, considerate, loving wife into a violent and ruthless killer.

What had caused the change? What concrete evidence did he have to back up his hunch?

He splashed the water in frustration. There was nothing that could connect Stella Blackmore to any of the murders. He had sightings of a female with two of the deceased, although each woman had been described differently, and Stella was the wife of one of the victims. The main concern to him was the fact she was missing.

No body, no ransom requested, no hints that she fitted the profiles of the other dead victims.

If she'd been killed it would only have been because she'd been present when the killer wiped out his intended victims.

Carter let out a long sigh.

The doorbell rang in the background. Taking his time, so as to avoid slipping on the ornate wooden bathroom floor, he grabbed a bathrobe and went to answer his door.

Rebecca stood before him, looking drawn. It was very obvious she'd cried tremendously since the burial of her sister.

"Becky!" he said in a surprised voice.

Rebecca gave a brief smile, "Didn't expect to see me, did you?"

"Not really. After the funeral you didn't even acknowledge me."

"Can I come in?"

"Jesus, I'm sorry. Please, please come in."

Rebecca slid past him, gently brushing herself against him as she did so. He caught a whiff of some expensive perfume, but had no idea of its name.

"Mark, I'm so sorry," she said wrapping him in a tight hug.

"Me to," was all he managed to reply, knowing if he started to say anything else his tears would flow freely again.

"Take it you told people to stay clear of the funeral."

He detected the hostility in her question, "I had to Becky. You know that."

"I know my *sister* was buried today, without any of her friends being there to say goodbye."

Mark broke free of her vice-like cuddle and looked deeply

into her eyes. "I told you why it had to be the way it did. We'll have a proper get together for everyone to say bye in a day or two."

"Great."

Carter understood the way Rebecca was feeling. He would've buried Mandy in a different cemetery, with all their friends and family present and it would've been a less morbid affair, just as she'd have wanted.

"Becky, you knew what we started when we decided to keep our relationship secret from our jobs. Mandy, and to a certain extent me, would have gone through a lot of shit that to be honest we didn't need at the time. Perhaps if we'd known what was going to happen, it would have been different. Mandy wanted it the way it was."

"Oh that's bloody brilliant, blame Mandy for the whole cock up."

Mark sat down, holding his head in his hands. He rubbed his face hard before leaning back into the couch and placing his palms on his thighs. "Go on then. If it makes you feel better, have a go at me. Get it off your chest. Blame me for everything, I mean do you really think I'm glad my girlfriend's been murdered and nobody at my work has any idea what she meant to me? Do you think it's easy investigating your own partner's murder? Give me a break. I often suggested we told people, but Mandy refused. It was like she was ashamed of me or something."

Rebecca now saw the emotion and the pain written across his face. She had come to shout at him, to blame him for Mandy's death, to tell him that she and every other one of their friends and family had thought all along that the secrecy pact they'd had was a crock of shit. Now as she watched him practically age before her very eyes, all she felt was remorse at her self-centered actions.

"I'm sorry Mark. I didn't fully understand what you were going through."

"That's just it, Becky. Nobody does. Not one person in my investigation team will ever understand what I'm going through. Do you want to know the worst part?"

Rebecca nodded.

"Worst part is I think I know who the killer is, but my team doesn't want to listen. No evidence you see, but because Mandy's dead, I can feel something they can't."

"How can you Mark," Rebecca asked curiously.

"I know who killed her because the same person murdered the man Mandy was having an affair with."

The words ripped into Rebecca's heart, "Mark!" she shouted. "What're you saying?"

He'd known his revelation would come as a shock. He also knew how much it would hurt Rebecca, to hear that her sister was cheating on him. The words had left his lips, coated with satisfaction. She'd come to hurt him and now the boot was on the other foot.

"Things hadn't been right for a while. She was staying out late, we hardly spoke when we were together and our sex life was non-existent. I was going to confront her when, when all this happened."

"Oh God, Mark I'm so sorry."

"You and me both," Carter said quietly.

Rebecca joined him on the couch, leaning sideways and resting her head on his shoulder, "What are you going to do now?"

"Catch the person I believe to be responsible."

"But if nobody else thinks it's who you suspect, how are you going to do that?"

"That's the current dilemma. I've no idea."

She awoke in time to hear her own scream fade into the quietness that is the night. The bed was wet with sweat and her nightgown clung to her body as if she'd been wrapped in cellophane.

Lying still, listening to the thumping of her heart caused her to shiver. Stella sat up and pushed the soaked bedding away before swinging herself round and out of the bed. She quickly threw off her drenched attire and replaced it with dry, warm, comfortable clothing. A T-shirt and track suit bottoms would scare away the chill.

Moving to the kitchen section of the caravan she filled the kettle, plugged it in and waited for it to boil before she put the heaped spoonful of coffee into her mug. It was only 3:10am and although she knew she should go back to bed, she also understood that sleep was as far from this caravan as it could possibly be.

Finally, and to her great relief, she sat holding the hot welcoming drink. She couldn't recall the last time she'd had a dream let alone one that she could remember. The one that had woken her tonight she could repeat as if it was a story she'd learned in childhood, sitting on her father's knee.

It had started calmly enough with her making a call to the hospital informing them there was a lady with serious head injuries at 89 Oak Avenue. She omitted to tell them they'd also find a dead body at the scene as well.

The next thing she knew was the police were kicking in the door to the caravan and she was desperately trying to make her escape by squeezing her small body out an even smaller window.

Amazingly she got away and then the chase began.

Stella swallowed a mouthful of her coffee as memories of her flight briefly flashed before her eyes. Shaking her head vigorously she tried to remove them.

Her brain rattled inside the confines of her head causing the blood to spin round, dizziness jumped on the merry-go-round and Stella released her grip on the handle of her mug. Burning hot liquid fell onto her thighs and ran down her leg, before splashing on to the floor.

Stella screamed. She tried to stand up to remove her track suit bottoms, but her head still spun violently.

Crumpling in a heap back into her chair, she dropped her head towards the table. It landed with a sickening thump. The pain took a second to register and then it hit her, spreading across her temples and traveling down her neck. This coupled with her burning legs brought her back to her senses quickly.

Leaping to her feet she practically ripped the offending trousers from her legs, throwing them against the far wall before striding to the sink where she took great handfuls of cold dish water from the basin and threw them on her scalded thighs.

Once the pain had died down sufficiently enough that she felt the need to cry had passed, she took a cloth and soaked it in the water. Taking it, dripping from between her fingers, she lay on her bed and pressed it to her forehead. She felt the large bump which had already formed and cursed out loud, "Stupid bloody dream," she muttered loudly.

Stella, angrily lay for some considerable time, before the sleep she thought had traveled far, returned to haunt her once more.

Mary Gage was hooked to so many monitors, she resembled a human octopus.

"Stupid question, but are they all really necessary?" Carter asked waving his hands at the offending wires and drip lines.

"Stupid question," Doctor Ramesh retorted with a smile on his face.

"It just looks so unreal, having her connected to so many machines."

"I know where you're coming from Detective Inspector, but without them she would be dead. As you are aware her skull is fractured in two places and she's having some difficulties breathing on her own. I know how badly you would like her to sit up and tell you who bumped her on the head, but it's not going to happen overnight."

Carter knew what he was hearing made sense, it was just difficult to accept bearing in mind there was a good chance she'd seen her attacker and he was certain he knew who that was. "Okay Doc, you win. I'll stop hassling you, just promise me you'll call if she so much as blinks."

Once again with a friendly look in his eye, Doctor Ramesh said, "To get you to leave me be, I would promise you anything."

Carter stuck out a hand which the Doctor squeezed without hesitation. They'd met on three other occasions, all linked to violent crimes, both men in their own ways wanted the same result at the end of the day. Patient cured, villain caught and locked up.

Walking out into the bitterly cold wind, Carter tried to barricade his neck to the elements by pulling up his jacket collar, but this only served to create a wind tunnel which resulted in the cold air streaming down the back of his shirt.

Stella Blackmore was out there somewhere and he was going to find her and soon. He knew the caller to the hospital was her, what he couldn't fathom was why she'd rang. After all she'd murdered the husband without a second thought.

The case grew stranger and stranger with each murder. What hadn't changed as far as he was concerned was the person committing the crimes. After the phone call, even some of his team were at least thinking about Stella as a suspect.

That, as far as he was concerned, was a start.

Stella ran for her life. Where did the police get the guns? Shots flew over her head, narrowly missing her. Her lungs had extended themselves to bursting point and her heart couldn't take much more punishment.

She stopped to try and catch her breath; the pursuers had fallen back slightly.

Stella doubled over, hands on her hips and took in huge gulps of air. Her thighs were on fire and her mouth was as dry as the Sahara desert. She imagined she could taste the fine grains of sand rolling about on her tongue.

Another bullet passed by, inches from her right leg. Frantically she scrambled down a grass embankment, landing on the concrete driveway at the bottom. She moaned loudly as she tried to regain her footing.

It was no use. Her ankle must have turned in the fall. Limping badly she set off in an effort to put some distance between herself and the police chasing her down

Stella had parked her car at the top of Marshall Street and if she could get to it, she may yet escape.

Her leg hurt her more and more with each step, blood trickled down her chin from a small cut caused when she'd bitten into her tongue during her fall.

She could hear shouts behind her. They were closing on her, fast.

Stella let a sigh escape her lips as she spotted her vehicle in the distance. Smiling she limped forward.

Her body was on the brink of collapse with both physical and mental exertion. Reaching the car she fumbled with her key, trying to open the door.

"Well, well, Mrs. Blackmore. We meet at last."

Turning, she saw the handsome man standing less than ten feet from her. She watched him flick some of his thick black hair from his face, "Who are you?" she asked puzzled.

"I'm the person who's going to take you down."

Stella knew the game was over. She slid down the body of her car and watched the man come towards her, "Suppose its prison for me then," she said in an attempt to sound both sarcastic and carefree at the same time.

"Prison," he scoffed. "People like you don't go to prison. You go to hell."

Stella looked up and saw the man raise the pistol in front of him, he was so close she could almost reach out and touch the barrel, "Noooo," she screamed into the wind and rain that had started to fall.

Her scream was lost on the night air and it disappeared from trace to be replaced by the manic laughter from the man before her.

Stella could see his teeth through parted lips, could see the hatred in his eyes and understood that this was personal.

A blinding flash of light told her she was about to die.

Screaming into the darkness, she opened her eyes. "Shit," she moaned into a sweat drenched pillow, "Just another bloody dream."

41

The team had worked every minute of every day in their attempts to obtain information that would lead to the arrest of the worst serial killer the area had ever known.

Carter had been to daily meetings with Chief Superintendent MacDonald who somehow always managed to make him feel as if he was achieving something, such was his positive attitude towards the case. Carter, however, could detect the underlying fear in his boss's voice that they would all suffer for the rest of their lives if progress wasn't made soon and the case put to bed. He understood the pain, guilt and pressure that the policemen involved in the investigation would feel if they failed to catch the murderer.

He walked from the office nodding at some of his team who were sitting behind a mountain of witness statements. As he passed he could barely see the top of their heads above the paperwork.

The journey he was about to undertake, was a re-run of the one he'd made on each of the past four days. Mary Gage had been in a coma ever since her arrival at the city hospital, however over the past two days there had been signs which suggested that she may be about to surface from her injury induced sleep.

He edged his Toyota Supra out into the morning traffic and almost immediately came to a halt in the slow crawling early rush hour. He didn't mind as it gave him a chance to mull over what he had so far in the way of evidence against *his* suspected killer. He could understand why he still had limited support regarding his theory that Stella Blackmore was the guilty party as what he had consisted of nothing more than odds and sods and a whole pile of circumstantial evidence. He *was* disappointed in their lack of enthusiasm because so far they'd no-one else that could be linked to the case.

One of the leads he'd asked MacDonald to look into was whether or not any of the officers currently being investigated by the Criminal Complaints Department could be in the frame as the killer. These inquiries had led him to believe there was more chance they could become victims rather than the prime suspects. Casual surveillance had been set up on all the officers concerned, just in case.

As he crawled along he started from the beginning with the first known crime. Tony Asque had been seen in a Chinese Restaurant with a mysterious woman who by all accounts appeared to have been his date for the evening and had been a very sexy lady. No two witness descriptions of her were the same. The men seemed to have been engrossed in what she'd been wearing, and the women for reasons better known to themselves, had apparently shut their eyes to her such was the limited information that they'd passed on. The body was found stabbed to death in the car park by one of the staff and no forensic evidence had been found.

The second victim Annie Walsh had been a drug pushing hooker who'd been killed at her flat, again stabbed, again no evidence. The third had been her pimp, who annoyingly to Carter still hadn't been named. He'd had his head sliced almost in two. The killer had cleaned up Annie, but had obviously been in to much of a hurry to do the same for her pimp. As before there was nothing to link the killer to the scene.

Meredith Rogers had been stabbed in her car and they had a good description of the lady with whom she'd left the office. This didn't fit the description of Stella Blackmore, but this woman had used Mrs. Whitemore as her name to see the solicitor. That was far too much of a coincidence for Carters liking.

The three dead bodies at Arcadia Drive, including Mandy had two shootings and a stabbing between them. Same gun used as in the most recent murder of Glen Gage.

This crime fascinated Carter the most. Why had the murderer blown away the husband, seriously injured the wife, but then telephoned the hospital, a fact that had saved her life? Why hadn't they shot her as well?

They hadn't found Stella's body, no-one had told them they had her as a hostage, so where was she?

Although they'd found blood at Arcadia Drive and later in an abandoned car that they suspected belonged to Stella Blackmore, Carter believed she was in hiding, planning the next part of whatever her game seemed to be.

By the time he reached the hospital he felt very frustrated at the lack of physical evidence to support his theory.

When he entered Mary Gage's room, he found Doctor Ramesh sitting beside the bed. He was holding her hand and was talking quietly to her.

What Carter heard was music to his ears. Although her speech was mumbled Mary Gage was to some extent replying to what the Doctor was asking.

Ramesh turned to see who'd entered the room, "Ah, Mr. Carter. You've saved me a call. I was just about to give you a ring to tell you our good friend Mary here is awake and wants to talk to you."

Carter approached the bed and smiled down at the battered woman lying there, "Hi I'm Detective Inspector Mark Carter from Westville Police Station. It's great to see you awake. How are you feeling?

Mary gave him a tentative smile in return and slowly lifted her hand to him which he took in both of his and squeezed reassuringly.

"Do you remember anything that happened?"

Mary turned her head away and he noticed as she returned to look at him she had a tear in the corner of her left eye.

"Hey, we don't have to chat today. We can do this later if you like?"

Mary gave her pained little smile again, "No it's okay. I want to talk to you."

"That's good, the sooner we catch the person responsible the better it will be."

Doctor Ramesh interrupted, "I'll leave you two alone for five minutes. That'll be enough for the first day. Fair enough?" he asked both at the same time.

Mary nodded politely and Carter responded by saying, "Sure thing, Doc."

Ramesh bent over Mary and whispered in her ear although it was loud enough for Carter to pick up what he'd said, "Take it easy and don't exert yourself, deal?"

"Deal," Mary said and touched his forearm.

Ramesh left the room and Carter moved forward and sat on the edge of the bed. "What can you remember Mary?" he asked bluntly.

"This is very difficult detective. She murdered my husband"

"I know it's hard trying to recall things that have hurt you."

Mary sighed heavily, "No you don't understand. I know who did this to me. I don't know if I want to tell you though."

Carter felt someone had stuck a serrated edged knife deep into his stomach and was slowly twisting the blade, retracting it, and pulling his innards out the hole in his belly, "What're you saying Mary?" he asked in shock.

Mary heard the frustration in his voice, understood what was going through the policeman's mind, but felt terrified that somehow if she told him the name of her attacker, Stella would find out and come back for her. She really was confused as to what she should do or say.

"I'm sorry, I need time to think some things through."

Carter felt like his world was about to end, sitting on the bed of a victim who knew the name of her husband's killer, knew the name of her attacker, could seal everything about his theory, but for some misguided reason known only to her she wasn't going to tell him.

"Listen Mary, there's some stuff going on here that I don't understand. This person who beat you up and killed your husband has also killed six other people including members of the police force and a solicitor. Whoever she is can be classified as extremely dangerous. I believe if we don't stop her she'll kill again and again. You don't want that on your conscience do you?"

Mary felt the icy daggers stab at her heart. The policeman had said 'she', did that mean he knew the name already? Stella hadn't said she'd murdered anybody else apart from her own husband. She certainly hadn't mentioned the murder of any police officers. Her head started to ache under the pressure. Still something held her back from passing on the name.

"I'm sorry," she said, "I can't help you yet. I need to think things through."

Carter threw his head back and blew out a powerful breath, "Christ Mary you could get arrested for obstructing the police here. If you know who did it, please tell me."

Mary turned her head away from him again and he knew he'd lost her. Carter needed to give it his best shot, "Listen Mary, I'm going to tell you something that nobody else knows. This is only in the hope it will convince you to help me."

Mary turned to face him, and she saw the moisture in his eyes.

"I don't know why you don't want the murderer of your husband caught. Maybe you're scared, I don't know, what I can say is I loved my girlfriend very much and I didn't want her to die, but this bastard who hurt you, who murdered your husband in cold blood, who has killed five other people also shot dead my Mandy. This is personal for me too, so please, I'm begging you tell me who did this to you."

Mary tried to pull herself up a little, but slumped back down the bed. Carter bent forward so she could speak in his ear. What he heard was the sweetest two words he'd ever heard.

Mary whispered, "Stella Blackmore."

Carter fought the urge to grab Mary's head and kiss her repeatedly. "Thank you, thank you so much," he muttered as the tears flowed freely.

Doctor Ramesh returned to tell them time was up. He walked in to find them both sobbing quietly into each other's arms.

42

Stella lay on the small uncomfortable couch, with her arm bent under her head for support, staring blankly at the screen. The set was difficult to watch at the best of times, but with vision blurred by one of the many empty bottles of Cabernet Sauvignon lying on the now heavily-stained carpet beside her, focusing was impossible.

Stella continued to stare at the tiny screen, eyes wide, as if some masochistic person had taken a staple gun to her eyelids.

The programme had a Professor of Human Biology telling everyone prepared to listen that we'd evolved from bugs and spiders and not as commonly agreed by the masses, the monkey.

At the present time Stella felt more like a direct descendent of *Quasimodo*. She still couldn't believe she'd been stupid enough to telephone the medical staff at City Hospital, and tell them that Mary was seriously injured at home. She'd been convinced the reward for sparing this woman, would be her silence. She'd felt certain that Mary had been living a lie, pretending everything at home between her husband and her was all sweetness and light when in fact she was living in a world of pain and abuse. The truth when Stella had heard it on National TV had cut her to the quick. Mary and Glen did have a perfect marriage, and Stella had misread their situation totally. She'd killed an innocent man, and spared the one who should have died for sleeping with her husband, even though apparently, as discussed on TV it had been a drunken mistake.

Now, sprawling and drunk, from alcohol and the misery at having had her name broadcast to the world, as a vindictive, manipulative and bloody murderer, she felt as if her world had collapsed around her ankles.

The questions that burned away at the inside of her brain, like two huge pus- filled sores, stinking and waiting to pour out their gangrenous liquid, thus drowning her mind forever in torment. Why in God's name had she told anyone? Why hadn't she just blown Mary away?

Stella rolled off the couch, falling awkwardly on top of the discarded bottles that'd given her a period of blissful emptiness before the agony returned. "Stupid, stupid, stupid bitch," she yelled out in hatred at herself, tears of rage streaming down her aged cheeks.

The early evening news bulletin had long passed by. The night's remaining hours had given her more than enough time to come to terms with what she had done. Midnight until the breaking of dawn had merely rammed the knife of truth deeper into her belly.

Her error was Major League and she knew it.

The ceiling looked closer than it was and she instinctively reached up to touch it, knowing it was fruitless. Both hands waved in the air before her, hands that had slain her enemies, were now the hands that had betrayed her.

Momentarily she thought about removing them, chopping them off one by one, guilty of the offence of treason against the rest of her body. Then she erupted into hysterical laughter when she realised it would be impossible once she'd removed the first one. Still chuckling like a hyena, she rolled over onto her front and once again caught sight of the television set sitting on the sideboard, smugly gazing down at her, judging her and finding her guilty of stupidity.

Stella staggered to her feet as quickly as her drink filled body would allow. She grabbed one of the bottles and charged the few feet to the screen, where she whacked it with all her might. The display exploded in a million strands of glass.

Stella watched in fascination as the floor disappeared under a blanket of shining shimmering fragments of glass.

"Pretty," she mumbled as she climbed to her feet, careful not to stand on the debris. Gingerly, she made her way to the bedroom where she fell face down on the bed and started to cry. Everything had been going so well until she'd decided to revert back to the nice person she'd been, the one who took beatings as often as a junkie takes a fix, the one who did exactly what she'd been told to do without question, the one who she'd always hated. That person had died when she'd killed her husband so why had she brought her back, even briefly?

Stella's body shuddered with remorse. She couldn't believe or understand why she'd committed suicide without even the need for a weapon.

The office had been a hive of activity since he'd burst through the door and yelled, 'Stella Blackmore' across the room.

Now, the day after, the atmosphere although still highly charged had reverted back to a calm working environment.

The emergency news bulletin had resulted in hundreds of calls, some of them helpful, but many about as useful as matches at the scene of a forest fire.

Carter discussed in great detail with WDC Forsyth the merits of the public, who more often than not report information that had absolutely nothing to do with the crime under investigation. No doubt, as Janet had pointed out to him, some smart Behavioral Psychologists would know the answer as to why they did that.

The jovial atmosphere that had followed the early calls was soon replaced by dejection as nothing concrete resulted

from any of them. Everyone had been convinced that
somewhere out in the big bad world, someone would have an
inclination as to where their suspect was hiding.

Six hundred and seventy three calls had resulted in them
being no nearer to finding Mrs. Blackmore than they'd been
before their appeal for witnesses.

The scores of files had been gone over yet again, witness
statements checked and double checked, descriptions of
female sightings compared with Stella Blackmore and still
there was no breakthrough.

"She must be disguised to the hilt," Billy Johnstone put
forward.

"Agreed," replied Janet. "But where is she now?"

"Need a bloody magic wand to answer that one," moaned
a junior detective from the other side of the room.

Several people turned to give him a filthy look, "Sorry,
just thinking out loud."

"You were thinking! Christ, the world is looking up,"
Johnstone said wryly.

Laughter filtered through the smoke-filled office.

Janet Forsyth glanced over to where Mark Carter sat
quietly listening to the conversation. He was a strikingly good
looking man and she wondered if he had a girlfriend.
Perhaps after the case was over she could persuade him to
take her for a drink. After all she'd turned down nearly every
man in the room who'd asked her out in the past, so why not
go out with a Detective Inspector? It might even help her up
the promotion ladder, although that wasn't the reason she
fancied him, oh no that would be his tight looking bum and
his shock of thick black hair and dark eyes. She caught him
flick a glance in her direction and smiled broadly back in
response. He had a hidden sadness in him that Janet
believed she could help.

Somebody cleared their throat noisily in the background
and the disgusting sound snapped her out of her fantasy.
"Who was that?" she asked, before adding, "Disgusting pig."

"Come on you lot. Let's concentrate on the task at hand,
shall we?" Carter shouted across the room.

"Gov," asked Derek Randall, the other detective sergeant
on the case. "What can we do now? Everything has been
covered time and time again."

Carter could hear the disillusionment in his colleague's
voice. He could feel it in his own heart. "I know, Derek.

Everybody has worked their socks off. All we can do is wait for something to turn up. In the meantime we'll just keep ploughing through the information we have and try to siphon something off from it."

Getting to his feet he walked past Randall, patting him on the back as he passed him, "You're doing a great job, Derek," he said, not waiting for a reply. Instead he carried on out the office and went to the control room where all the calls regarding the case were being taken. Popping his head around the door he asked to no-one in particular, "Anything new yet?"

He found himself staring at the rear of over twenty shaking heads. "Damn," he whispered and closed the door. "Where are you?" he groaned as he began his walk to see MacDonald and inform him about the latest developments.

As soon as Carter had left the room, Johnstone gestured Mike Grady over to him.

"Listen now he knows who the killer is we have to try harder to keep him away from her, otherwise the whole C.I.B shit will start up again."

"What do you intend doing Billy?" Mike asked in a worried voice.

"Just keep on doing what I've been doing all along."

"Yeah, but apart from hide a witness statement and hack off Asque's penis, you've not had the chance to do much else...have you?"

Billy tapped the side of his nose, "When we were at that toffee nosed solicitors the other day, I ripped a page out of her office diary. Silly cow had written in her appointment with Mrs Whitemore, but had crossed the white bit out and substituted Black over it. She'd known who was going to pay her a visit."

Mike was shocked, "Why the hell did she go with her then?"

"That my friend is a mystery, and we'll probably never find out what really happened, especially if we never catch Stella Blackmore. With us both doing what we can to screw things up, *never* could be a very, very long time." Smiling broadly he added, "If she's smart enough to use disguise then she could be very difficult to find anyway. Besides apart from us I doubt anyone else has ever seen her in the flesh as Brian kept her out the way most of the time."

"Yeah, and we're definitely the only one's that've seen her in the *flesh*," Mike said and grinned like a schoolboy.

43

Another day had passed by in a blur of anger, frustration and hatred. Only the bottles of wine and whiskey had caused momentary lapses in her feelings towards Mary Gage.

Her head pounded from the latest hangover, her eyes felt as if someone had scraped the top layer of her retina away with a blunt razor blade, and her body ached from lack of proper sleep and the poison she'd poured into it over the past five days.

Deep down Stella fought with her emotions; it was a constant battle deciding what she really wanted to do next. She'd even contemplated suicide such was her despair. She'd briefly thought about giving herself up. In a rare sober moment she'd grasped her next move from oblivion, plucked it from a higher place and was now blissfully clear about what she had to do next.

Mary Gage had betrayed her and for that she would receive her punishment, *Death*.

How she planned to carry out the task, aware that the hospital would be crawling with police still had to be thought through carefully. She was, however, sure she could fulfill her obligation to Mary.

Stella knew she'd have to put everything else on hold. The list would need to be completed later. In the meantime she had to work on getting to Mary Gage. Stella had always known how she was going to escape the clutches of the police, but she'd hoped to implement her escape clause after she'd cleared her list. Now that idea looked impossible.

Slowly she shook her head. Perhaps it was better this way. After all she'd made an almost fatal blunder and if she'd carried on, she might make another and this time not get a second chance to redeem the situation. At least going out in her own time gave her the satisfaction of calling the shots.

Her dreams came back to haunt her, causing an involuntary shudder to descend along her entire body. She would end this her way, there would be no chase through the streets of London and certainly she wouldn't give any policeman the satisfaction of gunning her down in some dirty thoroughfare.

Stella intended to carry on as she had been since shooting her husband. She'd been in charge since then, and she intended things to stay that way.

Constable Colin Brennan leant on the nurse's station, he was twenty-three, single, very good looking, and had a way with women of all ages. Tonight, he was charming Sister Denise Codd, who at thirty-four was lapping up the attention from a younger man.

Denise laughed at all his jokes, twisting her short dyed-blonde hair between long slim fingers. "Stop it," she said, "My sides are hurting."

"Good, you looked as though you needed cheering up tonight. Bad day with the old man maybe?"

"If you're searching to see if I'm attached, then the answer is no," Denise teased.

Colin smiled. "What! You trying to tell me there isn't a man in your life?"

"God you're such a smoothie."

"Well you know what they say?"

"No, but I guess you're going to tell me anyway."

Colin moved closer and whispered in Denise's ear, "There's only two certainties in life. One's death and the other's a nurse."

Denise playfully punched him in the arm, "Colin that's terrible."

"Ah, but do you deny the charge?"

Denise could feel her cheeks redden. "Depends doesn't it."

"Depends on what?" Colin played along.

"On whether or not I feel I've been wined and dined enough beforehand."

Looking around to make sure nobody could see them, Colin took hold of Denise's hand and rubbed it gently as he said, "Denise, can I take you out for a meal when all this security bullshit comes to an end?"

"That would be lovely Colin," she replied as she slipped her hand out from his.

"Great, we can sort out where and when later on."

"Okay, but first it's your turn to make the tea," Denise said as she gently pushed him towards the kitchen.

"I can't leave my post," Colin protested.

Denise pushed him harder. "You've already left it, you chancing git. You shouldn't be here talking to me in the first place. Come on get your sexy butt in the kitchen, half a sugar for me, please."

Colin turned and bowed gracefully, "Your wish is my command."

"Promises, promises," Denise said with a chuckle.

Colin walked away to make the tea. He could feel Denise's eyes burning into his back. He liked older women and had been out with quite a few. The things he liked about Denise already were her attitude and great looks which belittled her true age. Colin, for the first time since he'd been given the posting, found he was enjoying himself.

It had taken Stella a long time to clear her head of the demons she'd installed there over the past six days. Her body still ached and she was covered with bruises, the result of all the falls, when under the influence of one of the many bottles of red wine consumed during her depression-filled days.

She stood in the reception area to the City Hospital and stared at the huge circular clock that hung over the exit doors. The hands told her it was nearly 2.45am. The hospital out-patient area was deserted.

Many times she'd visited family and friends in such places. Indeed she'd spent weeks of her life lying in one of the wards, reflecting on her latest beating. She knew the best time to try and get to Mary Gage would be in the dead of night.

Stella expected a police guard, but having talked to her husband in the past about security on various jobs he'd been involved in, she'd rationed the facts down to there probably being only one or two officers with Mary. They may be armed, but she doubted it. The police would believe that now she was a named suspect, she wouldn't take risks which might lead to her arrest.

Yet again, she hoped to prove them wrong.

Standing in what little light the area provided she thought back to the earlier conversation she'd had in the day.

The phone hardly rang at the other end. It was if the

person had been sitting at the other end of the receiver waiting for her to call.

"Hello. City General, how can I help you?"

Stella had laughed at the stuck up voice at the other end of the phone, "Ah yes," she said in an equally eloquent voice. "My name is Susan Willowberry, and I'm the sister-in-law of Mrs. Mary Gage. I've just heard the awful news that she was involved in a terrible crime last week. I've been out of the country on holiday, Tanzania actually. Anyway, I would like to come and visit my dear relative tomorrow. Would it be possible for you to inform me as to which ward she is in please?"

The silence at the other end had briefly suggested her request would be turned down, possibly owing to police procedures.

However, the silence had been broken quickly enough, "Certainly Mrs. Willowberry. Mary is in the Constance ward which is in the west wing of the hospital, floor three. It's a private ward. Visiting hours are midday to three and four thirty to eight o'clock."

"That's most kind of you. Thank you for your help."

Stella had replaced her receiver as she'd heard, "That's no prob..." from the other end.

She'd been surprised at how easily the location of Mary had been given out. Having mulled it over for a few minutes, she decided that it was either a trap, or they weren't expecting her to show up at the hospital.

Feeling the sense of excitement building, she'd prepared for her nocturnal visit to the City General.

Stella moved towards a map of the insides of the building. Her entrance had been easy. She had merely slipped in through accident and emergency and walked without challenge along the corridors to where she now stood.

Constance ward was three floors up. The easiest way was via the elevator, but she knew that would warn the people on the ward someone was coming. If, and she doubted it very much, there was a trap waiting to be sprung, chances were someone would be keeping an eye on the lift.

No, she would climb the stairs to the ward, hopeful that way she wouldn't meet anyone on route.

As she climbed she could almost feel the tension in her body increasing with every step, the still atmosphere adding to her chilled nerves.

Level one passed without problem. Stella stopped to listen for any noise, checking if anyone was approaching. Silence greeted her straining ears, and she felt herself relax slightly, although her heart still pumped furiously and her breath left her pale lips in shallow gasps.

Moving upward Stella grasped the railings tightly, trying hard to stay calm. This was going to be the most difficult task she'd under taken and she knew it could all end right here with one wrong move.

Stella was three steps from reaching the level two entrance when she heard the distant voices. Stopping dead she craned her neck in an effort to pull the words closer. Everything was garbled, nothing came gift wrapped ready to hear. She moved up the remaining stairs and waited to see if the owners of the now loud voices were heading to where she was standing, like a statue in an ornate roman garden, or whether they'd headed off in another direction.

The footsteps growing louder made her jump into action. Turning round she bolted down the steps to level one where she quickly threw herself behind an old hospital bed she'd noticed on the way up. It had looked strange to her, sitting in the hallway, alone and deserted. When she crouched beside it she saw the broken front wheel for the first time. Momentarily she wondered what happened to sick hospital equipment.

The voices were descending downwards and she recognised the sound of two women engrossed in a deep conversation, something to do with the way you steam cabbage, if making a particular Chinese dish.

The women walked slowly past her hiding place, far too wrapped up in their own world to notice the quivering wreck behind the bed.

Stella let out a relieved sigh. She had no idea what she'd have done if they'd spotted her. Dusting down, she started to make up the lost time.

After what seemed like hours since she'd arrived at the hospital, she reached the door leading into the level three corridors.

The Constance ward lay off to the right, four doors down. From the layout of the Sycamore ward which she'd surveyed on the ground floor earlier, she was aware that the nurses' desk sat approximately one hundred feet along the ward on the left hand side. There were twenty-three private rooms on this corridor and Stella didn't know where Mary Gage was being treated. There was no alternative, but to search each room until she found her.

Cautiously, she entered the ward through the unlocked double, swing doors, fully aware of the immense risk she was now taking. Owing to her rubber soled trainers, her footsteps were silent as she inched forward. She was more concerned that her heart hammering against her ribs would give her away.

Every step drew her closer to the desk. Stella had no way of knowing how many people might be working there. She hoped the police wouldn't have any inclination she'd pay Mary a visit so soon after she'd been named as the prime suspect, and therefore the ward would have minimum staffing on duty.

What she saw when within twenty feet was one solitary nurse, drinking from a mug while engrossed in conversation with a young uniformed police officer.

Stella glanced up at the ceiling. Could it be *God* was on her side?

The possibility that it could still be a trap crossed her mind only to be dismissed without much thought. Apart from the room Mary slept in, there was no where else the police could be. That and the fact the officer was obviously having so much fun chatting up the nurse persuaded Stella that security was poor.

The gap closed to fifteen feet. Still she hadn't been spotted. As she stalked along the corridor she peered into the gloom of each room she passed. So far there had been no sign of Mary.

Ten feet and still undetected, Stella was amazed she hadn't been seen or heard her by now; she could feel her heart thumping furiously, she felt the moisture in her mouth evaporate and she became aware of the sweat on her brow.

When she was almost close enough to tap the officer on the shoulder she caught sight of the camera directly above the nurses' desk. Panic rushed through her veins. The bastards had been watching her approach all along.

Stella had been hunched over on her way along the

corridor, trying to keep herself small, now as she straightened up to her full height, the policeman, who she saw was only a kid, turned round and ran towards her, screaming at the top of his voice, "Call for back up. Stella Blackmore don't you bloody well move."

Stella saw the tension and fear edged into his smooth features as he grew nearer, she recognised the hatred and loathing in his eyes and briefly imagined he was the one in her dreams who finally shot her. From behind her back she produced the shotgun and leveled it at his waist.

Constable Brennan saw the weapon, realised she would have no hesitation in firing it at him, wished he was carrying a firearm, and knew he was about to die all in the time it took her to squeeze the trigger. He fell backwards and slid ten feet along the corridor on his own blood blown out the large hole in the centre of his chest. He came to a stop when he crashed into the nurses' reception desk.

Denise leaned over to see him and screamed. When she looked up Stella had both barrels rammed into her face.

"We can do this the easy way, or you can die right here. What's it to be?"

Denise lost control of her bladder, understood the signs of shock her body was sending her, stared into Stella's eyes and crumpled unconscious at her feet.

"That's just great," she moaned in annoyance. Turning round she heard the shouts coming from all the patients' rooms, and could hear sirens piercing through the night sky. She knew she had seconds to find Mary Gage.

Quickly and with great urgency she kicked open any doors where she couldn't look clearly into the room. One by one she ran along the corridor peering at the terrified patients in their beds. Mary Gage was nowhere to be seen.

The last room was empty. Stella could feel her blood boiling. They'd tricked her after all. Furious she made her way back onto the stairs and jumping down them two or three at a time rushed back out into the car park.

Stella reached her car and climbed in. Her last thought bounced around the inside of her head like an out of control rubber ball. She ran the facts over and over. There had only been one policeman, one nurse, and Mary Gage hadn't been there.

She suddenly realised she'd been right all along, the police hadn't suspected she would try and kill Mary.

Stella grabbed the sides of her head and slumped forward, cracking her forehead on the steering wheel. Mary had been there, she'd just not seen her. Maybe she was hiding in the toilet. All private wards had en-suite bathrooms. Stella groaned loudly before she started the car and heading back to the New Forest.

Pandemonium had broken out at the City General. Chief Superintendent MacDonald, Mark Carter, DS Johnstone and four other detectives had attended within minutes of the call being dispatched.

MacDonald was furious an armed guard hadn't been placed on Mary Gage's door.

"But Gov," said Carter, trying to pacify him whilst glaring at Johnstone, "We didn't think she'd be stupid enough to come here."

MacDonald tried to keep his anger under control. "That's just it. Not one of you gave it much thought; otherwise you'd have planted a guard on her door. Super glued his arse to the seat in fact.

"What do you want us to do know?" he asked dejectedly.

"Find this psycho before she kills anybody else would be a good place to start."

The detectives watched MacDonald storm off along the corridor.

Carter turned to Johnstone with his eyes blazing, "You were told to arrange an armed guard. Why the hell didn't you do it?"

Johnstone had to think quickly or he knew he'd be in serious trouble, possibly even thrown off the case. "After what we talked about the other day, I was certain she wouldn't come here. I tried to find MacDonald to get authorization to issue a weapon, but he'd gone home for the night. I was going to speak to him when he came back. I'm sorry, I just didn't think she'd come here." He looked down at the floor and tried to act guilty, hoping the hang dog attitude would score him some house points.

DC Dodds shrugged his broad shoulders, "Where do we go from here then Gov?" he said, trying to defuse the situation.

"Get the uniform over here pronto. Someone must have

seen her coming or going from the hospital. Somebody must have thought it kind of strange, a woman walking around the hospital grounds carrying a shot gun."

"Do you think anyone did see her then?" Johnstone asked.

"Not really, but it gives them something to do in the meantime, while we think how the hell we're going to catch this cow. Fuck sake Billy, I can't believe you've screwed up this badly."

Johnstone stared down at his feet. He knew the reason why.

Stella drove into the caravan park just as the sun had started to throw fingers of light through the canopy of trees that surrounded the site.

As she bounced in and out of the mud filled ruts which littered the track leading to her van, she checked to see if there had been any new arrivals during her time of inebriation from the world. She was pleased to see nothing, but empty pitches and the three caravans that had been there ever since her arrival.

Stella glanced at the one nearest her own. It belonged to Matt and Elsie whose surname she'd never found out. They were an elderly couple in their seventies and stayed on site for most of the year, only leaving when they ventured to visit their son, now living in Australia. She'd seen them once since her arrival and had exchanged a few words with them. They had no idea who she was and therefore provided no threat to her security. The remaining two were empty and she assumed they were summer plots, deserted and left to gather winter dust.

Parking the hire car which she'd obtained from a less than professional outfit on the outskirts of Southampton, by pretending to cry when asked to produce her driving license and telling them she must have forgotten it when she'd come all the way from Scotland on holiday, therefore could she provide a large cash deposit as security until she had her license posted to her. The thousand pounds she placed on the counter took away any objections the spotted young assistant might have raised at the time. Especially when she'd told him he could keep it for being so nice to her, provided he supplied her with a car.

Stella had phoned the company the previous day to ask if

they'd received her license as yet. When told no, she told them it was on the way, which seemed to satisfy the person she spoke to. She intended to dump the vehicle over the next couple of days anyway.

She grabbed a mug and the three quarter empty bottle of Bells No 8, and poured until the whiskey reached the rim. Slumping down on the couch she drained a third of the fiery liquid in two large mouthfuls and shuddered when it hit her stomach.

Mary was still alive and the police would intensify their efforts to catch her after her visit to the hospital. Time was running out and she had to escape. After all she'd only undertaken her game, safe in the knowledge that when push came to shove, escape was precisely what she intended to do.

44

During the three days since Stella's failed attempt to kill her, Mary had run over the events a dozen times. When she'd heard the gunshot, she'd just finished paying her beautifully decorated en-suite bathroom a visit and was in the process of returning to her bed, which had been proving a difficult task, because she was still linked to a drip and her head still throbbed with such intensity it felt as if a corkscrew was being twisted in her skull every time she moved.

The loud blast, followed by the scream took little more than a second to register in her mind what it all meant. Mary had been clay pigeon shooting on a number of occasions and knew a gun had been fired, the hysterical screaming and distant voices had told her Stella had come to kill her

Ripping the thin tubing from her hand, she'd pushed the trolley away from the bed and crawled underneath. She'd lay still with her eyes shut, trying to pretend that if she couldn't see Stella then Stella couldn't see her. As she'd shaken with fear, cold sweat had run down her back, dripped from her forehead to pool on the hygienically scrubbed floor beneath her quivering frame.

Intense shouting from the corridor outside, had burst into the darkness of her private room, she'd already switched the lights off from her bedside control panel, before taking up her hiding place.

The sound of wood against wall, as each door exploded under the forceful kicks that they were receiving reverberated around her head, the noise sounding like cries of pain in the eerie gloom of Constance Ward.

Mary had felt like a small child trying to hide from the bogey man, knowing he would find her, but having nowhere else to go.

When Stella had entered the room, Mary had taken a large intake of breath, pushed her face into the floor, smelt the disinfectant and tried to tell her heart to stop thumping so loud, for fear of giving her away.

Unable to look up, she'd heard Stella muttering to herself, heard footsteps in front of her, bedclothes being thrown back and a final moan from her intended killer, before silence had descended briefly, until the door to the next room was kicked open.

She'd remained under the bed for what seemed hours, only venturing out when a strong arm reached under and slowly eased her body back into the light, telling her it would be okay now as he was a detective with the Metropolitan Police.

Mary hadn't the nerve to mention she'd supposedly, already been protected by one of his fellow officers, who she assumed was now dead, lying in a pool of blood outside her door.

She found herself shivering as the recollection replayed itself again. Try as she might she couldn't prevent it coming back to haunt her.

Mary couldn't help wondering if Stella would try again, after all she was clearly insane and insane people do totally irrational things.

The doctors had told her she could be released within a day or two and the police had assured her they would give her ample protection, but she knew that if Stella wanted to kill her, she would try again whether she was guarded or not.

Silent tears of fear slowly trickled down her cheeks before dropping onto the crisp white sheets that she'd pulled up around her neck, another memory of safety from her childhood.

Mary wished more than ever to be back in the time when monsters had two heads, were pink in colour and chased you around the garden, instead of stalking you through life, carrying a shotgun and wanting to blow you away.

45

The scream cut into his so far peaceful nights sleep, pulled him up from the depth of darkness with such a start, that when he opened his eyes he momentarily forgot where he was. Rubbing his eyes to remove the crusts of sleep from the corners, he tried to focus on what was causing his girlfriend's hysterical wailing.

When he managed to peer far enough into the gloom, and focus on the far side of his large bedroom, he could see she was being held tightly by two burly men, one on each side.

Mickey leapt from the bed and naked charged across the room to dislodge her captors.

What he'd failed to see was the third man standing in the doorway to the en-suite. As he ran past he was caught with a heavy blow to the top of his skull which rendered him unconscious on impact.

When he awoke much later he found himself on familiar territory, although his head felt as if it belonged elsewhere.

He was sitting on a chair, dressed crudely, with the lights in front of the Panel blazing away at him. Driscol tried to stand up, but found he was heavily strapped to the chair, by both feet and ankles. "What the fuck is this?" he demanded to know.

"You're on trial son, that's what this is."

The voice sounded as if it had come from behind him and he strained his neck to try and see who was back there. He gasped when he saw the room was full of faces he knew. "What's going on?" he asked this time his voice showing signs of fear.

The first voice from one of the Panel members spoke, "Mickey we think you've tried to shaft us. This is your chance to tell us otherwise."

"You've got a strange way of showing it," he said sarcastically.

The second member spoke this time, "Well Mickey if you can't convince us otherwise...then you're screwed son."

The implications of what had been said rammed into his gut and he felt his bowels loosen. "I'm Mickey Driscol for God sake. I'm too big to be sitting here in front of a kangaroo court."

Laughter filled the room until a voice from the front shouted, "Enough!"

Silence returned and a quiet voice spoke from within the bright lights. "Mickey, no doubt your own brother felt the same way right up until the point you placed the gun to his head and pulled the trigger. No-one is too big to suffer the consequences of betrayal."

"But I haven't betrayed anyone," he said in a frantic voice.

"That's what we're here to try and find out. You can start by telling us what you were doing at the nick the other day, and what you were discussing with Billy and Carter."

The fact they knew he'd been into the police station caused grave concern. Who had told them? Had Billy grassed him up?

"I wanted to try and throw them off track regarding all the murders. I thought the more shit they were trying to wade through would make it easier for me...us, to go about our business without the old bill sticking their noses in."

"So what did you tell them?"

He needed to think fast and his brain felt as if it was being suffocated by a large fluffy pillow. Stalling for time he said, "What do you mean?"

"What did you tell them?" an angry voice yelled in his ear.

The loudness of the voice made him jump in the chair and he winced as the bindings cut into his flesh. He couldn't think of anything to say that would make it any easier for him so he told the truth, only bending it slightly. "I told them someone else had killed the two coppers, one of Bernie Reece's men. I thought they'd go off on a wild goose chase and that would give us more time to sort out the mess on the estate and to cover up the involvement within the force itself. I mean maybe it's time we got rid of the coppers we deal with. They're a liability." He felt reasonably confident he'd escaped the net tightening around his neck. The only way they could prove he'd said anything else was if Billy had told them. Smiling smugly he relaxed into the chair.

Silence followed with only the odd murmur from the Panel breaking the eerie atmosphere inside the smoke filled room. Finally when he felt his nerve would break the lights before him went out.

Before him sat three empty chairs, he caught sight of the door directly behind them closing, and heard the faint words as the Panel disappeared from his view. "Take the Judas out of here."

Driscol screamed hysterically after them, "No! I haven't

done anything to you." Then he felt several hands grab at his body along with the chair he was sitting on, felt it being lifted into the air and understood they intended to take him outside still shackled to it.

At the rear of the club he could see a dirty white transit van parked, but with the engine running. He was unceremoniously bundled into the back, the chair falling onto its side, causing him to crack his head on the metal floor. He screamed out in pain.

One of the men who got into the van after him said, "Practice the screaming Mickey, you'll be doing a lot of it soon."

Mickey tried to act the hard man. "Piss off," he said, but deep inside he was trembling like a little boy. He'd been in the game long enough to know he was being driven, tied to a chair, on the floor of a grubby van, to his death.

Johnstone had asked for the meeting with Carter in the hope he could pacify the man's anger towards him. The last thing he needed was to be thrown off the case, where it would be impossible to know what was going on regarding the murders and the C.I.B investigation.

When he entered Carter's office the older man was busily hammering away on the keys to his laptop.

"I'm sorry Sir," Billy began, "I don't really know why I didn't try harder to get the firearms issued. I guess deep down I still couldn't picture Stella Blackmore as a cold blooded killer."

"That's not the point though is it Billy? Whether you believed it or not, I told you to get permission from the Chief to issue firearms. You deliberately disobeyed my instruction."

"But that's just it Sir, I didn't disobey you. I went to see Mr. MacDonald, but he'd gone home. That's when I should have either got in touch with him, or told you what had happened. I thought she'd be safe until morning. I was wrong and I'm sorry. I'll have to live with the young constables' death for the rest of my life."

Carter sighed.

"Are you going to throw me off the case?" he asked in a defeated voice.

"I spoke to Mr. MacDonald about thirty minutes ago. We

need you on the team Billy, you're a good detective. If you screw up again I'll personally see you not only thrown off this case, but thrown out the force. Got it?"

Billy fought back the urge to smile. "Sir," was all he managed to say.

"Get the fuck out of my office Billy," Carter said his voice filled with disappointment.

Billy left feeling like he'd just won the pools.

The van stopped at an old industrial estate on the outskirts of Hendon. Once more they carried him in like one of the Roman gentry or a sick version of the pope. Large iron double doors were pulled shut behind them once the entire party was assembled.

Mickey looked round and saw that the inside of the warehouse they'd entered was empty except for a massive piece of wood abandoned in the centre of the large floor space. Mickey believed it was an uprooted tree trunk. He was surrounded by eight men who he knew worked for the Panel. "So what now?" he asked trying once more to regain his composure.

"Ever seen the film, *The Mummy* Mickey?"

Mickey shook his head. "No. Why?"

"Well in the film one of the Pharaoh's high priests betrays him so he has him executed..."

"I haven't betrayed anyone," Mickey interrupted agitated.

"Shut up you piece of shit and listen. In the film this priest had his tongue cut out so he couldn't scream, then whilst still breathing he was thrown into his coffin and covered with scarab beetles which ate him alive. We couldn't get the beetles."

Loud laughter echoed around the warehouse. Mickey tried to see how he was going to get out of this and knew it was hopeless. "Look, I've got about thirty-five thousand pounds in my safe at home. I know I'm going to die, but if you agree to make it quick, I'll give you the combination. Nobody needs to know."

"I see no reason not to accept your kind offer. Tell me the numbers."

"Okay, fifty-four left, twenty-six right, eighteen right and twelve left. Shoot me now, get it over with." Mickey felt almost relief it would all end soon. He'd been caught out and knew why he had to die. It was an example to others. He, like many before him had underestimated the members of the Panel.

"Okay boys, Mr. Driscol won't have any need for his tongue now. Cut it out."

Mickey's eyes opened wide with horror when he saw three of the men move towards him, one holding a large hunting knife that sparkled even in the low warehouse light.

"You promised me you bastards," Mickey screamed at them as they approached.

Fingers pulled his mouth open, one went inside and he bit down with all his might, he heard the bone snap, heard the man scream in agony, felt he'd got a little of his own back.

Then he felt the knife cut deeply into his cheek, it was his turn to scream and the second he did so, someone grabbed his tongue and pulled it forward where the man holding the knife began to saw through the flesh.

Mickey shook his head violently from side to side, trying to shake them off. More hands came forward to hold his head steady, he felt the skin of his tongue give way, felt his mouth fill with warm blood and made loud mumbling sounds into the air.

He opened his mouth and watched in horror as fountains of blood washed over his chest. Someone came at him from behind and stuck tape over his mouth, wrapping it round his head to prevent it slipping off.

Almost immediately he started to gag. He was going to drown on his own blood.

Mickey would have settled for that if he'd known what was going to happen next.

"Got to make this a good example Mickey my friend. Nothing personal you understand."

Everyone grabbed him and he was cut loose from the chair, he could feel his strength draining away and put up little resistance. He saw the large lump of wood as he was placed beside it. God they were going to burn him.

He could feel himself drifting away, but knew he was being turned upside down. He felt his shoes and socks being removed, closed his eyes as unconsciousness beckoned and then had it snapped back as the agony shot through his body. He'd heard the distant crack that sounded like a gun being fired; now he knew what it really was. He'd been nailed to the wood, through his feet by a nail gun. The bastards were crucifying him upside down. His hands were pulled out below his head but he couldn't struggle such was his weak state. The gun fired and this time he hardly felt any pain. Mickey Driscol knew he was on his way to meet his brother.

46

Elizabeth Brooks sat slumped in her favourite black leather reclining chair, duster in one hand, tin of polish in the other. She ached from head to foot such had been her efforts to clean the layers of dust from the living room furniture.

Normally a very house proud woman, she'd let her standards slip over the past week. She wasn't ill or anything remotely like that, she hadn't got out of bed one morning and found herself, somehow changed into a lazier person, it was just the fact she'd found herself glued to the television set, watching each news bulletin with an almost morbid fascination.

Stella Blackmore had been portrayed, at first as a person who the police were very concerned to trace, having found her husband dead alongside two other people. The police wanted to find her to ascertain if she was aware of the terrible events which had taken place inside the house at Arcadia Drive. She was not a suspect, merely a missing person.

This had all dramatically changed with the announcement she'd murdered a man named Glen Gage and had seriously injured his wife, although when the broadcast was made it had been suggested she was in no danger of dying.

Elizabeth had sat in practically the same position ever since Stella Blackmore had been named as a suspected serial killer. She'd moved only to fetch some nibbles to eat and to visit the bathroom.

Living alone as she did, her husband having died, the result of injuries sustained in a motor car accident, there was no-one to tell her to do anything else. Especially keep the never ending dust at bay.

The advent of the 24 hour news programme had made it a must watch scenario. No way was she going to miss anything important regarding this case.

Fascinated she watched various reports portraying the wanted woman as firstly a bullied wife, someone who was a quiet person who'd kept very much to herself. Someone you would want as a friend. This theme had slowly been eroded to a scheming, deceitful, violent woman who would without mercy murder you where you slept, although the reporter had been careful to point out that none of Stella's victims had been disposed of in such a manner.

Elizabeth watched as photographs from the killers childhood were flashed across the screen, people who went to school with her were interviewed, and residents in Arcadia Drive were asked over and over what they thought had turned her into the monster she'd become.

Whilst digesting all the information that spewed from the set, Elizabeth waited for the moment that would change her life forever, waited with mounting dread for the announcer to reveal who she was.

Days had passed and as yet she had remained a nameless part to the puzzle. Why hadn't they mentioned her? Surely having spoken to so many people, someone out there must have given her name to the police. If so, why hadn't they called round to see her? It was only a matter of time before Stella Blackmore came visiting, she'd never been more sure of anything in her life.

In fact as she watched yet another TV special, she pondered why her sister hadn't called already.

Mark Carter gently rubbed his temples. Nothing was coming together and he felt the case slipping away from him. He'd spoken via the telephone to MacDonald earlier in the day and the news he'd received had gone a long way to create the depressing mood he found himself sitting in.

The Commissioner was threatening to throw both MacDonald and his whole team off the case, replacing them with detectives from Scotland Yard if a result wasn't forthcoming. How long their stay of execution would last hadn't been revealed.

His head felt heavy so he dropped it down onto his desk, feeling the cold from the wooded surface against his skin. His arms hung limply by his sides and he sighed heavily.

"That bad, Sir?" a female voice said over his head.

Sitting up he saw Janet Forsyth grinning before him.

"Something for you to smile about is there, Janet?" he asked before returning his forehead to its earlier cool spot.

"Not really. Just thought I'd pop in a see if you fancied a coffee or perhaps lunch with me."

Carter once again slowly lifted his eyes to meet her eager face, "Lunch?" he said quizzically.

"Yeah you know, sit down, and eat food, lunch."

"Forgive me Janet, but are you asking me out?" Carter teased despite his current apathy.

Janet smiled at him in a way he found sexually teasing, before replying, "Yes, for lunch."

"He straightened in his chair, "What's brought this on?" he asked.

"Nothing really, just thought you could do with being out of the office for a bit. If you don't want to it's no problem."

"But I do want to Janet. I haven't eaten properly for days."

She could see the glint in his eye. Maybe he did fancy her. "Okay, one o'clock all right for you?"

"That would be fine."

Janet smiled at him before leaving the office. The minute she'd shut the door Carter once more lowered his head to the table. It was the comfiest place he'd found all day. Besides he'd just been asked out to lunch by the prettiest detective at the station. Why he wondered had she asked him?

The wind and rain lashed against her windows, sounding strong enough to shatter the glass and carry the occupants away to their own dance with the devil.

Elizabeth, apart from her hurried cleaning frenzy earlier had remained where she'd sat almost constantly since the news of her sister had broken.

She was watching a repeat showing of *Dads Army* which had always been a particular favourite with the sisters, tonight though she found the laughter difficult to find. Channel flicking she tried to find something that would supply her with some form of relief from the tension that now constantly gnawed at her neck and shoulders. Locating nothing equal to the task she, for the first time in what felt like an eternity, switched the television off. The screen disappeared behind its own curtain of darkness, delayed only by the small white dot in the middle, which blinked a personal goodnight to the viewer.

Stretching her tired legs in front of her, she took her arms up over her head and tried to push both ends of her body as far apart as she could, releasing the stiffness from her joints.

Relaxing slightly she got up and walked to the kitchen where she opened the fridge and took out a small packet of turkey slices and a tomato. Buttering two slices of brown bread, she jammed five slices of the meat and the two halves she'd cut the tomato into between them. She poured a long glass of semi-skimmed milk and returned to her leather chair.

Her head buzzed with emotions. Why had Stella killed all those people? What was she trying to prove? Where the hell was she? No matter how she bent the facts, she couldn't come up with any plausible reason for what her sister was doing.

At first she didn't hear the quiet tapping sounds on her front room window, and then it grew stronger and stronger until it sounded like someone playing a drum solo on the panes. Placing her supper down on the arm of the chair she went and peered out the window.

Through the rain she caught sight of the back of what appeared to be a female. She had shocking red hair and was dressed from head to toe in black. Elizabeth spotted the large holdall she had swinging gently from her shoulder

She opened the door to tell the woman to go away, had started to form the words, when the stranger turned around to face her and pushed her way inside.

"All right, Liz?" Stella asked as if she'd seen her every week.

"No it isn't. What the hell are you doing here?"

Stella grinned at her, "That's no way to treat your own flesh and blood."

"Don't give me that bull. When did you last visit me here?"

Stella's grin grew wider, "Just before I married Brian, about a week before I caught you sucking his dick at my wedding."

There had been no anger in her voice which scared Elizabeth even more, just a calming tone answering the question asked.

"You know what happened. I tried to explain at the time."

"Yeah, right. How he'd some sort of power thing over

you, how you couldn't help yourself, how he'd told you we were into swapping and that I wouldn't mind. Yeah, you told me all right, a pile of crap."

Stella made her way into the kitchen and took out the same packet of turkey Elizabeth had used minutes earlier. Without fetching anything else she popped a slice into her mouth. "Tasty," she ventured.

Elizabeth sat down beside her, "So what do you want?"

Stella didn't reply, she continued to eat the turkey, one slice at a time.

"Stella, I asked you what you want."

Stella finished the packet, screwed it into a ball and flicked it at the bin in the corner of the kitchen. "Want! I want you to help me escape."

Elizabeth felt like she'd been punched in the guts repeatedly by Mike Tyson.

"How in God's name do you think I'm going to do that?"

"Easily, that's how," Stella said, the smile on her face bigger than ever.

"Just as easily as you seem to have stayed away from the cops?"

"Even easier than that sweetheart," Stella said smiling.

Elizabeth sat down. "Are you going to share this with me?"

Stella gave her sister a long look before answering, "Later. Now I just want to sleep for a week. I'm bushed."

Elizabeth put her hands on Stella's shoulders and stared at her intently, "I think if you want my help, I'm entitled to know what you have in mind."

Stella pushed her arms away, "Entitled! You lost any rights you had when you started to play around with my husband." She put her face as close as she could get it without touching Elizabeth's before continuing, "I've been very busy as you're no doubt are well aware. Don't think because we're related you will be treated any better if you piss me off more than you already have. Do you get my meaning?"

Elizabeth recoiled to a safer distance, "What, are you going to kill me as well?" she shouted, her voice containing no fear which surprised both sisters.

"Who said anything about killing you? Perhaps I'll just shoot off your legs, just like I did to Brian."

Elizabeth slumped into a chair. "You shot off his legs?" she asked in a shocked tone.

"Not intentionally. I was trying to hit him in the chest. First time I'd had to shoot something that moved. Gun was more powerful than I gave it credit for."

"How did he die then?" Elizabeth asked quietly.

"Left him to bleed to death on the floor where the pig belonged."

Elizabeth raised her eyes to meet Stella's and saw the hatred she'd felt for her husband at the end. It did nothing to ease the nauseous feeling she had in the pit of her stomach. She'd loved Brian Blackmore more than any man she'd ever met, with the exception of her late husband. No man deserved to die as he had, no matter what emotional pain he'd caused Stella by having his affairs. "You could have just left him Stella, got a nice settlement from the divorce. After all how many other men are sleeping around?"

Stella started to laugh in a way Elizabeth had never heard a sane person laugh before. There was no humour in the sound coming from her sister's lips. It was more like the baying sound of an animal. "Stella what's wrong?" she asked, her voice now filled with panic.

Abruptly the high pitched noise stopped. Stella looked at Elizabeth with reddened eyes and in a whispered tone asked, "All those times I spent in hospital with broken ankles, a punctured lung, multitudes of cuts and bruises, black and blue features and a face swollen like a football. How do you think I got there?"

"You fell down the stairs!" she answered in an equally quiet voice.

Stella let a few notes of the creepy laugh leave her lungs, "I was thrown, punched and kicked there by the man you slept with."

"Never," shouted Elizabeth in response to the allegation.

"Think about it. How many times was I there? How often can someone with half a brain fall down the same flight of stairs? Why was he always beside me in hospital? Even coming with me when I needed a pee, on the few occasions I was still able to walk. Think hard, Liz. Think very hard."

She knew the truth already, just didn't want to admit to herself that Stella was right. "You still could have left," she said in a feeble way.

Stella knew her sister would try and put a blanket over what her beloved brother-in-law had done. She also was aware Elizabeth knew she'd told the truth. "So you're going to help me then?" she said, knowing it wasn't a question, but an order.

Elizabeth nodded in defeat. What else could she do?

Stella walked to the window and drew back the heavy velvet curtains, which hung from long, wooden Indian carved rails and peered out. Very little movement could be detected. She hadn't disturbed any of the neighbours on her arrival and no police cars had slowly crept up on the house. Feeling safe she turned to where Elizabeth still sat and said, "I'm going for a lie down. Don't try and do anything stupid or I will hurt you Liz, please don't think I won't. This has gone a long way and I won't let it rest until I'm away from here. Understand?"

"Yes," Elizabeth replied, scared by the stranger in front of her.

"Clever girl," Stella said sarcastically, before climbing the stairs to the bedroom.

Left alone Elizabeth started to cry.

47

Carter had telephoned the office using the shiny jet black Bat phone his five year old niece, Emily, had given him the previous Christmas. It now had pride of place on his bedside table and he found himself involuntary smiling as he'd made the call.

Four hours had passed since he'd told MacDonald he'd be taking the day off work, owing to a severe migraine that had crept up during the night.

He was still lying fully clothed on top of the bed clothes, staring up at the aertex covered ceiling. There was no headache, not now and not earlier. He'd needed space and time on his own, away from the hustle and bustle of a busy CID office to think things through.

Carter had joined the Metropolitan Police Force, three weeks after his eighteenth birthday and had been involved in a love affair with the job ever since. It had been all he'd ever wanted to do as a boy growing up in London, and he'd told his career master at Grovebury Secondary School he wanted to study the relevant subjects, that if passed, would enable him to gain entrance to the force without the need for any examinations.

Having played football, rugby and badminton for his County, he'd found the physical examination very easy, the medical had also been a breeze.

Quickly he'd found himself at Hendon Training College participating in the sixteen week selection course, after which he was posted to Kilburn Police Station to complete his two year probationary period.

From the start Carter wanted to be a detective, setting his stall out before him, he'd spent three years learning the trade on the crime squad at West Hendon before achieving his ambition in May 1984, nearly six years after he'd joined.

In 1986 he passed the Sergeant examination and had become a Detective Inspector in 1991.

During his twenty-two years service he'd investigated many cases, ranging from armed robbery, murder, rape, and sexually-orientated crimes. He'd never been involved with someone like Stella Blackmore.

He lay with his hands beneath his head, slowly running the facts of the case through like a well oiled-machine, taking one piece of the puzzle at a time, deliberating whether it was of any use or not.

If ever there had been a person he needed to put inside for the rest of their life, it was her. With one act, he would gain revenge for Mandy's death, get more job satisfaction than he'd ever dreamt of and once more regain control of his emotions, which were stretched like an elastic band waiting to snap.

He could remember the names of drug dealers, robbers, rapists, major villains he'd been responsible for locking up. None of them had caused him more personal pain, or more frustration.

How could this woman stay out there so long without capture?

What had changed her from housewife to murderer?

No stone had gone unturned in their efforts to bring her to justice, but so far all they'd managed was a fleeting glimpse of their prey.

Carter let out a long sigh. Yesterday he was sure they'd been given the information that would lead them to her. The manager of a local Southampton Hire Company called *Driveaway*, a Mr. Tom Wilson, had been horrified to find that one of his staff had hired out a vehicle to a member of the public without having first seen their driving license. The employee had apparently been given a large amount of money to keep if he released the car. From the man's description they'd ascertained Stella Blackmore had been the person responsible. The manager had sacked the worker and the Southampton police were looking into the offences concerned.

Carter and his team had descended on the area like a flock of hungry vultures. The car had been found abandoned less than three hours later, parked in a child's bay at a *'Toys R Us'* superstore. It'd been cleaned before being left to rust.

Carter shut his eyes tightly and allowed the days events to replay in his head.

Disillusioned the officers had gone to a local pub to discuss the next step. Carter and Grady had been standing at the bar when Detective Jason Sharpe had said, "You know Gov there are loads of camp sites around here. I've stayed at a few with the wife and kids. Thick forests surround most of them. Could be she's hiding in a caravan somewhere."

Carter had felt it had all fallen into place with that one observation.

Stella's caravan had been located when uniform officers interviewing the many occupants, spoke to Mr. & Mrs. Matt and Elsie Turner, an elderly couple who although couldn't name the lady in the caravan opposite their own, described Stella perfectly.

Carter remembered the words that came across his personal radio, "Inspector Carter from 345 receiving. We've found Stella Blackmore's caravan."

He closed his eyes and was instantly taken back to the raid on the caravan.

The thin fibre glass door provided little resistance to the heavy set detective who forced it open with his shoulder. Inside looked like a war zone, empty and partially-filled wine bottles were strewn around the combined space as if part of an elaborate collection of modern art. Crisp packets littered the floor looking like multi-coloured leaves from an exotic plant, several layers of dust had coated the entire interior surface making the place surreal, perhaps resembling the after effects of nuclear fallout.

One of the officers had found abandoned on the bed a single sheet of A4 note paper on which someone had doodled small intricate flowers in the middle of the page, the outside of which was bordered with the name of Mary Gage, written over and over in thick block capitals.

Carter had snatched the paper from him, while at the same time dialing the station, where he'd ordered extra armed officer's to guard Mary Gage in case Stella tried to kill her again. He'd been unable to prevent himself from looking at Billy Johnstone the whole time he'd been on the phone.

Carter recalled feeling the excitement rising in his team as each new discovery added another piece of evidence against their fugitive.

He sighed out loud as he recalled just how short the elation had lasted. Soon it had come to light that she'd left nothing to suggest where she was, or indeed what her next course of action would be. Once again she seemed to have slipped through their grasp.

Carter rolled over onto his right side, and groaned with frustration. The only positive achievement they'd completed the previous day, had been to seal off one of Stella Blackmore's hiding places.

The work carried out since had left him feeling more depressed and flat than at any time he could recall during his career. Endless door-to-door enquiries, news bulletins, countless statements being read and reread, outside agencies adding more men to the case, informants being promised the earth to deliver any information that would lead to Stella's arrest, had all resulted in dead ends.

He allowed a grin to pass his lips as he decided she was being as elusive to them as the *Scarlet Pimpernel* had been to the French. "They seek her here, they seek her there...," he said in a humourless voice.

Tossing himself over onto his left side with such ferocity he almost bounced off the edge of the bed, he once more let out a long groan, "Where the hell are you Stella? Is someone giving you a place to hide?"

Carter restless in his quest rolled onto his back and resumed tracing around the pattern in the plastering with his alert eyes. The United Kingdom was a very big island and unless Stella Blackmore decided to commit another murder, he believed it was possible for her to disappear completely.

"God help us," he muttered before closing his eyes, hopeful of sleeping the rest of the day away, perhaps dreaming she'd been captured, and awakening to find his dearest wish had indeed come true.

Thin trails of steam wafted up from the bowl of hot country vegetable soup, like fingers waving a temperature warning.

Elizabeth unconsciously watched them dance before her as she twirled her spoon around the lumps of carrot and potato. She failed to see them reach a certain height before disappearing from view forever. She was too engrossed in her current situation, numb with shock that her sister was a multiple murderer and now slept soundly upstairs as if nothing untoward had happened.

The clock on the kitchen wall had moved on slowly, and now the hands read 8am. She wondered if she could, should, contact the police.

Questions rattled around her head.

How could she live with herself if she didn't turn her in?

Would Stella *really* hurt her if she tried?

It would be easy to dial 999, or to open the back kitchen door, run into the street and scream for help...and yet. Blood is thicker than water so they say; she felt she owed Stella something for the affair with her husband, but did her guilt warrant hiding a killer or helping her escape justice?

She finally lifted the spoon to her mouth and sucked in some soup. It'd gone cold, but she didn't notice.

The threat had sounded real enough, but could she really believe Stella would harm her? After all she could have just killed her like the others. There again she'd said she needed Elizabeth's help to escape. Stella hadn't said how she could help her get away and Elizabeth hadn't a clue what was going to happen next.

Without realising she'd finished her meal and scraped the bottom of the empty bowl. Looking down she tutted, got up and poured the remaining half a tin into her bowl before placing it in the microwave and pressing two minutes on the timer.

Why she was eating soup this early in the day hadn't really been a question. Perhaps the arrival of her sister had shaken her up more than she cared to admit.

As she ate, Elizabeth stood at the bay window watching various people leaving for work. She saw the postman coming down Mrs. Stevens drive and caught his gaze as he glanced in her direction. Momentarily she went to mouth the word '*help*' to him, but as soon as she thought it the inclination passed her by. Briefly she waved at him before sitting down on the cream leather couch.

Stella had always been such a quiet child and had grown up exactly the same. Her current behaviour was totally out of character. This worried Elizabeth more than anything else. How could she trust her instinct where Stella was concerned, if the woman asleep upstairs was now a virtual stranger to her?

She put the bowl down on the oblong coffee table and slumped back into the couch. She felt like she wanted to cry, but her eyes refused to allow tears to fall. Her heart ached for her sister and it was now that she realised she'd have to do anything she asked of her. If she could help her escape she would. After all what else could she do? If she refused maybe, just maybe she'd die like the others. Her life wasn't everything she wanted it to be, but she knew more than anything else, she didn't want it to end.

When Stella came downstairs she found her sister slumped on her side, arm trailing the floor, dribbles of saliva trickling down her chin. She looked as if she'd been drinking heavily and fallen unconscious. Glancing round, she laughed when her eyes fell on the empty bowl on the table, she put her sisters condition down to severe lack of sleep brought on no doubt by her arrival. "Silly bitch probably sat up all night worrying whether I was going to kill her or not," she mumbled before going to the kitchen to fix herself something to eat.

She pulled out a twelve pack of *Walkers Crisps* and chose a bag of Smokey Bacon. Hungrily she tore open the seal and rammed a handful of the crisps into her mouth. More than half broke on impact and fell to the floor, Stella trying hard to catch them as they fell. Owing to her hunger it didn't take long to consume the packet so she opened another bag, this time Cheese and Onion. Taking greater care she popped the crisps in one by one.

Having finished she took out a bottle of semi-skimmed milk, gave the top a quick sniff to make sure it was okay and then downed the remaining half pint in four large gulps. Wiping residue from her chin she went back into the lounge and gave Elizabeth a gentle kick.

"Wakey, wakey," she said in a loud voice at the same time

as throwing herself down on the couch beside Elizabeth, pushing her outstretched legs out the way as she did so.

Elizabeth grunted like a pig and partially opened her eyes, "Go away, I want to sleep," she mumbled.

"Should have gone to bed earlier then, shouldn't you?" Stella teased.

"Yeah right, I could sleep really well with a mass murderer in my bed."

Stella roared with laughter causing Elizabeth to haul herself upright and stare at her with a worried expression.

"What?" Stella asked between fits of the giggles.

"You okay? I mean *really* okay?"

Stella stopped laughing, "You mean am I nuts, right?"

"Well are you?"

"Do I look nuts?"

Elizabeth opened her mouth to speak, and then closed it firmly shut, making Stella feel very uncomfortable under her glare, "Well do I?" she asked in a demanding voice.

"Probably not," Elizabeth replied.

"Probably, what the hell does that mean?" Stella asked angrily.

"Well you're not what *I'd* call off your head, but someone else might. Jesus Stella, you've killed people."

"They were pieces of shit," Stella responded defiantly.

"Others may see things differently."

"Why should I care what others think? It's not my problem is it?"

Elizabeth wanted to scream that of course it was her problem. After all she was the one who'd killed them, but she felt something that told her to hold her tongue, not to antagonise her sister when clearly, she was unstable and on the brink of blowing up.

"Okay, what do you want me to do, Stella?" she asked appealingly.

"Do! What do you mean, do?"

Elizabeth could feel the volatile atmosphere descending over them, and knew Stella was elsewhere, "What do you want me to do to help you get away?" she dared to ask.

"Nothing," Stella offered as a surprising reply.

Elizabeth slowly shook her head from side to side. She was confused by Stella's non-committal attitude. After last night's conversation she expected to be part of an elaborate escape plan. "I don't understand," she said sounding like a lost schoolgirl asking a teacher to go over her homework again.

"There's nothing to understand really. Not yet anyway. All I want to do is rest up for a while, do nothing I need to get my head round the next steps. That okay with you?"

Elizabeth nodded. What could she say? She already knew it would be futile to resist, may even lead to her death. Shrugging her shoulders she stood up and said quietly, "Let me fix you something hot for breakfast. Then we can watch a bit of telly like we used to. What do you say?"

Stella said nothing; she just looked up into Elizabeth's tired eyes and smiled.

Both sisters knew time would pass slowly between them.

48

The *Hinge n Bracket Public House* sat in a quiet part of Camden Town. Billy Johnstone and Mike Grady had decided on a night out to ease the pressure he felt under and also to discuss the situation so far.

"You were a lucky bastard he didn't chuck you off the case."

"Close call, luckily I'm a damn fine detective."

Mike laughed, "So oh mighty one, seeing as you're still with us, what's the latest on your sabotage job?"

"You wouldn't believe me if I told you. So I won't."

"Oh come on don't be shy," said Mike as he took a large mouthful from his pint of beer.

"Let's just say, I have a hunch on how she intends to get away with it."

Mike spluttered into the foam sitting on top of his pint causing it to swirl into the air and land on Billy's lap.

"Careful you idiot," Johnstone moaned loudly.

"Sorry mate, but you took me by surprise there."

"Not difficult is it?" Billy said sarcastically.

"That's not very nice."

"Come on I'm only joking, stop being so touchy. Anyway it's your turn to get them in." Billy waved his empty glass in Mike's face.

"Same again?" he asked.

"No, get me a whiskey this time. Make it a large one.

With all the money you'll make from running the Estate you can afford it."

Mike remained seated. "I want to talk to Mickey before I go in and arrange a new dealer. I have Sally Smithers sorted and also Neville Townsend, but I want to run them past Mickey first. Trouble is I haven't been able to reach him and there's a drop to be made on Tuesday."

"Have you tried him at the pub?"

"Yeah, pub, house and personal mobile. No answers and none of his lads know where he is."

"Probably down at the Maverick Club then, sorting through the books."

"No, phoned there first. Nobody has seen him since yesterday afternoon."

"Strange," Billy said as he tried to think where else the gangster could be.

"You don't suppose...no."

"What?" Billy demanded.

"It's her again do you?"

"Her?"

"Stella Blackmore," Mike whispered.

Billy burst into hysterical laughter. Mike joined him.

"Paranoid or what?" Billy said between intakes of breath.

"Might be."

"No chance, Mickey wouldn't fall for any set ups she'd come up with."

"I'd have said that about Brian and Tony if you'd asked me earlier," Mike said in an attempt to score house points.

Billy said nothing in response to the last statement, merely waved his glass again. This time Mike went to the bar to order their drinks. While he was there Billy wondered about Mickey Driscol and Stella Blackmore. As Mike returned, he thought he heard Billy say "*Nah*."

The distant ringing of Carter's front door bell slowly penetrated his mind, bringing him out of the deep sleep he'd drifted into earlier. His eyes snapped awake and he flicked a glance at his wrist watch. The luminous hands told him it was quarter to seven. He'd been asleep for over five hours. The ringing sounded far louder. Rising from the bed he went to open the door, shouting, "I'm coming, I'm coming." as he went.

Standing on the front step was Detective Janet Forsyth. She was dressed in casual black trousers and had on a cream woollen jumper that clung to her breasts invitingly. Her usually tied back strawberry blonde hair flowed freely around her shoulders, giving her face a much younger look than her twenty five years normally provided.

She stood smiling at him, allowing him to study her, knowing he liked what he saw. "Well," she finally said, "Are you going to make me stand on the doorstep all night?"

Carter shook himself as if trying to snap out of a dream, "Sorry Janet, I was fast asleep. Guess I'm still there. Come in please." He waved a hand at the room behind him, moving to one side to allow her to pass, felt her brush against his body and took in the sweet perfume she wore. "What brings you here?" he asked her to her back, closing the door behind him.

"Billy told me you were sick so I thought I'd pop round after work and see how you're doing. After all we had a lunch appointment, or had you forgotten?"

Carter had let it slip his mind because he'd wanted time to think about how he'd felt about Janet. Mandy had barely been placed in the ground and yet he found himself growing attracted towards her. It was obvious she was making a play for him and try as he might, he was finding it very hard to resist. Perhaps, he'd rationalised it down to the fact his relationship with Mandy was less than perfect at the time of her death.

"I'd not forgotten. I just felt so lousy this morning I was going to leave a message for you. That's the part that slipped my mind, especially as I fell asleep."

"Oh well I suppose I'll let you off just this once," She said sarcastically before adding, "How do you feel now?"

"Better, head and neck still ache a little though."

"Sit down on that chair over there," she pointed at the tall wooden stool beside the kitchen table, "I'll give you a massage."

"Can you do them?" Carter asked in a surprised tone.

Janet laughed a brief chuckle, "Not too difficult is it really. Come on take your shirt off."

Carter removed the badly creased shirt he'd fallen asleep in, and sat on the stool. Janet moved behind him and he felt her cool hands on his skin, causing him to shiver.

"Cold," she joked.

"I've felt warmer ice cubes," he joked.

"Shouldn't have left me standing in the cold for ages then."

"Fair point, but maybe the icy sensation will ease my pain," he said in a sarcastic voice.

"I can do other things to help you forget that," Janet said as she slowly slid her hands over his shoulders and down over his chest.

Carter jumped to his feet so suddenly he pushed the stool backwards where it hit Janet on the shin. "Ouch," she cried.

"I'm sorry Janet. Look, please don't take this the wrong way, but I can't carry on with where this is leading. Not yet anyway."

As soon as he said the last three words he realised he'd said the wrong thing.

"Not yet! What's that supposed to mean?"

"There are things you don't know about me, things that might put you off getting involved."

"Please tell me you're not the murderer," she pleaded in a jovial manner.

"Don't be daft. No seriously, I really like you. In fact I like you more than I should, considering... You'll just have to trust me on this one. Maybe when Stella Blackmore is locked away I'll be able to tell you the things I feel you should know."

Janet nodded, resigned to her fate, "Hey take your time. I'm not going anywhere. I think we could be good together."

"So do I," agreed Carter.

"Can we still go out, you know as friends?" she asked hopefully.

"Of course we can. In fact let me have a shower and I'll take you for a curry or something. I haven't eaten all day."

"Can I rub your back?" she asked cheekily.

"Tempting," Carter shouted as he left her standing in the kitchen while he went to clean himself up.

Stella and Elizabeth spent the next two days in deep conversation. Surprisingly the topic of Stella being a murderer hardly drew a mention.

The sisters talked about their childhood, growing up in and around the suburbs of London. They discussed the night Stella found their mother, dead in her bed having suffered from a massive coronary only six months after their father had died in a pool of his own vomit, after one drink too many.

They talked about the times one or both of them had been subjected to his vicious temper for no more than a minor misdemeanor, the occasion of *the* famous party, where both sisters had lost their virginity's to boys *ages* older than they'd been.

Elizabeth smiled at that recollection, "He wasn't that bad looking either was John. Your guy was a pig," she teased.

"Bloody cheek, he may've had a few spots, but that was all that was wrong with him."

"A few spots," Elizabeth shouted. "He could've been a living dot to dot."

Stella burst into laughter, which caused Elizabeth to gaze in astonishment at the woman sitting before her, wrapped up in the humour of the moment and yet the person responsible for so much death and misery.

Stella was oblivious to her sisters' intent glare as the tears carried on rolling down her cheeks. He'd been a pretty ugly kid, but when Elizabeth had confided in her she'd gone and had sex for the first time, there was no way she could let the rest of the night pass without living a similar experience. She'd grabbed the first boy who'd walked past her, dragging him outside and demanding from the bewildered youth that he deflower her, and quickly.

The laughter slowly died down, Stella wiped away the few remaining tears and said, "God that was as a funny night. I must have had a shag within a minute of you telling me you'd done the business. Wonder when I lost my pulling power?"

Elizabeth knew the answer. It was a few years later when she'd met her future husband Brian. He'd wrapped his arms around her so tightly it was difficult to breathe. It was an obsession that had always intrigued her. He was allowed to do anything he wanted and yet if Stella so much as breathed too heavily he brought his own form of justice down on her head, sometimes literally.

Elizabeth tutted to herself, why had she kept her eyes so tightly shut when deep down she knew her sister was suffering so much. Worse, how could she have committed the ultimate betrayal?

"Penny for your thoughts," Stella asked.

"Oh you know, mind just back there somewhere in time, that's all."

"Don't give me the bullshit my girl. You were miles away. Come on spill the beans."

"I was just thinking about all that's happened and why it's come to this. How the hell did we get here Stella?"

Stella threw herself back in her chair and looked up at the heavens before leaning as far forward as she could, closing the gap between them. "I let a man rule my life for far too long. I let him abuse me, beat me and allowed him to throw me to his friends as some form of sexual play thing. I'd ceased to exist as a human being. I was a nothing, a pile of crap. Nobody knew who I was, nobody cared. Then Elizabeth, I woke up."

"But why did you have to kill, not just Brian, but the others as well?"

"Easy really, when I sat down and thought it all through I realised that although he was the one who'd laid hands on me, all the others were almost equally to blame. Some gave him the drugs that made him violent or sexually aggressive and led him to threesomes and sick fantasies. Others participated in his games, taking him further away from me and closer down his own track to hell. Not one of the bastards gave a second thought to whether or not they were ruining my life. Not one."

"But did they know Stella? Did he tell any of them you were sitting at home waiting for him to come back?"

"Maybe he did, maybe he didn't. Some of the bastards knew because he let them shag me after he'd drugged me to my eyeballs. Christ Liz don't you think I suffered enough?"

"Stella, it's not that at all. Of course you've suffered, but to kill these people. Oh God Stella, what've you done?"

Stella saw the wetness appear on her sisters' face, stood up and walked around the table to where she was sitting. Gently she placed an arm around her shoulders and pulled her close. Leaning down to whisper in her ear she said, "I've made myself whole again."

"You'll go to prison for the rest of your life when they catch you."

"*When* is a very big word sometimes. Anyway I like to think of it as *if* they catch me. You see dear Elizabeth, like I said the other day. You're going to help me beat them. It's us against the world."

Elizabeth looked up at her smiling sister and again caught sight of the stranger she'd become, "This is all a game to you now," she said in an annoyed tone.

"Game! No, it was never that Liz, more a quest. A quest to clean myself of the filth I've lived in for far too long. Not a game because games can be lost. I don't intend to lose anything here, nothing at all."

Stella left Elizabeth sitting in her chair, both confused and frightened by the prospect of the task she was going to be asked to perform, even though she had no inclination as to what she was going to be expected to do.

As Stella made her way back upstairs to the bedroom intending to have another lie down, she smiled to herself as she pondered how the future events may look if her sister downstairs knew the awful truth, that she'd been the driver of the hit and run accident in which her husband had died. Retribution at the time had tasted so sweet.

Stella's smile grew broader as realisation dawned that even earlier in her life she'd the capacity to cold-heartedly seek revenge, and the ability to be a killer.

The *Himalaya* Restaurant was filled to the brim with different groups of people. In all the time Carter had been coming here, he'd never seen it so busy. The head waiter told him that there was a large computer convention on in town and that he also had two hen nights and a fortieth birthday party going on. He did state however that because Carter was a regular he would find a table somewhere for them.

In fact owing to the packed nature of the restaurant they'd been forced to set one up especially for them in a far corner.

"Very romantic," Janet said, smiling seductively at him.

"Yeah, isn't it just? I've never been here when it's been so busy. Still this is probably the best seat in the house."

Carter looked deeply at the woman sitting opposite him. His emotions were bubbling just under the surface and he could feel a tight sensation around his chest. His girlfriend was dead, he was hunting her killer and yet here was an attractive fellow police officer still coming on to him and he could feel himself rising to the bait. "Janet, you're a bad woman..."

"I try to be," she interrupted him.

"What I mean is you don't give up very easily do you?"

"Never have, never will. If I want something, or someone

I go all out to get it or them. I don't believe in pussy footing around. Life's too short."

The last sentence cut him to the core. Mandy's life had certainly been snuffed out several decades early. He understood what Janet meant because he'd believed in similar philosophies earlier in his career, before the climb up the promotion ladder abruptly came to a halt. Before the relationship he'd been in had started to drift away to the sham it had become.

Janet sensed the change in his mood, "You okay?" she asked worriedly.

"Sorry just thinking about something."

"Something or *someone*?" she asked quizzically.

"Bit of both really."

"Want to tell me about them?" she suggested hopefully.

"Another time maybe, let's live by your rules of life being too short. This might be the last chance we get to eat a proper meal for days if we catch Stella Blackmore soon."

"A very good point Sir, if I may say so."

"Creep," Carter teased.

"I didn't get to where I am today without being a creep, Sir," Janet said in a stiff upper lip sort of voice.

Both giggled happily. Carter who'd placed his hands on the table felt her fingers search him out and tenderly wrap themselves around his hand. He badly wanted to snatch his hand away, but somehow he found he couldn't do it. He was enjoying the touch of female skin caressing his own.

"Let's eat," Janet said smiling brightly before breaking her grip.

Carter lost in the moment stumbled out a reply, "Oh yeah, sure. What do you fancy?"

"I'm not into very hot food, so anything that leaves the skin on the roof of my mouth."

"So you want madras then?"

"But of course...Not," Janet played along.

Carter studied the menu like a student looking over a final exam paper before he finally suggested various dishes he felt Janet would enjoy. Janet wanting to make a good impression went along with all his choices.

"So," she said between mouthfuls of Chicken Korma, "Do you think we'll catch her?"

Putting his fork down on top of his heaped plateful of special fried rice, butterfly prawns, onion bajee and beef dupiaza, Carter thought for a second before replying. "I think she's close. Stella knows we're closing in and unless she plans to go underground, hiding for the rest of her life, I believe she'll slip up sooner rather than later."

"Do you believe all the nice things people have said about her, I mean all her neighbours and family friends we've spoken to think she's an angel, whose led a very hard life with her hubby. None of them can come to terms with what she's done."

With a half-filled mouthful of food, Carter answered the question, "I think somewhere along the line she's flipped and totally lost the plot. Now what caused her to do so?" He shrugged before continuing, "We might never find out. What I'd like, is for her to tell us why she's killed all these people. Perhaps then everyone else will understand who this woman really is, or who she has become."

Janet ate some food whilst pushing her rice into a large pile in the centre of her plate.

"Not enjoying it?" Carter asked concerned he'd chosen wrongly.

"Yes, it's delicious. Great choice, I always play with my food when I'm thinking. It used to drive my folks mad when I was younger. Probably still does, but I don't see them that often anymore."

He detected a hint of sadness in her voice, "I'm sorry. Can I ask why not?"

"Oh there's nothing to be sorry about really. It's my choice. They still treat me like a little girl when I'm there, drives me nuts."

"That's because you *are* their little girl."

"God, you sound like my granny."

"Don't know if I should take that as a compliment or the worse insult anybody has thrown my way," he said in a playfully hurt tone.

"Well, let's just say…"

The bleep from Carter's personal pager cut across her sentence. He looked down at the number on the small dial, "It's the station. Dig in, I've left my mobile in the car. Order me another shandy and I'll be back in two ticks."

"No problem," she called to his back as he quickly made his way from the restaurant.

He'd been gone no more than a couple of minutes when

the door to the Indian burst open and he came running across the floor towards her, grinning from ear to ear.

"What?" she shouted before he got within reach.

People at the various tables all stopped eating and watched the man grab the woman under the arms, whisper something in her ear and rush her from the restaurant, throwing a handful of notes at one of the waiters as they left.

Once outside Janet turned to him and said, "Did I catch you right? Stella
Blackmore has just given herself up."

His beaming smile gave her the answer, "I wonder why." She asked more to herself than Carter.

"Come on. Let's go find out." he replied as he took hold of Janet's elbow and steered her towards his car.

49

The journey back to the station passed in a blur of neon light and evening traffic noise, as Janet Forsyth forced their vehicle between the seemingly endless queues of weary drivers, hoping to make it home before their bodies gave up the struggle after yet another busy London working week.

Carter had his forehead leaning against the passenger window and seemed blissfully unaware as his head continually bumped the glass each time Janet deviated from her course.

"God this is so exciting," she said between tooting her horn at the elderly driver in front of her. "I can't wait to see what the bitch looks like."

Her use of the word *bitch* surprised Carter, as normally Janet was a fairly quiet officer who tried to be nice to everyone, be they police or criminal. It was the first time to his knowledge he'd heard her sounding angry towards Stella Blackmore. "Thought you didn't like miscalling suspects," he mentioned casually.

"Sorry, don't know where that came from really. Just seems to suit her bearing in mind what she's done."

"And you were asking earlier if I believed all the sickly sweet things her friends had said."

"Ah, but that's different. I was using the bitchy term myself."

"Suppose there's female logic in there somewhere," Carter said sarcastically.

The dig in his ribs made him sit up straight, rubbing his injured side, "Hey, what was that for?" he asked in mock discomfort.

"For being a patronising git, Sir," Janet replied as she maneuvered the car through a tight space between an artic lorry and a black taxi cab.

"Ever think about rally driving?"

"Are you asking for another dig?"

"Not if the first one was anything to go by," Carter moaned as he placed his forehead back on the cooling glass.

The car sped on its journey, he could feel the tension and excitement creeping up from his lower back, spreading outwards from his spine, could feel his throat start to tighten up as his saliva dried out, felt the tightness around his chest and wondered if he'd be able to control his temper when he finally met the person responsible for murdering Mandy.

How would it feel sitting opposite Stella Blackmore? Could he stop himself beating her to a pulp regardless of the fall out afterwards? Did he dare to be left alone with her?

His mind raced along almost as quickly as the police car. "How long before we get there?" he asked restlessly.

"Couple of minutes at most, you champing at the bit?"

He didn't reply, just shook his head slowly from side to side.

"Yeah right," came the response from the seat beside him, causing him to laugh under his breath. Janet had a way about her that was growing on him all the time. She seemed to know exactly what to say in response to whatever he said or did.

Carter smiled out the window. His agonies would start to heal soon. In less time than it took to boil an egg, he'd be sitting opposite Stella Blackmore. He couldn't think of anything else in his entire life that he'd ever wanted this badly.

Stella Blackmore sat in the interview room, consisting of a table and four chairs, a tape recording machine and a pile of forms, so high you could hardly see the person sitting in front of you.

She'd been formally cautioned and asked if she'd wanted her solicitor present. Stella had smiled when her answer of *no* had registered in the faces of the two detectives present.

Johnstone and Grady sat in silence before her, having returned in response to a page message received whilst buying their third drink. Luckily, they hadn't started it and didn't smell too strongly of alcohol. Billy had swallowed a whole packet of Polo mints on his journey to the station, much to Mike's amusement. They'd asked a couple of questions, but Stella had remained silent. It had been pointed out to her, that her silence could go against her in a court of law. She'd shrugged her shoulders casually as if rejecting the idea as unimportant.

When Carter and Forsyth arrived at the station they quickly asked the desk sergeant what had happened.

"Well Gov, she just walked up to me and said her name was Stella Blackmore and that we wanted to talk to her. I didn't say much, just called Billy Johnstone on the quick like. They're in interview room two at the moment with, Detective Grady."

"Thanks John," Carter said before turning to Janet. "Listen could you go and grab everything we've got regarding evidence that'll put her at the scenes of the crimes. Make sure you bring the Mary Gage statement. I can't wait to see her face when I show her that little beauty."

"Can you please wait until I get back before you start the interview. I'd love to listen in."

Carter paused for dramatic effect. "Well normally two of us would be enough, but seeing as it's you, I'll make an exception. Just hurry back here with the papers."

Janet turned and ran along the corridor, preventing Carter from seeing the smug victory smile that slowly spread across her lips. She was going to date a Police Inspector and already it was providing dividends.

His first impression when he opened the door to interview room two and walked in, was that Stella Blackmore was far prettier than he'd imagined.

Her red spiky crop gave her a 70's punk look, deep brown eyes watched his entrance intently and she was a lot trimmer than the mental picture he'd painted. She looked as different from a murder suspect as you could imagine.

He already knew a jury would sympathise with any abuse defense her counsel put forward. She looked like you could knock her over by shouting in her general direction. Her appearance unnerved him.

Both Johnstone and Grady went to stand up as he entered the room, but were quickly told not to bother by his raised hand. Billy Johnstone was the first to speak, "Mrs. Blackmore has been cautioned and offered her rights to a phone call and a solicitor. She's declined at this stage to enforce these rights and, in fact, has refused to answer any preliminary questions we've put to her. This is despite being told it could go against her in court should it reach that stage."

Carter gave him a look that said *oh there's no doubt she'll end up in court, in prison, and for the rest of her life.*

"Mrs. Blackmore, do you understand the seriousness of the situation you're in?" Carter asked as he pulled out a chair and sat down.

No reply.

"We have reason to believe you were involved in the deaths of your husband Brian, WPC Mandy Burrows, Scenes of Crime Officer Tony Asque, civilian Annie Walsh, an unidentified male, solicitor Meredith Rogers, civilians Teresa Day and Glen Gage and the attempted murder of Mary Gage. What do you want to say to me regarding these allegations?"

A long pause was followed by an even longer shoulder rise from Stella.

Carter could feel his anger rising, "Mrs. Blackmore we can't help you unless you speak to us."

Stella shrugged again.

"Okay, if that's how you wish to play it for now, perhaps some time of quiet contemplation might help you see sense. Mike put Mrs. Blackmore down in the cells would you?"

Johnstone was surprised at how quickly Carter had terminated the interview. He was also impressed at how calm he seemed considering the length of time they'd been searching for their elusive prisoner.

Grady gently helped Stella from her chair and with his hand tightly secured around her upper arm, led her away.

"What do you think of that then?" Billy Johnstone asked.

Carter sighed and rubbed the base of his neck. "She seems one hell of a cool customer. It might take ages before she opens up."

"So you think she'll talk then?"

"Sure, why not? Lets face it she'd be bloody stupid not to.

The court will see her silence as practically a confession of her guilt. Unless she wants to just be locked up for the rest of her life, she'll talk soon enough."

As soon as he'd finished answering the question, Carter felt a sickly feeling in the pit of his stomach that maybe she wouldn't talk, perhaps all she wanted to do now *was* to be locked away and forgotten about.

He was enjoying a coffee when Chief Superintendent MacDonald came rushing up to him, "Great news, huh!"

Carter raised his eyes and saw the overwhelming relief in his bosses face. "Certainly is," he said before taking another sip from his drink.

"You don't sound as pleased as I thought you'd be Mark. Is something wrong? Anything you need to tell me?"

"Not really. It's just she's playing dumb or games. I haven't been able to work out which yet."

"Probably realised she's in a whole world of pain," MacDonald said, trying to work up some enthusiasm from the younger man.

"Could be, but I don't think that's it. She seems to be really cool at the moment."

MacDonald sat down beside him, "Look Mark she's the biggest thing since Jack the bloody Ripper. You should feel proud you've caught her."

Carter sighed, "I didn't catch her. She gave herself up."

MacDonald laughed. "Technicality mate. I'll be attending a press release shortly with the Deputy Commissioner and trust me, I'll be praising you and the team to the hilt. Christ Mark, this is huge news."

"I know what the papers were saying, chalking up the body count like the latest football results, and I understand what this means for the Met Police, but I can't help the way I feel."

"How in God's name is that?"

Carter detected the frustration mounting between them, "I imagined her to be this vile ugly creature, with black holes instead of eyes, a wide slit for a mouth and quite possibly a couple of pointed horns protruding from the side of her head. I thought we'd catch her screaming abuse at us, spitting blood, trying to tear away our flesh. What do I get instead?

She calmly walks into the nick, looks like someone you could easily like and refuses to say boo. Bit of a disappointment let me tell you."

"Glad I asked."

Carter grinned at MacDonald, "Sorry but..."

"Yeah I know, you can't help how you feel."

MacDonald rose from his seat, "Okay listen, just do your job. I have every confidence she'll tell you everything you need to hear to get a conviction. In the meantime just keep the pressure on. I'll call you in the morning for an update and to let you know how highly the Deputy Commissioner regards you."

"That'll be nice."

"Sarcastic bastard," MacDonald shouted back at him as he walked through the canteen.

Carter raised the coffee to his lips, took a mouthful, spat it straight back, "Shit it's freezing," he moaned.

He was about to go and get another when Janet Forsyth pulled up a chair and sat down, bringing a replacement drink with her.

"I thought you might need this. Saw the boss talking to you, and I know how he can go on and on, never letting you pause for breath in his relentless quest for information. He'd have been shit hot during the Spanish inquisition."

"Yeah," Carter agreed without enthusiasm.

Janet could see the tiredness in his eyes. "Are you going to speak to her again tonight?"

"No, I think we'll leave it till first thing tomorrow. Let her stew for a while."

Janet quickly brushed his hand with her slim and delicate fingers. "If we're doing nothing else tonight, why don't we go and finish the meal we started earlier. I can read you a bed side story after if you'd like?"

Carter knew he shouldn't, but found himself incapable of refusing the offer. "Okay come on. Lead me to my destiny."

Janet was glad he'd taken up her offer, but for the life of her couldn't fathom out what his last remark had meant. Putting it down to a cocktail of tiredness and stress she waited until they were outside the station before she linked arms with him and tugged him closer. Briefly, she thought she felt him resist, but then he was as close as it was possible to get, whilst still fully clothed. That was something Janet planned to rectify in the not too distant future.

50

Mary Gage had been released from the City Hospital earlier in the day. Her head still felt as if it had been crushed under an elephant's hoof, but the doctors felt she'd recover more quickly at home, surrounded by the things she loved.

Tears had fallen as she realised her biggest love, Glen would never come home. Instead the house would be filled with memories and images of her horrific ordeal at the hands of Stella Blackmore.

She'd spent the day generally tidying up, taking her time and resting every twenty or so minutes as the specialists had recommended. She was amazed at the amount of dust that had gathered during her time in hospital.

Feeling hungry she'd made a sandwich of ham salad topped with a large dollop of salad cream and could now be found sat in front of the television flicking channels trying to find something to watch.

A cowboy movie was due to start at seven on BBC1 so she switched over to wait, catching the tale end of the six o'clock news. She hardly took any of the information in, until she heard the news reader saying that the police had detained a suspect for the recent spate of killings.

Mary knew it was Stella because when she'd spoken to detectives earlier, they'd told her Stella was their own suspect. She was now also aware that her two uniform constables weren't standing guard outside.

Mary hastily pushed aside her plate as she turned the volume up. She'd missed the main section, but gleaned enough to understand Stella was in custody.

Mary Gage ate the remainder of her meal as if she'd never tasted food before in her life; such was her feeling of total contentment.

When they arrived back at his flat having enjoyed a large meal washed down by a jug of the house red and several glasses of Indian lager, Carter paid the cab fare and invited Janet in without being fully aware as to where his actions could lead.

Janet who was feeling very heavy on her feet from having sampled the strong beer for the first time in her life, slumped onto the couch. She tapped an irregular beat on the cushion hinting that Mark should join her.

Carter was also feeling tipsy and so without a fight he plopped himself down beside her, almost falling on top of Janet as he did so.

"My God, Sir, I think we're pissed," Janet mumbled as she started to giggle loudly.

"As farts, Janet. Pissed as farts," Carter added as he too began to chuckle.

"What would old MacDonald think if he saw us like this?" she asked cheekily.

"Probably be pleased we're celebrating our great arrest in a manner he'd approve of wholeheartedly."

Janet burst into uncontrollable laughter, leaning over as she did so, and ended up with her head on Carter's lap.

"Evening all, what's going on down there?" he said between gasps for breath.

"What would you like to happen...Sir?" Janet teased, still laughing, tears streaming down her cheeks.

Carter abruptly stopped laughing, placed his hands on Janet's face and slowly pulled her up so that he could look at her fully. Without another word, he leant towards her and kissed her lips. Instantly he felt her mouth open and her tongue dart inside his mouth. He closed his eyes and enjoyed the sensations running up and down his body.

Soon everything descended into darkness as Carter and Janet lost themselves in passion.

As Carter made love to Janet, everything else was forgotten. The stress of the case, his murdered girlfriend, lost promotion and the never ending reports to MacDonald all floated away from within to be replaced by lightheadedness and pleasure.

When they were spent, they stayed silent, each lost in thought. As the minutes ticked slowly by, Carter started to worry about what he'd done. Soon his head was in turmoil, guilt and remorse battered his insides, causing waves of nausea to engulf him, and yet he'd enjoyed their liaison immensely.

Gently he pushed Janet to one side and stood up, stretched and turned to face her said, "Fancy a coffee?" he asked trying to sound casual when in fact his body trembled with mixed emotions.

Janet didn't answer him. She'd used up all her remaining energy to please him. She'd fallen asleep where he'd moved her to, naked in the glow of a solitary lamp, and now she had a spooky glow flickering its way along her body like the kisses of ghosts.

Carter shuddered. He suddenly felt cold. Carefully he draped a cover over Janet, bent forward and kissed her forehead and then headed to the kitchen to make a drink. As he waited for the kettle to boil he knew he was in danger of falling for his fellow detective. Maybe, he thought that was why he'd felt paralysed to stop her when she became so involved. Was it possible she'd cast a spell over him?

"Get a grip Mark," he said into the darkness that was the kitchen, "You need caffeine and you need it now."

Bleary eyed, they were met by knowing looks, nods of heads and the odd suggestive comment. Normally Carter would have taken the officers concerned to task, but he felt totally drained and all he wanted to do was shut himself away quietly in his office, swallow several mugfuls of strong black coffee, which would allow him time to get his head back in order before he faced Stella Blackmore again over the interviewing table.

"Johnstone," he called out, once he'd found his seat behind a desk piled high with case correspondence

Billy Johnstone walked into the office with an expression-filled face that said, *I know what you were doing last night.*

Carter noticed it at once, "Knock the smug look off your face, will you? We had a meal and a long conversation about the job, fell asleep in front of the telly and low and behold, found that we'd slept the night away. Believe me?" he said in a less than convincing voice.

"As much as I believe Stella Blackmore is innocent." Johnstone replied still smiling.

"Oh well, guess I'll have to admit we had a great time then."

Johnstone chuckled, "Broke a lot of hearts in this office I can tell you, half the guys have tried and failed to get anywhere near Janet."

"Must be the two pips on my shoulder then," Carter joked.

"Could be she just doesn't like young men."

"Cheeky bastard. Are we ready to speak to her again?"

"Yep, whenever you like."

Carter yawned, Billy laughed again.

"Get me some coffee in here first; I need to wake up a bit more."

"Do you want Janet to bring it in?"

"Piss off and get me a drink, otherwise you'll be handing out bloody parking tickets in the High Street before I've finished with you."

Johnstone clicked his heels together, did an elaborate Nazi salute and turned round marching out the office.

It was Carter's turn to smile.

He flicked open the typed notes from the earlier interview and saw the long list of no replies from Stella staring up at him. He hoped she'd be far more responsive when they had today's first chat. Carter already knew if she chose to remain silent, a lot of the evidence against her was fairly circumstantial. Only one witness could stand in the box and point her out as the person who'd committed a crime.

Johnstone returned carrying two steaming plastic beakers, placing them on the desk he blew on his fingers, "Shit they're hot."

Carter carefully blew on his drink before he slurped a small amount. Leaning back in his chair, as he pushed it away from the desk, he lifted his feet up and placed them on top of a stack of paperwork and let out a contented sigh.

"Feel better?" Billy asked.

"Much. Listen give me five and we'll get her out the cell. Okay?"

"No problem, I'll go and sort out the tapes."

The door closed behind the detective and Carter was alone with his thoughts. Janet Forsyth had gone out on another job and he was glad as it gave him an opportunity to focus on the case without this new distraction to cloud his judgment. She'd have wanted to sit in on the interview and that would've looked very bad from a professional point. No, it was better if he distanced himself from her at work, maybe even altogether until he sorted everything out. There were things happening in his life that were growing more complicated with each passing day. It wasn't really the best time to fall in love...again.

Custody Sergeant Scott Thomas was a burly man of around 210lbs and as he shook Stella Blackmore awake on her cell bed, both detectives were glad they had her as a prisoner and not the larger than life Welshman.

"Thanks Scottie," Billy Johnstone said as he was handed the still half asleep prisoner, "We'll take it from here."

"Make sure she confesses this time," the sergeant said in a threatening voice, no doubt put on to try and scare Stella Blackmore.

Carter looked at Stella and decided nothing would frighten her. She caught his gaze and smiled.

"Ready to talk Stella?" he asked hopefully.

"Nothing to say is there?" she said holding his gaze.

Something in her eyes told him she was mocking him. "You'll get a better deal if you co-operate."

Stella remained silent this time, merely allowed Johnstone to lead her by the forearm down the dimly lit corridor and into the interview room. She noticed it was a different one to the previous evening, smaller and with a multitude of paint flakes hanging from the walls, as if scratched off by the finger nails of prisoners during horrendous torture interrogations in days long gone. She sat down at the table, and watched Carter put a tape in the recorder, saw Johnstone place his paperwork on the desk, and listened once more to the formal caution which again told her it was in her own interests to answer the questions put; otherwise the court would take her silence as possibly an admission of her guilt.

Carter finished the formal introduction to the interview and said, "Would you like a cup of tea or coffee before we begin?"

Stella shook her head.

"Have you had breakfast today?"

This time Stella nodded.

"Okay Stella before I begin the interview, are you still adamant that you don't want a solicitor present during this interview?"

Again Stella offered a nod.

Carter turned to Johnstone who gave him a knowing look before passing him a statement form, which Stella noticed was completed already.

"Stella, this is a witness statement from Mary Gage naming you as the person who hit her over the head with a shotgun, and as the same person who murdered her husband. What can you tell me about the incident?"

Stella shrugged and shook her head slowly from side to side.

Carter described her actions for the benefit of the tape recording.

"Did you murder your husband using the same shotgun you killed Glen Gage with?"

Stella held his eye, but remained silent.

"Did you murder Teresa Day, Mandy Burrows, Meredith Rogers, Tony Asque, Glen Gage, Annie Walsh or the man found in her flat?"

Stella sat like a statue.

Carter, after each question, carried on describing her actions to the recorder.

"Stella have you ever met any of these people?"

This time he saw her lips start to move, was convinced she was going to at last answer one of his questions, only to be dismayed when all she did was break into a large yawn. He felt the anger surge through his veins, clenched his fist and brought it down hard on the table, causing not only Stella, but Billy Johnstone to jump, "Do you realise the seriousness of the situation you're in?" he exploded at her.

This time he noticed Stella's expression change, her bottom lip started to quiver and tears slowly began their journey down her cheeks. She made no attempt to wipe them away, just sat there and waited for them to drop onto the desk before her.

Carter took out a handkerchief and passed it across to her. She took it and mumbled, "Thank you."

"So you can speak when you want to?" Johnstone said in a friendly tone.

Stella sucked on her bottom lip, but said nothing.

"Listen, we can only help you if you help us. If you didn't kill these people tell us so we can go and find out who did."

Stella looked at him as if studying him, Carter felt her eyes burn deep into his soul. She said nothing.

"Okay, I think we'll just pop you back to your cell for the time being. Let you get used to the size and emptiness of a similar cell, in which you could spend the rest of your life. That's if you don't start to help yourself." He thought maybe this time she would open up to them. He was wrong.

"Interview concluded at 09.57," Johnstone said clearly into the tape recorder before switching it off.

Carter watched the woman sitting opposite scan around the room. No escape from here Stella, he thought. Stella finished her tour when he blocked her view.

"So Stella, you're not going to assist us at all. Are you?"

Stella shook her head.

"Why did you come into the police station if you have no intention of co-operating/"

No comment.

Carter turned towards Johnstone, "Put her back down," he barked.

Carter waited for him to return and when he did the junior detective looked disappointedly at him, "I don't think she wants to talk to us."

"I can't get my head round this Billy. Something's not right here."

"What do you mean boss?" Johnstone asked as he sat back down.

"Why would she walk in here and then say nothing? It doesn't make any sense. I'm going to see MacDonald. We're going to need an extension to keep her here after tonight."

Johnstone watched Carter run his hands through his thick hair before he rubbed imaginary sleep from the corner of each eye. "What do you want me to do now?" he asked helpfully.

"Go up to the canteen and order me the biggest plateful of cholesterol they've got. I'll nip to Macs and start the ball rolling. See you in the canteen shortly."

"Okay, see you there."

When Carter reached the little room on the top floor of the station, laughingly referred to as the canteen, he was slightly disappointed to see Janet sitting beside Billy. They were engrossed in conversation, no doubt about his liaison the previous night and failed to see him approaching until he stood beside them.

Janet saw him first and looked up sheepishly, "Oh hello, Gov," she said trying to sound nonchalant.

"Janet," he said as he reached behind him and dragged a chair from a nearby table across the linoleum floor so as he could join them.

"Nothing doing at Groggy Daves," Janet said to him.

"Eh?" was his less than enthusiastic response.

"The suspect for the dodgy motors," Janet reminded him.

"Oh right, sorry I've lost track on the other jobs you lot are doing."

Janet smiled at him. "No worries, everything else pales into insignificance anyway when you compare it to the great scheme of things."

"You been practicing that answer for days or what?" Billy Johnstone asked grinning at her.

"Every morning, you know me, efficient at everything."

The last six words were said directly at Carter, who could feel himself reddening.

"I'll leave you two to chat," Billy said without any subtlety.

Carter sighed, "Good idea," he said coldly, "Go and lose yourself somewhere. Meet me in *The Rose and Crown* at one o'clock. We can chat through any developments over a pint."

"See you later then," Billy replied before walking away.

"He really is suffering for his mistake you know?" Janet said quietly.

"Deserves to though, doesn't he? A young policeman's dead because he cocked up."

Janet could see he was angry and decided it was best to drop the subject.

"You're looking at that plate like you've never seen food before."

"I'm starving," Carter said as he cut through a slice of bacon before dipping it into a runny egg yolk.

"So I see. Get anything from her this time?"

"Attitude and a few tears. I don't think she's going to say jack."

"Will there be enough to charge her with everything?"

"I think MacDonald will want her charged anyway. The Crown Prosecution Service can have the headache of deciding what offences should be mentioned in court."

As Carter chewed his way through the breakfast the doubts regarding their collected evidence against Stella Blackmore began to deaden his taste buds. Before he'd finished half the food he put his cutlery down and pushed the plate away from him. "This is bollocks, Janet. We should have everything we need by now. How the hell has she committed all these crimes and left us with so few clues? We should have enough evidence to put her away and throw away the key. Something stinks here, and I can't figure out what it is."

Despite the packed canteen Janet placed her foot behind his left calf and slowly moved it up and down.

Carter, who by now could feel himself sinking into a sea of depression hardly noticed, although several others did.

Billy went down to the cells and found Sergeant Scott Thomas tidying up the custody suite, having just finished booking in a particularly smelly drunk. "Nice job if you can get it," he joked.

Scott Thomas glanced up at him and grinned, "Swap with me then would you?"

"In your dreams mate, in your dreams."

The sergeant laughed, "What brings you down to the dungeons this time?"

"I just want to put something to Stella Blackmore if that's okay with you?"

"Sure, I'll book her out for you."

"Hey, no need to do that, I just want thirty seconds of her time. Forget the paperwork this time, you've got enough to be getting on with," and he nodded at the mess on the floor.

"Lovely isn't it?" Scott Thomas muttered in disgust. "Sure go and see her, I've got no problem with that...no violence mind," he added in a jovial voice.

Billy walked down the cell passageway and stopped outside number four. He opened the wicket on the front door and peered inside the cell. Stella was sitting on the bed with her back leaning against the wall. Billy could see she had been crying.

"You're very good." he said.

Stella looked up at him and could see he was smiling.

"You don't have to speak if you don't feel in the mood, but I thought I'd stop by and tell you my little secret."

He waited for any response, receiving none he continued, "I was given the task of tracing Stella Blackmore's relatives. Fairly easy thing to do and it didn't take long to put together a nice long list of people who we needed to talk to." He could see he had Stella's full attention now. "I'm a bit of a bad lad I suppose, but I forgot to tell my boss's about her *sister*. The one that looks remarkably like her, the one who could *pass* as Stella in front of someone who hasn't met the *real* Stella before." Stella was leaning forward now, hanging on his every word. "See the trouble is I've met Stella Blackmore before. I've even been lucky enough to have shared her with her husband. She's never *really* met me though because she was drugged to her eyeballs. I know who you are lady."

Bloodshot, tired eyes met his and held his gaze for a full minute. "What are you going to do about it?" she finally asked.

"Nothing at all." Ignoring the gasp from inside the cell, he continued, "While Stella is free I can carry on doing the thing I like best, making money. So I'm even going to help your sister escape. Carry on with whatever you've planned and don't let Stella...or me down. Speak to you soon...*Elizabeth*."

Elizabeth listened to his footsteps as they faded away along the passageway. She couldn't understand why, but she felt even more terrified now a policeman had identified her and yet wasn't going to say anything, than when all she had to do was sit there and be silent.

51

They met in the pub as planned having spent the morning involved in various tasks trying to pinpoint their captive to all the crimes.

Mike Grady went with Janet to order the first round of drinks, Carter and Johnstone stood by the food bar deciding whether to have chicken salad or the rather nice looking mutton vindaloo.

"Right she's not talking, so we need to screw her down with forensic evidence and make what circumstantial stuff we have look better than it does. Does anyone have a problem with that?"

Shakes of heads greeted the question.

"Good. I think we have a chance here, but everything needs to be water tight. All the statements have to be collated and put in an order that would give the jury the impression it most certainly is our girl at each crime scene. Okay, I know some of it is weak, but it's all we have unless Stella Blackmore suddenly decides to open up."

"No chance of that, is there?" Billy asked, already sure he knew the answer.

"Doesn't look that way, but we'll keep her in for the duration before we finally charge her. Time to stew may get her juices flowing; besides the old man wants her hit with the lot."

It was Janet who asked the question none of the others had thought of. "Are we certain she carried out these murders alone?"

Everybody turned to look at her, but it was Mike that asked for them all. "What do you mean?"

"Well we've so many different descriptions and maybe it's because there are two, three, who knows how many people helping her. I just thought I'd ask because our only witness is sitting at home alone."

For a brief second she thought she'd asked the stupidest question in the history of the police, until Carter bailed her out. "Fair point. I must admit I'd not given a conspiracy theory much thought. What makes you suspect she's got accomplices?"

Janet twisted her face into a look that told them all she hadn't got any answers to the question.

"Okay then until anything turns up that remotely hints at a partner, we have to concentrate on what we've already got. It might be a good idea to put someone back on Mary Gage as I removed the protection when Blackmore gave herself up."

Janet felt she'd undermined him a little in front of some of the others, she hadn't meant to sound smart, but somewhere deep inside she felt Stella Blackmore had a few more surprises up her sleeves for them all.

MacDonald paced the floor behind his desk, hands clenched behind his back. Carter sat before him, having informed his boss what had happened during the first two interviews, brief as they'd been.

"So she's as tight as a Scotsman's wallet," MacDonald spat.

Carter tried hard not to laugh at the description, but found it was impossible not to.

"What's so bloody funny?" MacDonald asked.

"Your description, I'm wondering if I'd get away with using it to describe how the interviews went, when it's my turn to give evidence."

"Suppose it was rather stereotypical," MacDonald said grinning, "Better not take the mickey out of us Scots in front of your new girlfriend eh?"

"Christ news travels fast around here."

"Always has, always will in a police station son. You sure you know what you're doing, I mean with it only being a few weeks since..."

"I know, its bit sudden, but she's got right under my skin for reasons I can't fathom yet." Carter interrupted.

"Could help you get over things."

"Yeah, I suppose so, but still, should I really feel this way when I only buried Mandy a few short weeks ago?"

MacDonald stopped pacing to and fro, which pleased Carter who'd begun to feel dizzy watching the man put a groove in the thinly carpeted floor. "Life has many ways to surprise us, Mark. Look at Blackmore, no-one would have put her down as serial killer material now would they?"

"No, I suppose not."

"You just do what feels right. Now what the hell are we going to do with this stupid woman?"

Carter pushed a light brown file towards where MacDonald now sat. "That's the transcript from the tapes, gives us nothing new. Personally I think we should just keep her banged up for as long as the law allows and then get her remanded into custody. That way we give ourselves a shot that she'll crack and talk, or we get longer to find the missing evidence which I feel we really need to make it a sure fire bet she goes down big time."

MacDonald looked worried, "Don't you think there's enough there already?"

"Depends how a jury looks at it. There's a lots of ifs, buts and maybes. A smart lawyer may get her off with some of the crimes."

"Mark, we can't have that. The Commissioner would do his nut. Do what you have to, but for all our sakes get a result."

Carter nodded his head, affirming he would give it his best, before leaving his boss, who had his head in his hands, despairing as to what would happen to his career if Stella Blackmore escaped the total justice her crimes deserved.

Mary Gage lay awake in bed listening to the wind blowing through the trees outside her bedroom window.

It had turned into a nightly occurrence as she battled her mind for the privilege of sleep. She was finding it hard, lying alone in the large king size bed with no-one to cuddle up to. Each night she'd found herself finally drifting off, having first exhausted herself with more tears of sorrow.

Tonight strands of light from the moon danced on the walls opposite, creating abstract images that Mary imagined the great painter, *Pablo Picasso* would have been proud of.

The wind rustled through the branches, sending eerie noises into the stillness of the bedroom, causing shivers of fear to tremble along Mary's skin.

She felt hot and sticky, her throat was parched and her nerves had reached breaking point, such was the level of sadness that filled each passing minute she was alone. Combined with the now gothic atmosphere the elements were creating outside, she felt her stress levels zoom into the red.

She pushed the covers from her body and climbed out of bed, slowly making her way into the darkness of the hall. Carefully she stepped onto the stairs and begun her descent to fetch a drink she hoped would soothe both her throat and trembling nerves.

Halfway down she caught her first glimpse of the strange light radiating from the kitchen. Stopping in her tracks she craned her neck into the black void that was the night, trying to identify any sounds that may give her a clue as to the origins of the light source.

Silence beckoned her down.

The light flickered green across the hallway carpet, before creeping up the stair towards her. Three further steps down and she saw it glow on her toes.

Mary could feel her skin crawling with goose bumps that seemed alive as they jumped from place to place along her body. Her breathing had turned to a fast gasping sound as she fought to keep her increasingly fast beating heart in check. She licked her top lip in an effort to chase the dryness away, but it was no use, her tongue seemed stuck to the roof of her mouth.

Reaching the bottom step she again stood still listening. This time she thought she heard a faint sound like the distant buzzing of a bee. Edging herself forward, fighting the urge to turn and run, she made it to the doorway of her kitchen.

The fridge door stood ajar, like a gaping mouth waiting on its prey. Mary was certain she'd closed the door earlier, when she replaced the milk she'd used to make her nightly mug of *Horlicks,* before retiring to bed. She made her way into the room and with a trembling hand pushed the fridge door shut.

Darkness sprang from its hiding places to engulf her totally. She gasped in horror when she realised the light switch was out of reach. Fumbling before her she tried to relocate the handle to the door, but her efforts drew a blank.

Panic nibbled at her insides, feeding itself on her intestine which tightened with every bite.

Mary crept forward with her hands out stretched before her until she collided with a wall. Slowly she edged along it, keeping the flat of her hand tight against the cold paintwork, hoping to find the light switch that would chase the darkness away.

Just as her trembling fingers made contact with the switch a voice from behind her said in a hushed voice, "Found it yet?"

Mary jumped so high she felt her bones nearly force their way out of her suit of skin, a scream erupted from her dry throat causing a wave of pain to follow it.

Mary slumped down onto the floor still surrounded by the black of night.

Footsteps came steadily towards her, "Who's there?" she asked in a pathetic voice.

The lights burst on and she shielded her eyes against there intensity. The seconds passed as her vision became accustomed to the now brightly lit kitchen.

The owner of the voice had said no more, it was as if it was waiting for Mary to see it.

When finally the task became possible, Mary wished she'd been struck blind.

Sitting at the table, carefully drinking from the carton of milk she'd used earlier was Stella Blackmore.

52

Carter and Billy Johnstone sat in *The Rose and Crown* public house, two glasses of bitter sitting before them. Neither touched their drink and to anyone who passed them, it looked as if they were studying the pints, searching the smooth light brown liquid for something that had meaning only to them. Both men lost in thought.

It was Johnstone who eventually straightened up, leaning back against the hard wood, breaking the silence. "There's no point talking to her again is there? I mean that's five chances she's had to speak to us and all she does is sit and gaze around the room. You don't think she's gone nuts or something?"

Carter finally picked up his pint, took a long slow slurp and replaced the glass onto the wet circle it had left on the surface.

"Good shot," Billy said holding both his thumbs up in a mocking salute.

"What? Oh right. I agree there's no reason to speak to her again. I don't believe she's mad though. Something keeps niggling me, at the back of my head that it's the opposite. I think she's playing with us, but for the life of me I can't think why."

"What do you mean?" Johnstone asked enjoying the other man's torment.

"It's her mannerisms; nobody else I've ever interviewed has been so unattached to what's been going on. It's as if she feels she had nothing to do with what we're trying to talk to her about."

In mock horror Billy enquired, "You don't think we've nicked the wrong person, I mean, that Stella Blackmore isn't the murderer?"

"Oh no, it's her all right, but there's something else going on in that interview room that we aren't privileged to know as yet."

"What's the Chief said he wants done?"

"Charge her with everything and present what we have to the CPS. Hopefully they'll agree we've enough to go to trial with."

"But we don't, I mean on a couple of the murders the evidence is non-existent."

"MacDonald knows that, he just feels if we do our homework correctly we can provide just about enough to get the case before a jury. If that happens we'll stand a good chance of convincing them she's guilty of the lot, especially as she won't talk to us, won't defend herself at all against any of the allegations."

Billy sighed, took his glass in his left hand, raised it to his lips and threw his head back. Carter watched amazed as the beer vanished within two or three seconds.

"Wow," he said "How the hell do you do that?"

"Practice," Johnstone replied confidently.

"Another?" Carter asked, still with three quarters of his first drink sitting before him.

"If you're going to finish that one," Billy said nodding at his drink.

"I'll enjoy it at my own pace thank you."

"Better hurry up, the spiders already started to weave his web."

Carter fell for the joke and looked down at his glass.

As soon as his head dropped slightly, Johnstone yelled, "Got you." Then under his breath he added, "In more ways than one."

"It must be this case," Carter moaned in his defense. "Sucks your brains out and then spits into the gutter."

"Could be you're just getting slow as the years slip by," Johnstone said, adding insult to injury.

Mark Carter chewed on the remark for a moment before giving his response. "Bollocks," he said and went to get another round.

Rosie Lord had stood in the fine drizzle, slowly getting drenched for nearly five minutes. Her newly permed and dyed, dark brown hair, now clung to her head like a dead starfish. Strands hung limply over her face, dripping the rain in her eyes and causing more than was bearable to trickle down the back of her lime green winter anorak.

"Come on Mary, open up," she hollered, fighting against the rain as it lashed against the front of the property.

She groaned loudly as all that greeted her from inside the house was silence.

Rosie had telephoned Mary the previous night to confirm she was still required to attend to the large bunions Mary had suffered from for the past three years. Rosie had wanted to make sure her normal appointment would still be welcome after Mary's terrible ordeal.

Mary had assured her she'd love to see her as her feet were once again causing great discomfort, and she'd added it would be lovely to see Rosie again for a nice chat over a glass of wine.

Rosie had been a regular visitor down the years, and had never been let down by Mary forgetting an appointment.

The rain was falling much harder now, she bent forward, pushed the letterbox open and shouted, "Mary, it's me. I'm getting soaked out here, love."

When her pleas were met by only the whistling of the wind through the opening, she decided to take a look around the back of the property. Holding her briefcase over her head she sprinted to the rear of the house.

The large patio doors were open about six inches. Rosie thought Mary may have had to pop out on an errand and had left it open so she could wait her return. It was the sort of thing she'd do, being the nice lady she was.

Pushing the large double doors wide enough to step through, she entered the house.

At first glance nothing seemed out of the ordinary, she'd been inside Mary's home dozens of times and everything appeared to be in the correct places.

Rosie put her bag down and went through to the kitchen, hopeful of making herself a cup of tea.

The scream that left her mouth was loud enough to wake the dead. Lying on the floor was the dead body of Mary Gage. She'd been shot at close range; blood covered almost the entire floor, making it appear to be a red carpet on which Mary lay.

Rosie rushed forward, throwing herself to the ground beside her, checking to see if she could find any signs of life.

It was then she saw the sight that would haunt her for the rest of her life, although it took a few seconds before she recognised the small object lying on the floor beside Mary. Her tongue had been cut out and placed beside her head.

Rosie threw her hands to her face, trying to hide the monstrous scene before her, and screamed through her fingers.

Climbing to her feet, she tried to rush from the kitchen, slipping on Mary's blood as she did so, and nearly falling on top of her. She ran to the front door, threw open the latch, and ran into the street, screaming "Help me, help me."

Less than five minutes later, Carter stood over the body of his only witness to a crime committed by Stella Blackmore.

He felt physically sick, although not at the gruesome sight before him. It was the utter despair building up inside him, threatening to drown him in sorrow, taking his dead body away, floating down the river to his own private place in purgatory.

Somewhere during his life he'd committed such a terrible deed that God had deserted him. He wasn't a particularly religious man, but how else could you explain the events surrounding Stella Blackmore.

Pure evil was at work here and as he stood looking at the

piece of meat that had once been someone's tongue, Carter believed all was lost, and he badly wished he'd arranged the guard when Janet had suggested this might happen. Like Billy before him he hadn't believed fully what was going on. Stella was in custody, so why the need for a guard. He hadn't given a second thought to a possible accomplice.

The cell door was practically ripped from its hinges. For the first time the prisoner felt really scared.

Carter's eyes were blazing with a blood shot appearance that made him look like the devil himself. The woman police officer beside him looked equally as friendly.

"Get to your feet," Carter yelled at her.

Elizabeth did as she was told, and was immediately grabbed under her arm by the female officer.

"Ouch," she said as her skin was pinched. "You're hurting me."

The grip didn't loosen until she was frog marched back into interview room two, where she was practically thrown onto her seat, the tapes were slammed into the machine, the formal caution was read at breakneck speed, and everything seemed so much tenser than at any stage before.

"Mary Gage has been murdered," Carter spat, opening the interview. "Her tongue has been ripped out her mouth. What do you know about this"?

His prisoner appeared totally shocked by what he'd just told her. For a brief moment he thought maybe she didn't know anything. Then he was sure she did.

"Come on Mrs. Blackmore, we know it was you who murdered her husband. We know you are aware she is, was, the only witness to that crime, and we're not stupid enough not to believe now that she's dead, you arranged for someone to kill her. I want you to tell me right now, who murdered Mary Gage?"

She looked at him and then for a long time at Billy Johnstone, before shaking her head slowly from side to side. Carter thought she was going to remain silent again, but he was wrong.

"I don't know," she said in a very hushed voice.

"Please repeat that again for the benefit of the tape recording," the female officer asked her.

"I'm sorry, I don't know," She repeated.

Carter leaned towards her, "That's total crap and you know it," he rasped at her. "Give me the name of your accomplice."

"I don't know what you're talking about."

Carter clenched his fists under the table. How could she remain so calm? "You'll spend the rest of your life in prison when I'm finished with you. Do you understand that?"

Elizabeth could feel the hatred over the table, knew he wanted to get up and hit her, and could see the veins at the side of his head pulsating. This man was ready to explode. "I would like to help you, but I can't." She started to cry.

"Why in God's name not?" Carter yelled. "You're going to prison for the rest of your life. I've explained it to you over and over. If you want me to help, then give me something in return."

"You haven't got any evidence to send me to prison, have you?"

"What?" Carter said, shocked by what he'd just heard.

"You have to prove I killed someone. You can't do it now can you?"

Carter couldn't contain his rage any longer. He leapt to his feet and screamed, "This interview is terminated. You lady are going to burn in hell. Get her out of my sight."

Billy Johnstone accompanied the female officer out the interview room, waited until they way out of earshot of Carter and said, "I'll pop her back. You go and make the Inspector a cup of coffee. I think he badly needs it."

Elizabeth turned to him as they reached her cell, "I can't take anymore. I'm going to tell him who I am. Stella promised me she wouldn't kill anyone else." The tears were flowing heavily now.

Johnstone put his face as close as he dared incase anyone came round the corner and saw him giving her an apparent kiss, "Listen you stupid cow. If you tell him anything your sister will come after you. Don't you get it? The only way you'll live to collect your pension is if she gets away. Besides if she doesn't do you, I will."

Elizabeth felt the warm spit on her cheeks and imagined it burning into her soul.

It was then she understood that she might physically live through this, but she would be totally dead inside.

53

The office resembled ants inside a nest. People scurried round carrying bundles of paperwork, large containers filled with evidential exhibits were being pushed from desk to desk as various officers, dipped in and removed whatever piece of the large puzzle that they'd been allocated to prepare for the court hearing.

Carter sighed heavily, aware that this was an act he was doing more frequently now, than at any other stage of his career. This case was providing bands of tightness that threatened to cut straight through his body.

He spotted Janet bent over a plastic evidence bag that contained two large kitchen knives, removed from the Blackmore household during the search following the recovery of the three bodies found there. He stood watching her, taking in her shape. Her position had caused the material off her skirt to ride up her thighs and as he watched the muscles of her hamstrings moved gently each time she shifted her weight from one leg to the other. Her legs seemed to go on forever and were shaped to perfection.

Mike Grady came up beside him, luckily didn't see where Carter's eyes were gazing and said, "Everything all right Gov? Heard you were a bit tense downstairs?"

Carter turned towards Grady; he intended to tell him to mind his own business, but saw the genuinely concerned look on his face and changed his mind. "Yeah, feeling a bit tense Mike," he said. "Thanks for asking."

"No problem, Gov," Mike replied as he walked off.

Janet had stood away from the desk and was now talking to Billy. Carter ambled across. "How's it going?"

"Think things are falling into place. Just a few bits and pieces and we'll be there."

"That's great news Billy. Anything to add Janet?"

"Not really. The team have it all sorted as Billy's just said."

"Great. I'll have to present this mess to the court in the morning."

Carter walked off only to be caught by Janet before he left the office.

"Are you okay? I heard it got a bit scary at the interview."

"I'm fine. It's just all getting to me I suppose. I still think we're missing something, but I can't put my finger on it. Oh well, at least she goes down in the morning. We still need to catch her murdering friend though."

"You think Mary Gage was killed by someone linked to Blackmore?"

"Of course, I mean what other explanation can there be? I'll tell you this Janet, I'm going to catch the bastard if it's the last thing I ever do and then I'm going to personally watch them burn."

Janet moved closer than he felt comfortable with in the fully packed office, "Hopefully," she whispered.

Carter backed away slightly, shaking his head slowly from side-to-side, "I've never met anyone like her before. She's really asking for someone to give her a slap Janet. Smug bitch."

"Make sure it's not you then. Throw it all away if you hit her, the case, your job...*us*."

The last word surprised him, "Us?" he said confused.

"We won't be working together if you're inside for smacking a female prisoner now would we?"

"Oh I see, sorry I thought you meant..."

"Don't think daft at a time like this, Mark. Just concentrate on the job in hand. Speaking of which would you like me to take *you* in hand later?"

He nearly choked on her remark, "Jesus, you're subtle sometimes."

"I didn't get to where I am..."

"Yes we know," he interrupted her joking voice. "Come round about eight. I'll need company by then."

"Sir," she grinned at him before spinning round and walking away.

Carter watched her for a second, and then he headed home to prepare himself for the biggest trial of his life.

54

The Magistrates Court had its usual assembly of suspects loitering in the thinly built corridors. He recognised some of them from previous cases.

Janet had picked out a dark navy suit for him, with a striped maroon and black tie. It made him look smart, but not too officious she'd said. What that meant, he'd had no idea.

As he waited for the case to be called, he found a small space to the rear of the police room within the court, to put his feet up and reminisce over the happenings of the night before.

Janet had been there less than an hour before they'd ended up making love on his living room floor. It was frenzied, almost as if it would be the last time they ever had sex. Not together, but with anyone. It was a feeling he couldn't explain. Not that he really wanted to, the night had been one of the most satisfying of his life.

Mandy hadn't entered his head and now as he thought back he felt guilty. Should he feel this way towards Janet?

Maybe MacDonald had been right, perhaps it was the current situation he was in. Circumstances often make people do things they wouldn't do under normal conditions.

Taking a deep breath, he decided he would go with the flow, see what developed, and take a chance at finding the happiness he craved.

He was smiling broadly when the clerk of the court called his name.

Elizabeth climbed the stairs up from the holding cell, flanked by two burly officers of the court. Neither said a word to her on the journey.

The first thing she noticed when she arrived in the dock was the smell. Downstairs had been musty, slightly damp. Here it smelt clean, as if someone had newly-varnished the wooden box in which she now stood. There was a smell of pine hanging in the air and she breathed in happily.

The room was smaller than she'd imagined, about the size of her garden at home. She caught sight of the handful of reporters sitting to her left, saw the members of the public crammed into their tiny area and finally spotted Detective Inspector Carter at the rear of the court. He was glaring at her; even from a distance she could see his contempt.

She continued to soak up the atmosphere until she heard, "All stand."

A door at the front of the court opened and three people came in. She knew from watching an old programme that had been on the television years earlier that these were the Magistrates.

They sat in front of her like the three wise men, each looked old enough to be drawing their state pensions. She wondered if they're eyesight would be good enough to see her where she stood.

She watched them intently, *the good, the bad and the ugly.* She stifled a laugh as she thought they all looked like the *ugly.*

The main one, who sat in the middle, had the appearance of a bloated pig. He had several chins which dangled from his face as if preparing to fall off under their own weight at any second. His eyes were tiny slits, peeking out from the rolls of fat that was his face, and he was as red as any fire engine she'd ever seen.

The other two didn't look as bad, but still belonged in an episode of *Last of the Summer Wine.*

Elizabeth worried if they'd be strong enough for what was about to happen in their court this very morning.

She'd been appointed a solicitor from the pool supplied by legal aid. She was called Susie, and she seemed okay. While they'd waited to be summoned into court, Susie had gone over all the facts of the case, she thought there was a more than reasonable chance, that some of the evidence would be thrown out when it went to the Crown Court. She'd told Elizabeth to be prepared for the worst because she believed she'd be remanded into custody to await her trial.

The solicitor had been taken aback when she'd had told her not to be so sure.

The charges were read out one by one. On Susie's instructions Elizabeth pleaded not guilty to each one.

She could hear the murmurs coming from various places in the court, pencils scribbling down every word she said, tutting with each not guilty plea.

Elizabeth was amazed to find she was enjoying every minute.

All too soon Mark Carter was called to the witness box. As he was taking the oath, to tell the truth, the whole truth and nothing but the truth, he didn't take his eyes off her.

She could feel them burning into her flesh.

She listened as he went through all the evidence the police had collated. Susie kept glancing at her, shaking her head, reassuring her it was going to be okay.

The evidence seemed strong on certain points and very weak on others. The pattern was repeated with Susie sticking her thumbs up at her each time she felt the police were struggling to provide a case.

Finally, it was her turn to say something. The magistrate made an attempt at humour by mentioning the fact that she'd not had much to say during her stay at the police station.

Elizabeth stood up, looked directly at Mark Carter and said, "My name is not Stella Blackmore." She waited for the gasps to die down, waited for the colour to completely leave Mark Carter's face, and then added, "My name is Elizabeth Brooks. I'm Stella's older sister."

Pandemonium broke out in Number Two court as Elizabeth Brooks revelation started to sink in.

The Magistrates ordered her to be removed back down to the cells. As she was led away she kept her gaze fixed on the slumped figure of Mark Carter in the witness box. His eyes never met her own.

The Crown Prosecution solicitor and Susie were involved in a slagging match of momentous proportions, each blaming the other for the farce they'd just witnessed.

Court officers and policemen were trying to clear the courtroom; the Magistrates had already left, no doubt gone for a quiet cup of coffee while the situation calmed itself down.

Carter had sat down heavily on the narrow bench fitted to the rear of the witness box; he had his head firmly held between his hands trying to prevent the tremendous headache swirling around inside his brain from blowing the roof of his head.. He was staring down at the dirty wooden floor, absentmindedly counting the panels that ran horizontally before him, thinking about anything to keep himself from going insane.

The vision of Elizabeth/Stella's face slowly began to materialise through the floor. At first it was as if someone had drawn the image using charcoal or pastels, but then it became a three-dimensional image that smiled up at him in triumph.

Everyone present in the building would never forget the scream Mark Carter gave when he toppled over the edge, sitting alone, watching Stella Blackmore laughing at him from between his feet.

55

The news had reached the C.I.D. office at Westville Police Station almost as soon as the words had left Elizabeth Brook's mouth. Although everyone was shattered by the deception Stella and her twin sister had managed to pull off, they were more concerned by the news that Mark Carter had apparently had some form of seizure in the witness box.

Janet had rushed to meet him at the City Hospital where the ambulance called to Court would take him. Other officers wished him well as she'd sprinted out the station.

The only person who revelled in the situation was Billy Johnstone. Of course he'd added his words of regret, but inside he was bursting with happiness. Stella was long gone, hopefully making use of the two forged passports he'd left at Elizabeth Brook's home address. He'd no way of knowing for certain Stella would go there, but it was a chance he'd felt worth taking.

He decided to go for a victory pint and looked around for Mike Grady, but the younger man was out the office. Billy shrugged; he didn't mind drinking on his own. Slowly not to arouse suspicion he walked out the office and headed for the nearest pub, which was the *Horse and Hound*. He'd barely reached the door when his mobile rang. "Hello, Billy Johnstone here," he said.

"Billy, its Chief Superintendent MacDonald. Are you busy at the moment?"

Billy was surprised the Chief Superintendent wanted to speak to him at such a time. "No Sir. Like everyone else I'm just taking in the news from court."

"Terrible business Billy. An utter disaster. We'll need to catch this bitch now, for Inspector Carter's sake if nothing else."

Billy fought with the urge to switch the phone off, and merely said, "How can I help you Sir?"

"Good lad, Billy, that's the spirit. Do you know Blake's Industrial Estate in Hendon?"

"Hendon?" Billy repeated.

"Yes, meet me there in half an hour. I've found something I think will cheer you up."

"I'm intrigued Sir."

"Thirty minutes then." MacDonald hung up.

Billy looked at his watch. He'd be on time if he left

without a drink. With his deliberate mistake earlier regarding the armed guard he thought perhaps he'd better be on time. Quickly, almost at a jog he made his way back to his car.

The journey was swift owing to the early time of day. The roads had proved quiet and he soon found himself pulling into the yard of the Industrial Estate. He could see the Chief Superintendent was already there. Stepping out of his car he waved at the senior officer, who nodded back.

Billy went across to where he stood. "Sir," he said cheerily.

"Billy I had a tip from one of my informants, and don't look at me like that. Senior officers are still policemen you know."

Billy smiled.

"Anyway," MacDonald continued, "There is something I want you to see, and some people I would like you to meet."

Billy feeling full of confidence said, "After you Sir."

The two men entered the large warehouse and immediately Billy could smell death, although all he could see was a large object in the middle of the room, which had a blue tarpaulin draped over it. Nervously he edged further inside, towards the mysterious shape. MacDonald stayed close beside him.

When they reached it, Billy turned to his boss, who said, "Pull it off."

Billy yanked the sheeting hard and it fell away, revealing the decaying body of Mickey Driscol, "Holy shit!" he said in a barely audible voice.

"Don't think there's anything holy in this mess. Do you son?"

Billy turned to see that MacDonald had been joined by two other men. He could see from the uniforms they were wearing, that they were high ranking Metropolitan Police officers.

MacDonald said, "Let me introduce Commander Gibson and Chief Superintendent Blake from New Scotland Yard to you."

Billy sat down on the grime covered floor and started to laugh. "Complaints Department no doubt?"

MacDonald joined in with his laughter and soon the other two men followed.

Billy stopped laughing and felt uneasy as the three men

carried on for some time. Eventually it was Gibson who spoke. "Billy you've screwed up big time."

Billy was taken aback by the language used by the Commander.

MacDonald added, "The fact you're bent son is the least of your worries."

Billy got to his feet, "What do you mean?"

"You've lied and betrayed the very people who looked after you. Both you and the piece of shit attached to that piece of wood."

All too soon it became clear to Billy, "You're the Panel."

MacDonald smiled, "Afraid so son."

Billy gave a worried glance at all three men in turn. "I haven't done anything to upset you."

"Oh really? How about not telling us Driscol was going to set us up?"

"Yeah, but I knew he couldn't do it."

Gibson shouted, "But you thought you'd let him try anyway."

Billy could feel his legs turning to jelly, felt his throat drying up, could hear the beat of his heart increase in pace. "I covered up the club when he came in and made his stupid allegations. I even told Carter it was a load of shite."

"But you didn't come to *us* Billy. What you failed to realize son when Driscol was trying to stir up a hornets nest, was that he'd hit the nail firmly on the head."

"What are you telling me?" Billy interrupted, trying hard to stop himself shaking so much.

MacDonald continued as if he hadn't heard him, "Ascot and Green came to see me with a new list of names they were going to arrest that morning. You, Grady, James, Peters and Russell were on it. If you all went down, one of you could easily have told them about my monthly cut from the Stonewall Estate to save your lousy necks."

"But only Grady and I knew about that. We wouldn't say a word."

Not the point son is it? You and Grady could easily have told the others over a beer one night, given them some juicy information about their Chief Superintendent. Besides even if you hadn't, the investigation would have been intense. Christ, I shagged Mandy Burrows more than any other senior officer at the Maverick Club, I got rid of all Brian Blackmore's stolen goods for him, I helped *you* by keeping the Old Bill out of the estate, so you could run the drugs operation easier. How long before I got nicked, days, weeks?"

Commander Gibson came so close to his face he could smell the whiskey on his breath, "If Mac was arrested, we might follow suit. We can't have that now can we?"

Billy tried to clutch at straws, "Nobody has anything on you. Nobody knew if the Panel really existed, outside those who worked for you."

MacDonald shook his head, "You didn't come to us son, so we began to think perhaps you had a hidden agenda with that bloated scum bag over there."

Billy shot a glance at the rotting corpse and could see his head had swollen to three times its normal size as the blood had settled at the lowest part of the corpse.

MacDonald then delivered the words that sealed Billy's fate. "I shot Ascot and Green, having set them up on the pretext of giving them more names. Senior officers too I told them. Came crawling like the worms they were."

The other two officers laughed loudly.

Billy thought he was going to pass out. What he'd just heard rattled around inside his head. Pleading he shouted, "I'm loyal to you." He cried before he crumpled to the ground, sobbing before them.

MacDonald asked "Why didn't you tell us sooner you'd guessed it was Brian's wife who'd killed him?"

"I didn't think it mattered to you."

"What? One of our men, one of our main operators gets wiped out and you decide it doesn't matter. What gives you any right to make decisions without asking us?"

"I'm sorry, I won't do it again."

MacDonald laughed, "You won't get the chance son. Surely you don't think we'd reveal ourselves to you if we'd decided to let you live?"

Billy felt his bladder open and felt the hot liquid running down his leg.

Gibson said, "Not very brave officer."

MacDonald and Blake burst out laughing.

Billy made a bolt for it, guessing he could out sprint the three older men, get out, give himself up to the nearest policeman and try and live long enough to grass the Panel members up. He knew he could provide the evidence to do just that.

He made it to the entrance and ran straight into two of the bouncers from the Maverick Club, who each grabbed an arm, holding him firmly.

MacDonald slowly walked up to him, "You have to go Billy. You're a liability now. Without you and with Carter round the twist, we can concentrate on getting over this little blip. So long son."

Billy screamed until he felt the cloth being rammed into his mouth.

"Take him and the dead meat away and lose them somewhere," he heard MacDonald request as he disappeared from view. Billy struggled for as long as his life lasted.

The hot sun beat down onto her back, cool water lapped at her toes; her hand blindly searched for and found the large Pina Colada cocktail by her side. Sitting up on her sun bed she took a delicious sip from the crystal glass, before replacing it back in the shining white sand.

The sea breeze was warm as it tickled its way over her body, birds flew low in the sky making it appear as if she could stretch up a hand and touch them. The sapphire coloured sea gently caressed the shore and distant voices of happy people having a good time floated on the air.

Stella had reached her final destination by travelling on various forms of transport. On each occasion she'd used a different passport, sometimes she was herself, others Elizabeth. On two occasions she'd actually managed to change the name under her picture to a totally bogus one. As yet she hadn't used the mysterious gift she'd found lying on her sister's front door mat for fear it may be a trap. She'd been surprised at how lackadaisical some of the passport controls had been.

Stella had been glad her sister in the end wanted her to get away, wanted to help her escape. It had been her idea to play Stella for as long as she did. Stella had only asked for enough time to flee the country.

Elizabeth had said she would give her days rather than hours. What she hadn't known was that by giving her so much time, Stella would be able to finish her business with Mary Gage.

She knew her sister would be angry at her for the deceit, but she still figured she owed her for the affair she'd had with her husband.

The police would come after her, Interpol too.   Stella wondered if bigger organisations like the FBI or MI5 would join in the hunt.

She took another cool drink.

Maybe she could stay away forever that would be nice. Get a job somewhere and live like a normal person from day to day.

Stella knew it couldn't be.   She was no longer a person who could enjoy the normality's of life.

She had a new craving, one that had taken over her soul.

Stella watched as two small children ran past her throwing a ball between them as they ran.   Small particles of sand rose up from beneath their feet, hitting her in the face. "Brats," she shouted after them.   Her yell was greeted by the universal language of two fingers being thrown up in her general direction.

Stella grinned.

Her drink was finished, so she decided to walk the short distance to the bar on the beach.   Her savings would keep her going for some time and would allow her to concentrate on her new hobby.

As she strolled up the white sand, like any other holiday maker, she kept making subtle glances at the other occupants on the beach, wondering if any of them would care to play in her favourite game.

Murder...

Printed in the United Kingdom
by Lightning Source UK Ltd.
125322UK00001B/16-63/A